## Despite everything,
## he was a man of honor . . .

"What you see here are the northern lights, the merry dancers, we Gaels call them. They are beautiful, are they not?"

"Yes, very. Do you see them often?"

"Aye, when the night is clear." Calum laid his hand on Abby's shoulder, twirling a strand of her hair around his forefinger. "The first time I bedded a woman, we lay and watched the dancers in the sky all night long." He smiled, though Abby thought she detected a trace of sadness in his face. "Forgive me, mistress, for being so indelicate." As he spoke, he leaned closer and stroked her long, unfettered hair. "So beautiful."

Abby held herself perfectly still under his gentle caress. The fire she had never felt for her husband was burning inside Calum at that very moment, and in her, as well. She thought of slapping him, but something stayed her hand. The man was not impertinent, simply frank and forthright. He did not deserve to be slapped for his honesty, however uncomfortable it made her feel.

"Was the woman you bedded your wife?"

His hand roved on to her neck. "Nay, mistress. A tinker's daughter. I was a wild stud-horse in my youth, and I'm naught but a docile *gearran* now. My wife—why, I didn't wrap her until our wedding night. She was a proper lass, you know, not a trollop."

The word stung Abby. Was that what he thought her, a trollop, a doxie, a drab? Surely not. And yet . . . "And what am I, pray?" He stared at her blankly, the fiery lights of the northern sky blazing in his eyes. "Am I not a proper woman?"

He surprised her with a laugh. "Too proper, if anything. But more lovely, more desirable, more tempting than any woman has a right to be." His hand slid to her face and he cupped her chin. She held her breath and put her trust in him completely. . . .

**If you liked this book, be sure to look for others
in the *Denise Little Presents* line:**

# ROAD TO THE ISLE

# MEGAN DAVIDSON

**PINNACLE BOOKS**
**KENSINGTON PUBLISHING CORP.**

# Prologue

*Scotland, 1714*

*Damnable smoke! Damnable country! Damnable people!*

Major Racker rammed his fingertips against his forehead, closing his eyes against the sworls of black smoke that rose from the crackling thatch and nearly filled the glen. The worst headache he could remember was devouring him.

Footsteps approached, and Racker cracked open his eyes. Flashes of red pain danced before him, dappling the image of the wary-looking grenadier standing at attention only an arm's length away.

"Beg pardon, sir."

"Yes?" croaked Racker. Even his voice, he realized, sounded full of pain.

"What would you have us do now, sir? The men are finished eating . . . the fire seems to be going along well . . . we slaughtered what cattle we could find . . . the rebels have been taken care of . . ."

The frightened wailing of a child cut his words short. "Not every rebel," said Racker, through tightly clenched teeth.

"Yes, sir. The little girl," admitted the grenadier.

"She's as good as finished, sir. We are somewhat short on ammunition just now."

Racker struck his forehead with the flat of his hand, relieving the excruciating pressure for several tranquil seconds. The child's cries filled his head, echoing and multiplying, threatening to explode his skull. "Then you must find some other means to deal with the situation. You are a young man, unused to these creatures, unused to the necessity of reprisal. This rebellion—" He gasped as a dagger stabbed his brain. A rafter falling within the blazing house sent a billow of smoke and a spray of sparks into the sky. A bad smell, nearly as strong as that of burning straw and wood, filled his nose. "—is over. But others will arise unless the Jacobite menace is—" A bolt of white-hot pain. Incessant wailing, torturous, damnable wailing, from lungs far too small to hold such power. He bowed his head for an instant. He was a rock to his men, and rocks bowed not. "—crushed."

"Yes, sir," murmured the grenadier.

"Where is Campbell?"

"On patrol, sir. To the south. By the loch."

"Damn his eyes!" Racker's own eyes blinked and danced in helpless paroxysms. The Scottish lieutenant and his brutish troops were doubtlessly terrorizing the female population, when they should have been with him, dispensing discipline. "No matter." He squeezed his forehead between both hands; the pain wavered, dimmed, and surged back. Damnable wailing. "See to the child."

The soldier hesitated. "Sir?"

Racker fumbled for his pistol and pushed it into the trooper's hand. "You are dismissed."

The grenadier saluted, turned and disappeared into the smoke. Racker saw nothing but bursts of red light. The bawling stopped. There was a shot, then nothing but the gentle rippling of flames and the soft mutterings of soldiers.

Gradually his eyesight cleared and the pain, though severe, became more tolerable. A cinder blew into his eye. And Thomas Racker wept.

# One

*The Heart's-ease, Glasgow, 1715*

Abby gasped for breath. When she could finally speak, she cried out, "Lydia!"

But Lydia, she knew, was gone.

Tearing the ragged bedclothes from her, she struggled out of bed. Her heart was just as ragged. She was in the Rose Cottage; was she alone?

Terror gripped her, forcing her into a run that lifted her above the floor. She floated from the bedroom to Lydia's room, where early morning shadows slashed the walls and ceiling with great black streaks. Lydia's pallet of faded featherbeds lay in a corner, still smelling of sleeping child, still warm to the touch.

"Lydia!"

*Search the house, search the house,* said a voice, high-pitched and mocking.

"No!" shrieked Abby. "Lydia is not here! Where is Lydia? Do not distract me so!" She pulled at her hair until her long, brown braids became undone and her scalp ached from the raking of her nails. She had to search the house.

Lydia was not in the abandoned servants' quarters, nor the silent, upstairs bedrooms and sitting rooms, nor the hallway, nor the balcony overlooking the barren gardens. Abby raced down the staircase toward the entrance hall.

*No, not here either,* the banister seemed to chuckle as her hand glided down the silken mahogany. Not in the entranceway nor the dining hall, not in the scullery nor the parlor, not in the garderobe nor the pantry, not in the library, with its endless shelves empty of books. Even Tip, Lydia's little spaniel, had vanished like a dim recollection.

"I know she is not here!" Abby shouted to the echoing house. "Do not vex me so! Take me to her!"

Suddenly her shattered thoughts collected themselves for one glistening moment. "Roger!" she called out. Roger would know where their little girl was. Roger knew all, took care of everything, had wept when Lydia's pony had been sold, loved Lydia most of all. "Roger?"

It was absurd to search for her husband. She knew the search was a fool's errand but she could not quite recall why, nor could she stop searching, dashing again throughout the entire house, even peering under the few remaining sticks of furniture, remnants of rugs and bits of blankets. At last her searching brought her to the garden doors of frosted glass etched with irises. As Abby watched, the crystal flowers danced ever so slightly in a wind that she could not feel; then they froze again.

*Open the doors,* said the mocking voice. *Perhaps Lydia is just outside, amongst the roses, playing with Tip, waiting for you.*

"I don't believe you," Abby said firmly, but in an instant her mind was filled with a vision of Lydia, so beautiful and tender, her eyes far wiser than other children's eyes, her face glowing with the happiness of earlier memories. "Lydia, *Mama* is here!" she cried, grasping the brass handles of the double doors. They swung open onto a garden of winter-gray trees and withered rosebushes.

It was not Lydia who met her.

It was Roger. For some time Abby only sensed his presence; when at last he became visible, she saw him in small fragments, as if her eyes could not bear the sight of his entirety. She saw at first his burgundy velvet frock-coat, spattered with mud and splashed with gouts of brighter red. His jabot was threaded with pink. His eyes were full of self-hatred. His skull—his skull was cracked open, exposing gray velvet laced with blood.

No! Abby felt her mouth sag open.

"Abby, my love! I'm so sorry," he whispered.

A sound of some kind began to rise from her throat.

"You must believe me. My intentions were honest. My companions were not. My plans . . . destroyed!"

No! She clenched her eyes shut, but she could not block out the sight of Roger and the ruined garden.

"I'm afraid Lydia is gone forever."

"No!" Abby screamed into a garden suddenly gone black.


Abby lay as still and quiet as death. She was not in the Rose Cottage. She was in her tiny chamber at the Heart's-ease, on her bed of shame. Roger was gone, and in his place stood a young, pug-faced grenadier, his jacket lying on the floor at his feet, his breeches half unbuttoned. "Enough of your bawling now, Annie. You'll have the mistress up here if you keep that up. You've had a bit of a dream, I'd say."

"Abby," she whispered, amazed at the quietness of her voice. "Who are you, sir?"

"No matter," said the soldier. "Ye needn't say my name, Annie."

He was kneeling on the bed, half over her, before she thought of crying out. "Mistress!" she called. The man clutched her by the wrist. She screamed as if the dead had touched her. "Mistress!"

Her outburst completely stunned him. Doubtless he was quite unused to shrieking women. He paused, unsure of himself, backed slowly off the bed and stood cursing softly at her. Certain he would fling himself at her again, Abby drew the coverlet up in front of her, the only defense she could imagine. "I am not a drab!" she cried.

The grenadier cocked his head. "A woman in a stew and not a drab? Wha' are ye, then? Queen Anne come back from the grave?"

Footsteps clattered up the stairs and onto the floor of the corridor outside Abby's chamber. The door burst open, and a head surmounted by a mass of thick red hair thrust itself into the room. "Annie," sputtered a voice. " 'Tis Annie ye're wanting, lad, no Abby. This puir creature hasn't been properly trained."

The soldier snapped himself perfectly upright, as if he had been called to attention. "Ah, then what am I doing wi' her?" he muttered. In a trice he gathered up his musket, heavy scarlet coat and boots and pounded out the door, taking with him the pungent odors of cabbage, ale and suet. Abby sighed in relief as the door shut behind him and she was once again alone with her memories.

She wiped a tear from her cheek with the hem of the coverlet. The dream. The terrifying dream. It still vibrated inside her head like the sound of a badly tempered clavier. It was the third time she had had such a dream. The first had occurred only days after she actually had awoken in the Rose Cottage, just before Roger's death, to find Lydia gone. She remembered the menacing shadows, the feel of the banister against her hand, the heart-devouring panic that had driven her all around the empty house and garden, not twice, but many, many times, until weariness and despair had made her stumble and fall. She remembered identifying Roger's broken body later the same day. A fall from a horse, they had said, but the horse had not been bred which Roger could not ride.

Lydia, as a very little girl in a white muslin gown with pink ribbons at the neck and waist. Abby closed her eyes and could see the child quite clearly. Little Lydia was standing in the dovecote at Brenthurst, in the beautiful countryside of Bury-Saint-Edmond. Roger was there too, as handsome and merry as he had been when they'd first wed. He was teasing Lydia. She was laughing. She was on his shoulders as he cantered between the cucumber frames, neighing and whickering.

Soon Abby was with them, far away from her tiny chamber in the Heart's-ease, far from the dirty city. Away from Scotland altogether. She stroked the woolen coverlet and imagined the feel of the mauve-colored lamb's wool blankets Roger had bought for her when she had first arrived in Glasgow in the midst of an early snowstorm. "You'll see, my love," he had told her. "Our life will spring anew here." He had gone to Scotland hoping to escape his bad credit, his many debts, his love of gambling altogether, and at first it seemed he might actually succeed. He had established her and Lydia in Rose Cottage and talked of his plans to join a friend in a merchant venture in the West Indies. As with all his dreams, however, his new life never blossomed. Within a fortnight he was coming home at odd hours of the night. Gaming again.

Another scurrying of steps in the hallway startled her. Her eyes flew open, and for just a moment she could see the slow, broad smile of her dead husband.

The second time the dream had come to her was at the Heart's-ease, two weeks past, her first day at the brothel. Any day, she feared, Mistress would have some dragoon or grenadier or fusilier give her "proper" instruction in shame and debasement. Hundreds of soldiers roamed the city, now that the Jacobites had finally been put to rout. There would be no shortage of tutors for the lessons she dreaded so much.

"Lydia," sighed Abby. "Roger." How she needed them! She drew her blue satin nightdress about her shoulders and sank back against the linen sheets. Perhaps she should leave. But where would she go? With her parents and her husband dead and her few acquaintances unapproachable, she had no place to go. What would her poor mother think, had she been alive to witness her only daughter lying in a bed in a stew in a depraved Northern town?

*Courage!* Wasn't that what Roger had always told her? *Courage, Abby!* Even when he'd lost a hundred pounds sterling at the bull pit. *Courage!* Even when, at the very end, she'd had nothing to feed Lydia and had to barter her tortoiseshell hairpins for bread and milk. *Courage!* But when Lydia had vanished that last, terrifying day and Roger had been discovered dead upon the highway, she had broken free of her courage and fled into the streets.

A rap at the door scattered her thoughts. "Abby, are ye awake?" The door cracked open. "Ye're no afeared of me, are ye?" Without waiting for a reply, the flame-red head appeared once again in the doorway.

Abby smiled in spite of herself. "Janet! I am so very happy to see you!" She flung aside the heavy curtains and sat on the edge of the bed, grasping a bedpost for support.

By now all of Janet had entered the little room and indeed took up much of it. She stood as tall as a tall man—taller, if one took into account her hair, which rose like flames from her head. Of all the ladies at the Heart's-ease, only Janet had shown Abby true kindness. Even so, Abby could not bring herself to tell the woman about the dream of Lydia lost; it was too painful to recount. "Tell me, what happened just now?"

"Grenadier laddies," snorted Janet, with a wave of the hand. "They've sowens for brains. Somehow the brute misdirected himself to you, instead of Annie down the ha'. Ye should hae seen him, dearie, wi' his coattails flapping and his buttons all awry." Janet danced about the room, shaking the hem of her yellow dress and stamping her feet in a creditable imitation of an agitated man in boots.

Abby laughed, but she had not forgotten Janet's warning to the grenadier. "Janet, my dear friend. The poor soldier didn't frighten me half as much as what you said to him. 'Proper training,' you said. I lacked proper training. I know what training you must be speaking of, and I've known since I set foot here I'd be faced with it. But no one, not even Mistress, has mentioned it until now." Every day she saw the ladies take the gentlemen into their apartments, every day she heard the creaking of the mattresses and the nervous laughter of the customers. "Pray what is afoot? You may speak plain with me. I am not as delicate as Mistress would like to believe."

"Well, it has to be said sometime," murmured Janet, her voice suddenly empty of humor. "Ye're quite on the money, Abigail. Mistress is planning something for ye. She has been taking a slow hand wi' ye, as ye've seen, what with yerself as thin as a stick and not a fit supper for the cat when ye came here. But Nancy's taken ill with the ague, ye ken, and Margaret must be off to the surgeon's soon and won't be good for anything for at least a fortnight. So that's why I've come to ye, Abby. I'm here to warn ye: Mistress is on her way to see ye. And she's naething good to tell ye."

Abby stood up and crammed her feet into the tiny,

white silk slippers that lay by her bed. "I have expected as much for some time. Fetch me my dressing gown, pray, dear Janet." She pointed to the single chair in the room, covered by her silk robe, a white, pink and moss green confusion of flowers. Janet seized it and fairly threw it on her.

"Puir lass," she muttered, tugging on a sleeve. "Not even the clothes on yer back are yer ane."

"No, 'tis true," admitted Abby with a sigh. "I have nothing. Not since Roger died. Actually, much before that. The house, the horses, even Lydia . . . all gone!"

"Ye puir bairn! And now the threat of the Bad Disorder, on top of all the rest."

"The bad disorder? But of course! The harlot's plague! But . . . it's deadly!"

"Deadly by bits," corrected Janet. "Why, if ye didn't look too closely at Mistress, ye might nae notice it in her. As yet, in any case."

"Mistress has the Bad Disorder?"

"Indeed she does! Why, her hair and her right eye aren't her own, and I'll wager there's more about her isn't her at all. Weren't ye knowing that?"

"Only the eye. One cannot avoid noticing it."

"Well, ye know nothing about it, Abby, nothing. And see now . . . I told ye nothing."

Abby understood. She would have known nothing that happened at the Heart's-ease without Janet's help. The woman was her gazette, and Janet's secrets were safe with her. "Just as with Priscilla."

"Not a word of her!" Janet put her hand to Abby's mouth. "Let the poor wretch lie in peace, she that never had any peace while living."

Abby had only seen Priscilla twice, but she could never forget the look of sadness on the woman's thin, sallow face. Priscilla had died only days after Abby's arrival, and had it not been for Janet, who had seen the murder, Abby would have believed what Mistress had told her: Priscilla had tripped on her gown, fallen down the staircase and broken her neck.

Abby opened her mouth to speak, then stopped. There was a scent of jasmine in the room. Janet tipped back her head, inhaling. She had smelled it, too. "Mistress!"

"Wha' did I tell ye?" whispered Janet. "I'm gone as swift as the gentlemen." But, as the woman opened the door, Abby could hear the rustle of Mistress' brocaded skirts sweeping along the quiet, oaken floors and the soft pad-pad of her satin shoes.

"Janet, is it you?" came Mistress' golden voice.

"Aye, ma'am, but I was in the process of being gone."

Mistress appeared in the door, then in the room. Unlike Janet, the proprietress of the Heart's-ease was small and fine-boned, but somehow much more imposing than the big Scotswoman. Perhaps it was her Look, a confident gaze that seemed to reach into people's souls, searching about for the worst within them. The glass eye, which never seemed to be looking in exactly the same direction as the real one, made the Look even more ghastly than it had the right to be. Abby could not bear to set eyes on the woman's face for more than a moment.

"Go, then, pretty Janet," said Mistress softly, gesturing toward the open door. "An excellent gentleman is waiting for you below." To Mistress, customers were of only two types: excellent or interesting.

Janet disappeared.

Now that she was alone with her mistress, Abby could not keep herself from stealing glances at her stray eye and perfectly coiffed hair. Many people wore wigs, of course, but not because their hair had been destroyed by the Disorder. Abby had just discovered a small curl out of place when Mistress spoke. Abby's gaze dropped to the bed.

"Abigail, do pour me some tea, child."

"Tea, madame?"

"Yes, if you please." Mistress pointed to Abby's bedstand, where a china teapot stood, only its spout visible, poking out beneath a pink flannel cozy. The grumbling grenadier had made her forget its presence entirely. "I'm afraid it may be cold by now, madame."

"Nevertheless, will you pour me a cup? Cool tea is so refreshing." Mistress smiled and lowered herself onto the arrowback armchair which the dressing gown had so recently occupied. She spread out like a garden, magnificent in the weak sunlight which filtered through the bedroom's one small window.

Abby handed her a full cup, dutifully adding the four teaspoons of sugar that Mistress always demanded. Mistress sipped slowly and smiled once more. Abby startled, nearly dropping the sugar spoon into the teacup. Mistress' teeth were pearl white; were they false as well?

"Sit down, dear."

The sugar bowl still in her hands, Abby stepped back until her shoulders met the post of her bed. She perched on the end of the mattress, the sugar bowl trembling in her grasp.

"Do not be nervous, my pet," said Mistress calmly. She had been raised in London—the illegitimate daughter of a marquis, some said—and had the most elegant speaking voice Abby had ever heard, melodious, well-modulated and unhurried. "I am just gathering a little information. Well, you know yourself how short your stay with us has been. I hardly know you."

"Information?" repeated Abby, dumbfounded.

Mistress took another sip of tea. "Yes, that is, information concerning your . . . how shall I say it? . . . intimate experience with men, or lack of it. It will come as no surprise to you, I daresay, what role the young ladies play here at the Heart's-ease. It is a part that I think you might be rather good at, with the appropriate discipline, of course." With this she whipped a black lacquer fan out of her sleeve and snapped it open so rapidly that Abby gasped.

"Now, please allow me to speak frankly and I shall be very sparing of your time. Besides your late husband, how many gentlemen have you had delicate relations with? You may tell me all, my dear."

"Why, no one, if it pleases you, madame," said Abby. "I had thought I'd made that clear during our very first conversation, and I am sorry I did not."

Mistress gave one crisp, precise stroke of her fan. "What? Not one lover? A coachman, perhaps? A schoolmaster? A clergyman?"

Abby shook her head. "No one but my husband." Fear rose inside her at the thought of the dream-Roger, but she held herself in check. "This profession is quite new to me, madame."

Mistress' teacup rattled ever so slightly. For a moment Abby thought she might rise and be gone, but Mistress held her ground. "And it disgusts you, does it not? It is vile, repulsive, unseemly, demeaning, dangerous and, for that matter, quite unhealthy." Her good eye rolled in a half-circle, while the false eye remained stationary. "It is perhaps the lowest form of occupation a woman could fall to, wouldn't you agree?"

"Yes." The word was out of her mouth before she could stop it. She felt her face grow warm and her hands gripped the helpless sugar pot so hard she was certain she would break it. "That is to say . . . I am so unused to the idea . . . I mean no disrespect, of course . . ."

"Of course." Mistress rose, her skirt falling to the floor in graceful waves. "Come, come. An honest answer is always best. Though I would have thought, given your circumstances, you might have been more generous. After all, were it not for this accursed profession, you would still be sleeping in the stable at the Cock and Hen, stealing bones from dogs and cabbages from cows."

Abby squirmed on the mattress. It was true. During her very worst nights, after the bailiffs had chased her from the Rose Cottage and her faithless friends had refused to help her, she had crept into stables and slept in the straw next to the warm, uncomplaining horses. Janet had discovered her quite by chance while entertaining a groom. Yes, she was obliged to Mistress, but she was not obliged to like the duties Mistress was intent on forcing upon her.

"You are correct, of course," continued the woman, with one eye on Abby and the other on the far bedpost. "It is a horrid business. The weariness. The rapid waning of youth and beauty—not yet your worry, my dear. And perhaps the worst, the inconveniences."

Janet had told her all about the horrors the ladies endured, drinking vile potions or submitting to agonizing cruelties and indecencies to be rid of their "inconveniences." If she did become debased, she swore to herself, she would never leave her child lying in a pool of blood on a surgeon's table. "Surely there is some other way I can be of use to you," she began. "A chambermaid, perhaps, or a housekeeper. A cook, a laundress, anything you please."

Mistress smiled pleasantly. "There is only one role for you here, Abigail. And you know what it is."

"I am afraid of . . . disease."

"The Affliction. Janet has told you about my malady, I see. As you may know, some ladies use a sheath to prevent the sickness. An unfortunate practice, really. The gentlemen don't care for it, though Janet often has need of such a thing. She services the lowlife—dockmen, sailors, merchants and the like—those most likely to spread disease. But you . . . you'll have only the *crème de la crème,* quality gentlemen of the finest sort. How would the Scotch say it? 'The flowers of the forest.' We serve no miscreants here. You have no need for a sheath."

Abby, who had been staring in terror at the misplaced curl on Mistress' hairpiece, blinked and looked at the ground. How she wished she could bring herself to say, "No, no. Absolutely not. I will not be a whore for you or for anyone. I refuse, unconditionally. No, no and finally, no." But she could not. All her life she had been brought up to follow the demands of others: her parents, her tutor, even Roger. How could she do differently now? "I beg you to reconsider, madame. I am a very private person. I wouldn't be of any use to your customers."

Mistress put her finger to her chin, as if deep in thought. "How can you be so certain, Abigail? Stand up, child."

Abby obeyed, and obliged Mistress by turning whenever commanded to do so, her gown gently swirling about her, reminding her of the flowerbeds at Brenthurst. "Remove your gown, please. And anything else you are wearing, too, if you would be so kind."

"Remove my gown?" Abby stopped mid-twirl. She had never stood naked in front of anyone, not even Roger nor her serving maids. Even the midwife who had delivered Lydia had done so through a slitted sheet.

"But of course. How may I see you properly if you are covered up?"

For a moment Abby considered refusing. She had heard tales of ladies beaten, turned out on the streets, even murdered, like poor Priscilla, for impudence. Dare she tempt such a fate for the sake of modesty alone?

She dropped the robe. Then the blue nightdress. It looked as if the sky was lying at her feet, and she felt suddenly very hot and dizzy.

Again she turned this way and that at Mistress' behest, and though she carefully avoided the woman's steady, discerning gaze, she could feel it boring into her. At first Abby stared at the intricate patterns on the Turkish carpet, closing her mind against her almost overwhelming shame. But it wasn't long before she felt herself drift into the protective harbor of distance, a safe place none could reach, save her. She lifted her head then and concentrated on her visions of Brenthurst, the beautiful house just outside of London which Roger had bought for her shortly after their marriage. She could envision the irises which spread like blue fire in the gardens in spring, and remembered the time little Lydia had picked one and ran joyously toward her with it, holding it aloft in the sunlight. It was no wonder why people called the flowers "flags."

"Thank you, Abigail. You may make yourself decent."

Abby shook herself awake; the images of Lydia and the stately irises vanished suddenly, as if an unseen hand had plunged them back into her mind. She dared a glance at Mistress' face. The woman seemed to be frozen in thought, her false eye only slightly divergent from her good one. How strange to speak of decency at the Heart's-ease!

Abby quickly dressed herself, then again retreated to

the edge of the bed. Mistress appeared in no hurry to speak, and it was some time before the uneasy silence of the room was broken.

"You are really quite a comely young woman, Abigail," said Mistress at last. "Not splendid, certainly not exquisite like Pamela and Chloe, mind you, but very lovely, in a quiet way that many men would appreciate. Your hair especially is quite becoming, and just the shade of dark brown that men admire so deeply . . . precisely the color of the chocolate you are so fond of. You should wear it down always, even below in the parlor. Nevertheless," she continued, flicking her fan, "the way you hold yourself, as if your body is present but your mind is not, suggests you are not very comfortable within your beautiful temple. Am I correct?"

Abby again felt her cheeks glow with embarrassment. Mistress was, of course, quite correct. Except during baths and childbirth and intimate moments with Roger, Abby had not even been especially conscious of her body. "As I have said, I am a modest person," she admitted, "and . . ." She hesitated, unsure that Mistress would appreciate her next comment. "And a God-fearing person."

"But of course," said Mistress softly. "You will have noticed that my ladies go to church each Sunday without fail. They procure some of the best gentlemen that way."

A sudden shout rattled the panes of the tiny window. Abby jerked her head up, and Mistress' good eye veered toward the sunlit glass. Another shout rang out, then a musket shot, then laughter, a horse's nervous whinny, a series of whoops and catcalls and buoyant curses, and a string of bleating notes played on a fife.

Mistress smiled politely. "Celebrants," she explained, though Abby needed no explanation. "They are so glad the hideous Jacobite brutes have been put down that they simply cannot restrain themselves." Then her face slowly relaxed and brightened, her natural color glowing through the rouge on her cheeks and the white lead on her forehead. "That is precisely what you need, Abigail."

Abby shook her head. "Madame? A celebration, you mean?"

"Ah, no, dear," laughed Mistress dryly. "Indeed, rather the opposite. A Jacobite. You need a Jacobite or a similar ruffian to teach you the ways of the world . . . that is to say, the world at the Heart's-ease. Someone too spirited to let you get the better of him by pretending he is simply not there. A Jacobite, yes. There must be some prisoners about, although a free man would be preferable. I understand they are so fierce they cannot be held long in captivity."

Abby shuddered and rose again, gripping her hands together before her lest they tremble and betray her fear. "I pray you, madame, do not bring any Jacobites to me. Many years ago, in the first uprising, my father . . . my father was killed by Highland soldiers. Of course, not all are so vicious, and yet . . ."

"You needn't worry at all," soothed Mistress with a little laugh. "I would never let anyone harm you." She surged upright, her skirts rustling like iris leaves in a high wind. "Do you think I would do anything to endanger any of my ladies? You are my life, my dear, all of you. I have nothing else, save you."

"I give you my word, madame, I shall try to do whatever you wish. *Whatever* you wish." She could feel the pounding of her heart as it strained to break free of its prison. She was not yet one of Mistress' ladies. But for how long? "Only please . . . no Gaels."

Mistress smiled, and her glass eye rolled upward. Then

she touched Abby's arm, and her voice was serious again. "I shall take your whims into consideration, my sweet." Then, with the smile still lingering on her face, she drew back the black fan and whipped it against Abby's cheek.

Abby cried out, hated herself for crying out. Her face burned. Tears filled her eyes. She had never been struck in the face before. The thought of it, more than the pain, made her angry and ashamed. "Madame," she gasped, "what have I done?"

"Why, that is for disturbing my delightfully peaceful afternoon, Abigail," explained Mistress. "You'd not thought I'd forgotten your screaming, had you? It's not allowed, you know." And like a great ship with varicolored sails she glided out of the room without another word.

But the fragrance of jasmine remained, mixed with a musty scent Abby could not quite identify nor the jasmine completely conceal. It was something like the smell of old hair and dry bones and dead skin. As Abby snorted to dislodge the odor from her nose, a tear fell onto her hand. *Courage,* she told herself, but another tear fell, and another, until her cheek tingled with pain. Shouting rose again from the street, and Abby drew heavy velvet curtains over the window to shut out the noise and her disgrace.

*Roger. Lydia.* If only she could bring them back, the way they were before their troubles started.

# *Two*

*Young Calum, Son of Red Calum*

The next evening, Abby visited the chocolate house, accompanied by Chloe—next to Janet the least objectionable among the residents of the Heart's-ease. Mistress allowed all the ladies one extravagance, no more—a lapdog, a caged bird, a weekly allotment of lace, ribbons, sweetmeats or, in Janet's case, black tea liberally laced with Highland whisky. Chocolate was Abby's passion, and the only peace she knew was at the chocolate house of a Saturday, listening to the educated gentlemen of Glasgow engrossed in their conversations. She loved to breathe in the wondrous, sweet aroma of cocoa and watch in fascination as the proprietor mixed the dark powder with hot milk and sugar to create a potion truly fit for gods. Although she always wore the insignia of Mistress' trade—kohl, lead, rouge and powder—the gentlemen drinking chocolate and coffee hardly appeared to notice her. She guessed they were much too entranced with themselves and their own scholarly preoccupations to pay much attention to a pair of wretched drabs.

On the way back to the Heart's-ease, Chloe kept to the rear and Abby walked boldly in front, a pint of the delectable drink safe in the handled flask she kept especially for the purpose. A swirling breeze blew a handful of dry, brown leaves against her skirts, then on down the filthy close. Two grimy children scurried past her, also brushing against her clothing, imprinting it with black smudges. Laughing, the children hurried on in pursuit of the leaves.

*Soon it will be winter,* thought Abby. *What will Lydia do?* If she were really in the far north—a rumor Janet had heard—what then? She wasn't a very strong child. It would be quite cold in the wilderness, and Lydia suffered in the cold. At Brenthurst this time of year the child was swathed in furs, velvets and woolens. *Poor thing,* thought Abby. *Surely those responsible for her care now will see she is kept warm. They must.*

Lydia was still very much in her thoughts when she looked up and saw the small wooden sign that bore the name of Mistress' establishment in large, graceful letters underneath a painting of a nosegay of violets, faded blue and yellow. Her brief respite was over already. Then she noticed Janet standing at a side door, the entrance to the ladies' quarters; the front of the building, which housed a perfectly respectable tavern, was for customers alone. "You are undone!" whispered Janet, fairly lunging at Abby's free arm. "She's found a devil for ye! In your chamber this very moment."

"Oh, Janet!" Abby's hand shook so badly she very nearly let go of the flask. "A Jacobite?"

Janet's eyes opened wide. "How am I to be knowing that? But I know he's the one, the one to tame ye. Mistress looked most full of herself when I saw her with him. She flitted about the man like a bum-bee on the heather."

"Does he seem very vile indeed? Are his legs bared? Did you get a noseful of him?"

Janet was about to answer when the side door opened,

framing Hugo, the barkeep. He stretched his huge hand out toward her and frowned. "Come, Abigail. Ye're wanted."

Abby hurried up the steps to meet him, Janet at her heels. It would not do to keep Hugo waiting. A patient, slow-thinking man, he nevertheless stood well over six feet tall and had a temper just as sizable as his frame. A few days earlier Abby had seen him pick up one bothersome gentleman and pitch him out onto the street with less effort than it took her to lift a full teapot.

"I'm to escort ye to yer chamber," muttered Hugo, wiping his arm across his mouth, and before Abby could press him for more information, he turned and trudged away.

She followed him up the wide staircase, Janet a step behind her, plucking at Abby's sleeve and mumbling, "A bad sign, a bad sign," all the way up to Abby's door. Abby knew exactly what she meant: Hugo's services were used only when trouble was in the offing. Abby had not expected Mistress to act so quickly, and now her mind was hunting this way and that for a way out of the coming ordeal.

"Hugo, I am really not well at all," she pleaded, laying her hand on his bulging forearm. "Pray let me speak with Mistress."

"The mistress is out the eve," he grumbled. "Now enter and see to yer business. I'll be direct below, should ye need me." He stamped once with his great plough-horse foot.

"The puir lass is not well," said Janet, shaking the big man fearlessly by the shoulder. "Ye can see for yerself plainly enough. Her face is as white as whey."

Abby at once raised her hand to her face. Was her fear that evident?

"Enough, hussy! She looks well enough to me," cried Hugo, and before Abby could gather her wits, the giant pulled open the door, thrust her into the room and shut the door behind her, sealing off any possibility of retreat or escape.

Abby stood stock-still, her eyes closed, her thoughts still scurrying about in fear and confusion. She heard Janet cry out, no doubt in answer to some indecency from Hugo, and then a flurry of steps down the staircase, Hugo's heavy boots pounding after Janet's lighter tread. But the room itself was silent, save for children's laughter and men's curses rising faintly from the street below.

She dared to open one eye. Her bed stood quite vacant, still a bit dishevelled from that morning, when Chloe had made use of it without Abby's permission. A handful of lavender lay on her pillow to dispel the scent of musk. A fire burned steadily in the fireplace, bathing the Turkish carpet and the surrounding paneled walls in a soft pink light. The room smelled of burning cherrywood, lavender, and, very faintly, of whisky.

Taking a deep breath, Abby risked opening both eyes.

She met the blue-green gaze of a man sitting in the chair Mistress had occupied the day before. She assessed him fully in a matter of moments. He continued to stare, holding a glass full of whisky in one hand, draping the other carelessly across a large, black book spread out on his lap. Thankfully, he wore breeches like any other man, though they, like his other garments, fitted him poorly, much too tight for his tall, broad frame. The buttons on his waistcoat strained to hold the cloth in place around his barrel chest, and the cuffs of his sleeves, free of lace or any other ornament, rode high on his wrists. His beautiful eyes and a generous spattering of freckles about his cheeks and long, straight nose made Abby think of schoolboys she had seen in London. Was this the face of a savage? Would she know a savage if she saw one? She trembled under his scrutiny.

"How do you do?" said the man, in a low voice. He rose, gave a brief bob of a bow, and stood expectantly, as if suspended in air.

He towered over her. Now that he was standing, she clearly saw just how thick his arms were, how muscular his legs. He was powerfully built, easily capable of doing whatever he wished with her. She would have to be wary indeed. "I'm very well, thank you. Please, sit down again if you wish."

He collapsed back into the chair, much to her relief. "Have you hurt yourself?" The Gael touched his cheek and grimaced.

"It's nothing," she squeaked. She cleared her throat; she had to know. "Are you a Jacobite?"

The man gave a slight jump; his whisky slopped over the side of his glass and ran down his hand, but he didn't seem to notice. He continued staring at her, his smile flickering but not disappearing altogether. Finally he dipped his hand into his coat pocket, drew out a silver snuffbox and handed it to her. On the lid was an embossed figure of a pelican pricking her breast with her beak to feed her young, and under that two words: *Iacobus Rex.*

" 'James the King'," she read aloud.

"You're quite the scholar," said the tall Gael, gently removing the snuffbox from her grasp and returning it to his pocket. "The crest is that of Clan Stuart, and I am its broken soldier. And now, m'lady, my life is in your hands."

"I thought it quite the opposite," muttered Abby under her breath.

"Your pardon?"

"I was not expecting your visit," she said, glancing about the room for any means of protection in case the man proved more vicious than he appeared. At last she remembered the chocolate canister. Surely scalding hot liquid was an excellent weapon. She squeezed the handle of the flask until her fingers ached.

The man smiled, exposing a full set of impossibly white, canine-looking teeth. She realized with some regret that, if the man had not been a savage Jacobite, he would have been rather handsome. "No good comes from hiding the truth. Even now soldiers may be searching the city for me. They had me all but captured when I slipped out of their hands."

Abby shook her head. She must not be hearing him aright. "A fugitive? I'm afraid I don't understand. What brings you to the Heart's-ease?" Perhaps the appetites of the Gaels were even more voracious than she had imagined. Perhaps they chose to risk capture rather than forego the pleasures of the stews.

The man laughed softly. "Not what you're thinking, I'll wager. I intend to sit here reading, speaking with you perhaps, and wait for night to fall. Half the soldiers will not have the wits to look for me here, and the other half will be loath to enter the place. When it's almost curfew, I'll slip out and take my leave of your lovely city."

Abby nodded toward the bed.

The Jacobite did not understand her at first, and when he did a roar of laughter surged from his throat. *"Mo Dhia,* woman, and me a married man! With four weans, no less!"

Abby smiled. She began to suspect the creature had never visited the stews before. "I'm sad to say that many of the gentlemen who come here are married."

"Married, yes. Highland, no," said the fellow, flashing his dangerous grin. "It's said Gaels makes the most faithful husbands. We mate for life, like eagles. Formulation is not to our liking."

"Fornication," she said, unable to suppress a little smile. Not only did the man's clothing fit him poorly, his language did as well. Abby felt her entire body relax, beginning with her nervous, twitching hands and ending at the very tips of her toes. "I'm quite glad to hear it. It's not my preference, either."

"Nay, I can see it's not," said the man gravely. "You have a genteel look about you, m'lady. And you are Saxon, not Lowland. I can tell by your speech. Even with all your paint you look more like a queen than a . . ." He hesitated. "My English is good, I think you'll agree, but I'm missing a wheen of words. What is the word you use?"

Suddenly she felt extremely relieved and incredibly weary. This was no monster at all. An awkward, ignorant fellow, perhaps, but no brute. Taking the chocolate with her she walked to her bed and seated herself carefully on the edge. "There are many, actually, most of them rather vulgar. Bawd, drab, slattern, trollop, trull, strumpet . . ."

"Ha!" he interrupted her. "That is what my people say, *strompaid.*"

". . . Whore, wanton, slut," she went on, ignoring his rude outburst. "I fear it's a long and ugly list, though I am not quite yet part of it. You see, when I first came here, I was near death with starvation and fever. Mistress took me in, and at first I was beyond caring where I was or what her profession might be."

"Not quite yet a strumpet, you say? But soon to suffer

the same vile treatment as the wretched females I saw below?"

Abby smiled sadly. "Indeed. And you yourself were to dispense that treatment."

"Myself?" The Gael laid his hand on his breast, not an affectation, she guessed, but a true gesture of surprise. "But I'm no whore-monger."

"Mistress doesn't know that. She saw in you the perfect instrument to train me in my proper duties at the Heart's-ease, Mr. . . . Mr. . . . ?"

Again he rose, the book—her Bible, she noticed—still in his hands, and gave another painful bow. "Forgive me for not introducing myself," he apologized, and proceeded to pour forth an exceedingly long string of words that set Abby's mind whirling.

This must be what Roger had spoken of, she thought. "Gaels have no names," he had once told her, "but patronymics. They will be most happy to recite their entire pedigree for you at the drop of a glove. Iain son of Iain son of Iain, *ad infinitum*." She had heard snatches of Gaelic from Roger's Highland gaming friends, and words here and there from customers at the Heart's-ease, but to her they sounded no more like speech than the screaming of hawks or the nickering of horses. "Again, pray, sir. And much slower. I am completely unaccustomed to your language."

The Highlander obligingly repeated his name, lingering over every arcane syllable. *"Calum Og mac Chaluim Ruadh mhic Chaluim Mhor Ruadh mhic Dhomhnaill Ruadh Og mhic Dhomhnaill nan Choinn . . ."* He continued a good minute by her estimate, and just when she felt she could not tolerate another *"mhic"* he stopped abruptly, his beautiful eyes wide open. "But your people would call me Calum MacDonald."

"Mr. MacDonald, then?"

"Nay, just Calum, if you please. My race has no use for surnames. 'Tis you Saxons who insist on them. And how shall I call you, mistress?"

"Abigail Fields." She dropped a curtsey, merely from habit.

"Miss Fields?" he ventured, seating himself yet again. His nearly nonexistent eyebrows arched high on his forehead.

The man was beginning to unnerve her. What was he doing with her Bible? And even more to the point, what was *she* going to do with *him? "Mistress* Fields," she replied, as calmly as she could.

*"Cead mille murthair!"* cried the Gael, setting his whisky down so quickly half its contents flew onto the floor. "A married woman, and your man allows you to be treated thus? Where is this creature? Bring him to me! I'll have a word with him myself. What sort of man . . ."

"I should like to be able to bring him to you," said Abby, pushing down the rage she felt rising in her breast, "but alas! He's gone." Her voice broke, and she had to touch the smooth skin of the flask and feel its searing heat before she could continue. "My husband is dead."

The Highlander sank back in his seat, his broad face caving in with embarrassment. "A thousand apologies, Mistress Fields," he whispered. "I meant well enough, you'll warrant. Your husband—was it an illness that took him?"

Abby shook her head. "They say he fell from his horse, but . . . please, I'd rather not speak of it. It's not been three months since . . . since it happened."

The Jacobite reached for his whisky, one hand still

holding his place in her Bible. "As you wish," he said, quaffing the contents of the glass in one swallow.

"I crave your pardon, but would you mind putting that aside? The Bible, yes. It was his. I like to keep it—" She hesitated. She had almost said "clean." "—to use it as little as possible."

The man gently placed the book on the washstand beside the chair. "It's sorry I am, mistress, but I cannot see a book without picking it up and reading it. A bad habit, but I suppose there are worse. I was just after wondering why the Lord worries about the foxes destroying the vineyards, though foxes neither eat fruit nor drink wine. Well, it's no great concern. You have children, of course."

"Children?" Abby tugged nervously at the cascade of lace at her bodice. Why didn't the confusing fellow simply go away? She had no desire to speak to a stranger, and the stranger had no desire for her, apparently. And yet, she did find him amusing. At least she was fairly certain he was not dangerous. "Only one."

"Male or female?"

"Why, a little girl, Lydia. She's very nearly twelve years old. We had a son as well, but . . . but he died before birth. My poor Lydia! I fear she's just as lost to me!" She twisted her fingers together until they hurt. How could she distract the brute?

"I'm sorry to hear it. And where . . . What are you doing now, mistress?"

She had begun bouncing gently on the bed, drawing forth a diffuse music of creaks, squeaks and thuds from the bed slats, floor and featherbed. The song of the mattress, the ladies called it. "Why, Hugo is listening below us. He'll expect to hear something, so I am providing him with what he wants to hear."

The Gael's face expanded into a huge grin. "Faith,

mistress, you do me an injustice!" In a trice he was beside her, bouncing as merrily and lustily as a child. His long sandy hair, tied in a queue at the nape of his neck, danced against his back. But after only a short while he slowed and finally stopped, his hand on his chest. "I am a bit weakened, I fear."

His face was as red as a turnip and glistening with sweat. "When did you last eat, sir?"

"Why, a day ago, mistress. I stole an apple and some bread."

"Stole? But you must have had silver or Mistress would not have let you in my chamber."

"Aye, I stole that, too. But after the food. I am no thief, but a man must eat."

"And drink?" She pointed to the empty whisky glass.

"Well, 'tis good to have a dram. I was aching for whisky. So when the ladies offered me some, I could hardly refuse, now could I?" Calum's smile became a wince.

Abby recognized the look of hunger at once. She herself had lived with it, slept with it and awakened with it for many days before coming to the Heart's-ease.

"Ah, these pains in my belly," he groaned. "Forgive me, mistress."

"Forgive you? Indeed! I shall feed you." Abby went to the wall, tapped three times and waited. Three short taps answered back from the wall of the adjoining room. "There. Celestine is unoccupied. She will have some food sent up directly. In the interim, would you care for chocolate?"

She held up the canister. He eyed it suspiciously. "What is it? A liquor?"

Abby laughed and poured the steaming liquid into two china cups. A skin gathered on the surface, which she shaved off with a spoon. She inhaled the fragrance of the rich, frothy mixture, sweet, milky and comforting. Even if she had been deprived from drinking it, just to smell it would have been treat enough. How strange that, only minutes earlier, she had considered using it as a weapon.

The Highlander sniffed at his cup. " 'Tis sweet," he muttered, sipping at the pale brown foam. "And hot." He grimaced. "Not for me, I think. What is that?"

Abby peered over the bed to see what he was speaking about. Horrified, she seized the wrinkled object by its very tip, picked it from the floor and took it to her washstand. "I'm terribly sorry. Chloe must have dropped it."

But the Gael was too curious to let the matter drop. "And what is it, mistress? I've never seen such a thing. It's no a creature, is it?" He craned his neck for a better view.

"Hardly that," she answered, hearing just a trace of laughter in her voice. She was trying very hard to be exact and grave and proper with the brute, but he was like no man she'd ever met before. She didn't quite know how to be with him. "It is called a sheath. A gentleman wears it to prevent disease."

"Wears it?" gasped the Gael. One eyebrow rose and his mouth dropped open. "You must educate me in this, mistress. When it comes to the business of this house, I know nothing."

She held it up for him to examine. It was still damp and greasy, and clung to itself in a ghastly mockery of manhood. "It is worn by a man over . . . over . . ." Even her experiences of the past two weeks had not made it easy for Abby to use the words that came so glibly to the other ladies.

"His pintel," guessed the Highlander. Abby nodded

gratefully. "What a crazy-mad idea, wearing a snood over one's *slat*. Only the English would think of such a thing! A man could not make children wearing this, I'm thinking."

"That is correct."

"My Catriona would never understand the need for it."

"She would if she knew there were no other prevention against the Great Pox," said Abby grimly. "But unfortunately I am not allowed to have it. Mistress forbade it."

The stranger shook his head. "I knew a man who died of this disease," he said softly. "A terrible, terrible thing it is. In the end he was blind and as mad as a hare." Then he raised his head and looked full into her face, and she could see he was indeed a handsome man, although much different from Roger. Her husband had had perfect, even features, the face of a prince from a picturebook; the Highlander's visage was rugged and masculine, his cheekbones unusually high. She could not tear her eyes from his.

"Ah, Mistress Fields! What a time you've had of it! 'Tis a pity to see a fine woman like you in danger." Abby was touched by the sorrow and sincerity in his voice. No one had grieved for her since Lydia had disappeared.

"Thank you, Mr. MacDonald."

Someone rapped on the door.

"There's your supper," cried Abby, and she hurriedly threw her silk dressing gown over her clothes. "No one must see that I'm still clothed," she explained to the puzzled Gael as she opened the door and found a large silver platter draped with a piece of white linen. She carried it inside to a little table by the window and withdrew the cloth. A cloud of steam rose from the two china plates underneath, carrying the smells of butter, freshly baked bread and cooked cabbage throughout the room.

A thin stream of saliva trickled from the corner of the Highlander's lips. He brushed it away with his sleeve. "Milk and bannocks and butter and kale," he said appreciatively. "Only what is this?" He pointed to two small slices of gammon nestled beside the cabbage on each plate.

Abby chuckled to herself. The poor man was certainly encountering a wealth of objects outside his experience. "Gammon steak, well cooked. Ham, they call it in the colonies. A favorite of mine."

He wrinkled his nose. "It's the flesh of a pig, isn't it? Devil the bit I'll have of it then, mistress. Pig is unhealthy, unclean meat. My people never eat it."

"As you choose," said Abby, biting her lip to keep from reminding him that he was no better than a beggar and hardly in a position to choose. Using a fork she edged all the offending meat onto one plate and heaped the other with bread and vegetables. The Gael pulled the chair to the table, paused as if gathering himself for battle, then attacked the food, first with knife and fork and then, when that proved too cumbersome, with his hands. Abby, seated on a brocaded stool, sipped her chocolate and nibbled at the gammon. She understood hunger.

A rhythmic slapping sound came from the window, which grew and grew until it became a thunderous tramping of boots. The shrill cry of a fife stabbed the air.

Too late Abby remembered the reason for her visitor's presence. She stretched her hand toward him and opened her mouth to say, "The King's militia on their rounds," but the Gael was already on his feet. An innocent pitcher, jarred by the sudden movement of his hand, flew from the table and shattered on the floor. He did not seem to hear it, but stood quivering, every inch of his being attuned to the martial sounds beneath the window.

*"Saighdear Ruadh!"* he whispered. "Red soldiers! Quickly, mistress! Do you have a sword about you?"

"Why, certainly not!"

The Gael drew a steel pistol from his coat and aimed it toward the window.

"Please, desist!" Abby said, rising so quickly she upended the table and sent it crashing onto the Turkish carpet. "Heaven save us! It is only the militia! They march past here every evening! Look! They are already gone." She patted his arm, and when at last he stopped trembling and lowered his pistol she went to the window and peeked down into the street. It was vacant, save for two drunkards lying by the roadside and a small, ragged boy Lydia's age, standing under the window gazing up at her with perfectly round eyes.

"Gone," she whispered.

A thumping on the stairs was followed by an even louder thumping on the door. "Is there need of me?" bellowed Hugo. "Are ye in distress, Abigail?"

Abby turned on the stranger. "See what you have done, you brainless ox," she hissed at the Scot, now standing sorrowfully with his chin on his chest. She turned to face the door and the sound of the barkeep's anxious voice. "There's naught amiss, Hugo. All is well. I stupidly upset the table and the supperware. That was the noise you heard. I shall clean it myself. It's nothing, nothing."

The thumping stopped, as she was sure it would as soon as she had mentioned the possibility of straightening up a mess. Hugo hated keeping things clean and neat. She listened as he grumbled and thudded his way down the staircase. Two raps came from Celestine's wall, and Abby answered with two raps. Yes, everything was really quite all right.

The Gael lifted his head and sighed deeply. "Forgive me, mistress. I am most ashamed." He tucked his pistol back inside his coat. "What can I do to offend the situation?"

"The situation is offensive enough as it is," sniffed Abby. "But if you wish to *amend* it, please have a seat and remain seated. Engage me in conversation."

They resumed their seats amid the rubble of dishes, food, silverware and spilled chocolate. "Now," began Abby, "I want you to know I am ever so grateful that you are not about to force yourself upon me. You could, you know, if you wished, with complete impunity. Tell me, how did you come here? Where are you bound?"

He tugged at his breeches, clearly uncomfortable with the feel of fabric against his legs. "Well, mistress, as I said before, I came to the city after I fled the red soldiers. It was some days after a great battle at Sheriffmuir where the forces of King James fared very badly indeed. It will be some time, I'm thinking, before a Stuart bottom will be warming the throne. Many men, my kinsmen and friends among them, lost their lives. And I carry something to remind me of them."

The man turned his face to the left and drew back a handful of long, ginger-colored hair. Just above his ear was a purple gash as long as his forefinger. Abby gasped, unable to look away. For a moment she could think of nothing but the dream-Roger. The Gael let his hair fall back over his scar. "A memento from one of your countrymen, an officer," he said, his voice calm and steady, without a breath of bitterness. "A saber wound. Very clean. He meant to cleave my head in twain, of course,

but his aim was none of the best, luckily for myself. I
hope it is not too repulsed."

"Repulsive," corrected Abby in a whisper, instantly
hoping the fellow had not heard her. She felt a burst of
sympathy for the poor man.

"Yes, repulsive," he repeated. "Pardon me. In any
event, I was not in the best of health nor the best of
mind. I admit, I lost my bearings and almost walked into
a troop of grenadiers. I outdistanced them at Craig-
nalughd, and lifted this coat—" he picked at the shoulder
"—and this pair of breeks from a poor addle-brained
souse at the changehouse there."

"You stole them."

"Aye, but I could scarcely wear my own plaid and
tartan hose, now, could I? When I came upon another
troop I had the good fortune to be passing a group of
laborers, and I joined them and entered the city in their
company. It was from them I got my hat—" he picked
up a disreputable tricorn from the floor and set it gently
on his lap "—and my new hose and blouse and shoon."

Abby glanced at the broken-toed brogues and tattered
stockings. It was a pity none of Hugo's clothing would
fit the man any better than the rags he wore. "Now you
are here, but where are you bound?"

The Highlander's face took on a dreamy, distant look.
"Ah, mistress. Home. Home to Loch Shiel and my family
on the road north, the road to the isles that the cattledrovers
take during their long summer journeys. Home to my Catriona and little Calum and Anghas and Morag and Mairi.
The name of my house is Bailebeag, in Glenalagan, just
north of the loch in the land of Clan Donald. I trow that
means nothing to you. Let me see . . . 'tis not far from
Glencoe, four days' march from the mountains you call
the Trossachs . . ."

"I'm afraid I know very little of your country."

". . . And only three days' march and a short boat ride from the outer islands, the isles of Skye and Lewis and . . ."

Abby felt the blood rush from her face. "I beg your indulgence. Did you say the Isle of Skye?"

"Aye, indeed I did, mistress," said the Gael, watching her carefully. "Skye, the winged island, they call it. Is aught the matter? You no look well."

Her hands began to tremble and her eyes filled with water. "Lydia!" she blurted. "Lydia is on that island. With a man, a chieftain, I believe. Duninnis is his name. He . . . my husband, that is, gave him our daughter."

He frowned and scratched his chin. "Your husband gave Duninnis your daughter? You mean Duninnis took her as his foster daughter?"

She shook her head. Fostering children with relatives was common among the Gaels, she knew. But Lydia's disappearance had been sudden and unplanned. How could she explain it? She herself did not fully understand it. "It wasn't fosterage."

"Is this an English custom then, mistress?"

"Indeed not. Lydia's misfortune had something to do with her father's debts. I believe he meant to accompany her but, you see, he was struck down. I would not have known any of this had my friend Janet not overheard two gentlemen discussing the matter at The Mermaid. She knows how deeply I love Lydia, and she told me forthwith. But until now I had no notion at all where the Isle of Skye might be or how to get there."

"You'll note that you still do not know where it is," the Gael reminded her, leaning back in his chair. From deep inside his coat he pulled a clay pipe and a sack of tobacco, then proceeded to fill the bowl and light it with a tinder box. "I know this Duninnis," he said slowly. "He is not a bad man. In fact, he and I are distant kin."

Abby leaped to her feet and quickly sat back down. "But this is incredible good luck! You know the island! You know the man! Absolutely amazing! Take me there at once!"

To her dismay the stranger burst out laughing, sending clouds of tobacco smoke rolling from his mouth. "Mistress, mistress! Now you take your ease! I cannot let you come with me on the road to the isles. It's a dangerous, difficult journey, not for a woman, especially a city-bred woman such as yourself."

Something within her struggled to say, "Very well, if you think so," but she managed to thrust it away. This time she was not going to let her timid self get the best of her, not where Lydia was concerned. "I was born in London, but I have lived most of my life in the country," said Abby, remembering the rolling green fields around Brenthurst and the orchards of her parents' country home. "I venture to say I am as hardy as any Scotchwoman."

The Gael nearly choked on his tobacco. "I intend to move swiftly. And I will be sleeping outdoors at night, on the stones and in the heather. Is that to your liking?"

"I am a very swift walker when I choose to be," said Abby, drawing herself up as tall as she could. After all, she and Roger had walked in the garden every day at Brenthurst. "And I will sleep anywhere you ask me to, as long as I know Lydia is my destination."

"I shall be eating raw oatmeal soaked in cold water."

"Food is of no consequence whatsoever," said Abby. She briefly thought of chocolate, then dismissed the thought. "I will eat anything and be happy."

He looked at her sharply. "You're quite serious, I think."

"Oh I am, indeed! Nothing is more serious to me than finding my daughter."

The Gael shook his head. "Nay, mistress, it isn't natural. You're a good woman, I trow, even though you were born south of the Highland Line. But your people made the blood of my people flow like a river at Sheriffmuir. I can never forget that."

"You trust me not!" she cried in disbelief. "Yet you revealed your identity to me the moment I entered the room."

"I can never refuse a forthright question," he answered, fumbling with the empty whisky glass.

"You should know," she continued coldly, "that my father was killed by the very people you cherish so highly." Her voice trembled at the memory; she had been only seven years old, and all she could recall of her father's death was her mother's black gown and broken face and the constant weeping that had kept her awake until daybreak for many, many nights. "And that *I* shall never forget."

For several minutes the room filled up with silence. The Highlander puffed on his pipe while Abby stared at him fiercely, challenging him with her eyes. "I know you love your daughter," he said at last, when his pipe had died out, "and your wish to find her is admirable and seemly." She waited, her hands clasped before her. "Saxon or no, you've no deceit in you, it's true. Why, you've had chances galore to play me false. But even so, mistress, I cannot take you. It would not be right nor decent. Besides that, I wish to be with my family. Taking you to Skye would take me away from them. And should

I fall to the soldiers, what would happen to you then? Nay, it's asking too much of you and of me."

Perhaps the man was lying to her. Perhaps he was not in the least related to Lydia's captor. No matter. "Take me only as far as you wish. I will travel the remaining distance on my own." She took a deep breath. "Have you considered," she said carefully, "that a man may travel far more easily in the company of a woman than he can when alone? You could be my husband, my servant, my brother. Who would suspect you of any disloyalty to the crown? But a man by himself—he above all others is suspicious. And besides, your pursuers are looking for a lone man."

"There's something to what you say," muttered the Gael, lifting a bannock from the floor and stuffing the morsel in his mouth. "You are a very clear thinker, for a woman." He peered out the window. "See you, it's completely dark now. The curfew is at ten tonight. Have you a timepiece?"

Abby pointed to the black and gilt enameled clock upon the mantel. "It is just past nine o'clock. Give me your acceptance, and I shall have my belongings packed and be at your service before the clock strikes the half hour."

"You are not going with me," he growled, but she thought his voice lacked conviction. Burning with inspiration she went to the washstand, opened a small drawer and withdrew a stringpurse made of jade green silk. "Silver," she said, holding it up for his inspection. "Two good-hearted ladies here, Janet and Chloe, give me a few coins now and then. Mistress knows nothing about it. There's a gold florin as well, a gift from an acquaintance of Roger's, here just last week. You'll need some coin, won't you? You can't undertake extensive travels without silver, can you?" She shook the purse so that it jingled pleasantly.

"Aye, it would help," he drawled. "But I still feel that this journey's not best for you."

"And this . . . this is better?" She swept her arm around the tiny chamber. "To live like a lapdog? Worse than a dog, really. Always at the command of others. Like a slave. Always debased and abused and degraded." She lowered her voice. "Not a week after I came here a woman was killed only two doors away from this very room. Priscilla was her name. She said the wrong thing to the wrong gentleman, and he struck her. Dead. Oh, afterward it was handled very quietly and discreetly. Happenstance, they called it. But Janet saw it all. And Janet told me." She touched her flaming cheek. "This mark? It's the work of my mistress."

She looked at him intently. He pulled at his breeches again and seemed most uncomfortable. She had affected him, but if she played him wrong she would lose him. "My dear sir. I know how absurd my request must seem, but I beseech you, hear me out. Lydia is life to me. I have nothing save her. Until you came, I thought I had lost her forever, but you have brought me the tiniest grain of a possibility that I might see her again. Please, don't take it from me." She paused, unable to tell if he were moved or not. "You have a daughter, have you not?"

"Aye. Two daughters. One very young, the other a big lass like your Lydia."

It seemed to her his voice was hushed and subdued. "Of course you must miss them. What if you thought you would never see them again? If they were completely lost to you?"

"Why, I would be next to myself with grief, I suppose."

*Beside yourself,* she corrected him silently. "Then you must know, must truly know and feel, what I undergo every day, Mr. MacDonald."

"Calum, mistress."

"Calum. And you must call me Abby. You know the pain in my heart that threatens to destroy me, to engulf me. You do know what I am speaking of, I trust." She held her breath. On an impulse she reached out and patted his hand.

The Highlander sat perfectly still for several moments, then without warning sprang to his feet and strode to the door. She was after him at once, only an instant too late to seize his arm and prevent him from leaving. The door closed against her face, its edge pinching the tips of her fingers as she tried to grasp it. He was gone! And with him, all hope of finding Lydia.

Her throat grew tight. Her aching cheek stung, as though anticipating the flow of her tears. How could she have been so stupid as to drive away her only hope of happiness?

She listened for the tread of his feet in the hallway, but all she heard were several doors creaking open as some of the more curious ladies doubtlessly tried to catch a glimpse of the ferocious Jacobite. Abby held her breath. One by one the doors closed. Suddenly the latch of her own door began to rattle. In one smooth movement Calum opened the door, entered the room, and shut himself inside.

His face was only a handbreadth from hers. His eyes burned green in the faint glow of the fire and seemed to have taken on a look of tenderness. "You would rather die than lose your child. I know the feeling well."

Suddenly his face changed. For the first time he glowered at her with menace in his eyes, and for an instant she glimpsed the warrior her countrymen must have seen at Sheriffmuir. "I might ravish you and abandon you on the moors."

"So you might, but I think not. And if you did, what of it? It could be no worse than being abandoned in Glasgow and ravished several times daily."

"You're not afeared of me?"

"Afraid of you? Only for the first few moments I saw you. But not now." Hopes of finding Lydia had made her fearless. "I daresay you are the least frightening man I have encountered at the Heart's-ease."

"You've a heart in you," he admitted gruffly, "not unlike my own Catriona. List, now. I have a plan for leaving the gates of the city. You could prove very helpful if you do just as I say and not be too English."

Was he agreeing to take her? She thought he must be, but she couldn't say for sure, his face looked so threatening. She was English born and bred; how could she not *be* English? "I promise you, I'll do what I can."

"And you'll not whine like a child nor complain nor try to change my mind after I've made my decisions?"

"Not at all!"

"Now I will not take you to Skye, you understand. Only to Bailebeag. You must go to the end of the road to the isles and make the channel crossing on your own. If any silver is left after our travels, you may have it. And I will arrange for a guide and a horse. Is that satisfactory to you?"

"More than satisfactory. You are most kind. I shan't be able to thank you enough." She felt her legs bouncing underneath her, ready to be off. "It was wicked of me to call you an ox. After all, it was I who spilled the china. Will you please accept my apology?"

"Well, then." He smiled again, and the ferocity drained

from his face. "I accept. But you are right. I was indeed an ox, a brainless one at that."

Perhaps, she thought, he had been gauging the depth of her decision. Perhaps his threatening expression was no more than a show. Without stopping to think, she took his head in her hands and kissed his broad brow. Immediately she backed away. "Oh, forgive me! It is this terrible business which has made me so bold."

He smiled sheepishly and his face grew bright pink. "Pay it no mind, Mistress Abby," he said, kissing her hand in return. "You are soon to be quit of it."

# *Three*

## *The New World*

"We must leave now, Abby."

Calum's voice seemed to come to her from a great distance. She shot him a rapid glance and continued to search her chamber for small items to place in the red leather portmanteau which lay spread-eagled on her bed. Thus far it contained only a few items of clothing, Roger's Bible, and some inks, pens and writing paper a kind customer had given her.

The Highlander paced to and fro across the Turkish carpet, his long legs traversing the room in four strides. She stole another look at his frowning face. Was he beginning to think, perhaps, that he'd given in too quickly to her passionate pleas? The mantelclock showed half past nine. She would have to make haste.

But she could not hurry. Too much held her back. She folded two linen handkerchiefs in neat squares and pressed them to her face; a faint scent of lavender still clung to them. "I must take these. Lydia embroidered them for me when she was very little. And this." Abby picked up a small gilt oval and unfolded it into a pair of miniature picture frames. There were Roger and herself in watercolor, their wedding portraits, as fresh as the day they had been painted. She held them up for the Gael's inspection.

"Is that you?"

Abby peered into the face of the younger Abby, a slender, slightly frightened-looking Abby, dressed in white lace and satin. "Yes and my husband, Roger." The artist had captured Roger's dark elegance and carefree heart, though the jabot which billowed under his chin was far too large and white and distracting.

"The fellow looks as if he had just caught sight of a beautiful woman," said Calum.

Abby felt her cheeks begin to burn. "I was prettier then. These were painted just after we had gone to live in Brenthurst. I was but sixteen years old, a child, really."

"And your daughter? Have you her picture as well?"

Abby unwrapped one of the kerchiefs. Inside was a lock of curly brown hair, tied with a lavender ribbon. "It's all I have of her. She favors me, though the curls are Roger's." Her throat tightened, and she struggled to keep back her tears. A woman about to set off on a perilous journey had to be strong, relentless, not given to swooning and weeping. There was no longer room for sentiment in her life. She placed the beloved treasures in the green stringpurse, along with her coins. "I brought this purse from the Rose Cottage," she sighed.

"Mistress, we must make haste. We cannot be on the streets after curfew." Giving vent to his impatience, the Gael leaned forward and shut the portmanteau with such a bang it jumped an inch off the coverlet. "Now then—we are ready to set off. Are you certain you'll be allowed to leave with me?"

Abby stared at him, conscious of her lips parting in amazement.

"Nothing is certain at the Heart's-ease," she replied

slowly. "But the other ladies are constantly coming and going, and I myself have never been challenged on the few occasions a gentleman has escorted me outside. Of course, I have never attempted to leave at such a late hour before, so . . ."

"Enough!" snapped Calum. "We'll leave as quietly as we can, then, and hope everyone else is too detracted with drink or other amusements to notice us. Come." He reached for her hand, but just as she touched it she gave a tiny shriek.

"Janet!" she cried. "I had nearly forgotten her." She opened the case and scribbled a few lines on a sheet of crisp gray paper.

"Pray don't forget the hour," growled the Gael.

"I'll just fetch my cloak."

Abby draped a cloak of thick gray velvet about her shoulders. The costly garment, lined with crimson satin and trimmed about the hood and cuffs with white seal's fur, contrasted oddly with her plain blue frock and sturdy, square-toed shoes. The ladies of the Heart's-ease dressed for beauty and fashion and ease of disrobing, not for long travels over hills and moorland. "Do you think this will do?" she said, whirling the hem of the cloak about her feet.

"Mayhap, for the time being. You'll not fare well in the winter on Skye in such fine dress. We'll get you an *arasaid,* such as the women of the district wear. But I will say this, mistress—you look quite fetching. My Catriona's not a jealous woman, but even she would envy you full sore. 'Tis well you washed the lead and paint and such like muck from your face."

Abby brushed her fingertips against her mouth, then stared at her hand. "It feels so peculiar to have my face clean again."

Holding a candle in a pewter sconce, Abby led Calum into the narrow hallway, then made straight for Janet's compartment. "The staircase! The staircase!" hissed Calum at her back, but she could not leave Janet without at least some brief word of thanks.

But Janet was not alone. Gruff laughter rang from behind the door, and Abby could hear her friend's voice, as quiet as a breath of wind, whispering, "Go to! Go to! The devil, you say!" She slipped her message under the door and hurried back to her impatient escort.

"Leaving your note, were you? We haven't time for such fancies, mistress." In the candlelight, Calum's face glowed scarlet and golden. Seizing Abby's hand, the Gael half-dragged, half-guided her down the shadowed stairs.

As she had hoped, at this late hour most of the ladies were in their rooms, occupied, like Janet. But the tavern in the front of the Heart's-ease was still doing excellent business. The chatter and laughter of unseen men rolled into the hallway, reminding Abby of the gaming houses Roger so liked to frequent.

*"Dia!"* gasped Calum. "This place puts me in mind of my grandmother. She was forever talking about the *shee* and restless spirits of the dead walking abroad. Fairy magic hid them from human eyes, but their voices might always be heard, chattering to each other."

"Please, no talk of the dead," whispered Abby, clinging to his arm. The darkened halls put her in mind of the burial vault that held her father and mother.

"Keep your bag well hidden 'neath your cloak, least someone spy us. We'll away now quickly, while we've the time."

As they turned into the passageway that led to the rear door, a giant rose out of nowhere to block their path.

" 'Tis Hugo," Abby explained to Calum. "The barkeep. We are undone."

The monster had just entered the very door they had intended to exit, on a visit to the privy, no doubt, judging by the disarray of his waistcoat and breeches. No taller than her Gael, Hugo nonetheless weighed a great deal more. His startled gaze and shaggy red hair and beard gave him the look of an enormous hound which had just discovered prowlers in his master's house.

"I thought I was after hearing footsteps on the stairs," he growled. "Where are ye bound, Miss Abigail? The mistress doesn't wish her ladies out so late the night, ye ken."

Abby breathed in deeply. "This gentleman wishes to introduce me to a friend of his at the Black Boar, Hugo. We shall return presently. Please stand aside now and let us past."

"Aye, fellow," added Calum. "Be a good lad and let us by."

"I implore you, hold your tongue," whispered Abby.

The savage ignored her completely. "Why, I'll have the lady back safe and sound—before curfew falls," Calum lied to Hugo. "Your mistress won't guess Abigail has even set foot outside." He slipped his hand into his coat and withdrew one of the coins Abby had given him earlier. "And here's silver to seal my promise."

The huge man craned his neck to inspect the coin in the dim light of the passageway, then shook his head. "The mistress would have my stones for disobeying her," he rumbled, "so stay here ye must. Yer friend, master, must wait 'til the morn."

A few idle drunkards had gathered in the passageway, drawn by the sound of Hugo's mastiff voice. Abby held her breath as Calum motioned them back. They gave ground, only to return a moment later. What time was it? Calum was right; she had lingered too long over her packing.

"Look here, man," barked Calum, stepping forward smartly.

"Calum, come back."

Again he ignored her. If he thought that Hugo would be cowed by a bold gesture, she was sure he was sadly mistaken. "If you refuse to listen to reason," said Calum, "then perhaps . . ."

There was a sudden movement in the shadows, a cracking sound, and the next thing Abby knew, Calum was lying on the floorboards, groaning. She watched him touch his nose; his fingertips came away red. The watchers skittered about him, gabbling nervously. "Fists! Fists! Fists!" cried one man.

Abby rushed to his side, pressing her silk kerchief gently against his streaming nostrils. She had to formulate a plan, and quickly too, before curfew was sounded. "Brute! Beast! Hobgoblin! Murderer!" she shouted at Hugo. "The poor gentleman meant no harm. Mistress will hear of this, I warrant you."

"Will she indeed?"

The voice was barely loud enough to be heard over the din of the large throng that now crowded the passageway, yet everyone immediately fell silent. Abby helped Calum to his feet. In the light of several torches and candles she could make out Mistress' pinched face and glowing false eye. Someone stood behind her, and as the flickering light shifted, Abby could see it was a woman, her head haloed by brilliant red hair. "Heaven protect me!" cried Abby. "Janet!"

The red-haired woman lowered her eyes. She would not look Abby in the face.

"Yes, Janet was quite helpful," said Mistress. "It was she who alerted me to your absence, Abigail."

Janet glanced up briefly, her face streaked with tears. "I thought ye were in danger of yer life, Abby. I had to tell someone, my heart."

"Enough of this," snorted Mistress, flicking her hand in Janet's face. Clad only in a gray silk dressing gown which revealed the tops of her bare breasts, the woman surveyed the scene like a master of hounds at the hunt. First she glared at Hugo, then Calum, and finally at Abby, her false eye veering off in directions of its own choosing. "Is aught the matter? Hugo, what is the meaning of this disturbance?"

"This man tried to take Abigail out of the house, Mistress," answered the barkeep, "so I stopped him. As ye'll remember ye'd told me, 'No ladies out near curfew,' and near it is."

"Stopped him perhaps too abruptly," observed Mistress, inclining her head ever so slightly toward Calum. "Are you all right, sir? Not seriously injured, I hope?"

"Not at all," said Calum.

*Yes, yes!* thought Abby, and she pinched the man's bare wrist. Calum turned sharply, groaning as he glared at her. "Ah, but he is injured!" she shrilled. "His pride covers the truth, madame. Hugo tried to kill my gentleman. Note my kerchief." She held up the bloodied cloth. "He's injured far worse than he'll admit. If you please, let me take him to the surgeon on Elizabeth Row, at least to make certain he is not in any danger."

Calum threw her a quick, approving look, and Abby returned it. Was he, perhaps, just a little proud of her dissemblance?

The Gael put his hand to his forehead. "Actually, mistress, I don't feel well at all. My head is throbbing something fierce, and I can't see very clearly."

"I swear I but tapped him," objected Hugo. Someone in the crowd concurred, and another disagreed. Soon they were bickering back and forth over the force of the blow, striking their palms with their fists to illustrate their opinions.

Calum gave a low moan. "Hurry, or he'll faint from loss of blood," pressed Abby. If he had not given her that one steely glance, she would have sworn that he was indeed badly hurt.

"I deplore you, let the woman take me to this leech of hers."

Mistress stiffened, and Abby could tell she was thinking of Priscilla. She surely wouldn't want to add another deadly incident to her credit. The building seemed to hold its breath as Mistress considered his request; even the tavern customers had stopped their palm-punching and arguing.

"Abby, see your visitor to the physician. But mind you not mention he was injured here. And return quickly." She turned to the growing mob behind her. "Gentlemen, the house will stand you each a drink." Almost at once the passageway emptied. Janet plunged after the men, her face in her hands. Besides herself and the Highlander, only Mistress and Hugo remained behind.

"Let me go with them, Mistress," growled Hugo. "If they are planning a mischief, they'll not get it past me."

"No, Hugo, you are needed here," she replied sternly. "Listen. Already your patrons demand your services. Little Tommy will be sore pressed to fill the glasses of so many. Do be so good as to apologize to the poor gentleman here, then make haste to attend to your customers."

For a moment Abby feared that the barkeep might challenge her, but it was not to be. Instead he muttered his apologies to Calum without looking at him and set off toward the front of the building, very nearly at a run. It must be humiliating, thought Abby, for such a big man to put himself at the service of a woman, even a woman as strong and capable as Mistress.

"Thank you, Mistress," murmured Abby, patting Calum's arm as if to comfort him. She could barely suppress the thrill of triumph in her voice. "You're very kind."

"Don't assume for a moment that I don't know what you are doing," said Mistress.

Abby felt a chill pass through her body like a knife. Calum's arm twitched once beneath her fingers. "You have no intentions of visiting the surgeon, and even less of returning. Am I correct?"

Abby thought best not to answer. She glanced at Calum and found him staring resolutely into Mistress' lop-sided gaze. "Protesting will do no good. I glimpsed your valise beneath your cloak, Abigail. Nothing, as you know, escapes my eyes."

*Your eye, you mean,* thought Abby, smiling half a smile.

"And yet you sent Hugo away," said Calum.

"Yes." She paused, and an odd expression crossed her face, neither a grin nor a snarl nor a pout, and yet something like all three combined. "I have no intention of stopping you."

The flickering dance of the candles in the wall sconces revealed only parts of Mistress' face at a time, giving her a ghostly, shattered look. "Do you mean to say we are free to leave?" said Abby.

"Indeed. If you wish. Why should I detain you? I see I have vastly misjudged the nature of this gentleman, or else you have charmed him into submission, at least for the nonce. No matter, Abby. You'll come back to the Heart's-ease, of this I have no doubt. If not on the morrow, then in a week or a fortnight or a month or two or three. Your spirit is not strong enough, you know, to let you live an independent life. Such as mine, for example."

Mistress drew a square of linen from her sleeve and blew her nose with such force that Calum fingered his injured nose and Abby felt her own nose tingle. "Where you will go and what you will do with yourself are your considerations now, not mine. Now begone, and quickly! You will be caught out past the curfew and spend the month in prison. Hurry! Begone!" She waved them away with the piece of linen. *"Adieu! Adieu!* Until we meet again, little Abigail. But if you should encounter difficulty, please—do not bring it back with you."

Abby bristled. How dare the woman insult her so! "I assure *you,* madame, I'll not be back." As Calum rushed her out the door, Abby caught a final view of Mistress' face, her mouth twisted into a frightful parody of a smile. At last she was free of this devil of a woman, free of this horrible place, free of a fate she did not even dare to imagine.

But her gallant Highlander was not quite free just yet. Once through the door and into the courtyard, she grabbed his hand and gave it a brisk shake. "Thank you, thank you, a thousand thanks," she sputtered. "Only one moment more, I beg you."

"We have precious few moments left, woman."

Abby stooped down and picked up a pebble from the ground. Drawing a bead on the swinging inn sign and its faded violets, Abby let fly with the stone. To her delight, it struck the weathered wood with a loud, satisfying crack, sending the sign into a fit of wild swinging and creaking. All the anger and disgust closeted within her for weeks flowed from her, and she smiled. Roger would have been proud of her aim.

"A thousand devils!" yelped Calum. "What a start you gave me! Why do that, woman? Are you lost to your senses?"

"Ah, I have never felt saner, Mr. MacDonald! But come! Why do you loiter? The tollgate is near! Make haste! Make haste!"

Out the door, down the steps, and into the close that ran by the building she made haste. It was all she could do. She stopped, panting. She could not move so much as her finger. She could feel Calum tugging at her hand and hear his agitated pleas to hurry, hurry, hurry, but her feet refused to listen to him.

She breathed in deeply. Never had the night air smelled so good! She thought she could make out the scent of salt from the sea and, much stronger, the odors of wet earth, stagnant water and manure. Calum's breath, full in her face now, smelled faintly of whisky. The scent of woodsmoke from a nearby fire was as sweet as rosewater.

A light rain was falling. She could not remember when she had enjoyed the feel of rain against her skin as much as she did just then. The raindrops trickling into her mouth tasted fresh and clean. The grim tenement buildings, faint lights still glowing in their windows, looked as full of warmth and human kindness as London at Christmastime. It seemed as if she had never seen, heard, smelled nor felt the city at all until that very moment.

Something struck her bottom with a hard smack, almost lifting her off her feet. "Heaven preserve us!" she cried out, more from astonishment than pain.

"Come, woman! We've no time to tarry. Come, come."
Again he pulled at her hand, and this time her feet moved
and she followed him, taking two steps for each of his.
They dashed through the almost deserted streets in the
wet darkness, once narrowly avoiding a bewildered old
man, another time hiding in the shadows as a mounted
officer cantered past over the glistening cobblestones.
Wherever they stepped, water sprayed up around them,
and soon Abby's sensible shoes were soaked through.

As they passed through a narrow lane, a casement
creaked open above their heads and a weary voice called
out, *"Gardy loo!"* Abby staggered backward at the warning, but Calum ploughed ahead. In an instant an arc of
filthy water and nightsoil fell at their feet, spattering her
gown and his hose.

Calum's roaring filled the passageway. He shook his
fists and stamped his feet, and several heads appeared
at several windows, cursing and muttering. It was just as
well Abby did not know his language after all, though
she could comprehend his meaning clearly enough. Once
his fury had subsided somewhat, she laid her hand on
his arm and tried to remind him of his mission. "The
tollgate, Calum," she murmured, "at the end of this lane
and to the right. We're nearly there."

"Are we now?" How quickly and cleverly he turned
from one tongue to the other, from fiery passions to gentle
thoughtfulness. She pointed down the cobbled path and
they continued, Calum pausing only now and then to slap
at the tobacco-colored stains on his breeches and hose.
When Abby saw the great stone archway of the tollgate,
the central portal in the city wall, she smiled to herself.
Here was the gateway to her freedom and to Lydia. Its
dark stones looked hazy and insubstantial in the thin veil
of rain. A lone sentry stood guard, his head down, his scar-

let jacket rust-colored in the shadows of the great gate. How odd that only one soldier should be on duty, but perhaps his fellow was about on an errand, or simply relieving himself.

Abby and Calum pressed close to the wall of a building opposite the gate. "What exactly is your plan?" she asked him.

"A plan? A plan of mine?"

"Yes, indeed. The plan you told me of in the Heart's-ease. You said I might be of help to you, do you recall?"

Calum nodded. "Aye, you're correct. It's much less a plan, mind you, than it is a prayer. Now just be walking forward up to the gate as though you had a right to, as far as the guard will let you. When he challenges you and asks why you'd be leaving the city so late, pretend you cannot understand why he is delaying you. Then leave the rest to me."

"And what will you do?"

"All will go well. I entreat you, don't ply me for explanations."

"I will! I must! What do you intend to do?"

"Play him for a fool," growled Calum, and she could get no further information from him. She walked forward warily, ready to turn and flee at the first glimmer of trouble. The Gaels, she decided, had an undeserved reputation for craftiness. She got no closer than a double arm's length from the sentry when he started, snapped his musket up tight against his chest and stared at her.

"Wha gaes?"

His sudden outburst forced her back a step. Well, who was she? Her mind raced for a suitable answer. Pretending not to understand, as Calum had suggested, seemed dangerous. What if the soldier thought her insolent?

Might he not simply shoot her? No, she needed a reason which might carry her past him.

"A midwife," she replied. "I'm needed just outside the wall. Come, I entreat you, let me through. Already the lady is in danger of losing her child." Had she taken her story too far? She could certainly not retract it now. She clutched her purse and tried to look honest and urgent.

The soldier squinted at her, lowering his musket by degrees until it was on a level with his waist. "Hae I seen ye afore, mistress?"

Fie on it! Had he been a customer? Abby could not remember him. "I am certain we have never met. Now if you please . . . a life is at stake, possibly two." That, indeed, was no falsehood.

"Wha went tae fetch ye? Whaever 'twas, surely he'd be wi' ye now," said the soldier, his voice rich with suspicion.

"Why, he . . . he took leave of me," stammered Abby. "Yes, I believe he went to have a dram at the Heart's-ease." What demon had made her mention the name of that wretched place? She shook her head. "Or perhaps it was the Black Boar."

"Ne'er fear, mistress," replied the soldier, lowering his musket still further. "When Archie comes back, me and yerself will visit both places and search the creature out." The guard grinned wickedly and seized her by the elbow.

As Abby tried to tug free, a hideous cry rose behind her and a broad figure rushed past, nearly bowling her headfirst onto the cobbles. "Egad, brute! Unhand the lady! I say, sirrah! How dast you!"

An Englishman! But no . . . his speech was much too ancient, though his accent seemed fresh from Vauxhall. She pulled away from the sentry just as her outraged rescuer let fly another volley of abuse. "Zounds, I say! I shall have you flogged, whoreson! Evissitated! Emasticated!"

Only one person she knew could mangle the King's English so splendidly. She peered at the wildman, taking in his bedraggled tricorn, tattered coat and spattered stockings. A dark crust of blood still rimmed his nostrils. He'd come within a hair's breadth of fooling her.

Calum had better luck with the Scots sentry than she had. No doubt the fellow was perplexed by the sound of gaming-room English coming from the mouth of a man with mountains, lochs and heather stamped on his face. The guard jerked his musket up before him, but his hands shook and his voice alternated between squeaks and thunder.

"Peace, sir!" he cried. "Enough, now! Take yer ease! Back! Back, lest I fire!" Abby glanced about nervously. The other sentry could not have been far off. Unless he was asleep or quite under the table, he would simply have to hear the uproar. Already several casements had opened in nearby buildings. Someone shouted an obscenity.

Calum's voice wavered, then suddenly grew soft. His ferocity all but melted from him. "Come, sir, no need for violence. A word with you in private, I pray." Pushing the sentry's musket from his face, he took the Scot aside, and when the two returned they were laughing and smiling like bosom companions.

Without waiting a heartbeat, Calum caught Abby by the arm and fairly carried her through the tollgate, the chuckling of the sentry echoing behind them. Safely on the other side of the gate, she clutched his arm to steady herself. Too much was happening too quickly; her head felt as light as foam on ale. "Good heavens! What magic did you use to charm the beast?"

The Gael held up the leather pouch he used to carry his share of Abby's fortune. "The oldest magic, mistress. Silver magic. Faith, that soldier-creature's a far sight more practical than your Hugo." He touched one finger to his swollen nose.

"Your language . . . your English . . . remarkable! Where did you learn to imitate an Englishman so well?"

"Why, from Englishmen, mistress. I can mock any voice if I but hear it once. Even your own." His last words were spoken in a clear, crisp falsetto, and for a moment Abby thought she was listening to herself.

"Magnificent!" Was there no end to the man's peculiarities?

The tap of bootheels on cobblestones caught her ear, but by now most people had covered their fires, leaving the city in darkness. Calum had hurried her into a tiny passage between two thatched-roof buildings. The smell was nearly more than she could bear: whisky, urine and the stench of a dead animal. She gasped, and Calum pressed his hand against her mouth. A red-coated figure rushed toward the tollgate, musket in hand, boots click-click-clicking. She could still hear them long after he had disappeared.

"The other sentry," whispered Abby, "and in a dreadful hurry, too. Wooing some wench, no doubt, or downing a pot of beer. He's quite gone now. Come, Calum. We must be off. Look you—what fortune! The rain has stopped." She grasped his hand but he refused to move, as frozen as she herself had been only minutes earlier. "Please, I beg you, come. Why do you hesitate?" In her mind's eye she could see Lydia, lonely and afraid, gazing out across a black wilderness for a sign of her mother. "We must make haste."

Still the Gael resisted. He would not budge from the reeking darkness of the passageway. "I want a sword."

"A sword? You haven't got one?"

"Nay, nor even a dirk. And my pistol is given to jamming. I must have steel, mistress, if I'm to lead us safely northward. Just now, when I ran up to the guard and he lifted his musket, I should have felt far braver if I'd had my broadsword about me. All I could think of was Sheriffmuir and the terrible fear and bloodshed and my many friends murdered."

"You were brave enough, I think," said Abby, "sword or no. To stand up to one's fears demands the greatest courage possible." Somehow she felt more certain of him now; his feelings were the same as anyone else's. "What shall we do then?"

He jiggled his head back and forth. "Find me a weapon, I imagine. By my troth, I'll not leave the city without a smallsword or a good hangar or a broadsword or a saber or *Dia,* even a foil or a dress sword."

"Surely you do not suggest returning to the Heart's-ease?"

"And have my nose broken this time? Indeed not, mistress!"

"What do you suggest, then?"

To her surprise he had a ready answer, as if he had foreseen the need for a good blade and had already conceived a course of action. "Is there no a tavern or changehouse or inn hard by? A place where drunkards go?"

"This part of the city is unknown to me," she apologized. "But the New World is near here, I believe."

"New world, you say?" gasped the Gael.

"Yes, Janet mentioned it often. She hated going there, but she was always certain of custom when she did."

"She went to the new world often?"

Calum stared at her, mystified, and suddenly she realized the source of his confusion. "Not the colonies. An inn. Just an inn. A dreadful, dirty, miserable inn."

"Aye, that's fine, then."

The New World was one of the many houses and business establishments that had taken root outside the granite walls over the years, as the city grew. Though Abby had never seen the humble stone structure before, she instantly recognized the sign over the door. Janet had described it quite clearly: a red savage, holding a sheaf of tobacco in one hand and the head of an unfortunate enemy in the other. "There you are!" she crowed in triumph.

But Calum had already passed the sign and the doorway and was trotting to the far side of the building. Abby hurried after him and found a small cobbled courtyard, barely visible in the occasional bursts of moonlight that pushed through the clouds. As her eyes grew familiar with the dark, she could make out vaguely human forms lounging on the ground. Sometimes a grunt or gentle sigh broke from the dark figures, disrupting the stillness of the night. Stepping forward in the shadows, she struck her toe against her portmanteau, knocking it over. She seized it, glancing nervously at the peaceful sleepers.

Slowly she became aware of another, far more active figure, maneuvering about the drunken wreckage in the courtyard. It was Calum; she recognized his awkward, lunging gait and long, copper hair. "Do be careful," she whispered, not loud enough for him to hear, but loud enough to make a comforting sound. She heard voices in the dark, Calum's and another man's, beginning soft and low and slow, then erupting in laughter. Another voice joined in with words too blurred for her to comprehend, and then another voice, and another. The still bodies began moving, first as ponderous as the waves of the ocean, then a little more quickly. Finally she heard a shout: "Damned Jacobites!" A flash of steel cut the darkness.

Mayhem exploded. The courtyard, as quiet as death only a moment earlier, was now a struggling mass of movement, noise and confusion. Indistinct human forms collided, cursed, and broke apart. A tin cup flew past her, landing with a clatter in the street. In nearby windows, candlelight appeared.

Where was Calum?

Abby fell back against the wall of the inn, flattening herself against the cold, damp stones. What had she done? How had she let herself become traveling companion to a warlike Jacobite who stole books and started melees among drunkards? She had known him less than five hours, and already he had probably gotten himself killed.

No, he couldn't be dead. Slain over nothing? A piece of steel? What would she do without his guidance? Where would she go? Certainly not back to Mistress. Abby scolded herself for letting Calum take such a risk. She should have thought of another way to provide him with a weapon, done anything, said anything, to keep him safe. Without him, she might as well have been in the center of the brawl now raging in the courtyard of the New World.

She twisted the strings of her purse round and round one hand. Only one thing could be done: she must seek him out. It was imprudent, even perilous, but she could simply not stand still and do nothing; her memory of Lydia called to her, and she had to obey.

As she stepped out into the dim moonlight, she stared into the boiling darkness of the courtyard, unable to force herself toward it. At first the brawl was all of one piece, but as she gazed in horror, a black shape disentangled itself from the whole, emerged from the chaos, and glided toward her. She turned to run just as it swooped upon her, snapped her up in its arms, and raced off down the cobbles, away from the tumult of the New World. Fright stopped her mouth; she could scarcely breathe, let alone give voice to her terror. With one fist she pummeled the stranger's back, clutching her purse and portmanteau in the other.

"Abby! Abby! 'Tis I! 'Tis Calum mac Calum! Be still! Deceased!"

"Desist." At once she wound her arms around the tall Gael's neck, by chance brushing her hand against his leather-hard scar. She did not flinch. When they reached the edges of the city, his frantic gallop slowed to a jog, then a walk. Gasping for breath, he finally set her down by the roadside, a stone's throw from the nearest house. The roar at the New World rose faint and dream-like in the distance.

She took a good look at his face. Blood again trickled from his nose, and again she dabbed it with her kerchief. Strands of wet hair clung to his forehead, and his chest heaved with every breath. But he was unhurt. "Calum! You're alive!"

"Indeed!" he puffed. "Alive . . . and victorious!" He held up a smallsword in one hand and a pint flask in the other. "Now I'll take on any man . . . or woman, for that matter. *Slainte!*" He drank from the flask, then offered it to her.

"No thank—My portmanteau!"

"You have it in your hand."

For the first time in many weeks, Abby laughed. The

sound of her laughter, so light with relief, made her mer-
rier still, and she laughed all the harder. "So I have!"

"Come, let me take it, lest in your grief you drop it."

Once again she burst out laughing, only to have sobs
interrupt her laughter, and the next moment she was
weeping in earnest, tears flowing off her face and onto
her sleeves.

Calum murmured something in his strange language
and pulled her against his chest. Steam rose from his
warm, damp body. "Take heart, Abby," he whispered,
patting her on the back. "You've lived an entire life in
one night. You did well, and now you are free for aye.
Soon we'll be traveling the road to the isles, and at its
end you'll find your Lydia."

Abby nodded, still weeping. She wept for Roger, for
Brenthurst, for the Rose Cottage she had left behind in
Glasgow, for Janet, who had betrayed her, for all the
wretched ladies and gentlemen of the Heart's-ease. She
wept for Lydia, alone without a mother, and for Calum's
children, parted from their father. She wept for the poor
drunken brutes battling each other in the courtyard of
the New World, and for Calum, a good man, savage or
not, wet, exhausted, and bleeding from the nose. But
most of all she wept for joy.

# *Four*

## *A Fire in the Heart*

Thomas Racker sat, his pen poised in his hand. A chill wind whistled through the flap in his campaign tent, fluttering the flames of the three candles on his folding desk. In a moment the wind died down, the candles once more blazed brightly, and the night lay calm and silent. The empty parchment stared at him, begging for words.

*Dearest Diana,* he began. It was not, he thought, a very comely name—too round, too feminine. He imagined his wife's face, as smooth and simple as an egg. He closed his eyes, breathed deeply, then continued writing in a script as graceful as any engraver's.

*How happy I am to have the opportunity to return your kind letter of November 10. You will have heard, of course, of our great victory at Sherrifmuir, and how the Jacobite rebels broke, ran and retreated from our superior forces. Unfortunately, many brave supporters of His Majesty also fell that day, but the victory ensured his safety on the throne, at least for the time being. These brutes are nothing if not persistent. You need not worry for me, by the way. I received nothing more serious than a scratch on the hand, though many Jacobites fell to my saber.*

*It saddens me deeply, and I know it will sadden you*

*as well, to report that my honest captain and dear friend, Edwin Richardson, was slain in the thick of the battle, just as he was alighting from his wounded horse to do combat on foot. A treacherous rebel cut him down from behind. I do not have to explain to you how this misfortune has affected me, since you yourself have often remarked on the good captain's excellent disposition and observed our deep friendship. He had a certain way about him, a courageous spirit and a noble nature not easily matched.*

A drop of perspiration fell onto the parchment, obliterating the "f" in "friendship." The major set down his quill, his hand trembling. Taking a silken kerchief from his wrist, he wiped his dripping brow and chin. His skin was rough with bristles; he would need to be shaved in the morning. Racker took a sip of Marsala from a silver flask at the foot of his desk and resumed his letter.

*I and my troop are currently camped just north of a valley named Glenfinnan, in the extreme west of this inhospitable, barbaric country. There is some unrest among my men, who decry the miserable weather and lack of proper victuals, though I am assured by reliable sources that the weather, as frigid as it is just now, will assuredly become worse.*

*If you wonder at the extreme northernness of my position, my dear, allow me to explain: I have been assigned the agreeable task of making certain that as many renegades as possible who participated in the uprising are brought to justice, and their families severely reprimanded. Agreeable, I say, not because this duty takes me away from you for an even longer period of time than I had anticipated, but because it is accounted a great honor, since few are deemed courageous enough to attempt it. Furthermore, by leading a peace-keeping expedition, I believe I can make some small contribution to the welfare of our beloved country and ultimately its future harmony by punishing those responsible for this treasonous act of insurrection. Already I have been able to rout a few of the miscreants and destroy some buildings where they are reputed to take refuge. As to the Pretender, the traitorous spawn of the wretched James, he has run like the dog that he is and is rumored to have already returned to France, deserting his supporters.*

*My new captain of my mission is one Donald Campbell by name, a Scotchman of few words and much muttering. A member of the Duke of Argyll's army, he is every bit as distressed to be assigned to my company as I am to accept his. He is a rough fellow, the opposite of Captain Richardson, and very nearly as savage as the Jacobites he tirelessly pursues. They are, I understand, members of clans traditionally in opposition to Clan Campbell, and therefore his natural enemies. You see, he is not quite the staunch Loyalist he avows to be, as he is driven more by old hatreds than by any love for His Majesty. Still, he is quite well acquainted with the region and has been, perhaps in spite of himself, most helpful to my purpose and the king's.*

A spatter of raindrops struck the tent. The major's hand jerked backward, sending a delicate spray of ink over his last paragraph. *Damnation!* A heavy rain began to fall, showering against the canvas like a volley of pebbles. The major's hand shook in a spasm of cramps. He clenched and unclenched it briskly, until it shook no more. The major did not care for rain. Like the ever-present mist, it hid too many secrets.

*It is my sincere hope this letter finds you well and that you are enjoying your stay with your sister in Oxsley.*

*You should be receiving this just as you return. I do hope
you have not spoiled your nieces and nephews to a great
extent, though I certainly will understand if you have. I
shall write to you again at the very next opportunity that
presents itself to tell you more about the details of my
expedition.*

*Your most faithful servant and loving husband, Thomas*

Major Racker blotted the letter with great care,
folded it and sealed it with red wax. He then drew a
small volume bound in burgundy-colored leather from
inside his coat and spread it out before him on the tiny
writing desk. He glanced about, listening, but heard
only the roar of the rain and the far-off neighing of an
unhappy horse. Racker retrieved his pen from the ink-
well. Again his hand was shaking, but he forced himself
to write.

*My dearest Edwin,*

*Dear God in heaven, I miss you, my friend! Only you
and you alone must realize the depth of my emptiness,
my ceaseless agony, worse by far than any head pain I
have ever had. A heart pain, if you will. With you gone,
my kindest Edwin, the hours creep by like some lowly
creatures sunk in mud, without the sweet anticipation of
an hour, a minute, the smallest particle of time spent
with you.*

*Where are you now? Hades, I have no fear of it, con-
sidering the very nature of our consort. And yet I would
gladly walk through a thousand walls of fire to but grasp
your hand again. Doubtless I shall meet you in flames,
when my campaigning is at a close.*

*I don't believe I ever told you my experience on first
catching sight of you. I was on my way to some important discussion when I beheld you, mounting your
horse. Such grace, such beauty, such angelic move-*

*ment! Man was not meant to look as beautiful as you did then. I stood transfixed as you turned the beast and cantered off, never even having noticed my wretched presence. For wretched I was indeed, and have been ever since, torn apart by an unquenchable fire that destroys my heart as well as my immortal soul. My dearest Edwin, would that you—*

Major Racker's quill skittered across the page as the flap to his tent shuddered, opened, and revealed a foot, a leg, a man's entire body. At once the major closed the journal over his hand to keep his privy words from smearing. "Campbell! Damn your eyes! Don't you people announce yourselves?" Doubtless the cur could not read, yet it was foolish to take risks.

The dripping Gael saluted with a listless wave of his hand, covering his face with a shower of water droplets. "I am announcing myself, major. Give me leave to speak, if I may."

The major felt heat rushing up his neck. Damn the man and his insolence! Yet there was little to be done about it. Without knowledge of the area supplied by the captain and his Highland soldiers, Racker would have to rely on maps for plotting his expedition. And the maps, drawn by men who had never set eyes on these forsaken mountains, were filled with errors. "Say what you will."

"Major, my men are very unhappy here. It's the homeland of our enemy, Clan Donald, and every rock and tree seems unfriendly to them. They are sick of fighting women and children and living out in the cold and wet, with nary a roof or a wall in sight. If you don't provide some distraction for them in the way of honest combat, you can expect to lose many. They will simply return to their warm homes and warm wives in Argyle.''

The major looked the captain over with utmost precision. Tall and stout. Ten more years and the man would be decidedly fat. His great bush of curly red hair, half hidden under a blue bonnet, was pulled into an unruly queue at the back. Given Campbell's belted plaid and warlike stance, it was all the major could do to refrain from reaching for his pistol. He detested all redshanks, even Loyalist ones. "Desertion is a serious offense."

"Indeed it is. And being deserted in a strange country, without benefit of anyone who can guide one through it, is also a serious situation."

The major folded his hands together. "Are you saying you, too, would desert me?"

The captain reared back his head, his eyes half closed. "Not a whit, major. I am only informing you that my clansmen are not above turning against me, slaying me and leaving you and your lads in breeks to find your own way about. I am therefore requesting a move westward, toward the coast and the Hebrides. The weather is warmer, provisions more plentiful."

"The Hebrides—the Misty Isles, you call them. Yes, I know the place you mean. And exactly what amusements will you be up to, Captain Campbell?"

The Scotchman took a deep breath. *You're wise to be wary of me,* thought the major. He stared at Campbell until the captain's gaze fell to the floor, then rose to the level of the major's chest. "Amusements, major? We were speaking of revolt, as I recall it."

*"You* were speaking of revolt, my dear captain, not I. If I am to suffer a mutiny, so be it. I cannot believe there is one man under my command who will judge me an

unreasonable leader." The major slipped his fingers from his journal so that it shut completely. The ink by now would be quite dry. "I have ridden through the jaws of hell at Sherrifmuir and survived. The men are well aware of that. They respect me for it."

"Aye, but you'll agree that we are short of provisions. And if you believe the weather is bad now, you will look back on it as pleasant in a fortnight or less."

"It's true," mused the major, tapping his fingers against his lips. "What boots it to stay here after all, when we have turned so much of the rebels' country into char? However . . ." Major Racker rose, clutching the journal to his chest. "I believe the welfare of your soldiers has little to do with this discussion of ours, captain. I believe a more personal reason lies behind your proposal."

"And the reason for your belief, major?"

"Why, merely a whim. Although I might point out your sanguine face, your trembling hands, your tightened lips. You are hiding your true purpose, captain."

Campbell parted his lips and stuffed his hand into his plaid. He peered at Racker through squinted eyes, as if taking aim at the major's forehead. "You enjoy telling people what they are thinking, do you, sir?"

"Come, come, Campbell! Prove me wrong, if you can." Racker jabbed his forefinger into the captain's fleshy waist. The major's pulse raced, his groin tightened. He could almost smell the exquisite fragrance of the captain's anger. "You won't enlighten me? Then I shall guess. A grudge of tremendous proportions. Someone inhabiting the west coast has stolen some cattle of yours. No? Then he has slain a friend. Or broken an oath. Cheated at whist, perhaps? No? Come, tell me! What did the whoreson do to you? You surely did not think you could avoid keeping the truth from me?" The captain's lips curled upward in half a snarl, and the major drew back ever so slightly. "Out with it!"

"There is a woman in Ardnamurchan," croaked Campbell. "My wife knows naught of her." He laid his sizable hand across the hilt of his broadsword. "Only a man weary of living would inform her."

"An affair of the heart! But of course! How deucedly stupid of me! You may trust me implicitly, of course. Ardnamurchan, you say? What lies there, captain, other than your *paramour*, that is?"

Campbell stammered and shook his head, trying to collect his paltry wits. "Still Jacobite territory . . . the land of Clan Donald. Plenty to keep my lads busy making good on old debts. Corn and beef . . . whisky galore. At least enough to last through Candlemas."

Racker laid his hand on Campbell's shoulder, but recoiled at once as his fingers sunk into the captain's sodden plaid. The major wiped his hand on a blank sheet of parchment. "Your foresight is commendable, captain. I have intended for some time to march westward, into the belly of the beast. This should make for excellent sport and temper the worst fears of the men as well."

"Then we are to go to Ardnamurchan?" blurted Campbell.

"Yes. For God's sake, man, you're trembling. I'll fetch the Marsala."

The major handed Campbell the flask. The Highlander sniffed the rim. *"Slainte mhath,"* he muttered, then flung back his head and drank deeply.

" 'Tis a *fait accompli*. Tomorrow we'll march west. Me, to greater military conquests . . . you to conquests of a different sort."

The captain downed the rest of the wine. In no condition to continue the conversation, he blundered out
of the tent into the rain with the barest semblance of
a salute and a muttering of Gaelic. The instant he left,
the major closed his eyes and clearly saw the captain,
stripped of his heavy plaid and jacket, writhing naked
and bleeding in a field of heather. He opened his eyes.
The saber.

Yes, his saber was still where he had sequestered it,
wrapped in a length of good English broadcloth inside his
traveling trunk. The entire tip of the blade was russet-red,
stained by the blood of the man who had slain Edwin.
Racker had misjudged only one stroke that day at Sherrifmuir, but he had won some small consolation: while he'd
not quite finished Edwin's murderer, he'd most assuredly
sheared off a quarter of the bastard's face.

He had a hazy memory of the man's face, too surprised
to even look surprised. Weary, yes, confused and angry.
A flash of flame-colored hair framing azure eyes and a
firm, fierce jaw. That jaw had twitched when the Gael
cocked his head at the very moment Racker's saber had
begun to fall. The flash of silver blade, a burst of red, a
wailing scream, bagpipe-shrill.

Damn his head pains! He could remember little else.
The force of the blow had carried him forward over
the shoulder of his horse, through the air, onto the
ground. The fall had saved his life, for all had thought
him dead.

Racker kissed the rust-red blade and returned it to its
nest within the trunk. Briefly he considered telling Diana
about the incident, but no, she would not understand.
Instead he scrawled a few lines to Edwin in the leather
notebook, recounting the adventure.

When the major woke in the morning, he was still at

his writing desk, the closed journal pillowing his head. He found the letter to Diana, balled it up and tossed it to the ground.

# Five

*Untying Riddles*

Abby awoke to the smells of woodsmoke and roasting meat. She had had a vague dream of trotting and stumbling through the darkness down a dirt road that stretched on and on. As she sat up and rubbed her hands against her cheeks, she realized she had been remembering the journey of the night before.

She glanced about and saw she was in a stone building. An inn, she judged, ruined and deserted: shards of glass and broken bottles lined broken shelves, and a very large cast iron pot, almost big enough to allow her to climb inside, lay up-ended in a corner. One stone wall and a huge rafter were scorched, and it occurred to her that someone must have attempted to set the building alight. A torn whisky-skin on a peg on the wall reminded her of Calum, but she could not see him. She resolved to ask him about this place and what had happened to it.

A number of straw pallets lay scattered about the flag floor; she had spent the night on one of them. She ran her hand over the brittle grass straws. They were not yet musty, and their faint, sweet scent reminded Abby of the nights she had spent in the hay of the stable at the Cock and Hen.

Forcing herself to her feet, she shook her head to clear

it of fatigue, and her cloak to free it of straw. The smell of food was stronger now, and saliva gathered in her mouth; she had eaten nothing since the meager, disastrous supper with Calum the night before. She stepped carefully into her shoes, still cold and wet from the night's journey, and made her way through the half-light toward the charred door. It swung open on one hinge.

Calum crouched over a little fire in the center of the barren courtyard, his back toward her. Smoke carrying a delicious smell swirled up from the flames and straight into her nose. Beyond the fire lay an ocean of mist, dull gray hilltops and, above them, a paler, duller sky. The dampness crept under her cloak, chilling her to the quick. "Good—" She stopped, shocked by the cold air in her mouth. The Gael swung around with amazing speed, blinking at her. Abby had caught him completely unaware. When he recognized her, his ferocious grin lit up his face. His tricorn, perched sideways on his head, made her recall an illustration she had seen as a child, the portrait of an infamous pirate. "Morning."

"Well, Mistress Abby! And a fine morning it is! I see you don't believe me, but mind you, the mist will clear soon and we'll have a fine, brisk day. You slept well, I trust? Here now, have a seat on this stone. Your breakfast is nearly ready."

With a start she realized he must have spent the night in the inn with her, though it was of no great consequence anymore. How close had she come to losing every particle of integrity at the Heart's-ease? She didn't care to think about it. That page of her life was behind her.

She walked forward and sat on the stone beside him. He had somehow managed to catch a hare, which he now turned on a spit over the fire. As the carcass cooked, grease dripped from it, sizzling in the red-hot coals. Abby's stomach growled. She asked a hurried question to hide her embarrassment. "Calum, what sort of place is this?"

"Why, if it please you, mistress, an inn. At least, so it was. This place is known as Aberness. 'Tis some ten miles from Glasgow."

"But what has become of it? It's torn to pieces. Is this the work of robbers?"

Calum laughed, but there was no humor in his voice. A tiny ripple of fear ran down Abby's throat. "Faith, mistress, not robbers at all but good Loyalist troops. The landlord of the inn, you see, was a Jacobite. A Lowland Jacobite. Yes, it's not only we Gaels who wanted to bring King James back to the throne."

"I'm afraid I don't understand. Jacobites are rebels, are they not? If you were apprehended, you would be hanged for treason. This James must be the 'Iacobus Rex' upon your snuffbox. You would have him be king?"

"Devil take it, woman, James *is* the king!" Calum shouted into her face, the force of his passion blowing her backward.

"Please, a little more patience with me, I pray. I haven't a good head for politics, you know." She had tried to develop one, years ago, but whenever she had asked Roger or his pot companions to explain the decisions of Parliament, the rumors surrounding the king's health, the latest rumblings of dissension in the North, they would praise her gown, her coiffure, her perfume, and tell her not to bother with such inanities. "Now, I have but one king, and he is King George. Your king is James the Second, is that correct?"

"Not a whit! James Stuart was driven from the throne many years ago. He tried to recapture it but failed. James

Edward Stuart, the son of James the Second, is my king, or would have been. The Pretender, your people call him. Think of it, Abby. You might have had a Stuart king, not a German, like your Georgie Hanover, but a Scottish king. Like his father. Were you not taught all this as a child? Long before there was the House of Hanover there was the House of Stuart, with the Orange king and poor little Queen Anne in between. How could you live in England, mistress, and not know this?"

"I'm afraid, Mr. MacDonald, I have been taught it is not my place to know. But," she went on briskly, "you can undo that teaching. To begin with, you can tell me what happened here." She waved her hand toward the devastated building.

Calum fell silent for a moment, rotating the spit. When at last he continued, his voice was much too calm. Abby could almost hear the rage bubbling within him. "Mistress, what happened here is the beginning of the end for my country. Or perhaps Sherrifmuir was the beginning. So many men from so many clans following their chiefs, without question or hesitation, into the maw of death itself. That was Sherrifmuir. Death itself. I saw my cousin's head torn from his body by grapeshot and my own brother scattered into a thousand pieces by a grenade. Death for my family, for all Clan Donald, for Clan Stuart, Clan Cameron . . . even Clan MacGregor, what was left of it. I myself slew many of your countrymen, but they were like blades of grass in a meadow, too many to conceive of. What happened at Sherrifmuir was no less than the death for our hopes of a Scottish king for Scotland."

Abby thought of Roger, his head cracked like an egg, and her mother dressed in black, weeping. All these people she had loved had suffered so much. "I am sorry for you, Calum."

"Reserve your tears for my poor clansmen. We lost the day, we lost our lives. We failed ourselves, our chiefs, and King James. My own chief, MacDonald of MacDonald, got down on his knees—his *knees,* mind you! The chief of the great Clan Donald!—to beg King Jamie's officers to carry on, but they withdrew to France. James hadn't the money to rebuild his army nor the heart to lead it. Many chiefs were quick to part company with him when they realized half their clansmen were lying at Sheriffmuir and the living half spread over the entire countryside.

"And this?" He spat toward the inn. "It's what the English call a reprisal, though the devil the bit of 'prize' I can see in it. The landlord was a Jacobite, and Jacobites are not fit to live, you see."

Abby shook her head. She had heard of military acts of vengeance against the Jacobites and their supporters, but this was the first reprisal she had actually seen. "Whoever did this was no gentleman." Calum laughed, though she could not see why. She had meant what she'd said. "Where is the landlord now?"

"Slain, I hear, along with his wife and children. The eldest son fled north, but Lord save him! 'Tis no safer there. My father was in the first rising for King James, in sixteen-and-eighty . . . well, years ago. He told me how scores of families, many in Glenfinnan, my own birthplace, had their homes burned about their ears, just as this poor man had."

Calum's neck turned pink, then crimson. Abby could tell the fire inside him was not easily contained. But she could not stop the flow of her questions. "Why, Calum, why? Women and children are not at war. What's to be gained by slaying innocents? I don't see the sense to it."

"Because there is no sense to be seen, woman." Calum

sprang to his feet, then crouched low again, rose once more, stalked once around the fire and again sank down beside it. "In wartime, there are no innocents. Not to your people's way of thinking. I can see you don't believe me, but 'tis true." Calum's voice grew to a rumble, then a roar. Abby braced herself against the storm of his rage. "My countryfolk are no more human than stoats and badgers to the red soldiers. You English and Stout Georgie will not stop until they have turned the beautiful mountains of my land into so many cairns to mark the graves of the Gael."

"You must not speak of my country this way, nor His Majesty," said Abby softly. Try as she might, she could not make sense of the situation. Why, her own father had been in the military. He would never have slain private citizens, Scotch or English. "You have no right to speak harshly of others, when it was your clan, your army which destroyed the peace and threatened the unity of the realm." She trembled with passion, remembering her father's death.

"Daughter of the devil!" shouted Calum. "We were for restoring unity, not undoing it." In an instant he was on his feet. Abby rose, suddenly afraid. Calum stared at her, his mouth slightly agape. Then he brought his fist down on his palm with the force of a pistolshot. *"Cead mille murthair!"*

Abby bolted. How could he have fooled her so! He was a savage or, worse yet, a lunatic. She had not run far when she realized she was running into a bank of mist. She looked back and gasped. The inn had completely disappeared. Before her, through a shifting gray-white veil, came the sounds of running water. The country was devouring her, taking its own vengeance.

*You must call Calum,* she told herself. Abby bit her

lip and kept silent. Being lost in a strange country could be no worse than being attacked by an even stranger man. A movement in the mist startled her. She took a step back. The mist shifted, and she stepped back again, this time colliding with something hard and warm.

"Mr. MacDonald!"

"Calum. I apologize for frightening you, mistress. You know I would never harm you. We'll not speak of kings and government and battles ever again."

The Gael took her by the hand and led her back to the inn, striding through the mist as if he could see through it. Inside the ruined building they found two wooden trenchers, a carving knife and a fork with only two tines. Returning to the fire, Calum thrust the fork into the blackened flesh of the hare and broke off a fore-leg. He turned to Abby and smiled. She felt her mouth fill with water. " 'You eat with me but I never eat with you. Who am I?' "

A riddle? Yes, of course, it had to be. And the answer was a knife and fork. But she would not spoil his jest by answering too quickly. Questions and answers, she was beginning to see, was a dangerous game to play with Calum MacDonald.

The Scot waved the knife in slow circles. "This, of course. Do you fathom it? You eat with a knife, do you not?"

She paused, pretending to think hard, then smiled. "Yes. A pity we have no linens."

"Mistress Abby, we are no in your fine Benthorse now."

"Brenthurst."

"Aye, aye." He wrenched a joint of meat from the roasted hare, flung it onto the wooden plate beside the knife and thrust the trencher into her hands. Then he proceeded to cut bits of flesh from the carcass with the knife and toss them nimbly into his mouth. "Eat well. We've a long road ahead of us, and we'll leave after eating."

The meat was tough, dry and gamy. She thoroughly enjoyed every bite. More than once she burned her fingers and her tongue in her haste, and though she thought how dreadful she must look and how much her beloved mother would have disapproved, she could not for the life of her keep from hacking and gulping her food exactly as Calum did.

Callum had spoken nothing but the truth about the long road ahead of them, though he did his best to make the journey bearable.

"Here is one for you, Mistress Abby. 'I am ancient, but every month I am born anew. What am I?' "

Abby scarcely heard him over the clanking of the iron skillet, wooden spoons, griddle, carving knife and tin cup he had carted with him from the ruined inn. He wore them all suspended from his belt, along with his smallsword and a peck of oatmeal in a muslin sack, just as a hunter carries a day's spoils at his waist or shoulder. Her portmanteau, its red cheerfulness covered with mud, swung from his hand, occasionally striking the skillet with a resounding clunk. "Must you make such a din?" she grumbled.

"Faith, mistress, if you don't like me now, you'll not like me much better when I've my proper arms about me. One well-armed Gael makes as much noise as an army of Englishmen. Hazard a guess?"

"The riddle? I'm afraid I must concede." She stood on tiptoe to stretch her aching feet. Every toe was swollen and tender, and a blister on one heel made her shoe an instrument of torture. With every step she took, branches of dry heather tore at her long skirts. Her fingers were freezing inside a pair of cotton gloves, and cramps ran up and down her stomach. She could not even distract her mind with thoughts of Lydia. It was well past noon, and already she and Calum had walked countless miles, without pausing once. Some chocolate would have been lovely.

"Calum, please, I must rest. Just for a few moments, I promise you. I am so very weary of walking on this horrid ground." As she spoke, one foot sank deep into the boggy soil. With a mighty tug she managed to retrieve her foot, sans shoe, as the ground let go with a hostile, sucking sound.

The Gael stopped, then crouched low on a windswept tangle of cottongrass, his accoutrements clattering about him. "As you wish," he muttered, "but there's rain in it soon." He pointed to an angry, ink-black cloud billowing toward them. "And we without shelter. Rest for a moment only, now." He broke off a stem of grass and chewed it thoughtfully. "The moon."

"The moon?" Abby pulled her shoe from the mud and sank down beside Calum. Her entire body relaxed at once, and even her feet stopped hurting. She removed her other shoe and wiggled her sore toes. "The moon?"

"Ancient, but reborn every month."

"But of course! You must forgive me, I am without a brain when I'm this weary." She drew her hood away from her face and breathed in a great draught of air, so clean and tart it fairly burned her lungs. *Yes, the moon,* she thought, gazing out over the moor, softly rolling, endless and brown, a sea of dead heather and bracken. In the distance stood a long, low mountain of charcoal gray granite, disappearing into mist at the very top. *I may as well be abandoned on the moon.*

She had seen only four other people since she had left

the city, and those at some distance: two young boys gathering wood, a farmer riding a harnessed pony, and a very thin woman standing at the doorway of a decrepit cottage. Amazingly, all of them had seemed to stare straight at her and her dissonant companion, but none had said one word. She guessed they must have taken her and Calum for tinkers.

On an impulse, she looked up at his face, shadowed beneath the tricorn. "Calum, where are we?"

"Why, some four leagues north of the city, mistress, if you please. This place is called Bas-Allan's Heath, and that big hill is called Allan's Nose. There's forest galore just over the ridge here, and there we'll take shelter and I'll make you a meal of some sort. A fine, slow, easy pace for your first full day on the road."

"The road?" Abby sat up straight and looked about right and left, forward and behind. She could not remember seeing any trace of a path, let alone a road, since she had left the inn that morning. "Are we near this 'road to the isles' you spoke of earlier?"

Calum stopped chewing his grass stem, then smiled and spat it out. *"Arrah,* mistress, we've been traveling it these several hours past."

A twinge of pain shot up her leg. Surely this was another of Calum's wordplays. "Speak plainly, pray. I cannot riddle just now."

"There's no riddle to it. We are on the road to the isles, and it will take us northward."

Abby clambered to her feet, her shoes in her hand. "But . . . but you must point it out to me, then," she stammered. "I see nothing anywhere but brown moor and black rock." A raindrop struck her nose. From overhead came the faint growl of thunder.

Very slowly the Gael pulled himself upright and shook

himself with great vigor, his pan and utensils rattling forth a bold thunder of their own. "The road is not so much out there," he said, pointing to the infinite moorland, "but in here." He tapped his temple. "I've traveled the route many years as a boy, southward and northward, following the cattle droves. Sometimes you can see a track though the heather, sometimes dried dung. Sometimes not. It makes no difference. I know quite well where I am going."

"You mean to say there is no road to speak of, only your memory of how to proceed?" No road meant no relief from walking through heather, mud and rocks and, worst of all, no well-defined direction, no clear path to Lydia. Without a road, they could become lost forever in forsaken wilderness. Abby held her breath, waiting for his answer, although she already knew what it was.

"There is no road," he said calmly. "Not the sort you mean, anyway. *Dia!* There are no roads in the north at all! *Criosd agus Mairi!* Your face is aye as white as death, mistress. Come, you have nothing to fear." He squinted at her. "You trust me, do you not?"

Abby took another deep breath. Did she? She had little reason to, but then, she had little recourse not to. He had not taken advantage of her, after all, as many a man in his place might have done. "Implicitly." He cocked his head, as if to hear her better. "Yes, indeed," she tried again.

"That's fine, then."

Raindrops spattered lightly on her head.

Calum took her hand and led her forward at a trot. "Come, woman," he puffed. "Road or no, run you must. Would you be drowned in the storm?"

"Please! I'm too tired to continue! It's scarcely raining

at all." She dug her stockinged feet into the ground and threw her weight backward.

"Do not be English with me!" he commanded. She had not the slightest idea what he meant, and was about to ask him when a great crack of lightning split open the sky, sending her leaping toward him in terror.

They ran together over the heath and up and over a gentle ridge, Abby kilting her skirts with one hand and holding her shoes in the other. Just beyond, as Calum had promised, lay a dense forest. Abby could smell its sweetness as she ran, gasping and panting. Calum dragged her into the fragrant embrace of a broad pine tree as the rain arrived, light enough, but steady and cold. Abby collapsed at the foot of the tree on a bed of dry, brown needles while Calum dashed back out into the rain. "Wait for me," he called back over his shoulder. In a few moments he returned with water in his cup and skillet.

Abby's stomach turned upside down with anticipation. Hot porridge was not to her liking, but she knew she could eat anything just then. "Shall I gather tinder for a fire?" she asked, hoping he would refuse her help. It was cozy and dry beneath the tree, and she felt her spirits begin to brighten. She rubbed a little water on her face so vigorously her cheeks smarted afterward.

" 'Tis too wet to start a fire. Whatever you might wish to burn is much too damp to light." To her puzzlement, Calum dumped two handfuls of meal into the skillet and swirled it about in the water with his fingers until it congealed into a nubbly gray paste. In color and texture it was not unlike the mixture of sand and bonemeal the servants spread on the kitchen garden at Brenthurst. Abby watched, repulsed, as he sucked his fingers clean and handed her the skillet and a wooden spoon. *"Bro-*

*chan,*" he explained. " 'Broken stones,' we call it. Catriona says it is good for the stomach."

"Your wife has an iron stomach, then. One cannot possibly eat this uncooked."

"One can," he said firmly, and demonstrated by eating a spoonful of the substance. "Take it, now." He pushed the skillet toward her. The smell of clay filled her nostrils and she backed away.

"No. It is inedible. I'd rather go hungry."

"Go hungry and get weak," he muttered. "Get weak and you'll not reach Skye at all."

"I will reach Skye, but not half poisoned!" Calum offered her the *brochan* once again, but as she raised her hand to fend off his generosity, her wrist struck his and the skillet fell to the ground. The gruel oozed out onto the pine needles.

*"Dabhaill! Mac na Dhabhail! Cead mille deamanchean!"* Calum righted the skillet in an instant, scooping the spilled *brochan* back into the pan, pine needles and all. He glared at her, shaking his long forefinger in her face, scolding her in his native language with such vehemence that droplets of saliva struck her face as he spoke. At last, apparently exhausting his supply of epithets, he fell silent and began eating the porridge himself.

Suddenly Abby understood. She had been horribly wrong to refuse the food. He had nothing else to offer her, and little of what he had—so little that even fouled food could not be wasted. "I'm so sorry," she murmured. After all, she was no stranger to unwholesome food; she had stolen victuals from beasts at the Cock and Hen before Mistress had found her. A mere five weeks of decent food at the Heart's-ease had spoiled her for hard living. And to think she had told the Gael that food mattered nothing to her. "Please, forgive me. It was an accident, I assure you."

He looked up from the skillet. "It won't happen again, will it now? You'll eat whatever you're given?"

"I give you my word, no more arguments regarding food or anything else. Perhaps . . . perhaps you'd let me have a taste?"

Without a moment's hesitation, Calum thrust a spoonful of the mess at her, the very spoon that had been in his mouth only moments before. She closed her eyes, trying to shut out the earth smell of the *brochan*. Then she ate it.

It was not horrid at all. Tasteless, if anything. She devoured the entire contents of the skillet. What a fool she had been to create such a tempest over such a trifle. As she handed the skillet back to Calum so he might prepare his own supper, she realized how she could make amends.

"Here is a riddle for you, Calum. 'I am the beginning of eternity, the end of time and space, the beginning of every end and the end of every race. What am I?' "

"Aye?" said Calum, without looking up from the skillet. "Eternity, you say?"

She repeated the riddle. "But I caution you, do not try to solve it in your native tongue. Its answer depends on English."

Calum snorted. "Are you saying the Gaelic isn't good enough for your riddle?"

"Not at all." What ill luck. She had offended him further. "Yours is an excellent language, and I should like to learn it myself. Nevertheless, the answer to this riddle must be in English. It is an English riddle, after all. Surely there are some jests in your tongue that cannot be translated."

"Perhaps." He nodded slowly as he finished stirring his food and popped a spoonful of it into his mouth. " 'The beginning of eternity, the end of time and space.' Well, if Catriona were here, she would say 'love' is the answer, women being such seminal creatures."

"Sentimental. Love is not the answer," Abby replied, not much pleased with the sound of her words. "Not this answer, leastways. And you are untying the riddle, not Catriona."

"The Lord Almighty, King of Heaven, then."

"A wise answer, but alas, quite wrong. He is perhaps not the very end of *everyone's* race."

"Hope, then?" Abby shook her head. "Power? Truth? Whisky?"

"No, no and no. Whisky?"

"If you were a Gael, you'd understand," he explained. He made several other guesses, each of them as errant as the first. Between answers he gobbled down the *brochan* as if he had no concern save his belly, but it was clear she had confounded him.

"You must be less of a philosopher and more of a prankster to riddle this one," she offered, enjoying his confusion. "Shall I tell you?"

"No!" Calum was about to say more, but instead snapped shut his mouth and sprang to his feet. Abby glanced about her, startled, but all she could see was mist and the blurred images of trees and rocks. All she could hear was the monotonous dripping of the rain and an occasional breath of wind in the highest branches of the big pine.

"What is it, Calum?" Visions of wolves, wildcats and outlaws leaped into her mind. "Do you see something?"

"Listen, mistress," he answered. "A drum." He was alert and watchful, but he made no move to draw a weapon or dash away. "The jangling of a horse's bit. The tread of many feet. Put your hand to the ground. You will feel it trembling."

Abby knelt and did as he bade her. The earth vibrated under her hand, just as he had said it would, and she, too, could hear the sound of a drum and the clink of metal. She looked up and saw a tiny patch of red advancing slowly toward her through the mist. As it came closer, the red patch grew and grew until it was clearly discernible: a scarlet-coated troop of Hanoverian foot soldiers, led by an officer on a stately black horse. At the front trudged two Highland soldiers, muskets on their shoulders, plaids drawn up over their heads against the rain. Scouts of some sort, she reckoned.

The horse let out a shrill whinny.

"They will come straight past us. Say not one word unless you're asked to," Calum counseled. "Whatever I say, pay me no mind. If I say I can fly, nod your head in agreement. And none of this smiling and bobbing and curtseying you English are so quick with."

"Mayhap we can fade back into the mist. They shan't see us." The sounds of the patrol came closer, and Abby could make out about thirty soldiers, besides the officer and the Scots.

"Nay, Abby, nay. No time for that. They have already seen us. Draw your hood over your head, woman."

"I shan't be able to see very well."

"There'll be nothing to see. Now cover your head. There's no way of knowing how long these fellows have been out on the moor without female companionship."

"Surely the officer will not allow any indecencies."

"A short life to you, creature! List to me! Cover your head!"

Abby pulled the hood low over her face, taking her time.

The Highlanders were the first to reach them. They stopped and peered through the rain long and hard at Calum, then at Abby. Finally the taller of the two addressed Calum very briefly in Gaelic. From the way the man spoke, Abby thought he might be asking a question. She didn't care for the way they stared at her, and she looked to Calum for a clever response.

"I nae hae the Gaelic," he answered simply, in a very tolerable imitation of a Glasgow accent.

The Highlanders exchanged glances and shrugged in unison. "Ye look as if ye might," said one.

By now the officer had ridden up, calling his troop to a halt just behind him. Abby glanced from Calum to the other Gaels, back to Calum, then to the officer and again to Calum. What, if anything, was happening?

"Bound northward?" the officer called to Calum. Abby could see he was quite young, perhaps in his early twenties, a captain, from the looks of his uniform. His oilskin cape and dripping tricorn framed a handsome face and round, gray eyes. It was all Abby could do to keep herself from dropping him a curtsey. Then she noticed the lace on his jabot was covered with rust-colored spots. She held herself motionless. Mud, no doubt, and yet . . .

"Indeed we are, sir," answered Calum. "To my wife's sister in Corrielorgan."

The captain glanced at the Highlanders. They nodded.

"Anghas and Dughal seem to have heard of the place," said the horseman. "Tell me, Jock, what happened to your face?"

Abby's eyes flew upward. She checked a gasp. Calum's hat had pushed his hair well back, exposing his scar. He tapped the wound with his fingertips, and she could tell his mind was racing to find a suitable explanation. She drew her hood back a little so she could see him more clearly. Her chest felt tight. She tasted the bitter tang of nausea.

"A friend cut me, maister," said Calum.

Abby looked at the handsome officer. His eyes were wide open. "A friend? With friends who lacerate your face, you need no enemies."

Calum, encouraged by the officer's reply, warmed to the story. "Aye, but he is a gude friend. It's only when the whisky's on him that myself never kens wha himself will be doing. I wuld nae gie him silver for mair drink, and that angered him."

One of the Gaels rolled up his sleeve. A thin, dark line ran from his elbow to his wrist. "My own foster brother did this to me wi' his dirk."

"A violent race, indeed," muttered the captain. His gaze met Abby's, and she looked away, tugging down her hood. "What beautiful eyes your wife has." His horse shivered and pranced in the cold rain, but the Englishman sat his saddle with ease.

Abby turned toward Calum for a sign. The captain's words troubled her; what would make a gentleman speak so boldly? Should she address him, tell him to mind his tongue around ladies? Then a terrible thought occurred to her: what if the captain discovered their ruse? She was English, yes, but she was an Englishwoman consorting with a Jacobite, a fugitive, an enemy of King George. Surely she would be shown no more mercy than he. The thought stoppered her throat and killed even the possibility of a reply. For an instant she was gripped with the desire to run away into the mist and be free of her dangerous companion. But she could not move. She could not abandon him.

"Aye, that she has," drawled Calum. "Beautiful eyes. 'Tis a pity she's sae ill. We are bound to her sister's to seek a cure."

Before the captain could point out that she looked in the peak of health, Abby decided to at least sound ill. She covered her mouth, clenched her eyes shut and fell into a fit of deep coughing that made the captain's horse throw back its head and roll its eyes.

"The coughing sickness," Calum explained.

The captain paused only a moment. "Lead on." He urged his horse forward, and the Highlanders spun around and marched on without a word. In a matter of moments the whole troop had passed by and dissolved into a red blur among the pines.

Abby sighed. The tenseness in her chest and throat had vanished. "Well done, Calum! Both your scar and my 'sickness.' Your accent was on the mark, too. Why, you sounded just like Hugo." To her astonishment, Calum stumbled back against the tree trunk, his eyes glistening, his face pasty white. "Calum, are you ill?"

As if in answer, he darted away from her into the rain. Even though she couldn't see him through the mist, she could hear him retching. *Poor man,* she thought. When she remembered his tenseness at the Heart's-ease and his memories of Sherrifmuir, his sickness made sense.

In a few moments he returned, wiping his mouth with his kerchief. "A thousand pardons, Abby, but it's the red soldiers that do this to me. I cannot even abide looking at them. All I smell is blood, and all I think of is death and disgrace. *Arrah!* I very nearly wet my breeks when that creature asked about my scar. He must have been far north for a long time not to have heard about me. Oh, for a skinful of whisky just now!" He took a sip of water from the tin cup. "He called me 'Jock.' Had he thought I was a Gael, he would have called me 'Donald.' He would never have had the decency to ask me my name."

"Nevertheless, you were magnificent," murmured Abby.

"You're no stranger to craftiness yourself, mistress," he said, with half a smile. " 'Twas your coughing that drove them off. But you should have kept your head covered, as I told you. I believe they'd have marched straight by had it not been for the two Campbell creatures."

"Campbell? The Highland soldiers, you mean? They asked you a question, didn't they?"

"Aye, my name. You see, my people can tell each other just by looking at the face. Clothes mean nothing to them. I gave them a start when I answered them in the English, and I'm not certain they believed me at all. But for now, until we go further north, I am Lowland, and so are you. It is safer."

"There was something on the captain's jabot, did you see?"

"Aye, something. Blood, dirt, whisky, gravy . . . who can say? Little good comes of imagining too much. You noticed, I hope, he was traveling southward, so if he *has* been spoiling his lace with my people's blood, he will probably soon stop."

The rain settled down into a light, steady drizzle. Abby and Calum set out into it, heading directly toward the hill Calum had called Allan's Nose. Abby could tell that their brush with the soldiers had made the Gael wary. His gait was slow and measured, and he spoke but little. Once he turned to her and said, "Courage."

At first she thought he was trying to raise her spirits, as Roger had. Then she realized what he meant. "No.

That is not the answer. Courage is certainly not the beginning of every end nor the end of every race."

Calum turned wearily and shambled on.

They continued northward, the countryside changing from thick forest to bleak, stubbled fields. Abby saw more people, or at least the signs of people: distant cottages, clouds of peatsmoke, walls of stones piled on stones, ponies and cattle grazing in the heather. Once a dog ran up to Abby, barking and snapping, and she could not move until Calum had driven the beast off with well-aimed pebbles.

That night they slept in the cottage of an old couple Calum called Seanair and Sean-mathair, grandda and granny, he explained, not actually his grandparents, but distant kin. The old man and woman doted over Abby, fed her bannocks and butter and milk and soothed her tortured feet with poultices made of nettles. She lay down for the night on a featherbed, with three thick, woolen blankets atop her. Lying in the soft bedding in the warm room, breathing in the strange, sweet scent of the peat fire, Abby began to feel she had become accustomed to hardship. *For Lydia, I can manage any obstacle the journey might place before me,* she mused. She had, indeed, already withstood disgusting food and a long, hard march in cold weather over treacherous ground, nearly ruining her shoes. Worst of all, she had endured loneliness, with no companion save a demi-barbarian who did not believe in creature comforts. She wished wild Janet from the Heart's-ease were with her, to make her smile.

The morning was frosty, and the woman of the house fretted about "the puir Sassanach leddy, wi' the frost bitin' her hands and feet." Abby pleaded with Calum: couldn't they stay one more night?

"And strain the kindness of these good people?" he replied. "The less time you stay in one place, the sooner you will see Lydia. Only two days' march to the Trossachs, Abby, and the Highland Line."

"I'll go, then, but I must have new shoes soon." She held up the remnants of the shoes she had once considered brutishly sturdy.

"I will get you shoon," he promised, "even though my own Catriona goes barefoot, no matter the weather. But she is a Gael, and stout of heart."

"And I am not?" fumed Abby. "Consider what I have been through."

"But you are English," he said mysteriously, and Abby decided to let the matter lie.

He led her out into a white world glittering with frost. Ice glazed every blade of grass and crackled underfoot. Pine trees shimmered like a starry sky. Abby remembered the stories she had told Lydia, stories she had heard from her own mother: Jack Frost, who painted leaves and windows with icy patterns, and tiny frost fairies, imperceptible in a frosty landscape until their movement betrayed them. By midmorning, however, the frost had melted and, though her toes and fingers still ached with cold, Abby was sorry to see the ice go. For a short while, it had allowed her to escape to a sweeter time.

At noon they crested a little hill. Before them lay a rocky valley—a glen, Calum insisted—cut through by a stream in spate, wild and white. When Calum saw the stream, he emitted such a shriek that Abby immediately cringed and stepped back, expecting government soldiers or worse. To her astonishment, Calum caught her by the waist, picked her up and kissed her full and hard on the lips. The smell of whisky clung to his breath.

"Calum!" She slapped his cheek. He scarcely seemed to notice. What lunacy had she stepped into?

*"Conneag Uisge,* the Rabbit Water," he cried. His cheeks were both so red it was impossible to tell where she had struck him. He set her down, gave a joyous leap straight up in the air and let out another shriek.

Abby backed away again, shaking her head. He must have drunk whisky back at the cottage and gone completely mad.

Calum stretched out his hand toward her, suddenly calm. "Don't be alarmed, Abby. Forgive me if I gave you a fright just now and took improperties with you. You did right to put me in my place with the palm of your hand. But look, woman! That is the Conneag Uisge . . . Conneag Uisge. We are closer to the Highland Line than I thought."

"I implore you, do not take such liberties again." Was he thinking of the Heart's-ease? Had he lost his respect for her somehow? Surely not; he had been nothing but a gentleman to her up until that very moment. Evidently the Gaels were simply people of great passion and emotion, quick to act and slow to think. Calum had given her ample proof of that, yet she was no longer afraid of him.

The man nodded at her, turned his gaze toward the glen and finally back to her. "My apologies, mistress. Do you know what runs and has no feet?"

Abby peered into the dark glen, illuminated by the raging, ice-white stream. "Water, of course. Is this the Highlands, then?"

Without replying, Calum turned and plunged down the

hillside, his peculiar, lopsided gait swallowing up the heather.

She had no choice but to follow. Her sore toes struck rock after rock as she half-ran, half-slid down the scree-covered hillside. This miserable land! She should never have set foot in it. Soon she'd have no feet left at all, to set anywhere.

Abby stumbled to the bottom of the hill, puffing and gasping. She patted her hair, only to find it had pulled itself completely free of its pins. She felt stray locks sticking out all over her head, like the fur of a terrified cat.

"Come, Abby! Here's the ford," called Calum. She hobbled over to where he stood beside the frothing water, and suddenly her heart sank to the rock beneath her feet. The Rabbit Water was no rabbit at all but an untamed white stallion, a raging wildcat, a dangerous silver serpent. Its waters swirled black and white within a pool, then plunged down a hillside in frenzied delight. She had crossed many streams before with Calum, a few without the benefit of a bridge, but none quite so turbulent as this.

"Are you certain it is not named the Rapid Water?"

Calum shot her a crooked grin and, as Abby stood rooted to the rock, tossed her portmanteau across the water with one graceful motion, then her purse. Both landed within a finger's length of the water, on the far bank. Then, with three great, graceful leaps, the Gael followed her possessions to safety. Safe on the opposite bank, he turned to face her, one foot on dry rock and one halfway in the stream.

The distance across the streambed was scarcely more than two ells, but the ferocity of the water and the weariness of her journey made Abby draw back. *This is how the River Styx must look,* she told herself. "I cannot do it. I refuse. I must have a bridge. Just look at these!" She gripped her skirts and raised her many petticoats an inch above her shoes.

"Throw me your cape," Calum bellowed above the thundering of the stream. He extended one arm toward her.

Abby did as he bade her, but the cape was heavy and her throw was none of the best. The tail of the cape landed in the water, and Calum jerked it away. "Now kilt up your skirts and come across," he shouted. "You saw where I placed my feet. Do you the same, and I shall help you." Again he stretched forth his arm, reaching even further toward her.

As he explained it, it sounded simple, but still looked impossible. Abby glared at the churning water. She thought of the little house where they had stayed the night. Were she back there, she could rest in the soft bed, her feet in poultices, and let Sean-mathair take care of her, just for the day. Now she would likely get both feet wet and come down with the grippe.

Clutching her skirts about her, she started forward, then stopped and backed away. "It is much too wide and swift."

"You needn't leap across. See you the tops of rocks in the water? You've but to walk on them, then give a bit of a jump when you near me. I'll pull you over from there."

Abby hesitated. There were rocks rising from the water, but their granite pates were shiny and black. The stream splashed at her feet. She could almost hear it laughing at her.

Calum said something in his own language, then continued in hers. "Devil take it, woman! Would you let a wheen of water keep you from finding your daughter?"

"Do not mock me!" she cried. For Lydia she would ford every watercourse in Britain, laid side by side. *Cross this brook,* she told herself, *and you will be that much closer to Lydia.* She hopped onto the first rock, then the next. The water rose around one shoe, entered it and surprised her with its ice cold touch. Without looking, she leaped toward Calum's outstretched hand. Her fingers grazed his, and she caught sight of his face. In an instant his expression turned from calm concentration to bewilderment to anger.

"Abby!"

Her feet came down, not on rock, and once again the chill of the water startled her. The stream rose around her with a tremendous roaring and rushing, sucking her under. She heard the bubbling of her own breath. Then she was floating, pitching headlong toward the rocks, tumbling and tossing hither and thither at the whim of the water. She was going to die, to split her skull, just as Roger had split his. A strange feeling of peace came over her. Her journey north was over. *I'm so sorry, Lydia. I'm so very sorry.*

The stream caught her and carried her forward, shoving her down its steep embankment. She swallowed water and vomited it out. Panic replaced her odd serenity, and she thrashed and kicked and paddled in the tumultuous water. "Calum!" she cried, as rocks reached out on either side to bump and bruise her. "Dear God, Calum! Assistance, pray!"

Calum scrambled over the rocks, following Abby's course down the hillside. The water was not very deep but quite fast, and Abby was just terrified enough and English enough to get herself drowned if she worked at it. Crouching on a rock, he reached out his coat to her. *"Gamh mi do labh!"* he shouted, and then, "Take hold, take hold!" But the water was perhaps in her ears and she tumbled past him, staring and gasping like a fish, flailing the water with her arms, missing his coat entirely.

*"Suidh! Suidh!* Sit down and then stand up!" he cried. "The water's no deep! Climb out over the rocks!"

He thought he heard a word float back to him, carried on the wind: "Skirts!"

*Ah, well,* he thought, picking his way down the hillside, *she's through the worst of it now, and she must stop when she comes to the loch.* Then she might be able to walk out of her own accord. With any luck he needn't get his feet wet.

The cascading stream emptied into a little loch, no deeper than the brook itself. And there, not a double arm's length away from him, was Abby. She was stranded in the very center of the loch, immobile. Her skirts and petticoats had swelled up all around her, so that she resembled the inflated sheep bladders Calum had played with as a child. Above the billowing skirts, her arms shot out straight on either side, her hands clenched in fists.

Try as he might, he could not restrain himself. He laughed.

Abby turned toward him, and he could see from her face that she was in a wretched way, indeed. Water—whether tears or no—streaked her face, her eyes were as red as neaps, and her hair clung to her head and neck like tendrils of brown seaweed. "Brute! Savage! Barbarian!" she screamed at him and, perhaps, the world at large. "I hate you! I detest you. I detest all men!" Her voice broke apart in sobs.

With a mighty effort, Calum fought back his laughter. He slipped off his hat and shoes and unrolled his hose from his feet. "Abby, forgive me." He stripped his heavy coat from his shoulders, unbuckled his belt, and dropped his skillet, griddle and cups to the ground. "Take courage, my calf." *Dia!* He, too, had been up to his neck in water at Sherrifmuir, with his own skirts floating about him. Later, mayhap, she'd see the humor in the situation. "You're not hurt, are you?"

The poor woman gave a long, high-pitched wail. "I'm bruised, bruised, bruised all over!" Again a wail. "And sore. Please, for the love of God, Calum, assist me!"

"Aye, aye. Wait a bit," he muttered. There was nothing for it but to do what had to be done. Taking a deep breath he jumped feet first into the pool. A sheet of water rose up around him, and when it cleared he could see Abby, sputtering and gasping, within easy reach. He was standing against her billowing skirts.

Calum tugged at Abby's hand, but the woman would not budge. He pulled at her elbow. Nothing. "My skirts!" she wailed. "They are preventing my movement!"

He assessed the situation. The woman was right. How could she take a step with all that weight about her? Working his way back to the shore, he scrambled atop the rocks, snatched the kitchen knife from the pile of discarded utensils, and leaped back into the loch, the blade aloft.

A terrible screaming pierced the roar of the cascade. A handful of water flew into his face.

"Daughter of Hell!" he sputtered. "Wretch! Pestilence! I am helping you, woman!"

The screaming stopped abruptly. With one swift stroke he stabbed Abby's captor skirts, ripping a vent in the heavy fabric. He did the same with each petticoat as the linen layers rose to the surface like curious trout. As the last petticoat gave way, Abby stumbled backward and would have fallen had Calum not caught her. The ballooning skirt buckled and swung behind her like two enormous wings. "Come! Walk!" he shouted, and Abby walked, gripping his hand with all ten fingers, shoving herself through the water on stiff legs. He pulled her ashore, dripping, shivering, and sobbing, and into his arms. For a few moments he held her against him, enjoying the warm, wet smell of her, until he thought of Catriona, lying without clothing under a plaid, waiting for him. Gently, he detached Abby's grip on his sleeves. "We'll make you a fire, hellion," he murmured. "Not that you need it, mind you. You've fire enough inside to keep you warm."

"Nearly quenched, I should think," she gasped through chattering teeth. "My purse . . . my portmanteau. Where are they?" She glanced about nervously.

"They are on the bank where I tossed them, safe and sound," he assured her, "along with your cape, which you sorely need. But first, a fire. Then, you must strip."

Calum found his coat and draped it around her shoulders. Abby's mouth was blue, her eyes the size of walnuts, and her brown hair dripped water into her face. In a strange way she looked very bonny indeed, something like Catriona surprised by a rainstorm. He thought of the morning, at the head of the glen, when he had foolishly kissed this Englishwoman. He must never let himself become so careless again. What would he do with the love of two women? And yet it had been sweet, that stolen kiss. He cherished it as much as his hidden snuffbox.


As good as his word, that was Calum. Once he'd built the fire, he trotted off, only to return in a short time with her portmanteau, cloak and stringpurse, all three slightly damp to the touch. While he stood with his back toward her, she removed her ruined gown and petticoats, sodden stockings and dripping camisole. How she shivered! Perhaps it was the cold, or perhaps her sense of modesty that Mistress had found so amusing. She pulled the cloak about her and crouched beside the crackling fire, stretching her hands into the warmth of the flames. It was delightful, like nestling with Lydia under the mauve blankets at the Rose Cottage. For a moment she was far away from the glen, at home with Roger and Liddie. The embers made a thumping sound as they shifted, and she looked up.

Calum stood on the other side of the fire, his back still toward her. But now his back was bare and pale, as well as all the rest of him. Except for his tricorn, the Gael had shucked off every stitch. Abby started, but halfway to her feet she sank back down again, her eyes on the dancing red flames. "Calum, for the sake of all that is decent, please put on your clothing."

"Decency or no, mistress, my clothes are soaking wet." She heard him quite clearly; he must have turned his head in her direction. "And they are wet not of their own choosing, mind you, but because I leaped into the Conneag Uisge with them to secure your safety. So do not disturb their depose." He pointed to his drenched garments, spread out over rocks beside the fire, like the skins of wretched animals. "They have earned it."

"Your coat!" she cried. "It was quite dry. You used it to cover me."

"Aye, it's true. It was dry, but after lying on your wet frock it's no dry any longer. It's stretched out here at my feet, if you'd care to look."

"No, thank you," said Abby, still gazing at the flames.

"Another thing you should know, mistress: my backside is becoming quite warm. I shall have to turn presently, and you'll not be liking that, I'm thinking."

How odd that she had spent so many days in the company of fornicating men and women and now could not abide the sight of one harmlessly naked man. But Calum was no ordinary man. He was her guide, her companion, her tutor in the ways of the wild. And he was something else, besides. Abby remembered Calum's kiss from that morning, so fresh and caring and full of joy, so unlike any kiss forced upon the ladies of the Heart's-ease, even sweeter than Roger's kisses. No, Calum was not one bit like Roger or the gentlemen of the Heart's-ease. Perhaps that was why she could not look at him now.

"I shall find you something myself," she muttered, rifling through her bag. The two frocks she had packed were both velvet, much too elegant for traveling attire, but warm and almost dry. Both smelled just a trifle fusty, and the blue one, the least fashionable of the two, was damp at the waist. The petticoats and stockings she had brought with her were dry enough, though, and she laid them out by the fire to warm. The moss-colored gown was her favorite, edged about the hem, cuff and bodice with lilies-of-the-valley and jonquils embroidered in white and yellow silk. Shutting her eyes, Abby balled up the frock and held it up, away from the grasping flames. "Take it. Cover yourself."

She waited. After a bit she heard his footsteps, felt the cloth tug in her hand and pull free, heard the sound of the fabric rustling and flapping. The Highlander must have snapped the frock in the air and shook it out. A hushed but rapid flood of Gaelic followed, punctuated by snorts and whistles and high-pitched eagle cries as the man cursed the clothing. There was a short pause, followed by much grunting and gasping and a few incomprehensible rumblings that might have been words.

When the sounds ceased, Abby opened her eyes. A chuckle rose in her throat, exploded, and poured out of her mouth in a stream of laughter. "I beg . . . beg your pardon," she stammered, then sunk her head in her hands to bury her laughter.

"Pray, what is so humorous?" growled Calum. He stood facing her, the moss-green frock wrapped around his waist like a makeshift plaid, its beribboned sleeves dangling about his knees. "You don't care for my attire? You chose it, after all."

Just when Abby concluded she had insulted him, Calum smiled his fierce smile and doffed his tricorn. Abby sighed with relief and laughed with him. "Indeed, Mr. MacDonald, I never know what to make of you, whether I've grieved you or amused you."

"Calum. Aye, and that makes for interesting company, does it not, mistress? Devil take it! There's the answer to your riddle: a good humor. What better beginning for eternity?"

"None, indeed, but you are still off the mark. You may throw me back into the stream, I fear, when you hear the correct answer."

"Nay, nay. I shall fathom it effectually."

Abby laughed. It was good to riddle and chat with Calum. In his own way, he was a gentleman, perhaps more of a gentleman than any other man she had ever known, Roger included. But if that were true, why did the military persecute him and his people so? "Calum, not long ago you said the English consider you and your clansfolk as no more than brutes. I know this is true. I believed so myself, for a time. But now I see that's not at all so. How did such thinking begin?"

Calum glanced to one side and pursed his lips. "Now there's a riddle I cannot answer. It's just how life is, mistress. There's no way of knowing why one people detests another." He pointed to her portmanteau. "Nothing damaged, I hope?"

"Nothing ruined, but . . ." Suddenly Abby remembered the stringpurse. She snatched it up from the ground and hurriedly searched its contents. "These are a trifle damp," she said, arranging Lydia's handkerchiefs on a stone beside the fire. "The watercolors appear to be unharmed, however, and . . . oh!"

A drop of water had trickled over Roger's face, blurring his bright eyes and distorting his smile into a vague snarl. She blotted the picture with the hem of her cape, without effect one way or another. "What a pity! Still, it could be worse."

Calum looked at the smudged portrait and snorted. "Murdered, you said?"

"No, I never did say!" Abby snapped the twin frames shut. It was infuriating the way the man always seemed to know more than he should. "But it's true. At least, I believe so. He owed a great many people a great deal of money. Any one of them might have arranged his death and blamed it on a fall from a horse. Tell me, what made you think Roger had been murdered?"

Calum shrugged. " 'Tis unlucky to speak ill of the dead, mistress, but I'll just say he has the look of a man with a hundred enemies."

"A hundred enemies, and as many friends, all one and the same," murmured Abby. It had taken her years to realize that the very same people who drank to Roger's health with his own wine would just as soon have drunk his blood. When luck was with him, those people fairly shoved each other aside to have a private word with him, but when luck was against him, which was often, they passed him in the street without a glance. She had seen it happen time and again. When his luck did not pick up, the carriage and horses had been the first to go, sold to pay his debts. Then the furniture. Then the servants left. Then . . .

A great empty space opened inside of her, and Abby felt her eyes fill up with water. Then Lydia had disappeared. Roger had lost her somehow. Surely he had meant her no harm, but had been overpowered, duped or forced into giving up Lydia. What a shame that he was not alive to explain it all.

She felt the pressure of a hand on her shoulder and looked up into Calum's sky-colored eyes. "I am sorry, mistress. Come, I'll cook some meal on the griddle and you'll feel better."

Calum's griddle cakes were delicious, crisp and brown on the outside and steaming hot and soft inside. Abby had never eaten anything like them before. By concentrating on the food she found she could hold back her tears and, for the moment, her longing for Lydia.

"Quite fine," she praised the Gael, between mouthfuls.

Calum, still clad in his outrageous, unmanly garments, nodded and smiled. "Excellent, you mean to say. Catriona taught me. She told me, since I had shown her how to fire a pistol, it was only fair that I learn how to make oatcakes." He eased a cake from the griddle and picked it up with the sleeve of the frock. Abby frowned but said nothing. After all, who in this wilderness would care about or even notice the condition of her gown?

"Did you mean what you said, mistress?" asked Calum, breaking open his cake and sniffing the fragrant steam.

"I beg your pardon? Said about what?"

"About learning the Gaelic. You said you would like to learn to speak it."

"Did I?" Abby considered. She must have shouted some such nonsense during her travail in the stream. "I don't remember." Still, it was likely a good idea to humor the man who had, if not quite saved her life, certainly brought it to safety. "Why, yes, I would. It would be helpful, I think. Just a few words. 'Here, there, yes, no' . . . the like."

Calum burst out laughing. "Have I already made an error?" she snapped.

"There is no 'yes' or 'no' in my language, Mistress Abby, so you cannot learn either."

Abby stared at him. This would not be a simple matter, this language of eagles' screams. "But how may one negate and confirm things, then? Or can one?"

For some reason Calum also found this humorous, and it was some time before his laughter subsided. "Here, mistress, say this: *Bha me anns an Conneag Uisge an duigh.*"

He repeated the phrase slowly, and slower still, as she spoke it back to him, syllable by syllable. The result made him howl with merriment. "This is no an easy task for you, is it, Abby?"

"It is not seemly to make light of another's efforts, Mr. MacDonald. Now pray tell me, what have I just said?"

" 'Today I was in the Rabbit Water.' "

Abby laughed in spite of herself. He might be dangerous company, but the man was amusing. He could pull her away from the verge of tears and make her laugh at herself, as no one had ever done before. "How does one say this? 'I owe my life to you.' "

Calum's face turned bright pink, just as she had hoped

it would. The man was the soul of humility. "Get away with you," he muttered. "You owe nothing of the sort." He bit into his oatcake. The Gaelic lesson was over.

That night was very cold, and Abby slept in fits and starts, sheltered only by the rocks of a shallow cave in the hillside. Now and then she could hear Calum beside her, mumbling in his sleep in the peculiar, nasal tones of his mother tongue.

Then she was back in Rose Cottage again, sunlight streaming into her eyes . . .

"Lydia!" she cried. She raced to the child's bedroom. Everything was as it should be: Lydia's canopy bed, her curtains, two velvet chairs, her little writing desk, even Tip, asleep on a cushion beside the bed.

But no Lydia.

"Tip, where is your mistress?" Abby stroked the dog, and her hand leaped aside. His fur was icy cold. The room darkened, and Abby noticed long, red streaks on the walls. As she watched, the streaks grew wider and wider until the entire room was filled with red blotches, all spreading out like ink spilled on paper. Abby ran from wall to wall in search of the door, but there was none.

"Lydia is gone."

Tip was speaking. The dead dog was staring at her, his eyes white and glaring. His jaws moved with mechanical steadiness. "Gone for a walk. Gone to the park. Gone to fetch the poor dog a bone."

"Lydia!"

The room seemed much smaller now. The walls, Abby realized, were moving slowly toward her, closing in on her. Soon she would have no room to breathe . . .

\* \* \*

"Abby! Is aught the matter?"

Abby awoke sobbing. Something dark and warm came close. She hesitated only a moment before throwing herself against Calum's chest.

"Abby, you've been dreaming, *mo chreidhe,*" he whispered. "All is well now." He folded his arms around her, and she sank into their hard, protective clasp.

"Lydia! I saw Lydia. No, I didn't see Lydia. That was it. She was gone. Tip was there, her little spaniel. He was dead, but speaking. 'Lydia is gone,' he said. The walls, all red and moving toward me. I couldn't breathe. And Lydia . . . Oh, Calum! Lydia is in danger! She must be!"

Abby felt his huge hand engulf her own. She thought of the cruel words of the grenadier at the Heart's-ease, after she had awakened from her other dream. Calum was different. She grew warm, remembering his exuberant kiss at the Rabbit Water. It was not lust that had powered that kiss, but life itself.

"*Arrah,* Abby, there's no good comes of desperate thoughts. Your dream shows nothing but your own fear and worry. Duninnis is a good man. At least, I'm certain he'd do nothing to harm your daughter."

"Perhaps you are right." A tremor ran through her from the base of her neck to the tip of her tailbone. More than anything else she wanted to believe Calum, to feel relief and trust and hope, but she could not rid herself of the sight of Tip's unhinged jaws or his growling message, innocent enough, surely, but devilish and menacing: "Gone, gone, gone."

She shuddered again, and Calum wrapped his fire-warmed coat about her shoulders. "Lie down, lie down now, mistress. I've sung many a wean to sleep, and I warrant I can do the same for you."

And Calum sang, a gentle rush of words and music she could not understand but loved to hear. Once he paused, just as she felt herself poised on the edge of sleep, and, to her surprise, she began singing.

> I have a garden, a garden so rare,
> Filled with roses, fragrant and fair.
> Each a beautiful thing to see
> But none as dear to my soul as thee.

Calum's fingertips brushed her forehead. *"Gle bhodaich!* Very pretty. An English song?"

"Yes." She fought back a wave of weariness. "A very old one. I sang it to Lydia when she was little. She is still quite fond of it."

"Someday you will sing it to her again," he promised.

"God willing." *I believe him,* Abby told herself as she sank into sleep on Calum's salt-scented coat. She had to believe him. She would see her daughter again.

*Six*

*The Beginning of Eternity*

A little girl had attached herself to Abby's skirts and would not let go. A tiny boy, naked despite the cold and barely able to toddle, had made a game out of hugging Abby, backing away from her, and bumping into her. Three older children chased themselves round and round her, as if she were a tree or stump.

She loved children, she told herself. She truly did, though she was not used to loving quite so many lively youngsters at one time. "Children! Children! Behave yourselves!" she cried, clapping her hands. The wild games ended. The little troop turned their grimy faces toward her, exchanged knowing looks with each other, and burst into laughter.

A shriek cut through their merriment. The children scattered as their mother emerged from the black house, screaming at them in Gaelic. Only the naked baby remained, too amused by his new game to desert it. Abby picked him up and handed him to his mother, who apologized, or appeared to. Abby recognized only two words among the spate of sounds that flowed from the woman's mouth: *clanna,* children, and *dorrach,* bad.

"Where . . . is . . . the . . . gentleman?" asked Abby, reining back her quick speech to a sensible jog. She

pointed to the stone house, built so low that Calum's
head would brush the ceiling if he stood erect. "May . . .
I . . . go . . . inside . . . now?"

Of course she knew the mistress of the house knew
no English. Calum had explained that few people in the
wild hills of the Trossachs knew Abby's language. Still,
she reasoned, one never knew what people could deduce
from intonations, gestures, and inflections. The woman
stared at her blankly. Then Abby remembered. *"Duine?"*
she ventured. "The gentleman? *Duine?"*

She had to repeat the word several times before the
woman understood, but when at last she did, her face
broke into a smile and she began chattering like a mag-
pie, her little boy echoing her words and gestures. "Shentlemun, shentlemun," cried the mother, nodding toward
the black house.

"Shentle, shentle," laughed the son.

Before Abby could decide whether to enter the house
or remain outside as Calum had bidden her, a man
ducked through the low doorway and strode toward her.
Was it the woman's husband? Abby backed away as he
came closer. The man seemed familiar and strange at the
same time. He was tall and broad-chested, dressed in a
full belted plaid, jacket, and short hose, the same sort of
garb that Roger's visitors from the north had often worn.
A blue wool bonnet slanted over his face. His hair hung
in red-gold waves to his shoulders, and his chin was spotted with red where he had cut himself shaving. Strength
and manliness clung to him like an odor. Within a short
distance of her he stopped, tilting his head like a robin.

Perhaps he was waiting for her to address him. Desperately Abby tried to recall one of the greetings Calum
had taught her. *"Gle mhath,* no, I mean, *lath mhath."*

"You'll have to practice that a bit, mistress. You are

still saying 'law' instead of 'lah'. Faith, 'tis a pity you don't speak my language as well as I speak yours."

Abby blinked. There stood her dear companion, no longer a brute ill at ease in ill-fitting rags, but a Scottish gentleman robed in magnificent blue-and-gray-striped tartan. While the old Calum had always walked as if drunk and stood as if carved of stone, this new Calum was at home with his clothes, his body, and his surroundings. He moved with careless grace, much like the wild-cat she had glimpsed one morning as it had loped through the heather. The more she gazed at the Gael, the more he appeared to fade into the granite-gray slopes and valleys of the mountains behind him, at one with his country. Even Roger, as handsome as he was, had never looked so splendid.

"Inspect me long and well," he said, smiling ferociously. "It's your silver that has paid for all this. Listen to my sporran." He shook the leather pouch that hung before him on his belt. A few coins jangled inside. "The lady is a weaver, and a good one, too. I had to force the money on her. Because she is a second cousin twice removed, she would have given me clothing out of respect for our kinship, but that she can ill afford to do, what with her husband dead nigh two years."

"She's welcome to it," said Abby, still awed by Calum's wild elegance and his amazing skill at recalling his kith and kin. Since Roger's misfortunes at the gaming table and her experiences at the Heart's-ease, Abby had little desire for riches. "I was hoping to find some way to repay you for your kindnesses. Let this be your payment. Do you think whatever you paid might cover the cost of a pair of shoes for me?" She stretched one foot forward; the sole of her shoe was completely worn away and her toes peeped through the tattered leather upper.

The weaver stared at Abby's shoes intently, lifting her skirts to expose her own bare, muddied feet. Calum and she traded a few words, and at last he nodded. "A nice surprise is in store for you, mistress, but you'll have to give my kinswoman the shoon you're wearing now."

"With pleasure! But why?" Surely the woman didn't intend to wear the torturous things.

"If she pounds the leather flat with a mallet, she can trade it to the tanner. He'll give her cotton thread, which she sorely needs."

"Calum, here's a riddle for you: what has a tongue but cannot speak?"

"One's shoe, of course," answered Calum. *"Arrah,* Abby, that was nothing. Though Highland shoes have no tongues, nor heels, neither." He extended a leather brogue so she might see for herself. "I'm still chewing on the beginning of eternity, though."

Now it was Abby's turn to step inside the black house with the weaver and leave Calum in the cold. Two half-grown girls stared at Abby with fearless curiosity as the weaver helped her remove her sodden dress and ruined petticoats in front of the fire. *"Broghan,"* Abby reminded her, pointing to her wretched shoes. The woman smiled and nodded as she slipped a linen shirt over Abby's head and wrapped her in a long, white cloak striped with thin blue lines. A few words from the weaver made Abby understand she was the new owner of an *arasaid,* part gown, part cape, a garment as soft as lambswool but much warmer and heavier. She had new shoes, too, light leather brogues laced up the instep and tied round the ankle, very similar to those Calum now wore. They had belonged, it seemed, to the woman's husband. Only a little too large for her, the shoes felt delightfully roomy and soft on her aching feet.

Outside, Calum bade her turn around so he could examine her. *"Gle snog!* Very nice! You cut a bonny figure, Abby, when dressed propitiously."

Appropriately? wondered Abby, holding up her heavy skirts for Calum's and the weaver's inspection. With a sudden pang of shame she remembered the evening at the Heart's-ease when Mistress had observed Abby's nakedness with sickening pleasure. But this was different. She was dressed. She was respected. She knew Calum and his kinswoman had only her comfort in mind, and she loved them for it.

The flock of youngsters had wandered back, drawn by the sight of Calum's and Abby's new clothing. They whistled and shouted their approval of the strangers' transformation from Englishfolk to Gaels. Abby smiled and inclined her head toward them. She noticed that the clouded sky had broken and a streak of blue cut across the endless gray.

What charming children! What generous people! Her journey was progressing exactly as she had wished it to, except for the incident at the Rabbit Water. In no time at all, no doubt, she would be holding Lydia in her arms, drinking chocolate once again.

After a pleasant night in the weaver's cottage, they traveled on, deeper into the forested hills of the Trossachs, following the 'road' in Calum's mind. Sometimes Abby found herself walking alone and would take advantage of her privacy to relieve herself among the rocks and heather. Calum always came back to her after a few minutes.

Abby saw very few people, even on the road, and passed few dwellings. Rarely did anyone approach them, call out to them, or indeed take any notice of them whatsoever, save to turn away. She began to miss the crowded streets of Glasgow and the sounds and smells of masses of hu-

manity. Even the Heart's-ease seemed friendly compared
to the Highland wilderness. Now and again they would
encounter a band of half-grown boys, who would shout
profanities after them or pelt them with pebbles and balls
of dirt. One quick movement of Calum's hand toward his
smallsword, however, and the pack would scatter.

So it was Abby's great joy and relief to spend the night
with a man and wife as kind as the weaver, still more
of Calum's very-much-removed relatives. The fellow's
name was Duncan Mor, a "child of the mist," as Calum
called him, a MacGregor clansman. After a pleasant meal
of venison and oatcakes, Duncan's wife and eight children took to their beds. And what beds! Abby had never
seen anything like them. Each family member slept in
his own wicker frame, not unlike a basket, covered with
plaids against the cold.

Duncan kept Calum and Abby company by the fire.
The air was blue with peatsmoke, which burned Abby's
eyes and made the entire room reek of burning earth. It
was warm by the fire, so warm, Abby noticed, that both
men stripped off their plaids and sat down beside her to
visit, dressed only in their long linen shirts. Abby, in
great discomfort, averted her eyes whenever the men
crossed or uncrossed their legs, momentarily exposing
themselves. She remembered Calum's sense of delicacy
at the Rabbit Water, when he had been forced to stand
naked before her. His modesty then made his present
behavior all the more baffling. However, she thought, Calum had been a stranger in an unfamiliar land, wearing
Lowland clothing and speaking in a foreign tongue. Now
it was she who had to adjust to primitive customs and
peculiar sensibilities.

Calum and Duncan passed the whisky-skin between
them freely and now and then, to Abby's amazement,

broke into song or wild laughter. The sleepers continued to doze through this uproar, while Abby, listening for familiar words, was soon drowned in a sea of Gaelic.

When Duncan at last joined his wife in bed, Abby pulled at Calum's sleeve. "They seem to lead a happy life."

"*Seem* to, aye, but you must understand, mistress, we are a diversion and they are making the best of it. 'Tis our custom to make a guest welcome, even an enemy, but day to day, Duncan and Morag lead a hard life. They are, after all, MacGregor folk, as are most of the people in these mountains."

"Are MacGregors not just another clan? There are many, I understand."

"Aye, but only one like the Children of the Mist. They are the only people not allowed to use their rightful name."

Abby laughed nervously. "I cannot believe such a thing! Not allowed to use their name! But why?"

"Many years ago, even before James was driven from the throne, Clan Gregor engaged Clan Colquohon in combat. Well, such warfare was common enough back then. Entire clans were sometimes destroyed. The men of Colquohon fared badly, but instead of accepting their fate, they petitioned the king, the Stuart, James, to punish Clan Gregor. Some MacGregor clansfolk were slain, some sent to the tropics as slaves. The name was banned by royal decree. They cannot even bear weapons, by law, in any case." Calum took a swallow of whisky, as if to wash the taste of the story from his mouth. "A terrible thing. Very unfair. Every clan, Clan Donald not excerpted, has done the same or worse to at least one of its enemies. But only Clan Gregor has been broken this badly."

"Duncan appears to be decent and law-abiding," observed Abby.

"He is," agreed Calum. "But others of his clan have been driven to crime—cattle thieves, robbers, reivers, murderers."

"But . . . but what if we come across them?"

"Why, they may rob us, kill us, rape us, aye, *us*. But I believe we can avoid them, mistress. I know their haunts, their hideaways among the hills. What's more, no Gael, no matter how low, would be apt to bother a poor man and his wife traveling the road to the isles. Keep your florin well hidden. Truly, I'm more concerned about the red soldiers. Duncan here told me he has seen them about. Moving southward, he hopes, out of the cold. The government aye loves to hound Clan Gregor, good Jacobites, by the bye, and the clan has had more than their share of reprisals over the years. Don't fret. Duncan has armed me well with a musket and powder and a good sword." Calum reached behind himself and produced a long-barreled Spanish rifle, a powderhorn, and a Highland claymore, a broadsword with a silver basket hilt lined with red leather.

"Not allowed to possess weapons, you say?"

Calum smiled and pointed to the ceiling. "He hides them in the thatch. *Arrah!* A man has to hunt to feed his weans."

"One does not hunt with a sword."

"Aye, but it's good to have one, in case you are the hunted."

Abby ran her finger over the intricate designs incised in the hilt of the claymore. How well did Calum handle a blade? She remembered he had refused to leave the city without a sword to defend himself. But, attacked by trained troops, what kind of protection would he afford her, or himself, for that matter? She would have done well to think of those questions back at the Heart's-ease.

Though doubts sometimes plagued her, Abby knew that her best hope was with Calum, and her best chance of survival. She rose just before dawn, eager to be on her way. The morning was gray, cold and dry, good traveling weather, according to Calum. They left Duncan and his family waving farewell from their black house and set off over the undulating moorland. The weather worsened as the day progressed. Snow fell, turned to sleet and pelted Abby's hands and face until she cried out in pain. Calum wrapped his plaid around her and together, in the middle of the bare moor, they waited out the storm.

The weather changed again, and as suddenly as the sleet had begun it ended, melted by wan sunlight and warm winds that breathed a sense of life into the land. Mountains rose out of the mist. Abby had never seen their likes before, and she did not know whether to fear them or admire them. Sunlight and shadow chased each other over the crags and checkered the glens. A hillside glowed in the sun one instant and fell dark the next. "The Lord must have changed the weather just for you," jested Calum, untangling his long plaid from Abby's shoulders. "He wishes you to see how fine the mountains of my country can look when not viewed through rain and snow. If you find this pleasant, you will love my Bailebeag."

Abby shuddered. The solemn, brooding mountains were not to her liking. "Is this the Highlands, then?"

Calum laughed. "Yes, it is what your people call the gate to the Highlands. *Dorus do Thuadh,* we call it. The little wood just before Duncan's house marks the border between the northland and the lowland."

"Why did you not tell me?"

"In truth, I meant to, but it loosened my mind."

"Slipped your mind, you mean. Really, you are exasperating, Mr. MacDonald. In the future, you must let me know where we are. Assuming you know where we are."

Calum bowed low with exaggerated humility. "Indeed I shall, Mistress Fields. My apologies."

Abby smiled.

The day passed quickly, full of shifting light and clouds and the constant threat of rain. For the first time in her life, Abby saw the Highland breed of cattle, great, hairy beasts, duns and roans. They approached her along the trail, swinging their scythe-like horns. They looked so fierce and wild, she shrieked when she saw them, but Calum made her understand she had nothing to fear. One shout from him sent the herd lumbering away.

By evening they came to a herder's abandoned hut, and there Abby suffered through a chilly, dream-filled night. Awakening before Calum, she went outside to scrub her face. The sun had just risen, and though the air was cold, the sky was clearer than she had seen it since the beginning of her journey. She was searching for a likely place to make water when a red fox trotted in front of her. *Why, it doesn't see me,* she thought. It didn't scent her, either. Such a beautiful creature! Its eyes shone yellow in the morning light, and its tail streamed behind it like a banner. Where could it be going with such strength of purpose?

Over broken granite, through dead heather, and past a grove of bare-branched rowans, Abby followed the fox. It moved slowly, a red tear trickling over the gray face of the hills. At last it stopped, sniffed the air, and bolted.

"Come back!" cried Abby. She scanned the heather for a glimpse of the fascinating animal. "Come back!" What a ninny she was, shouting for a wild beast to return.

If anything, she was driving it away. A red patch on the hillside caught her eye, and she scrambled toward it.

It was not the fox. It was a person. Two people.

The stench of gore filled Abby's nostrils. She turned away, splitting the air with a scream of horror. Yet she had to look again. Again she screamed. The third time she looked, she did not turn away. The poor creatures!

The bodies of a man and woman lay before her, the man atop his lover, still joined to her in the act of love. A single musketball had killed them both, shattering the back of the man's head before plunging into the forehead of the woman. Her long, yellow hair lay spread out above her head like straw upon a blanket of blood.

Who could have done such a thing?

"Adults." She jumped at the sound of Calum's voice stabbing the air behind her. He was developing an unpleasant habit of showing up when she least expected him. "That is to say, adulterers. Adultery. Some jealous husband is weeping now for the wife that betrayed him. *Mo Dhia!* What a sadness it is!"

"Poor things! You must attend to them, Calum," whispered Abby. "Don't leave them out here for the beasts to maul."

"And me without a spade, woman!" Calum shook his head and sent his bronze-colored hair flying about his neck. "It's not my work, mistress, to bury them. Let their clansfolk attend to that." Calum came up close to the bodies, then slowly walked around them. "A bonny shot. I wish I had made it. Not that I would have slain them, mind you, though being eaten by wolves and crows is no less than they deserve. My people do not take betrayal lightly."

"Your people are brutes, then!" cried Abby. "Yes, these people did wrong, but they have paid the ultimate price. They deserve Christian decency, not condemnation."

The Gael had just begun to speak when Abby noticed yet another patch of red. This one was far away but moving closer, fading in and out of view behind trees and heather. "Pray look behind you, Calum," she murmured.

Calum spun around, gazing down the glen. Almost at once he stiffened, then clasped Abby by the waist and propelled her up the hillside, into the cover of a little stand of pines. "Red soldiers?" whispered Abby.

Calum rolled his eyes in disgust. "Aye, the very worst sort of Hanoverian lowlife. Clan Campbell. See how ragtag they are? Deserters, perhaps."

Abby squinted and soon made out the shapes of four Highlanders, dressed very much like the scouts she and Calum had encountered near Allan's Nose but filthy and tattered. The four made their way toward the corpses, then spent some time circling them and prodding them with sticks. All the while the soldiers kept up a steady chatter of Gaelic which Abby could not understand.

The soldiers finally left the way they had come, but Calum refused to budge from the little wood. He and Abby rested an hour while a light snow fell, mantling the lovers' bodies with a veil of glittering crystals. When Calum decided all was safe, Abby knelt by the bodies and wept, all the pain and worry she had stored inside finally finding release. "You must do something for them," she sobbed. In the end, Calum pulled the plaid from the man's body and covered both corpses with it.

"You and I were a heartbeat away from joining them, y'ken."

"What do you mean?"

He looked at her, puzzled by her confusion. "Why, the soldiers. Had they seen us, they would have killed us for spying on them. Even your Englishness would not have saved you from them."

"Yes, I'm well aware of that. I'm sorry to have put you in such danger." For a moment, she had thought he had meant something altogether different.

Calum led the way steadily northward over increasingly rough, wild country, and Abby soon found that modesty was a virtue that a Gaelic man could ill afford. The wind often tore at Calum's plaid, revealing his thighs. Once he slipped on wet stones and fell on his face. His plaid, billowing up over his back, revealed everything: his legs, buttocks, stones, *membrum virilis*. Abby watched through squinted eyes, loath to look, but afraid he had hurt himself. Laughing at his clumsiness, the hardy Gael simply picked himself up and walked on.

As they traveled, Calum pointed out landmarks, beasts and birds to Abby, always in Gaelic. *"Beal dubh,* the Black Mouth,"* he told her, as they crossed the flimsiest of plank bridges over a deep, narrow chasm. Abby dug her fingers into the thick sleeves of his jacket. She could well imagine a huge tongue emerging from the depths of the pit and pulling her and Calum into the blackness below. A petrifying fear possessed her, but only for the few moments it took to cross the gorge. She heard the wind sigh, and thought it might be the fissure itself, panting like a hound.

"The Beal claims several lives a year, so I'm told," continued Calum, in a steady voice. "Hunters find the bodies far below, every bone broken."

"Calum, pray keep silent if you can say nothing cheerful," muttered Abby. The sight of the slain lovers was still fresh and red in her mind and colored all her thoughts with foreboding. To make matters worse, she had lost her portmanteau and skinned the palms of her hands after one of her many falls on the rocky path.

"Faith, don't be so English, Abby! My country is invaded by the soldiers of your German king, and my people are being shot on sight. What cheer is to be found in that?" Calum pointed toward the peaceful glen. "Beautiful, aye. But what good is beauty without freedom, without life? That is my inheritance—fear and captivity. And there's aye little that's pleasant about it."

"And what of me?" cried Abby. Calum was not the only one in the process of losing his country. "I cannot even show my face to my own people. Traveling with you, I have lost my right to be what I am. An Englishwoman."

"No harm done to you, then," chuckled Calum. The man's moods shifted as abruptly as the sunlight. Abby was thinking of a reply when a shadow crossed Calum's face. He looked up. *"Iomhlair."*

Abby followed his gaze. An enormous bird glided high above the glen, its pinions spread wide. "Oh! An eagle! It won't harm us, will it? What did you call it? Yoolur?"

Calum laughed and shrugged. "That will do for now, mistress. It's looking for its supper. As you should be, too. Soon we'll come to the house of Catriona's cousin, and there we can spend the night. She has many children, a husband who loves to tell stories, and plenty of food to share. Come! 'Tis but a few miles distant."

The prospect of hot food and good company thrilled Abby, and she forgot why she had been angry with Calum. The blisters on her feet, protected in the supple Highland shoes, were quickly healing, and the beautiful *arasaid* kept the wind and cold at bay far better than any cloak or frock.

"Let's hurry, then! I shall at the very least amuse your friends with my attempts to speak your language."

"You shall indeed. Tell me, is it constancy?"

"Constancy? Oh, my riddle. But of course not." The man and woman on the fox's hill preyed on his mind, too. She glanced at him just as he turned toward her. She lowered her eyes, and she and Calum walked on in silence.

It was nearly evening when they reached a heap of stones which had been a house. Only one wall was still standing. Charred thatch and the great black splinters of half-burned rafters littered the ground before it. Abby smelled smoke and wet straw and the dusty smell of scorched stone, though she guessed the outrage had taken place some time ago. "A reprisal," she whispered. Calum sighed and waved his hand toward the ruins, as if trying to will them back into a structure. "I'm so sorry, Calum, but we can't do anything to help. And night is coming apace. We mustn't tarry."

Calum kicked at a blackened windowframe. It fell apart under his foot. "And where would you be going?"

"Why, to . . ." The words she was about to say stuck in her throat. This pile of rubble—this testament to military thoroughness and reparation—*this* was the house of Catriona's cousin. Calum turned, and Abby thought she saw water glistening on his cheek. "Oh, Calum! I'm so terribly sorry!" She rested her hand on his shoulder, but he gently pushed it aside.

"This house was more than four score years old, mistress, but took only half an hour of hatred to destroy. And it was your people did it."

"Mayhap. Mayhap it was your own, the Highland soldiers we saw near Duncan's house. That's not important. But at least your kinsfolk are safe."

Calum's eyes narrowed as he returned her gaze. "Clan Campbell and my people are two different races. But tell me . . . how can you be certain my relations are alive?"

"Why, they would be clearly visible." Abby remembered a fire years ago in the stables at Brenthurst. Seven horses had been roasted black, trapped in their stalls. "There would also . . . also be an odor."

"It's true, I believe you're right. I don't smell the stench of burned bodies." Calum walked carefully around the standing wall, and for the next several minutes occupied himself overturning bits of debris and digging a stick into piles of ashes, until his legs and stockings were black with soot. Abby joined him and found nothing but a cracked jar, a steel pistol that fell to pieces when she picked it up, and a large brass button. At last she satisfied Calum that his people had escaped.

"Well, sit down by the wall, then, away from the wind, and I'll fetch some water for *drammach.*" Calum nodded toward a pile of half-burned sticks that had been furniture. "We've plenty of dry wood, if nothing else."

"Sit by the wall? You mean to stay here tonight? What if the soldiers should return?" Abby glanced about. Perhaps soldiers were encircling them even now, watching.

But Calum had already disappeared.

Abby insisted on cooking, and Calum gladly showed her how to measure the meal in the skillet and heat it over the open fire without scorching it. After eating, Abby lay down, but it was some while before she fell asleep. The wind seemed to walk in boots, and the shifting embers of the campfire whispered of vengeance and destruction.

She awoke to the sound of Calum screaming.

Abby jumped to her feet, then knelt down beside him. He was sitting with his back against the blackened wall, his plaid wrapped tightly around his shoulders. Even in the dim light of the dying fire, Abby could see his face was ash-white. "Calum? What is it? Did you see something? Were you dreaming?"

The Gael pointed to his sword and a whisky-skin that Duncan had given him. Abby pushed both into his hands. Calum took a pull of the liquor, gripping his broadsword with his free hand. "I saw Catriona."

"In a dream, you mean."

"A dream, a vision . . . call it what you will. I saw her, standing before me. She was bidding me farewell. Farewell, she told me. *Slan leat.* Farewell. Farewell forever. Farewell for aye. Imagine that, mistress! My own wife leaving me. And the children! They stood at her skirts, stretching out their hands toward me while she pulled them away."

Abby stroked his arm, but he stared straight ahead into the darkness, focusing on something she could not see. "Nothing but a dream, Calum. I have them, too, as you know. They're nothing but shadows and delusions. You've said as much yourself."

He turned toward her. She was relieved to see the color had come back to his face. "What meaning can it have? Catriona would never desert me."

"Of course she wouldn't, Calum. The dream has no meaning at all. No more meaning than red stains in Lyddie's bedroom, or talking dogs or moving walls. Now please, I beg you, go back to sleep. It's this place that has broken your dreams and disturbed your thoughts." The Gael's face looked distraught and bewildered, and Abby thought of Lydia, who had been so frightened when she woke one morning to find the parlor and dining hall stripped of all their furniture. Reliving the child's terror,

Abby took Calum's hand in hers and kissed his calloused knuckles. "I promise you, all is well."

"We shall see," whispered the Scot, reaching his hand up to stroke her cheek. His touch was wondrous tender, considering the roughness of his hands. "The world is not always as English as you would like to have it, Mistress Abby, for shadows and spirits sometimes walk and talk like living folk." A deep sigh shuddered through him, and he lay down and curled up in his plaid. Abby bathed his face with cool water, but before she could dampen her kerchief a second time he had fallen asleep.

She nestled down beside him, listening to his deep breathing and the ragged bits of Gaelic he flung about himself in his sleep. What had he meant, that shadows talk and walk like the living? Was brave, practical Calum as nervous about ghosts and demons as so many of his countrymen? Once he gasped aloud, still sleeping, and she pulled back a lock of his red-gold hair that had fallen into his mouth. She imagined Catriona a few days hence, lying in bed with her husband, secure in the warmth of his love and loyalty. *It would be good, sometime,* thought Abby, *to have such a life again.*

In the morning she awoke to a strange sight. A gaunt young woman clad in nothing but a tattered *arasaid* stood over Calum as he slept, staring at his face with great interest. Abby cried out. The girl slowly turned toward the sound, her eyes remarkably blue but as blank as a schoolchild's empty slate. Then, just as slowly, she turned away, her attention drawn back to the sleeping man.

"Calum!" shouted Abby. "Calum, awake, pray you!"

The Gael snorted, rolled over, and sat up abruptly, nearly tossing the watchful girl onto the ground. When he saw her, he leaped to his feet and fired a string of questions at her in his native tongue, too rapid for Abby to follow.

But the girl did not even seem to hear him. She looked into his eyes for a few moments, with all the intensity of a sparrow eyeing a cat from a safe distance. Then she turned away, keeping her gaze fixed straight ahead of her. She must be blind, thought Abby, just as the girl proved her wrong by neatly avoiding a stone in her path. Calum caught the mysterious creature by the arm, but he could not detain her. Wherever she was going, she had set a firm, uncompromising course.

The young woman walked around the blackened ruins of the house three times, right past Abby, searching for the nameless something that might put her mind at rest. Then she trudged off into the hills and faded away in the gray distance.

Abby shivered; the morning had become very cold, and Abby fancied the girl had brought the chill with her. "Who was that, Calum, and where is she going?"

The Highlander ran his hand over his face and swore under his breath. "I've seen poor lost souls like this before. What we call a *triegte,* a forsaken one . . . what would you say in English? Hmmm, a *survivor.* But as you can see, she hasn't survived very well. She's naught but walking bones. Her family has been killed, I trow, and she is still looking for them. Perhaps a disease or accident took them, perhaps a reprisal. It hardly matters."

Abby stared long and hard where the girl had disappeared into the mist. The strange waif made her think of herself, lost and abandoned, though under much different circumstances. "Is she mad?"

"Well, in a manner of speaking. Mad with grief and sorrow, more than her mind could bear."

Abby brightened. Calum and his people had done so

much for her—rescued her from the Heart's-ease, kept her alive, clothed her in protective woolens, raised her spirits—even made her believe that she might see Lydia again. By helping this girl, Abby knew she could repay some of the kindness of those who had helped her so much. "Calum, we must come to her aid. Surely she has kinfolk here. We'll find someone to return her to her people and . . ."

Calum shook his head. "No, Abby, no. We can't. She won't let us help her, won't even let us get close if she suspects something's afoot. She may have relations . . . or she may not. But no one can save her now. She's lost, Abby, lost."

"How can you be so cruel?" She had overestimated him and his kind. They were savages, brutish and compassionless. "The poor child needs our help."

"Very well. You will see for yourself," muttered Calum, and slinging his musket over his back he marched off in the direction the *triegte* had taken, his back pine-tree straight and his plaid swirling about his legs. Abby trotted to keep up with him. When they finally saw the lost girl again, Abby was gasping for breath. Her legs felt like pudding. The girl plodded ahead in a straight line over the moor, to all appearances oblivious of the presence of strangers.

"Let me . . . let me speak with her," Abby asked Calum, who had already begun walking toward the waif.

"As you wish," mumbled the Gael, and he stopped to let Abby precede him.

"Halloo, halloo!" called Abby. The girl turned and stared at Abby, her dead blue eyes sunk deep within her smoke-stained face.

Abby addressed her in Gaelic, then realized if she were to say anything further it would have to be in English.

She smiled and stretched out her hand. The *triegte* took a few slow steps in her direction. By heaven! thought Abby. A gentle voice and an outstretched hand had helped her coax dozens of dogs and horses toward her; why not innocents? "Come here, lass," she crooned. "We shan't hurt you. Are you hungry? What is your name?"

A flash of fear lit up the girl's eyes. To Abby's surprise, the outcast walked straight up to her and gazed into her face. For a moment, Abby glimpsed the intelligence and kindness which had no doubt once burned like a bonfire in the young woman's heart. The next instant, Abby screamed in pain.

The girl had slapped her hard across the face. Abby's cheek smarted and grew hot. Through the tears rising in her eyes, Abby saw that the face of the girl was as blank as before.

Behind her, Abby heard Calum give a shout. He loped up to her, then past her, then stopped as he neared the maddened girl. She stood still, so still she didn't seem to be breathing. Perhaps she was too frightened, too distracted, or simply too weary to run from her countryman. For some minutes all three stood, wary and alert, watching each other.

Finally Calum pulled a rust-red hunk of smoke-dried venison from his sporran and offered it to the girl. *"Sithionn?"* She hesitated only a heartbeat, then snatched the meat from him and devoured it. *"Am bochd!* The poor thing!" he murmured to Abby. "She's half dead with hunger."

"But I was trying to help her, Calum," wailed Abby. "I would have offered her food. Why . . ." She raised her hand halfway to her throbbing cheek. "Why did she strike me?"

"Mistress Abby," replied Calum, "you cannot help it.

It may well be that her family was slaughtered and her home burned to the ground by soldiers who speak as you do."

"My English! My English words! I frightened her with my English words!" moaned Abby. Still, she felt relieved; the unfortunate had been lashing out at fearful memories, not at Abby herself.

"Perhaps," said Calum tenderly. "It's in-material. Come. If you wish to help her, fetch me some water. I will make a fire and boil some *drammach* for all of us. I can think of nothing else to do for the wretch."

The *triegte* stayed with them through the night and followed them up the glen the next day, walking barefoot over frost-silvered ground and rock. Abby noticed the girl never came closer than an arm's length, even during meals. She was with them the next morning, too. When they paused for their midday meal, Calum sent the *triegte* to a nearby spring for water. She never returned.

Abby did not know what to make of the girl's disappearance. Was she frightened? Ungrateful? Bereft of all her senses? Or was the desire to find her family, however hopeless, too strong for her to resist? "We would have done anything for her," she complained to Calum that evening, after he returned from searching for the wanderer. "She would not let us be of assistance."

"You must remember, Abby," said Calum, "she is a Gael. She's not an Englishwoman. You yourself were deserted, were you not? Yet you found people to hold you up, keep you alive. People to depend on, even if some of their motives were not the purest. You did whatever it took to keep yourself alive. But Gaels can't do such a thing, can't depend on strangers for their existence. 'Tis a failing in the race, you see, and one of the reasons we are so easily destroyed." He sighed deeply and touched his hand to his forehead. Was he thinking of Sherrifmuir? she wondered. "Only rarely will one clan come to the aid of another. A son of Donald, for example, would never help anyone . . ."

"And the *triegte*," interrupted Abby, "she would not let anyone close to her. She had lost all, and would prefer to lose her mind trying to recapture her life rather than start life over again." She paused, amazed at what she had just said. Never in a hundred years would she have thought to refuse aid when she knew it was needed. She had lived too many years under the fuss and care and doting affection of her parents, of Roger, the servants. It was only Calum who had treated her differently, yet she relied on him, too.

"Oh, Abby, I'm sorry for you! There are some things can't be changed, not by you nor anyone else. Don't take it to heart. The *triegte* is part of the land now. The land will take care of her."

"You mean she'll freeze," sniffed Abby, grateful for the warmth of his arms and the music of his voice. "Or starve. Or fall into the Black Mouth. Oh, Calum! She reminded me so of Lydia!"

"No," said Calum firmly, "she should not. You can do nothing to help the wandering one, but Lydia needs your help as much as a child ever needed her mother. Come now, let's be going. We're so close I can almost smell Catriona's oatcakes on the griddle and hear the children laughing."

"We are so near?" Abby raised her head, expecting to catch the scent of baked oats and the happy sounds of Calum's household.

"Well, not so very near. But not so very far, neither. Come, let's speak no more of death and destruction. As you have seen, my poor country is too full of both to lift up its head and be happy. But we will soon be warming ourselves at a fire at Bailebeag, I'll be playing with my weans and Catriona will be looking you up and down with no small twinge of envy in her heart. And then . . ."

"Then we can continue on to Lydia."

"*You* can continue, though I shall find a guide for you, as I promised."

They returned to the cattle track, sidestepping mounds of frozen dung. Once Abby thought she saw a ragged, human shape on the ridge above the glen, but she did not pause or wave or call out to it. It was no more substantial than her dreams, no more real than her memories of Brenthurst.

*Racing. Racing, flying, fleeing. Racing the damnable wind.*

The wind caught the major in the face, chilled his teeth, burned his eyeballs. Even in the semi-darkness of the evening, he could see steam rising from his horse's neck. Any moment the beast would take a false step, lose a shoe, step into a hole, collapse. He would fly from its back, fly into blackness, fly toward forever. Toward Edwin.

The major laughed. He clapped his spurs against the animal's flanks, and it leaped over a nonexistent obstacle.

A movement caught his eye.

A hare? A roebuck?

Racker tugged at the reins. The horse slid to a stop. Foam flew from its mouth and spattered against his sleeves.

"Campbell?" he called. No, not Campbell. The captain was a mile behind, quartered just a day's march from Ardnamurchan with his Highland soldiers and the grenadiers. Campbell had tried to stop him, though he knew it was the major's custom to ride fast and hard, especially over unknown ground. "You'll break your neck, sir," the Scot had told him. "Too many rocks. You'll no see them in the twilight."

"I can see in complete darkness," the major had replied.

"You'll lose your way."

He had followed the course of a stream, a stream that now shone silver in the waning light. Only a short distance ahead, it rose in a mass of white spray and disappeared over the edge of a rocky ridge. Racker wheeled his mount to the left.

The horse whinnied. Again a movement, the faintest flicker of red and white against the brown and gray of the halflit moor. The horse, its ears bobbed in the style of a proper hunter, pricked up its remaining stubs of flesh. The major followed his mount's gaze. Another flicker, then a shape. A rustle of clothing, a startled breath.

Racker grasped the hilt of his saber, then released it. He urged his horse forward at a gallop. The shape swung to the right. The major pulled up and veered back toward it. He could see very clearly the form of a man, his bare legs flashing white as he sprinted away. As Racker rode forward, a shadow soared toward him: the man's plaid, thrown off to blind the horse. The beast shied. The major struck it on the head with his fist and coaxed it back into pursuit.

The man ran naked over the moor. He swerved to one side, then another, but the major followed. He drew up close behind his panting quarry. Pulling the horse's head up high and straight, Racker dug his spurs into its side. The terrified creature sprang forward.

The force of flesh against flesh vibrated in Racker's tailbone. A sharp sound like the snapping of a stick came from the horse's hooves, then a squeal, then a thud. Racker lurched forward. The animal stumbled, regained its footing, and galloped on.

"Jacobite," the major explained to his mount, to the wind, to Edwin's ghost. "Likely a Jacobite. And if not, what loss to anyone?"

# Seven

## A Little Gold

" 'Tha an cu aig an dorus. Tha an chat aig an tiene. Tha na chlainn a'cluich aig . . . aig . . .' Help me with this bit, Calum. How does one say 'floor' in your torturous tongue?"

Abby paused on the path and turned to look behind her, but Calum was gone. Not a minute earlier he had been at her side, coaching her through the series of snorts and whistles that constituted his native speech; now he had disappeared.

"Attending to his privy needs," she thought aloud. She knew she had but to follow the faint track that led north through the dead heather. He would be back beside her before she began to worry about him, criticizing her pronunciation of every Gaelic word she knew.

Thinking she might do well to take advantage of her solitude, she scanned the hillside for a private place to relieve herself. A heap of broken rocks not far down the path caught her eye, and she hurried toward it, singing under her breath. If she could only find a spring or a stream, she thought, she might wash her hands and face. She might actually begin to feel like a normal, happy woman again.

When Abby came to the rocks, she thought she heard

the roar of water. She looked up and spied a waterfall on the cliff above her, shining like a golden thread in the morning sunlight. Glancing about for Calum and not finding him, she climbed a short distance up the brown slope toward the dancing water. A little further still, and she could hear it roaring and sighing as it tumbled down the rocks. She imagined she could smell its freshness and taste its sweetness. But she could find no stream. Likely the water flowed into a cavern or fissure underground, a subterranean river. Intrigued, Abby climbed higher still, until she found herself at a little pool, its banks encrusted with ice. As she stared up at the falls plunging down the hillside, spray flew into her face. She laughed wearily.

The falls were dappled in warm, yellow sunlight and black shadows, a sight so striking that Abby could not tear her eyes from it. With a pang of guilt she realized it was the first time she had found true beauty in Calum's country, though it had been far kinder to her than the stews of Glasgow. She was sorry Calum was not beside her so she could tell him how lovely the falls were, how much she admired their glory.

Kneeling carefully on the mossy shore, Abby scooped a handful of icy water into her mouth, then another onto her cheeks. The water burned, and she felt the shame of the Heart's-ease slowly melt away from her. She thrust both hands into the pool, sending ripples over her reflection.

She stared, squinting at the strange water image before her. What had happened to her during her long journey? Her hair was brown no longer, but red and wild. Her eyes were small and dull. Had hardship changed her so drastically that she could not recognize herself? No! This was not her face!

As Abby spun around, something as solid as a stone struck her jaw and sent her sprawling over the mossy rocks. She lay dazed, marveling at the salty taste of blood in her mouth, forcing her eyes to focus. And then a great weight fell on her. Hands tore at her *arasaid*. She smelled the sharp stench of sweat and whisky. "Calum?" she cried out. Surely it was not he. But who, then?

*If you are in dire straits, bite the bastard,* Janet had once admonished her. A hand came toward her face. She flung herself on it, grasping a little finger in her jaws and biting down hard. The finger's owner screamed. Another blow caught her by the side of the head, and her jaws sagged open. Gaelic curses poured over her. Through a mist of pain and confusion, she smiled to herself; it was not Calum's voice.

The hands were now between her legs, wrenching apart her skirts. Another pair of hands held her arms, and she realized there must be two men, not one. Terrified, she remembered the horror of her first night at the Heart's-ease, when three men had forced themselves upon her. Hugo had saved her, ripping the men from her and dashing them against the wall. But Hugo could not save her now.

Abby looked up into the face of her tormentor, the same feral face she had mistaken for her own in the mountain pool. The stink of whisky and tobacco made her stomach lurch inside her. Pulling one hand free, she raked her fingernails across the man's cheek.

*"Mille murthair!"* he cried. A fist rammed past her head, sinking harmlessly into her hair.

"Abby! Abby!"

Had one of them called her by name? The man atop her raised his hand again, then held himself still and looked over his shoulder. From the corner of her eye,

Abby spied a chunk of granite just within her reach. Scrabbling for the rock, she grasped it at last and pulled it close to her. With the little strength she had left, Abby smashed the stone into the man's face. Agonized howling filled her ears. She felt the flesh collapse beneath her hand, and when she drew her arm away, her fingers were bathed in blood.

A red flash ignited before her eyes. When it cleared, both men were gone, and the air was filled with unearthly groans and the clanging of steel on steel. Her head throbbed. She inched herself into a sitting position, then hunched low at the sight before her. Calum and a tall, dark man were striking at each other with broadswords at the foot of the falls. They battered at each other with such ferocity that saliva flew from their mouths. The man's nose was straight and bloodless; Broken Nose must have fled.

At once she saw her fears about Calum's swordsmanship were unfounded. Although his rival was far taller and heavier than he, Calum matched the man blow for blow. Sparks flew from their swords. Ignoring her aching body, Abby searched her mind for some way to help her champion. Finally she threw a stone at the dark man, but it fell far short of its mark. As she watched, gathering the strength to rise and come to Calum's aid, her protector struck his adversary's shoulder with such force that blood sprayed forward, spattering the faces of both men. The wounded man tottered back, slipped in the gravel by the water's edge and tumbled hind end first into the pool. Struggling in his tartans, the fellow flailed and thrashed until he found land, then took to his heels, dripping blood and water as he ran.

Calum turned toward her, stumbled, and picked himself up again. His fine jacket was streaked with blood.

His face was as dark as a thundercloud over the mountains. "Did you have a pleasant diversion?" he growled, mopping his scarlet-spotted face with his neckerchief. "Did I not tell you to keep to the track at all times, woman?"

"I was not seeking diversion," she sobbed. "I was merely washing my face . . . then these men beset me and struck me." She gasped for breath; her throat was raw, and she realized she must have been screaming. She had to pull her spirits together. "Oh, Calum! I am so sorry! You've risked your life for me yet again. Are you hurt?"

" 'Tis nothing. A few scratches." Calum knelt beside her and took her hand. She looked back at him, unable to hide the pain and terror in her eyes. "Ach, Abby, my poor Abby! You're nothing but cuts and bruises!" He had not seen her face clearly until then; when he saw how badly she was hurt, she could see that he had to force himself to look at her. Her lips felt swollen, as if she'd been stung by a hornet. Blood matted her hair and dappled her cheeks. Bruises throbbed all over her body, and stings from scratches danced across her exposed skin. Worst of all were her hands, the nails jagged and broken, the fingers bright with blood. He folded her into his arms, and the strength she'd mustered vanished like smoke in a strong wind. Pain and fear and the thought of what could have been overwhelmed her. Again she broke into sobs and whimpers.

Calum held Abby close, astounded at the emotions rioting through him. *Devil take the creatures that harmed her! He'd break the bastards in half! Anyone who had struck the dear woman deserved to be gelded and have his privates thrown to the dogs.* "Did they hurt you intimately, *mo chreidh?*"

Abby shook her head.

"I should have slain them anyway, the sons of Satan. A short life to them! To do this to a woman! My God! Just look at you! Shall I go after them, mistress?" He rose and glanced about the waterfall. A trail of blood led up the hillside.

"And leave me alone? Oh, no! Please stay!"

"As you wish." Calum dipped his hand in the pool and dabbed the snow-cold water on Abby's swollen cheeks and hands. To his relief, her slender fingers washed clean. "God in Heaven, woman, you look as if you've been brawling at a change-house with twenty men. What a fool I was to let the one go, the *iargall!* Say but the word, Abby, and I'll run after both of them and finish them."

"No, Calum." Abby clutched his shoulders. Her eyes were red and bleary, but her voice had recovered some of its steadiness. "I believe I broke the nose of the red-haired man, you know."

"Did you now? Then that was his blood on your hands. Faith, you are a scrapper, aren't you? Tell me, can you walk?"

"Yes. But mayn't I rest a little first? My head is twirling like a teetotum."

He wondered what that might be, but his pride prevented him from asking. "Mistress, I fear we must leave. Unless I run after the brutes and slay them—which is no less than they warrant, mind you!—their clansfolk are likely to hunt us down and take their own revenge."

"Outlaws with a sense of justice?"

"Yes, indeed. It's the custom of my people not to leave wrongs unpunished. And you may be sure that, when those two tell their story, you and I shall be in the wrong."

Abby's eyes grew as round as curlew eggs. "What should we do, then, Calum?"

"Can you walk?" he asked again.

"I think so. Only please fetch me my purse. I can't continue without it."

Calum searched the rocks about the pool and soon found the green stringpurse. When he placed it in her hands, she sighed with content and seemed far less frightened. It was amazing the good a few happy memories could do for a body. "If you are feeling any better now, Mistress Abby, I beg you, let us be off."

The woman pressed her hands against her forehead. "A moment more, pray . . . There, I suppose I am sufficiently recovered." He helped her to her feet. "Oh, Calum! I ache all over and my head is spinning."

Calum pulled at his chin, trying to think clearly. They could try hiding from Clan Gregor, a risky business in such open, barren countryside. They might try quitting the road and striking out over the moor, but the poor *quean* would not last very long if they did. There was only one thing to do. "If you are well enough to walk some distance, we are in luck. A friend of my father's lives two miles from here, perhaps three. We'll be safe there, and you can take your leisure."

"Yes, I'm all right." Abby raised her sleeve to her face. Carefully she wiped the tears from her eyes and blotted the blood from her lips. "Oh, how my teeth ache! I hope I shan't lose any. Yes, yes, let us be off."

Calum offered her his arm. "Mistress, it must be a terrible thing, being a woman attacked by a man, not only the pain but the fear and the hatred. Now myself, there's naught I can do about my sex. I didn't choose it, after all. But if you hated me a small wee bit for being a man, I'd suppose I'd understand why."

He searched her eyes, but saw only pain and weariness. Then she smiled, just a shadow, a suggestion of a smile, and he knew she did not hold his maleness against him. It relieved and amazed him.

They set off down the slope, Abby leaning heavily on Calum's shoulder, and soon reached the track where he had left her. They continued through the glen, but Abby walked far more slowly than Calum thought a person could walk. She was as weak as a newborn mouse and could scarcely muster more speed than a turnip. "I'm slowing our progress a great deal," she fretted. "I fear we'll be overtaken."

"You're injured, mistress. Do the best you can, for you can't do any better than that."

They had covered a little more than a mile when Calum stopped and sniffed the air. Was it whisky he smelled? Before them, the trail dropped off steeply to one side, and was bounded on the other with huge rocks. He looked up and down, forward and behind, but saw nothing.

"What is it, Calum?"

"I smell whisky." Again he breathed deeply. Among the scents of the peat, the heather and the wet earth, he clearly smelled the tang of the water of life.

"Yes, I smell it, too. Where does it come from?"

As if in answer, three men suddenly appeared on the path before them. Calum thrust himself in front of Abby, his hand on the hilt of his broadsword.

"Calum, who are they?"

"Sons of Clan Gregor. See the oak leaves in their bonnets? Freebooters, from the looks of them, and dogs every inch of them."

The MacGregor men arranged themselves in a line,

blocking the track. They snuffed and snorted, struck fierce postures and shook their heads like nervous horses. Basket-hilted swords, steel pistols and long dirks in black scabbards rattled and clanked about them as they fingered and slapped their weapons. Calum waited.

"What are they doing, huffing and snuffing like that? Such passion! Why don't they speak?"

"They will, when they're ready. Whisht, now, and be still."

One man, a fair-haired fellow with a missing eye, stepped forward and began speaking so rapidly in Gaelic that Calum knew Abby would not be able to understand a word. "Who dares trespass in the Beinn Riaghall? Strangers in our mountains have been known to suffer unfortunate accidents."

Calum hesitated. If it had not been for the attack on Abby, he would have thought the fellow was bluffing. Traveling with a woman was a sure token of peace on the road to the isles. "We are not trespassing, but only passing through your Royal Mountains. My name is Calum Og mac Chaluim Mhor of Clan Donald, and I am a friend and kinsmen to many in your clan."

One Eye lifted his head, glared at Calum, and then at Abby. "Two clansmen of mine were brutally injured this morn at the falls by Linn Solas. You wouldn't be knowing anything about their misfortune, now, would you?" One Eye spat onto the stones at Calum's feet.

At once Calum glanced about, searching the rocks for the men that had mauled Abby. "A red-haired lump with a bleeding nose? A dark ferret creature with chin whiskers and a cleft shoulder?"

The outlaw shifted uneasily from one foot to the other but said nothing. He gave one swift nod and crossed his arms over his chest in a threatening way.

"Where are the farting sons of a dog?"

One Eye smiled, exposing a mouthful of broken teeth. "With the healer, having their wounds seen to. The one's nose was broken. Shattered like a stick, it was. The other nearly lost his arm. They'll neither be good for anything until St. Bridget's Day, if then. Was it you what did that to them, Connal?"

"Calum is my name. It was I, yes, who cut the one. And it was she who struck the other." Calum stepped aside and let the outlaws fill their eyes with Abby's misery. "The cowards set upon this lady with the lowest of intents. See what they did to her, the sons of hell. By defending her I did only what any decent man would do."

One Eye craned his neck to study Abby more thoroughly. "A wretched wench, indeed," he muttered. "Your doxie?"

Calum scowled. "A friend of my family."

The outlaw laughed and turned toward his fellows. At once all three fell to arguing, stamping their feet and drinking deeply from a skin of whisky. Though they spoke too softly for Calum to grasp more than a few phrases, he got the gist of their quarrel. One Eye, who seemed to be a man of influence, wished to let them pass. The other two reivers were in favor of defending their clansmen's honor by killing the son of Donald and the Saxon woman on the spot.

Abby tugged at Calum's sleeve. His own little daughter often infuriated him with exactly the same gesture. "They know I am English!" she gasped, with not a little pride in her voice at being able to catch a word here and there. "Calum, that fellow is hideous! Did you see? He has only one eye, just like Mistress!"

"Abby, we are in grave danger," whispered Calum,

without taking his eyes from his countrymen. "These are the clansmen of the creatures by the falls. As I feared, they've come to make short work of us. Now, I can best two of them easily enough with my sword, but the third will slay me."

The woman fell silent. Then she tapped him on the shoulder and pushed something cold and heavy into his hand. "Will this help matters any?"

When he saw what she'd given him, Calum snapped his hand shut. *God preserve her!* He had forgotten about the gold florin!

"Gentlemen, a word with you." Calum stepped forward. The outlaws leaned toward him. "If you'll not believe in our innocence, will you at least let us buy safe passage?" As he held up the gleaming coin, an admiring gasp dropped from the mouths of all three cattle thieves. Two of them made a move toward him, but retreated when he slipped his hand onto the hilt of his claymore. " 'Tis not worth getting killed over, is it, gentlemen? Still, you'd like to have it, wouldn't you?"

One Eye snorted and moaned and all but licked his lips, his lone eye fastened to the glittering gold. "Very well, Connal, be off with you, then, and take the *quean* with you. Hand me the coin, and you'll have no cause to fear Clan Gregor."

"Nay! Nay! Hand me the coin!" cried one of his cronies.

"Myself! Myself!" cried the other, and soon all three were pushing and tugging at each other. As they wrestled amongst themselves, Calum calmly strode to the edge of the trail and let the florin fall from his hand. It rolled and bounced from rock to rock down the rough slope, cutting a shining path over the dark granite.

"Oh!" cried Abby. "It's lost!"

"Son of the devil a hundred times over! A short life

to you, piece of dung!" cried One Eye, not even bothering to look Calum in the face. Instead he sprang over the edge of the path, his clansmen so close behind him that they brushed against his haunches.

Calum took Abby's hand and gently tugged her forward. "A body needs but little gold, mistress," he said with a smile, "but that little gold is priceless. Perhaps we'd best be on our way, while these hounds are hunting for their rabbit."

Abby mumbled something that sounded like agreement, but they'd only traveled a short distance when she stopped and tugged on his plaid. "Calum, the falls were beautiful," she said, looking full into his face. "I confess I am not used to wilderness, but your country is splendid. I am quite serious. Fierce and splendid. Dangerous and splendid."

"I cannot decide whether you are praising the land or cursing it," laughed Calum. "You've plenty of cause to hate it, I should think, but if you mean to compliment the Trossachs, I shall gladly say 'thank you' for them."

Was the woman trying to thank him for coming to her aid at the falls? Calum thought she might be. The English had odd ways of doing things. Despite her Englishness and the bruises and cuts and smudges of blood on her face, no other woman, not even Catriona, had ever appealed to him quite as much as Abby did just then. An icy shiver rippled through his belly. He tried mightily to ignore it. "Come, we'd best hurry."

# *Eight*

## *Fir-chlisneach*

A heavy rain fell for days. Abby did not mind. Warm and dry in the black house of Calum's friend, she happily whiled away her time practicing her Gaelic and entertaining the man, his wife and children with her broad English "ah's" and slow, round "oo's." She learned how to weave baskets using a wooden needle, how to bake bannocks, and how to join in on the choruses of half a dozen lovely songs. When the rain at last abated, her face had stopped hurting and her dizziness was completely gone. She could scarcely wait to be back on the road to the isles, where every footstep brought her closer to Lydia.

They left on a cold morning so thick with mist that Abby could not see Calum in front of her unless he was within arm's reach. By the end of the morning the mist had lifted, and Abby found herself high on a ridge overlooking a dark, dreamy glen flanked by jagged mountain peaks. "Where are we now, Calum?" she panted, scrambling to keep up with the man as he strode along with the confidence of one of Roger's stud horses.

"Why, this is called Glen Mhor, Mistress Abby. Part of the lands of the great Clan Donald. My people. The Trossachs are behind us now. We'll be at Bailebeag well within the week."

"A week past then, and I'll be on Skye," she thought aloud. "When I find Lydia, I shall kiss her a hundred times, a thousand times, for all the kisses I have missed from her."

Calum winked at her, as if he knew something she did not. "And after that? What will you be doing after that?"

"Why, I shall . . . I'm afraid I must think on that a while longer." In fact, she had not thought of that question at all. Where would she go and what would she do after she had found Lydia? She had no home, no country, really. No close relations, no friends. Save Calum, of course.

"Well, you may stay at Bailebeag as long as you wish," the Gael suggested, reading her mind, she was sure. "My Catriona would enjoy having another woman about the house—once she sees that I still love her above all—and my Morag and your Lydia would be sure to get on well together."

"Thank you. I shall consider it." How generous of the man to offer her food and shelter in a land that had so little of either. She wondered, though, about Catriona. Just how would the woman perceive her? As a rival? An enemy? A friend?

"Friendship."

"Beg your pardon?"

"The riddle."

Abby chuckled. "Oh, Calum! You really will put an end to me when you finally solve it. No, not friendship. Though you must know how much I value yours." To her astonishment she leaned forward, stretched as high as she could reach, and kissed Calum's rough cheek. With a start she remembered she had kissed him before, at the Heart's-ease, when he had agreed to take her north with him. "Forgive me, Calum."

The Highlander smiled and stroked the spot her lips had touched. With a little horror and a little satisfaction she saw that she had kissed him just below his scar. "Naught to forgive, mistress, I assure you. Indeed, I shall treasure it."

What should she do with the man, thought Abby. He frustrated her so; practical and level-headed one moment, full of feeling the next, plain spoken and frank one day, mysterious and guarded the next. She felt as if many men, not one, were guiding her through the mountains.

After two days of hard travel through the Great Glen, it seemed to Abby that the people they met were becoming friendlier and bolder. Men would hail Calum by name and speak freely with him. They'd slap his back, hug his shoulders and sometimes even kiss him lightly on the mouth. She had never seen such a thing, even among the most vulgar and deprived of London lowlifes. The idea of a man kissing a man repulsed her but fascinated her, too. An ancient, barbaric practice, she imagined.

Women did not kiss her guide, but they were not afraid in the least to approach him, offering milk, oakcakes, wine, even seaweed—a little of whatever they happened to be carrying. They all regarded her with wary courtesy, and only the boldest sniggered when she attempted to speak their language.

"It's lovely to see such friendly people!" Abby told Calum, after one especially amiable encounter.

"Aye, but something is wrong."

"What could be wrong?" Perhaps Calum had been away from his people so long he had forgotten their audacious customs.

"Indeed, I don't know. But when I ask about Catriona and the children, how they are and how they've been, devil the man nor woman nor child will tell me. They pause and look away and say they haven't had word of them. That's aye unlikely, near as we are to Bailebeag. I fear one of the family is ill and these good folk are reluctant to tell me. It brings bad luck, you know, to bear bad tidings."

Such ignorant rustics, thought Abby, but she held her tongue. There could not be anything wrong, not now, not so near Lydia and victory. "I'm sure it's nothing, Calum. Perhaps the weather has prevented any news of your family from reaching the people here in the glen. But, if you're worried, we can make haste. I'm much stronger than I was before. I don't need to be coddled."

Abby did feel stronger and healthier than she had since leaving Brenthurst. Even so, she was glad there was now no shortage of cozy places to stay the night. Calum's friends and relations welcomed Abby with all the affection of a truly generous people, feeding her ptarmigan, trout, scones, butter, honey and other delicacies until she could almost fancy herself back at Rose Cottage, cosseted by the servants. One woman made her brose, a rich concoction of cream, whisky, honey and oatmeal which reminded Abby of the syllabub her mother had made at Christmastide. If not quite as glorious as chocolate, the brose tasted far better than any other food she had eaten on her journey.

One evening, as they were hurrying toward a village and Abby was anticipating a cup of hot punch and a warm fire, a storm caught them out in the open moorland. Rain mixed with ice pummeled Abby until she could neither think nor see. "Calum! Where are you!" she shouted into the storm.

"Abby! Come toward my voice!" he roared. *"An tur, an tur!"*

*A tower?* wondered Abby. All she could think of was

the Tower of London; surely he didn't mean that. As she stumbled forward in darkness, trying to judge what direction his voice had come from, her vision cleared slightly and a dark mass of stone rose before her, indistinct and threatening.

It was indeed a tower, the sole remainder of an ancient fortress of Clan Donald, Calum informed her. Once inside, the Highlander managed to light a small fire with odd bits of sticks and peat. A blazing chunk of pitch-pine made a torch of sorts, shedding just enough light for Abby to notice a movement by the stairs. "A rat!" she cried.

"An offended field mouse, just," chuckled Calum, "but 'tis best not to stay down here in any case. The floor here is cold stone, and the floor above is warm wood."

Torch in hand, Abby crept up the crumbling staircase to a single large chamber, empty save for a broken chair, a table, and odd bits of clothing and weapons. A single window, partially covered by the pelt of some great beast, let in the chill of the night wind. On the floor—wooden and warm, as Calum had promised—she discovered an abandoned plaid. She rolled herself in it and, without a second thought as to who had last used it, fell asleep before she could bid Calum good night.

Sometime in the night she awoke. A sliver of pale pink light had forced its way past the pelt over the window and leaped into her eyes. She thought at first she was dreaming and trembled, remembering the vision of Lydia's blood-red walls. But no, the light streaming into her face was the color of the roses in the gardens at Brenthurst.

Abby stood up and inched her way to the window, careful not to awaken Calum, who lay some distance from her, arguing over the price of dream cattle with some dream companion. The pelt drawn down to block the drafts was damp and smelled like compost. Touching it was like touching the wrinkled skin of a very old person. She pulled it aside, looked out the open casement, and gasped.

The rain was gone, the night clear. The blue-blackness of the sky was streaked with ribbons of red light that shimmered and danced like ripples on a sunlit pond. At first she thought the hill must be on fire. Then she remembered: Roger had mentioned this marvel to her once in passing. For all their brilliant color and constant movement, the lights made not one sound, but stood tall and dignified, a thousand rainbows distilled into one iridescent mass.

Splendid. Remarkable. Mysterious. Beautiful. And no one to witness it save her. Abby felt a tear fall onto her hand. She had not felt so miserably alone since her last morning at the Heart's-ease.

*"Fir-chlisneach."*

Abby leaped forward, bumping her head against the pelt. When she looked over her shoulder, there stood Calum, directly behind her. Any closer, in fact, and he would have been embracing her.

*"Fir* . . . I beg your pardon?" Abby squirmed and wriggled, but she could not free an inch of space between herself and Calum. "I implore you, stop stealing up behind me."

"Did I frighten you?" whispered Calum, moving back a bit. "For that I'm sorry. This which you see here is called the *fir-chlisneach,* the merry dancers, we Gaels call them. Your people call them the northern lights. They're beautiful, are they no?"

"Yes, very. Do you see them often?"

"Aye, when the night is clear." Calum laid his hand on Abby's shoulder, twirling a strand of her hair around his forefinger. "So beautiful. The first time I bedded a woman, we lay and watched the dancers in the sky, all night long." He smiled, though Abby thought she saw a trace of sadness in his face. "Forgive me, mistress, for being so indelicate." As he spoke, he leaned closer toward her and stroked her long, unfettered hair. "So beautiful."

Abby held herself perfectly still under his gentle caress. She had not spent a fortnight at the Heart's-ease without learning a little something about the mysterious passion between men and women, the passion that had killed the lovers on the fox's hill. Such fire had never existed between her and Roger. Her love for him had been quiet and sedate; she had fulfilled the duties expected of a wife, but their intimate moments were for his pleasure alone, never for hers. The fire she had never felt was definitely burning inside Calum at that very moment, a loving husband but only a man, nonetheless. She thought of slapping him, but something stayed her hand. The Gael was not impertinent, simply frank and forthright. He did not deserve to be slapped for his honesty, however uncomfortable it made her feel. Some of that fire seemed to be warming her, as well. "Catriona?" she asked, playing for time. "Was the woman Catriona?"

His hand roved onto her neck. "Nay, mistress. A tinker's daughter. *Arrah!* I can't even recall her name. I was a wild stud-horse in my youth, and I'm naught but a docile *gearran* now. Catriona—why, I didn't wrap her until our wedding night. She was a proper lass, you know, not a trollop."

The word stung Abby. Was that what he thought her, a trollop, a doxie, a drab? Surely not. And yet. . . . "And what am I, pray?" He stared at her blankly, the fiery lights of the northern sky blazing in his eyes. "Am I not a proper woman?"

He surprised her with a laugh. "Too proper, if anything. But more lovely, more desirable, more tempting than any woman has a right to be." His hand slid to her face and cupped her chin. She held her breath and put her trust in him completely. "Abby, a strange fever has come over me and not for the first time, neither. Many's the night I've watched you in your sleep, your face lit by the moonlight, and longed to touch you, wake you. But tonight is different, and I am aye weak. My hands shake, my blood boils, and I wish Catriona were with us to prevent me from doing anything I might regret."

"Regret?" she squeaked. She would have to make a decision, and quickly, too. She knew she could not keep the Gael from doing whatever he wished with her, but he would never take her against her will. She could refuse him. He might be uncivilized by London standards, but he was a man of honor; he would never force himself on her. Indeed, he had saved her life on at least two occasions and guided her safely past countless obstacles. She owed a great deal to Young Calum Son of Red Calum, and she had but one way to repay him. "Surely you would not commit adultery?" She had intended the words to form a statement, but of their own accord they asked a question.

"Say but the word and I will not. I'd never hurt Catriona, but you have a powerful hold on me, mistress, a hold that no other woman ever had. If I but lay down beside you, my will might dissolve within your arms." His voice grew rough and breathless, as if he had run a great distance or fought a great fight. "Tell me to cease. Tell me to go back to my bed and fall asleep. Tell me not to love you. You are my chieftain, Abby, and I'll do as you bid me."

Now his hands were at her bosom, lovingly tracing the curves of her breasts within the loose confines of the *arasaid*. "I beg you, tell me to cease!" Abby held her tongue. She enjoyed the warmth of his hands, the intimacy of his touch. A warm, pleasant feeling was coursing throughout her body, a sensation completely foreign and not a little embarrassing, but thoroughly delightful. She did not feel lonely anymore.

He spoke in Gaelic, and she could not follow him. "A poet's song," he explained, panting. " 'My love's breasts are like orchard apples, her hair like willow leaves.' Abby, command me to cease, or I cannot promise what consecrations will follow."

The *fir-chlisneach* still glimmered in the distance, spreading their glow inside her. She truly wanted this man—it was a hunger burning deep in her being. If she let him take her, might he not feel somewhat obligated to her? She had seen it at the Heart's-ease: the women received all sorts of gifts and favors from admiring customers. One gentleman became so attached to a lady that he actually left his wife for the strumpet.

And did this Gael love her? Certainly he must. He adored her, as every uncivilized man adored women who were cultured, refined, well-bred, and English. Because he loved her, she thought she might be able to give herself to him and not feel violated. It wouldn't be the same as it would have been at the Heart's-ease, among the repulsive wretches Mistress styled "gentlemen." Calum was virile and comely and, in his own way, gracious. If she let him bed her, she'd never abuse his trust.

The thought made her decision easier. "Consequences? I have dealt with the worst of them. Do as you wish, Calum. I know you will do what is right, if not for Catriona, then at least for us. Tonight, this beautiful night, I can't, I won't refuse you."

Calum stared at her, bewilderment shining in his face. Suddenly he was upon her, pushing his mouth upon hers and lapping at her lips with his tongue. She parted her mouth, and his tongue filled it, dancing and flitting over her teeth and palate. The strange sensation, not unlike pain but a thousand times more agreeable, erupted again inside her. She shut her eyes, clutched his shoulders, and pulled him closer still, determined not to let him go until he bade her.

She felt herself rising in the air as he scooped her up in his arms, then lowered her onto the plaid she had used as a bed, his lips, amazingly, never once leaving hers. He lay atop her like a pile of plaids, warm and heavy. One hand strayed to her loins. She thought of the men at the falls and felt her body contract, much against her will. Calum must have sensed her terror, too, for he withdrew his hand and returned it to her breast.

Abby pulled her lips away from his. "I am recovered now," she whispered. "I promise you, if you take me, I shan't flinch."

"Mistress, I cannot."

"Cannot?" Abby heard a tremor of fear rising in her voice. Had he reconsidered? Or was she doing something incorrectly? "Cannot?"

"Aye," whispered Calum. " 'The mind decrees, but the flesh does not obey.' So the menfolk say, anyway, when they have drunk so much they cannot please their wives. In a word, I cannot enter you for I have nothing to enter you with." Calum rose and walked to the casement. "I'm a great fool, I fear."

Abby sighed, relieved. She had not been all that eager

to deceive Catriona, especially since she was certain she could not deceive a wife for long. But what did Calum feel? Something she had overheard in the Heart's-ease leaped into her mind. Celestine had been telling Janet that a particular customer was "as firm as hasty pudding," and Janet had replied, "Be kind to him, lass. Above a' else, naught embarrasses as man as much as a sleeping pintel."

"Not a fool at all. Far from it," said Abby softly. "It's no great matter, really. It shows nothing more than your excellence as a husband. You are no less the man for it, you know. Indeed, perhaps you are more the man for it." Poor Calum! He was too honorable to be a rake, even in the grip of passion. The image of the murdered lovers flashed in her mind. "Perhaps I failed you in some respect."

"Nay, mistress," sighed Calum, staring out the window at the fading lights, "I failed myself. Forgive me, Abby, I very nearly did the worst a man can do. I nearly took advantage of your kindness."

"And that is wrong?"

"It is. I would never be able to marry you, be a husband to you, even a faithful lover. And what if I got you with child? What would you do then?"

Abby didn't have an answer for him. The prospect of bearing Calum's child had never occurred to her. Was there room in her heart for a child other than Lydia? If circumstances were different, she might be intrigued to discover what sort of baby the two of them—so very different—might produce.

"Of course, there is Catriona, too," continued Calum. "I would well deserve to be lying dead in the open with my brains strewn about the heather if I did such a thing to her. For I do love her, Abby."

"I'm well aware of that," agreed Abby. "And a fortunate woman she is to have you." Abby had no one—save
Lydia, of course—who cared one way or another about
her. But perhaps now she had a small claim on the brave-
hearted Gael as well. She needed the man. "Calum, I
am so very cold, so very empty and alone. If you lie
beside me and hold me to keep me warm, that would be
no disgrace to Catriona, would it, nor to me?"

In the dim light of the *fir-chlisneach* she could see
him smiling. The Gael stretched out beside her and
wrapped his plaid around both of them until they were
enmeshed in a snug cocoon of tartan. The powerful fire
inside her grew dull and faded into a deep sense of peace
and admiration for this strange man who wanted to bed
her but could not, and finally would not. His warmth
enveloped her and she sank into a deep sleep, her head
nestled under his chin.


In the morning, Abby awoke to find the sky as gray
as pewter and Calum gone. She found him below, preparing a hasty breakfast. His voice was loud and jolly
but without affection, and Abby thought it unwise to
mention what had taken place between them during the
night . . . and what had not taken place.

Soon they were on the road north once again, Abby
stumbling through a dozen awkward sentences in Gaelic,
with Calum alternately encouraging her and laughing at
her. The quiet intimacy between them was lost, she
thought sadly. But what had been could be again, and
she began to long for its return.

Just before noon, Calum stopped so abruptly she
bumped into his back. He clapped his hand on her shoulder and smiled his broad, canine smile. Perhaps he has

reconsidered yet again, she thought. "Can you say, 'Yonder stands Calum's horse,' in my tongue, mistress?" he asked.

She hesitated, trying to recall the word for horse. *"Sud stad . . .* hmmmm *. . . ead aig Chaluim."*

" 'Yonder stands the jealousy of Calum'? Not likely, my calf. *Each,* not *ead.* Do you see?" Calum pointed to a rocky outcropping on a lonely hillside. Abby gazed for some time before she saw what he wanted her to see: a gray horse, the same color as the granite that surrounded it.

"A wild horse!" she gasped.

"Nay," murmured Calum. "My horse. My stone-horse, Luran. There's no mistaking his white feet and the white streak down his forehead. See his halter, mistress, with the lead rope hanging from it?" Straining her eyes, Abby thought she could make out the rope. What eyesight the man had! "He has chewed through his tether, the whoreson, as he's wont to do when the devil is in him. Do you recall the last village we passed through? Luran's favorite mare is there. 'Tis she he's bent on visiting, I'll wager." Suddenly he put his fingers to his lips and let loose such a shrill whistle that Abby had to clap her hands over her ears to protect them.

The horse flung back its head and answered its master with a high-pitched, bugling neigh. It swung around at a gallop, disappeared, and reappeared at the foot of the hill, streaking up the glen toward Calum.

"Take care!" cried Abby. She would have run off the path had Calum not gripped her elbow and pulled her toward him. The horse thundered nearer, its mane flying, its eyes rolling white. As she was struggling in Calum's arms, convinced the beast had murder on its mind, the stallion slid to a halt in front of his master and rubbed his massive head against Calum's chest.

The Gael released Abby and flung his arms around the horse's neck. She shook her head in dismay. Save for his large, intelligent eyes, Luran was quite plain, not at all like Roger's hunting and racing stock. His legs were short, his coat shaggy and matted, his hooves cracked and broken. He reeked of sweat and manure. Why, Roger would not have let such a nag spend one night in his stable!

Luran nickered as his master stroked him, and Abby was forced to admit the brute did seem to recognize the man. *"Ghille mhath!"* Calum whispered into the animal's silken ear. "Good boy!" He leaned forward and kissed Luran's steaming neck.

What a kind, loving man, thought Abby. He loves his horse. And I love him.

Abby blinked and shook her head. Her blood seemed to have frozen within her. What had she just thought? God in heaven! Was she in love with a wild Jacobite? She could not be.

Yet she could not deny it. When she tried to picture herself apart from Calum, she could not bear the pain of the thought. Was she truly in love with a half-naked savage who kissed his horse?

"My poor old Luran!" muttered Calum, raking his fingers through the stallion's tangled mane. "He's come quite a long way and is carrying half the countryside in his coat. You're no seeing him at his best at all, mistress, but what great luck it is to have him with us. Sit you on his back, and we'll be at Bailebeag by sunset."

Still stiff with the shock of her newfound feelings, Abby let Calum seize her by the waist and fling her up onto Luran's broad back. Her legs dangled over his belly. She could not even say for sure that they were her legs; everything seemed distant and foreign to her.

Calum grabbed the tether rope. "Come, lad. You may be giving up your sweetheart to serve the Englishwoman, but you'll find the *quean* to your liking. She's much lighter than I."

The Gael jogged forward, and the horse gave a great leap. Abby lurched sideways, clutched at a handful of gray mane, missed, and rolled off the stallion's back.

"Abby!" Calum sprang to her side as she sat up, brushing bits of bracken from her sleeves. "You're no injured, are you?"

"Only my pride." Abby looked up at the man, his blue eyes bright with concern. There could be no doubt in her mind now: she had never known she had the power to love again, and so soon after Roger's death. If she could, she would have wed this man, horse or no horse, on the spot.

But she could not. As Calum lifted her in his arms and once again set her on Luran's back, she made a silent vow. She would never again allow him to embrace her as he had in the tower. She would never again come between him and his wife, nor ever risk hurting him again.

Luran trotted forward, Calum at his side, Abby repeating her vow over and over to herself as the drab countryside flew past. The wind rushed against her face, and for the first time during the entire journey she realized how much she had slowed down her companion. Calum and Luran sped over the rocks and heather like two roebucks.

*He is hurrying home and hurrying away from me,* she thought. *But it is no matter to me. I will never again interfere with his faithfulness. I will never encumber him again.* Calum was Catriona's man, not her own. Her family was on Skye, and the sooner she saw Bailebeag, the sooner she would be with Lydia. A happy thought, but Abby did not feel happy. A darkness she could not explain settled over her and, try as she might, she could not dispel it. She did not try to comprehend it, but clung tightly to Luran's mane and tried to think of nothing but staying on his back.

# Nine

*A Letter from England*

*Very quietly now. Stealthily, lest they hear.*

Major Racker approached the door of the little stone house—a black house, they called it, because of the oppressing darkness inside. He held his breath, careful not to clack his bootheels against the frozen puddles of rainwater that pocked the yard. With feather gentleness he laid his hand on the plaid that served as a door over the low entrance. He would have to duck to get inside. No matter. His hand gripped the plaid. *One, two, three . . .*

"Campbell!" Racker threw aside the plaid, stooped low and burst into the room. As he had been informed by his lascivious sergeant, there lay Captain Campbell, as naked as a newborn, fully engaged with a disheveled woman in a like condition. The intermingled smells of musk and burning peat filled the little house. "Enough of this, Campbell!" shouted Racker, flicking his hand toward the captain. "I must have a word with you!" The major smiled to himself as the Scot glared at him, a ferocious snarl distorting his shaggy red face.

A strangled growl erupted from the captain, then a hideous stream of Gaelic, punctuated by whimpers from the female. At last the Highlander remembered his English. "Devil take you, major or no! A hundred thousand deaths to you! We are coupled, man!"

"Yes, so I can see," answered the major softly, letting his eyes play over his subordinate's gleaming body. With one wild, angry movement, the captain pulled a plaid over himself and his lady. "Well, the moment you are disengaged, attend on me at once at the house," continued Racker. "I have important matters to discuss with you." He turned on his heel and left the house, knocking his tricorn to the ground as he bent low under the doorway. He seized the hat and slapped it on his head. Laughter rose in his throat, but he made no sound. He was a master of silent laughing.

Two grenadiers with naught better to do stared at him as he strode past them. He barked something at them and they scattered, each throwing a salute and a "beg pardon, sir" after himself. They were among the sturdier remnants of his original patrol, once fifty strong, now reduced by desertion and disease and the occasional Jacobite retaliation to half that number. Campbell's troops still held their ground, though even their forces were greatly diminished. The major reckoned he might be able to muster forty, possibly fifty able-bodied soldiers among the lot. If their numbers fell much lower, they could easily become the prey and not the predator in this hostile country.

Racker hurried to the house he had chosen for his own billet, the largest and cleanest of the hovels in the village of Ardnamurchan. Not one soldier had to sleep on the ground; there was shelter aplenty, squat black houses with rounded corners and heavy thatched roofs. Some of the original occupants, most of them female, had objected, but only until the first blood had been drawn. Then all gave in to the major and his patrol, keeping to the shadows, cooking immense quantities of food for the victors without complaint and keeping their objections to themselves.

As he gained the doorway of the house, a young grenadier not old enough to grow a beard saluted and handed him a grimy paper packet. "A courier brought you this, sir," explained the boy. Racker dismissed him and entered the house, his feet sinking into the soft layer of bog myrtle spread over the dirt floor in a vain attempt to keep it dry. A Highland woman approached him, a pitcher of milk in her hands. Racker waved her away, drew his folding desk and campaign chair close to the fire and seated himself in the single spot of warmth and light in the entire house.

The letter was from Diana. It smelled of her, of lavender and violets. Racker snorted to free him from the scent. He nearly set the letter alight but then changed his mind and tore it open. He may not have felt deep affection for Diana, but he needed her.

A dull pain struck the center of his forehead and began gnawing its way deeper and deeper into his skull. The major pressed his fingers to his temples as he plunged into his wife's letter.

*My Dearest Thomas,*

*I have not heard from you in some time, no doubt because of your position so far north. I fear for your safety, though I am assured by reliable sources that you are well and have your situation well in hand. Captain Jackson swore on his honor he would see that you received this missive and, if you are reading this, he has succeeded. Neither I nor my family nor the servants are the same with you gone. Ivy House itself, even all of Norwich, seems the drearier without you. We all pray for your speedy return, by Christmas, with God's speed. The*

*Reverend Wapple comes to see me every other evening to join in our prayers. He is a very tedious man, but a gentle and harmless soul.*

*My sister Margaret visited here several days since with Theresa and Richard. The children are so beautiful and clever I thought of you when I saw them, for I know you would have wished to have them for your own. I know you are not keen on children, but I am told this is a common affliction among men, until they become fathers. I hope you will not think me ungrateful nor unsatisfied, yet being childless has put a great burden on my mind. Of course, there is no blame in the matter. The Lord in His mercy will do as He sees best, I am certain.*

Damn the woman! Two hundred miles away from her and she was still complaining about her inability to breed. In most matters, Diana was a quiet, long-suffering creature, not terribly intelligent but wise enough not to draw attention to herself. Let the conversation turn to progeny, however, and she was lost. The few quarrels they had ever endured were on the topic of children, or rather the lack of them. And there was nothing under heaven he could do about it. He saw to his husbandly duties regularly, a difficult task but necessary to avoid suspicion. That their congress had never produced a child seemed just and natural to him: he was not made to bed women nor to sire offspring.

A noise at the door made him start. Diana's letter drifted to the dirt floor, perilously close to the fire. Against his better judgement, Racker picked it up and stuffed it inside his coat. The boy who had given him the damned piece of paper was standing in the doorway, his back illumined, his face in shadow. "Captain Campbell to see you, sir," said the lad.

Red and green flashes of light interrupted the major's

vision. His head exploded in agony, then collected itself. He shut his eyes, and when he opened them, Campbell stood before him, one hand on his hip, the other making an attempt at a salute. It looked as though the man had clothed himself in the midst of a whirlwind; half his plaid dragged on the floor behind him, and his linen shirt was inside out, its seams plainly showing. The simpleton had believed the major needed him. "You would see me, major?"

"Would I?" Racker poured himself a bumper of Marsala and drained it off in two draughts. The pain throbbing in his forehead wavered, then shrank back, next to nothing. "I don't recall."

The Scot's small eyes flared wide open and his lips drew back in a wolfish grin. "I'll refresh your memory, major. There was myself and my beloved, in intimate embrace, and then yourself entering the house with a shout, and then myself, shouting back, and finally yourself requesting me to see you on urgent business. Surely you recall *now!*" The captain slammed the flat of his hand against the writing desk. The major jumped in his seat as the little wooden table folded shut with a snap and crashed to the floor like a stag shot in the heart.

"Yes!" gasped Racker. He sat back in his chair, clenching his hands to keep them from trembling, lest he give any sign of distress the captain might notice. "I wished to see whether or not, in a fair battle, you could defeat my folding desk, and I must say, Captain, you've given a good account of yourself."

*"Mo Dhia!* What a great fool I am!" Without the least effort, the Gael picked up the fallen desk, held it aloft and dashed it against the floor. The wooden tabletop cut through the myrtle, cracked, then splintered and flew into a dozen pieces. Part of an oaken leg shot past the major's

ear. He flinched but did not jump. A shriek filled the room. From the corner of his eyes, the major watched the Highland female race into the only other room in the house. "I could give a better account, major, were it you yourself and not your innocent furnishings I was tossing about. I could do it, ye ken. Drive you right into the dirt of the floor."

"Yes, and be hanged for it. But pray, hold your temper, Captain Campbell. Life here would be frightfully dull without you."

Campbell strode up to the fire, so close to Racker that the major recoiled from the stink of damp wool, whisky and the dark, sharp scent of musk. "Three men disappeared this morning. Your grenadiers. They could not abide the cold and bad food any longer, so their mates said. My gillies tell me King Georgie has no other troops for miles around in any direction, and it's their opinion we are here alone, without reinforcements."

The major poured another cupful of Marsala and downed half of it. "Possibly. What of it? I need no reinforcements. I am under orders to return south at my own discretion. And my discretion tells me to continue disciplinary actions among these heathens until they are brought to their knees."

"Aye," snarled the captain, "because your acclaim will be all the greater when you do finally drag your arse over the border. But I am asking you, Saxon—what will you do when all the little lads in breeks here give you the slip?"

The insolence of the wretched Scotchman was getting on his nerves. "I believe I am the one who need worry about the threat of desertion, captain, not you. Go back to slitting MacDonald throats or swiving MacDonald women or whatever it is your kind does best." The major finished his Marsala and turned toward the fire, away from the Scot. "You are dismissed."

Behind him, he could feel the blue eyes of the captain, glowing fiercer and hotter than the blues flames of the peat fire. The major fancied he could hear saliva dripping from the savage's mouth. When he turned back to the doorway some moments later, the captain was gone.

*Well done, Thomas,* the major congratulated himself. How much would the Scot take before he broke down and tore himself free, taking his brutish soldiers with him? Whenever this occurred, as Racker intended it surely would, he himself would have the pleasure of hunting Campbell down, forcing the dog to lead him safely southward, then handing him over to the authorities to be hanged as a cowardly deserter.

The fool!

Racker patted his coat, searching for his snuffbox to celebrate his triumph, when something crackled at his touch. Diana's letter! In the heat of his encounter with the Scotchman, he had cleanly forgotten it.

Racker pulled the paper from his pocket and smoothed it out on his knee. As much as he disdained his wife, her letters were his only contact with his home in Norwich, with England, with the sweet scent of beechtrees and the sound of the hunting horn on a crisp autumn morning. He held the page up to the light and read the last passage.

*Someday, it is my fondest hope, we will be blessed with a charming, gracious child, a son, of course, to follow a military bent and become your greatest source of pride. But sometimes I can almost see another child, a lovely girl-child with long, flowing hair, taking my hand and accompanying me through the streets of the town. And everyone who passes says, "My regards to your ex-*

*cellent father, the major, my dear." And this angel would smile at them and curtsey, and the love she held for you, my dearest Thomas, would be enough to melt the stoniest heart.*

*Yours in love and faithfulness and desirous for your safe return,*
*Diana*

The major stared at the letter for some time, then folded it in careful squares and fed it to the fire. He watched Diana's longings catch flame, curl into a black char and fall into cinders. Actually, it would be a blessing were he to impregnate the poor woman, a splendid diversion which would occupy her time and give her much less opportunity to bother him with her petty wishes and concerns.

Thinking of children made him think of one reprisal in particular. He drew his journal from an inner pocket and thumbed through it, taking care not to rip a page or smudge the cover. Now and then he would glimpse Edwin's name and had to force himself to continue his search. At last he found the entry he was seeking.

*November 30, 1715 Ballybeg*
*Burned to the ground the home and property of one notorious rebel, Calum MacDonald, a staunch supporter of his chief, Alan MacDonald of MacDonald. The house was some three hours in burning, as a recent downpour had given it a good soaking and therefore some protection from the flames. Family perished in the conflagration, all but one young girl-child, disposed of otherwise. Deuced headache, very bad.*

Despite the pain he had suffered that day, he remembered the little girl quite well. She had been wailing so loudly her cries had almost split his skull asunder. Yet she had been an exceptionally lovely child, with red-gold ringlets and pink, healthy skin, not unlike a very young, considerably prettier Diana.

If his brain had not been assailed by his demon head-ache, he could have made good use of that child, bathed her thoroughly, dressed her nicely, taught her a little English. Diana would have been delighted to have such an exquisite little thing to parade around the streets of Norwich. Why had he not thought of it before? Perhaps another child, equally well-suited and equally abandoned, would present herself someday. Then Diana could at least dupe herself into believing that she had what she wanted most in all the world: a loving family.

# Ten

## Five Cairns

Luran planted his feet in the heather, stretched out his neck, and whinnied. A faint echo whinnied back from all sides. Abby blinked, staring into the little glen before her. A wisp of blue smoke rose from a small gray cottage in the distance, all but hidden among the long shadows of the twilight. "Are we there? Is that Bailebeag?" She pointed into the glen. "Oh, Calum, it is, isn't it? I am so weary and hungry and sore. Tell me we've arrived."

The tall Gael laughed and tugged on the stallion's tether, urging him forward. "Nay, mistress, I can't tell you such a thing. But I'll tell you this: here we part company with the road to the isles. Yonder lies the house of Angus, my brother, the kindest, truest friend in all the world. There you can rest, while I go on to Bailebeag."

In a matter of minutes they were pounding up toward the house, Luran at a canter, Calum at a dead run. *"Aonghas, Aonghas, mo bhraithair! A'bhel thu dol dhachaigh?"*

Abby saw a movement in the doorway as Luran came to a stop. A pack of children streamed from the house and surrounded all three of them, crawling under Luran's belly and flinging their arms around Calum's neck, chattering all the while. She counted five little ones, the youngest two or three years old, the eldest not more than nine.

Above the din of the children, Abby thought she heard a thin cry like the call of a plover. She raised her head and beheld a stout, bearded man in the doorway, his arms stretched out in front of him, as though parting a cloud before his eyes. *"A'Chaluim? A'bheil thu ag beo samhach?"* he shouted. "Calum? Are you still alive?"

The two men ran into each other's arms and the children followed, until all were a wriggling, gibbering, joyfully weeping confusion of tartan and humanity. Abby could not fathom much of what they said, as all seven seemed to be speaking at once. She gathered only that the bearded man was Angus, and that he had been very much afeared that Calum had been killed at Sherrifmuir.

She was not part of this enchanted circle, Abby realized, yet she longed to approach it, to bask in the warmth of the reunited family. When their happy noise had faded a little, Abby slid off Luran's back and stepped as close as she could to Angus without pushing aside any of the excited children. She cleared her throat, though only the youngest child turned to look at her. *"A'bheil thu Aonghas mac Dhomhnail? Tha mi caraid ag Calum."*

At once the children dissolved in shrieks of laughter. Both men jerked up their heads and stared at her. Had she said something stupid, she wondered.

Calum brushed aside the two smallest youngsters and motioned Abby forward. "How inconsiderate of me!" he said in his most formal English. "Angus, this is Abigail Fields, an Englishwoman traveling to Skye to collect her daughter. She has been so kind as to allow me to guide her here. She's learning our tongue, as you can see, but perhaps 'tis better to continue in her own."

"I am Angus *mac Iain mhic Dhomhnail,* mistress, and

I am most pleased to meet you," said the bearded gentleman, in very tolerable English. His voice was quiet and solemn, and Abby knew at once she could have trusted him with her life. "You're more than welcome to my poor home." He made a little bow, and Abby curtseyed. The children tittered. Angus cuffed the nearest boy on the head. "These insolent creatures are Mairi, Morag, Coll, Diarmid and my little one, Sorcha. I fear they're aye ill-behaved, but pay them no mind."

"Have I made a great fool of myself?" asked Abby.

"Not at all." Angus took her hand between both of his and smiled. "But when you are calling yourself a friend of Calum, say *bancharaid*. *Caraid* is for a man. An easy mistake, mistress, in a difficult language."

"You are too kind." Abby glanced at Angus, then at Calum. The two looked as different as Luran and Roger's favorite hunter. "Is it true the two of you are brothers? Forgive me, but you look nothing alike."

"*Foster* brothers," Calum corrected himself, gathering Sorcha, the youngest, into his arms and tickling her until she screamed with delight. "But can't we continue all this chatter inside? I'm thirsty, Angus, and the lady is weary. You can give us both a bite of food and a dram, I ween, before I leave Abby with you and set out for Bailebeag on my own."

"Bailebeag?" said Angus. Abby thought he started at mention of the name, but in the semi-darkness of dusk it was easy to imagine things. The feeling of foreboding perched in her brain like an annoying insect. "You'd go there the night?"

"Aye, man," laughed Calum, whisking the children through the doorway ahead of him. "It would be wicked to keep Catriona waiting any longer. Tell me, is she well? Does she miss me? How are the weans?"

"Everyone is well," said Angus softly. "Everyone misses you."

*"Teine,"* said Sorcha.

"Did she say 'fire'?" asked Abby. Perhaps the tot was cold.

Angus took the child from Calum and all but thrust her inside the house. Then he slapped his tall kinsman on the back and laughed. "She's a proper hostess, just. She wants you inside by the fire, cozy and warm. Come in, then! Calum, have you slept at all since I last saw you? What happened to your face? God and all the saints! A sword wound! A token of Sherrifmuir, I'll wager. O, 'tis so grand to see you living, man! Come, now, both of you, inside. Don't worry yourself over the horse. Coll can see to him."

Something about the man's loud manner made Abby hesitate, but the prospect of a warm room and good food soon lured her inside. As in most Highland houses she had seen, there were but two rooms, one for the family and another for visitors and invalids. Abby seated herself on a low chair by the fire, her head just inches from the thick pall of smoke that hung over the room like a pungent mist. The children crowded around her, gently patting her fine *arasaid* and the faded stringpurse. But something—someone—was missing. She touched Calum's arm and whispered in his ear. "Where is Angus' wife?"

"Dead a year," Calum whispered back. "A fever took her. He misses her sorely, but he makes do well enough without her."

That was certainly true when it came to cooking, Abby soon realized. Angus plied her and Calum with delicious griddle cakes, turnips in butter, brose, and thin slices of mutton roasted on the fire. The men removed their plaids before sitting down to eat, but by now Abby was used to half-dressed males and did not turn away from them. She laughed to herself at the thought of gentlemen in London sitting down to tea without their breeches.

After supper, Angus fetched a small keg of French claret from the second room and, filling cup after cup for his "brother," engaged him in an endless outpouring of Gaelic conversation. In between sentences, Calum tossed down wine like water. Abby drank but little; as sweet as it tasted, the claret made her dizzy.

She was about to ask Angus where he had acquired such a luxury when Calum lumbered to his feet and stumbled toward the doorway, nearly stepping on little Sorcha, who lay curled up asleep beside Abby. His awkwardness reminded her of the ragtag stranger at the Heart's-ease, though he was still half-naked. "Baile-beag . . . I must be going," he muttered. "Abby, you'll be safe here. I'll send for you. Nay, I'll come to you. Nay . . ." Calum stopped short of the door, wavering like the trunk of a great tree in the act of being felled. "*Dia!* Why is the room jumping about so?" He laid his hand across his forehead and tottered backward.

"Calum? Are you ill?" Abby reached out her hand to him, but she was too slow. Angus was already on his feet and beside Calum, breaking the fall of the big man as he slumped to the ground and lay as still as a log.

Angus glanced at her as he covered Calum with a plaid. "Not ill, mistress. Too much wine and too much weariness. He'll sleep well the night. And you will, too, I'm sure."

Abby disengaged herself from Sorcha's grasp and inspected the prostrate Gael. His breathing was slow and steady. Angus was obviously correct, yet a persistent, fearful feeling made her believe he was not perhaps completely forthcoming. "You wished him to drink himself under the table, didn't you?" She stared the man in the face. While he was not handsome like Calum, Angus had a broad, open countenance that could not conceal lies. His eyes, only a shade lighter than Calum's, reflected a look of utter despair she had not noticed before. What accident, handicap or circumstance, she wondered, had prevented Angus from fighting by the side of his foster brother at Sherrifmuir?

"Something is very wrong, isn't it, Angus? Why, I believe you intentionally prevented Calum from leaving for Bailebeag. Isn't it so?"

A melancholy smile played across Angus' lips. "You're a canny one, mistress. I can hide nothing from you, I see. In the morning, I promise you, all will become clear. Now take your sleep, if you would, like dear Calum and the weans. You'll need your rest if you intend to travel to the Winged Isle in the next few days. Calum tells me your daughter's name is Lydia. You're aye fond of her, I trow."

Instantly the cloud of gloom that had made Abby doubt Angus lifted from her mind as she remembered Lydia a hundred different ways at once. Playing chess with Roger, riding her cockhorse about the garden, feeding tidbits *sub rosa* to Tip beneath the dining table . . . Lydia, the brightest star in her mother's darkest night. A sob scattered Abby's memories. She felt the tears break loose and course down her cheeks. "I'm terribly sorry," she said, dabbing her face with her kerchief. "You must think me an addlepate."

"Not I, mistress," murmured Angus, patting her hand. "We Gaels do not see tears as a sign of weakness, as the Saxons do. Why, after my Ailis died, I wept every night just at the thought of her. Sometimes tears are all that mark us from the brutes, I'm thinking." He showed her to her bed, a heather mattress piled with plaids, and kissed her hand before bidding her a good night. She sank back upon the plaids, half expecting to fall through them to the floor. Her body felt incredibly heavy, and her legs and bottom ached from the long ride over rough country. She wondered how Calum was faring, lying dead to the world on the cold, bare floor. And what had Angus meant, that all would become clear to her in the morning? Nothing was clear to her anymore, now that she knew she loved the Gael. Nothing but her longing for Lydia.

Abby drifted into sleep, and the face of her daughter flitted like a bird throughout her dreams.

Abby woke with a start. Where was she this morning? Angus' house, of course. Without knowing why, she was aware that everyone in the family was up and about save her. She smelled oatmeal porridge and coddled eggs and heard the gentle ebb and flow of many voices.

Angus, Calum and all the children greeted her, and the youngest boy brought her an earthenware basin half filled with water. Abby dabbed a little on her face. It was as cold as ice. Would she never again have a proper bath with soap and hot water, perfumed with a drop of rosewater? A thick towel, warmed by the fire? Hyacinth-scented balm for her hands and feet? A beautiful silk dressing gown, like the one which Roger had given her one Christmas, embroidered all over with blue iris and pink dianthus?

She forced herself to smile at the child and thank him. He rewarded her with a grin that engulfed half his face and made her ashamed to think of the luxuries of her past.

After breakfast, Angus invited Calum and Abby to join

him on a short walk. Taking Sorcha in his arms and leaving Mairi, the eldest girl, in charge of the other children, Angus ambled out of the house, with Calum at his side. Abby scrambled along over barren fields and moorland as best she might, far in the rear. Both men walked faster than she could run. Surely they were headed toward Bailebeag. At last she was to meet the woman that Calum could not betray.

As she trudged through the boggy pastures, she glanced ahead at Calum and Angus. The two had their heads close together, deep in conversation despite their rapid gait. Suddenly she heard Calum give a cry of horror. *"Mo chreach! Mo chreach an diugh!"* She had heard the words before during her travels. Now they made her freeze in her footsteps. *Alas! Alas! My complete devastation!* Calum bolted forward like a wounded deer. The painful feeling of despair she had sensed earlier enshrouded Abby again. She ran after the Gael.

Angus caught her by the arm and brought her to a stop beside him. "Let him go, mistress. He must see for himself, by himself."

"See what?" she panted, watching Calum disappear over a ridge.

"Bailebeag," murmured Angus. He glanced at Sorcha, but the girl was preoccupied sucking her fingers. "That is to say, where Bailebeag was. 'Tis gone now, burned to the ground by the king's soldiers two fortnights past."

"Burned? Bailebeag burned?" The earth seemed to tilt under Abby's feet, and she clutched at Angus' shoulder to steady herself. "But it can be rebuilt, can't it?"

"To be sure, but you'd need start from the ground up. There aren't ten stones still standing together in any of the walls."

"The people!" Abby persisted. "Catriona, the children . . . what of them?" She felt her grip tighten on Angus' jacket, as if some unseen force were squeezing her hand closed. Part of her believed Angus; another part did not want to.

"Gone also. Wife, weans, cattle . . . even the two hounds. All dead. The only creature that escaped was Luran."

"All dead?" gasped Abby. "Oh, my God in heaven! Not all dead?"

"All deat," little Sorcha repeated.

"I buried them, mistress," said Angus, his voice scarcely louder than his breathing. "It fair crushed my heart, what was left of it. I pray every day for the souls of the dead, for Calum, for the weans, for my poor country. For everyone. Even for those whose hands struck the fire."

"Who was responsible?"

Angus shrugged. "Soldiers, mistress, Saxon and Gael. Two gillies saw them torch the house and leave, once it was destroyed. The flames could be seen for miles around, yet no one could lift a hand to stop them. To do so would be to risk death itself."

"Then they should be brought to justice!" cried Abby.

"Nay, mistress, they are justice," sighed Angus. "At least, their sort of justice. And how might one pursue them, even if one didn't value his life? They are lost in the mist, many miles distant by now. Perhaps even back in England and Argyle, prattling on about their courage and manhood and loyalty to the king."

Angus shifted Sorcha onto his free arm and walked on toward the ridge. Abby followed him in a daze.

A terrible howl split the steel-cold air, the grieving, desperate wailing of the damned. "Calum!" cried Abby.

She gathered her skirts and sprinted past Angus to the crest of the ridge.

The smell of smoke hit her like a stone. In a moment her eyes took in the glen below her, a grove of naked trees, heaps of stone, a blacked square of earth. But it was Calum who drew her total attention. He crouched low in a heap of soot and cinders, picking up handfuls of black dust and letting them run through his hands. His face, hair, legs and hands were black with soot. His wild wailing never stopped, but continued in waves, each cry ending in a strangled gasp before starting anew, high and shrill and broken-hearted. "Calum!" she shouted again and took a step forward. Suddenly the image before her shifted and she saw not only the man but his bleak surroundings, a jumble of blackened stones and wood. It was all very clear to her and no mistaking it: the ruins that held Calum captive and seemed to consume him had once been a house.

"Bailebeag," she whispered to herself.

"Aye, Bailebeag," echoed Angus, plodding up beside her. "See you the cairns?" He pointed to five conical piles of stones, a little removed from the ruins of the house. One rose much higher than the others, yet was no taller than Abby herself. "There sleep Catriona and her little ones. They're not very much, these cairns, but they are the best that myself and my clansmen could do to honor the dead. *Och, am bochd!* Poor creature! Look at him! Hark to him!"

Calum rose and half-crawled, half-ran to the five cairns. In a frenzy he clawed at the stones of the tallest heap, sending many crashing to his feet. Then, like a child caught in a mischief, he replaced the stones with great care and embraced the reconstructed cairn. The sound of his sorrow poured from his mouth. It undulated

# We've got your authors!

If you seek out the latest historical romances by today's bestselling authors, our new reader's service, KENSINGTON CHOICE, is the club for you.

KENSINGTON CHOICE is the only club where you can find authors like Janelle Taylor, Shannon Drake, Rosanne Bittner, Sylvie Sommerfield, Penelope Neri and Phoebe Conn all in one place...

...and the only service that will deliver their romances direct to your home as soon as they are published—even before they reach the bookstores.

KENSINGTON CHOICE is also the only service that will give you a substantial guaranteed discount off the publisher's prices on every one of those romances.

That's right: Every month, the Editors at Zebra and Pinnacle select four of the newest novels by our bestselling authors and rush them straight to you, usually *before they reach the bookstores*. The publisher's prices for these romances range from $4.99 to $5.99—but they are always yours for the guaranteed low price of just *$4.20!*

That means you'll always save over 20% off the publisher's prices on every shipment you get from KENSINGTON CHOICE!

All books are sent on a 10-day free examination basis, and there is no minimum number of books to buy. (A postage and handling charge of $1.50 is added to each shipment.)

As your introduction to the convenience and value of this new service, we invite you to accept

## 4 BOOKS FREE

The 4 books, worth up to $23.96, are our welcoming gift. You pay only $1 to help cover postage and handling.

To start your subscription to KENSINGTON CHOICE and receive your introductory package of 4 FREE romances, detach and mail the card at right *today*.

high and low, soft and loud. Little Sorcha, frightened by her uncle's wailing, broke into sobs of sympathy.

"Calum's children . . ." Abby thought of Lydia. She felt the sting of angry tears burn across her cheeks. What dastard would slay a child, any child? "Catriona?" Abby's vision blurred, and she rubbed her eyes with the back of her hand. Now Calum's wife would always be a mystery to her. A selfish, vicious thought sank its teeth into her mind: with Catriona dead, Abby was free to love Calum. But what good was such freedom when the very man she loved was as ruined as Bailebeag?

How the Gael grieved! He grieved as no Englishman could ever grieve, no matter how devoted to his family. He grieved with wordless roaring and moaning, with death-white ashes under his nails and in his mouth, with froth clinging to his lips. Poor Calum! Beloved Calum! His entire world had disappeared while he had been out fighting to preserve it. A lifetime of love and effort, gone in the time it took to set fire to the thatch.

*Calum needs comforting,* thought Abby. *Calum needs me.* The thought sent her racing toward the cairns, her feet crunching through a sea of cinders.

Calum raised his head. His lamentations wavered and faded to a halt as he stared at Abby through red eyes glinting with tears. When she was so close to the Gael she could almost touch him, she stopped and drew back. A feeling of despair, as thick and real as a stone wall, blocked her path. She could get no closer to him.

"Calum . . . ? Oh, Calum, I beg you, let me help you! Tell me, what can I do?" Her words sounded empty and helpless in the loud silence of the glen. She thought of the ruined cottage in the Trossachs and the *triegte,* the forsaken girl forever in search of her lost family. Like the *triegte,* Calum might despise the sound of Abby's English. He might very well despise her as well.

Gathering all her memories of Calum's tenderness and trust around her, Abby stretched out her hand toward him. She blinked tears from her eyes and they ran into her mouth. *"Tha mi gle bhronach, a'Chaluim Og,"* she murmured. "I am so very, very sorry. Oh, Calum, my dear, dear friend! Believe me, I am so very sorry."

A low wail began to rise from Calum's throat, but as it rose, so did Calum, ripping himself away from Catriona's grave with great effort. At last he stood erect before her, still moaning, black with soot from his bonnet to his shoes. Abby began to feel the unseen wall between them crack and fall asunder.

He clutched her hand.

In a instant she was on her knees and Calum was huddled in her arms. *How I love this Gael!* she thought, but dared not speak a word for fear of driving him from her. Instead she cradled his head in her lap and stroked his hair, now more black than red. Soot covered them both.

Abby remembered one beautiful autumn evening only months ago. Roger, hollow-eyed and burdened with the weight of his gaming debts, lay his head in her lap and wept, begging her forgiveness for some transgression he could not explain. She had patted his head, told him she loved him and sung to him, and before long he rose and walked toward the stable in the moonlight. She hoped he would turn around, speak to her, tell her to get her bags ready, that all three of them were leaving Glasgow for good.

But he had said nothing. It was the last time she had seen him alive.

" *'I have a garden, a garden so rare . . .'* " she sang to Calum, but her voice broke as she began the second line and she could not continue. No soft words, gentle music nor reassurances of affection could help Calum through this outrage. It was murder, it was unspeakable horror, it was everything that Abby abhorred most, and all of it as senseless and ghastly as Roger lying still and white in the bare courtyard of Rose Cottage or the slain lovers, linked in blood on the fox's hill.

A hand clapped her on the shoulder. She looked up into Angus' strong, sad face. "You have done him a magic," he said. "I did not think it possible."

Abby looked down into her lap. Calum lay with his head and one hand on her knees, his mouth agape, his eyes tightly shut. Asleep.


For two days Calum slept, as still and silent as a dead man. Abby and Angus took turns watching over him, keeping him warm and coaxing a little water down his throat.

One night, well after the children and Angus had gone to sleep, Abby was bathing Calum's forehead with cool water when he awoke with a start. "Calum!" she cried and tried to touch him, but the man rushed out of the house, to the midden, she guessed. He was some time returning, and when he did come back, she thought he looked at her in a peculiar way, as if she were a distant relation he could not quite recollect. His lapis-colored eyes, sunk deep in his gaunt face, burned with frightening intensity.

"Calum?" she repeated softly. "Are you feeling any better now?" As soon as she'd spoken, she realized what a stupid thing she'd said. She braced for his anger, remembering something her mother had told her long ago: words were not dogs; once slipped, they could never be called back.

"Better? Feeling better, mistress?" His voice was like the roar of the falls at Linn Solas. "Why, do you mean better than broken-hearted or better than wishing to lie down and die? How better can one feel when one's life has been torn up in pieces in front of one's face?"

"I meant no offense," whispered Abby. In the darkness, the children groaned, shifted in their beds and fell silent. She heard Angus call out Calum's name, then he too fell back asleep.

"Fetch me some whisky."

Abby took a deep breath. She recalled what Angus had told her earlier: feed him when he wakes. "Wouldn't you care for some oatcakes? Or some sowens? I think there is some milk . . ."

"Whisky!"

Abby flinched. He had never before spoken to her so fiercely, not even at the ruined inn that first morning on the road. Rummaging about with a tallow candle, she located a skin of Highland liquor and sat with Calum as he drank it dry, right from the hide. About a good English quart, she estimated, by the weight of it. How could anyone consume so much liquid of any sort?

When he had finished and tossed the skin aside, she tried to touch his shoulder. It was a grave mistake. Calum jerked his arm away. To her utter amazement, he snapped at her, just like a beaten hound, his teeth clipping the air, inches from her face. "Leave me be!" he snarled. The wall between them had returned, as she had feared it might.

Of course, she knew it was the whisky, coupled with his grief, that made him so ferocious. She had seen Roger's friends affected in similar ways; in fact, Roger had once been bitten by a pot companion steeped in too much Madeira. There was nothing she nor Angus nor even Calum could do save let his distemper run its course. With tears in her eyes, Abby left the Gael alone and retired to her bed of heather and plaids. She had won him, only to lose him, and to his wife, at that. No bonds were stronger than those forged by a sudden death. That she knew only too well.

The morning dawned wet and cold. Stray snowflakes drifted through the air and melted at once on the rocks and heath. Abby watched the children racing about the yard, trying to catch the ice-lace in their mouths. She remembered Lydia throwing snowballs at her father. Angus had cautioned Abby that, if she did not leave soon for Skye, she would not see her daughter until the spring thaws.

She felt a hand on her arm. It was Angus. "Calum is awake now," he said in a weary voice, "but I am worried for him. He says next to nothing, he desires nothing and he does nothing but lie in his bed. 'Tis understandable, for certain, considering the circumstances, but 'tis so very unlike Calum."

"It's true," said Abby, "but he will recover, be himself again, in time. Time is his friend, but it is my foe. Oh, Angus! I hate to leave you and Calum and the children, especially now, in your sorrow and with Calum so despondent. But what else am I to do? I must seek Lydia!"

Angus nodded. "Indeed you must. And you will." He patted her hand. The man was small but very powerfully built, like Calum, and his touch was just as tender. "I spoke with a man I know, a drover, who plans to travel to Skye in two days' time. A gentleman owes him money, and he would be more than glad to escort you over the sound to Duninnis' fortress and bring you back here. He is a decent, honest fellow I would trust with the lives of the weans, so I'm sure you'll have no reason to find fault with him."

"If you speak for him, Angus, then I'll go with him wherever he leads me. But I would like a horse as well."

"Take Luran, then. He's swift and well-mannered, smart and frisky." Angus glanced at Calum, motionless upon his bed. "Besides, his master has no use for him now."

"Thank you, I shall take you up on your kind loan, Angus. And I promise you'll get Luran back in good fettle, whether I return with him or not."

"You're no coming back to Glenalagan?"

"I don't know." Abby remembered Calum's invitation to her, but he had offered it before he'd known of the tragedy awaiting him. As much as she wanted him, she was no longer sure he wanted her. "Perhaps. On the other hand, perhaps Lydia would feel happier back in England. In any case, I shall never forget your kindness."

The next two days, Abby set about repaying Angus' hospitality. She could not recall having ever worked so hard before in her entire life: stacking peat, milking the family's lone cow, carding wool and cooking every meal. When Angus objected, she persisted, suggesting that Angus could find better use of his time by talking with Calum and playing with his children.

The second morning, she returned from fetching kindling to find Angus lying in the middle of the floor by the fire, thrashing about like a fish in a basket, groaning and squealing. The children stood in a circle about him, very alert but not afraid, well out of reach of his flailing hands and kicking feet. And in their midst stood Calum, with Sorcha in his arms, keeping close watch on his foster brother.

Their inactivity enraged Abby. Why didn't they help

the poor man? Dropping the kindling on the floor, she rushed to Angus' side, only to receive a fist in her stomach. The blow sent her staggering back and pitched her onto her bottom. "Abby, keep away!" cried Calum.

Abby stared at him. He was speaking to her!

"Angus will be all right. He has the falling sickness. These fits come on him when he's weary or distressed. He means you no harm."

Abby sat perfectly still, breathing in the sound of his voice. Not kind, loving words, perhaps, but not growls, either. And had he not called out to her to prevent further injury? It was a feeble reason to hope, but a real one.

By and by Angus' wild movements slowed, then stopped. He lay sprawled on the floor, shaking his head and moaning. Abby rose and went to him, though Calum and the children kept their places. "Poor Angus! What has happened to you?" she cried, helping him into a sitting position.

Angus took one look at her, another at Calum and the children, and immediately lunged to his feet. *"Ceud mile math,* a hundred thousand pardons, mistress. Did I alarm you?"

"A trifle, yes. You have an illness, Calum said."

"Aye, but 'tis nothing." Angus brushed the ashes from his clothing and dispersed all the children with a wave of his hand. It was clear he did not wish to speak of his infirmity. "Now and then I fall down, but there's no danger in it, save the shame of not being able to serve my chief in battle. But brave Calum more than makes up for my absence."

Calum gave his brother the fleetest of smiles, then turned toward Abby. His face was grave. "Is it true that you're leaving us tomorrow?"

Abby folded her arms across her chest. Facing his expression was like facing a row of armed men, or a gaggle of gossip-mongers at the theatre. She felt she was utterly defenseless in the grip of his gaze, nor did she understand the ill-contained sound of anger in his voice. "Yes, it is true. I must leave, Calum, before bitter weather prevents all travel. Angus has procured me a guide and made me a loan of Luran. With your leave, of course."

"Will you be returning?"

"I . . . I can't say for certain." Did he wish her to return or not? Abby could not decide. She thought of asking him to accompany her, then dismissed the notion as cruel and absurd. "I can't say what will happen when I reach Skye," she continued. "I'm not even sure Lydia is there. But whatever befalls me, you must understand how highly I value our friendship, Calum, and I shall never forget you. Despite what has happened, I wish you great happiness, and I am certain it will one day be yours."

"Leave, then!" roared Calum. "Go on with you! Do you think you're wanted here, Englishwoman? Go, take my horse. Take all you please, but spare me your patrontudes!" The Gael snorted and spun about sharply. Without a word he stalked out of the house into the cold, wearing only his shirt and jacket. Abby's throat tightened, and she turned away from Angus so he would not see her weeping.

"Pay him no mind, mistress," said Angus softly. He held her by the shoulders until she had fought her feelings back into control. "Calum's no brute, and 'tis most unlike him to bully a woman. It's his grief and anger that are talking, not himself."

*I was not patronizing him, I was not speaking platitudes,* Abby reassured herself. Yet, when she rethought what she had said, she could see how he had misread her. He had mistaken her love for mere pity.

* * *

To take her mind from the painful thought of leaving, Abby threw herself into preparing a fine supper for Angus and the children, and Calum, should he deign to eat with her. While she had never cooked a meal at Brenthurst and only a few during her last days at Rose Cottage, she had seen cooks preparing food all her life and had some idea of what could be done with plain victuals to make them appetizing. Realizing that Christmas must have been close, she baked a cake of sorts in a skillet over the fire, using oatmeal ground fine, sweetened with honey and dried apples. Angus had shot a roebuck, and she dressed it herself, slicing the meat thin and roasting it over a bed of hot coals. The children enjoyed their food so much that, after the meal was over, they hugged her about the shoulders and patted her hair with their greasy hands, purely from admiration. Abby held her tongue. Several times throughout the ordeal she even caught herself smiling.

She had a present for each child, a silver coin from her lean purse. It was clear from their cries of disbelief that they had never received a gift of any sort before. More troubling, however, was the fact that, though Angus was fond of calling himself a devoted follower of *Criosd,* his brood had not the slightest idea what holiday the Saxon lady thought she was celebrating.

As Abby rose to gather the wooden bowls from the table, Calum's deep, familiar voice rumbled from the shadows. *"Agus mise? Cha bheil tiodhlac aig mise?"* His meaning sprang into her head at once: "And me? Have you no gift for me?"

Angus' dirk lay on the table, its blade still glistening with venison fat. Seizing its hilt in one hand, Abby grasped a thick tress of her long brown hair in the other and shoved the dagger under it. Pressing the blade against the bundle of hair, she severed it in one stroke and nicked her thumb in the process. *Truly a dangerous weapon,* she marveled as she sucked at the tiny cut.

Abby tied the lock into a knot and held it out toward Calum. "Here is your gift," she said. "Pray remember me, my dear protector."

To her relief, Calum took the knot from her hand, examining it in his palm a moment before raising it to his nose. "How sweet it smells!" he whispered. "I shall remember you, mistress." As he spoke, his face seemed to crumble and fall apart. He rushed into the second room before she could beg him to remain.

Later that night, long after Angus and the children had fallen asleep, Abby lay wide awake, listening to the wind blowing through the thatch and Angus' deerhound whining in his sleep as he lay by the fire. As much as she wanted to leave Glenalagan, she hated the thought of the morning, when she had to say farewell to Calum. There was no foretelling the moody Gael's behavior. He might be tender and understanding, distraught with grief, formal and distant, or surly and ill-tempered. She supposed he had a perfect right to all those disparate feelings, though she wished she could be certain of them in advance.

Abby could think of only one solution. She had to bid Calum farewell before he expected it.

In silence she stood up, wrapped a plaid around her shoulders and edged toward the entrance to the second room, where Calum lay sleeping. The brief journey seemed to last an eternity. Each step was painful; the dirt floor made her bare toes curl with cold. Angus' hound stirred as she passed him, cocked one ear, but did not awaken. Silently she crept into the little room and knelt on the floor beside Calum's bed. His back was toward her. She could hear his even breathing and just make out his plume of red hair above the darkness of his plaid. "Calum?"

"Abby, is it you?"

His voice caught her off guard, but she refused to back away. "Yes, indeed. I've come to say farewell." For days or forever, she still could not say.

Calum rolled over until he faced her, then pulled one arm out from his plaid and stretched it wide in welcome. "Come to me, mistress. Let me keep you warm. I promise you no mischief." Without hesitation Abby lowered herself into his embrace. The wall was down again, for how long she could only guess. For an instant she remembered her vow to never again come between Calum and his wife, but it no longer seemed a very practical sort of promise and she promptly dismissed it.

" 'Twas I that slew them, ye ken."

Abby felt her mouth fall open in dumbfoundment. "What?"

"I slew them. As good as slew them, Catriona and the weans. Had I been home, where I should have been, instead of chasing after a dream for a spineless Stuart king, I might have saved them. I might have led them to safety."

"Or died with them."

"Aye, perhaps."

"Then I should have been very heartsick indeed," whispered Abby, "for I would never have known you. Calum, you are not to blame for what happened, any more than I am." She gulped and looked down at her trembling hands. Many an unkind person, she realized, would have held her guilty by association. She was a Saxon after all, wasn't she?

"Abby, I'm a man accursed. First I have lost my Catriona, and now I am losing you. I can't ask you to stay, yet I don't wish you to go. Please . . . don't part from me just yet. Come morning, if you must, but not just yet."

"Not yet," she promised. His words made Abby's heart give a cautious leap of happiness, and she burrowed herself deeper into his grasp. He smelled of warm wool and damp earth, and her skin tingled from foot to crown at the thought of always being wrapped in those scents. Perhaps he still loved her. She could not tell for certain, though. Rather than risk his mockery should she be mistaken, she thought of ways to buy herself some time to think. "Here is a riddle for you, Calum. 'I am a word of single number, foe of sweet and peaceful slumber. But add a single letter more, and bring a plural to the fore, make joy where there was woe before.' Think in English, pray."

"English, English," he grumbled. Abby felt his skin ripple beside her. Although she had not given it a thought before, she realized now that the arms which held her so gently were completely bare, which likely meant the entire man was bare beneath his plaid. She stiffened for a moment, then relaxed. She was not in England anymore. In the north, she'd discovered, modesty had less to do with revealing one's privy parts than revealing one's privy feelings.

*"Arrah!* This is difficult."

"Not so," she answered. "But it is fitting."

"By God, I have the answer," murmured Calum. " 'Cares' is the word. 'Tis single, and by adding the single letter 's,' one spells . . ." He looked full in her

face, his eyes glowing in the semi-darkness like a cat's.
" 'Caress.' My God, my God! Caress!"

"That is correct," murmured Abby. If only she were
bolder, she thought, she'd ask him to demonstrate the
answer.

Calum cupped her face in his huge hand. Abby felt
the weight of a hundred worries, sorrows and forebod-
ings fade from her mind, but still she could not summon
the courage to tell him of her love. *Take me, right now,
here in this room,* she wanted to say, but the fear that
she might offend him prevented her. Less than a week
had passed since the dreadful morning they had walked
to Bailebeag.

"I could bed you this moment, you know," he said.

What strange powers the man had! He could read her
thoughts! "Will . . . will you?"

"Nay, but not because I cannot." In the moonlight, she
thought she saw him wink. He kissed her forehead.
"Abby, it would not be right. I would, mind you, if I
thought you and I could ever be man and wife. But I
don't know, mistress. You yourself aren't certain you'll
be coming back. You have your own battle to wage. And
I have mine. You might come back to Glenalagan and
find me gone."

A freezing tongue of fear ran down Abby's spine. Her
head jerked back, out of his grasp. "What can you mean?
What are you speaking about? What can you mean, you'd
be gone?"

Calum leaned forward, so close she could feel his
breath against her eyelashes. "I am going to kill him.
And doing so, I risk my own life. God in heaven! I'll
do what I should have done in the first place. Fight for
my wife and weans."

"Fight him? Kill him? Kill whom? Oh, Calum! Speak plainly, I beg of you! We've no need for riddles now!"

"The officer who killed my family. That is the man who ordered their deaths. Those who set the fire are no more than hounds attacking a stag at their master's command. But the master! The officer . . . him I'll have. I'll device the most painful death possible for the son of the devil. And if I die, well, at least my weans and wife will rest easier in paradise." While Calum spoke, his eyes took on a fierce glow. His fingers clutched Abby's wrist so hard she almost cried out in pain. Instead, she touched his hand, and he broke his grip. "Forgive me, Abby."

"An Englishman?" she ventured.

"Aye, so I believe. A government soldier, in any affair. Angus spoke with a man who saw the brute, riding away from Bailebeag on a defigured horse."

"Disfigured?"

"Aye, sorely maimed. Its ears and tail were missing, if the man spoke the truth."

Cropped ears, cropped tail, thought Abby. Roger had once owned such a mount, an elegant hunter, a very costly beast. Such a steed was much in vogue with country squires and men of substance. "This is a gentleman's horse, Calum. The man is surely gentry, perhaps even a great lord. To slay him would be tantamount to writing a death warrant for yourself. I beg you, reconsider!"

"There is nothing to reconsider," said the Gael firmly. "Whoever did me this woe must be repaid, no matter how many lands he owns and no matter how English and noble and fine he is. 'Tis the way of my race. Leave no wound unpunished. I only regret I had not slain him before he took my family from me."

"You will be killed!" Abby wrapped her arms around his neck. Gently he disentangled her. Tears choked her throat, and with a shock she realized she must risk all to keep Calum from risking his life. "Calum, come with me to Skye."

For some time there was no sound save the whining of the wind in the thatch and the sighing of the sleepers in the other room. "My heart, I cannot," he said at last. "Not just now, not with Catriona's murderer wandering free. I must find him. It can't be helped. But if I succeed, you'll find me here, and if you come to me then and ask again, I will take Skye apart piece by piece for you until I find your daughter."

Abby swallowed hard. She could not wait that long. "Calum, we have been through a great deal of suffering, you and I, together and separately. I beg you, accompany me. I can't tell you why, but I feel in my heart of hearts it is best for both of us." Calum shook his head. Abby pushed her face into his hair, where it lay on his neck, just above his shoulder. He smelled of black earth, wood sorrel, dogbane, globeflower and cotton grass. "Then what am I to do?"

"Why, what you planned on doing all along, woman," said Calum. "Go to Duninnis and retrieve Lydia. You have no need of me. You are the strongest woman I have ever met, and Duninnis will tremble at the sight of you. You English females think you must have a man next to you, helping you with every step down the lane. 'Tis not needed."

"You know I don't think that at all," whispered Abby. "I want you with me because I crave your company, not your assistance. Oh, Calum! We have conquered so much together! Come with me!"

She leaned forward, and suddenly her lips met his yet again. He lapped her all about the face and sucked so hard on her mouth she was sure he was sucking the very life from her. But just as suddenly as he had begun, he pulled away, leaving her with the taste of his tongue on her own. "No, my heart, I cannot go, I will not go. And not even you nor your honey kisses can persuade me from seeking the devil that destroyed my weans. Please go back to your bed and sleep, now, *mo lurag*. In the morning, with the light, you'll see clearer and think straighter."

Abby's eyes smarted with the sting of tears. "There is nothing wrong with my thinking," she said, her sobs catching in her throat, "Nothing, save mayhap that I thought you bore me some modicum of respect, some morsel of affection." Tears blurred what little she could see of Calum's face in the dark room, and she thought for a moment he had vanished completely. A strange terror she could not name made her raise her hand and strike out into the darkness that had swallowed her love. She heard a sharp smack, then a soft cry. The pain in Calum's voice terrified her still more, and she scuttled off the bed and into the other room.

This time the deerhound lifted his head and stared at her as she hurried past the fire. She flung herself on the heather bed and wept as quietly as she could for what seemed like an eternity. No one woke to speak with her or comfort her, though once the dog shoved his cold nose into her hand and licked her fingers.

She wanted Calum with her. Forever. He had to go with her. What if he were killed? What would she do? She would never love another man again. Was it really true she had struck him? How could she have been so insane as to strike someone she loved so deeply? It was she who was the savage, not the Gael.

Sometime before dawn she was roused by a hand on her shoulder and woke to ink-black darkness and the faint smell of whisky. "Calum?" she whispered, still half asleep. The darkness wavered and seemed to retreat. *This is nothing but a dream,* she thought, and fell back asleep at once.

In the morning, during a breakfast of beef broth and turnips, Abby was introduced to her guide, a drover of Clan MacGregor. His name was Niall, and he instantly put her in mind of Duncan, the "child of the mist" she had met in the Trossachs. Niall had Duncan's same quick smile and gentle way of speaking, though he knew not one word of English other than "Devil take it!" and other curses he would not repeat in the presence of a woman. Traveling with the drover, Abby decided, would place a great burden on her small store of Gaelic.

When at last it was time to leave, Calum himself offered Abby his arm and led her outside where Luran stood, his breath forming a column of mist in the chill air. A sheepskin lay on the stallion's back in place of a saddle, and leather bags full of provisions were draped over his withers and croup. No heavy cruel bit dangled from his mouth; Luran wore a halter only, with deerhide thongs instead of proper reins. The horse's charcoal gray mane was braided with bits of red wool, the ungainly work of the children.

Calum caressed the horse's great head, then took Abby's hand. In the clear light of dawn, she was ashamed to see a pink streak across his cheek, a token of her fear from the night before. "Your face . . . I'm sorry, Calum . . ." she began, but the Gael held his finger to his lips and she fell silent.

"Think nothing of it, mistress. I frightened you and, for that, it's *myself* that's to blame. List, now. You'll be going back to the road to the isles now. It leads over mountains many miles through the land of McDonnell of Clanranald to a little frith, the Kyle of Lochalsh. At the kyle, a boat will carry you to Skye. Pay good heed to Niall. He's a thoughtful fellow, and his counsel is good. Give Luran his head downhill and be patient with him on the uphill. With these two looking after you, I have no doubt but that you'll get to Skye and bring Lydia back to the mainland well before the snows come."

As if to mock him, a stiff wind sprang up from the north, sending a shiver across Abby's shoulders. She gripped the front of Calum's jacket, surprised at her own ferocity. "Calum, come with me."

"Nay, mistress, it cannot be. If you can, return to Glenalagan. If I'm still with the living, I'll be here to greet you, I promise you that."

Abby released her grip, and her hands sank into his. What was she to do without him? But no, she must not think of that. She must think of Lydia, and nothing else. "Oh, Calum, if I must go alone, then . . . then *beannachd Dhe leat*. God be with you!"

"You're improving, mistress," he said, with a wry smile.

At the sound of her words, the children swarmed over her, smitten with the sudden, concerted realization that their amusing Saxon guest was truly leaving them. They shrieked and chattered like rooks, jumping up and down as they tried to stroke her hair or pat her arm. She hugged each one and tried to console them all as best she could. Her heart ached at the thought of leaving them, and it startled her to think of how quickly she had grown to love the children.

Angus pried his two youngest offspring from her and clasped her to him in a farewell embrace. "Godspeed,

Mistress Abby," he murmured. "Take these with you to make your journey easier." Into her outstretched hand he placed a tartan pouch, half the size of her treasured stringpurse.

Abby turned the gift over and prodded it gently with one finger. "Thank you, Angus. What is in it?"

Angus retrieved the pouch and poured its contents into the palm of his calloused hand. "Why, to be sure, mistress, charms for traveling, and most excellent they are. See you here!" The Highlander picked up a stiff, gray feather and thrust it in front of her. "An osprey's flight feather. That's for speed. And here's a bit of shoe leather, so your feet will not pain you. And this is a dried bog violet. Very lucky for wayfarers." Abby stood on one leg, then the other, shifting back and forth as Angus described every item in the pouch. His thoughtfulness touched Abby, but the odd array of wild things with their wild, musky smell bordered too closely on the heathenish to give her any comfort.

At last Angus produced a lock of ginger-colored hair from his sporran and added it to the contents of his palm. "Why, it's Calum's, isn't it?" she gasped. "That's surely not a charm."

"No, mistress, 'tis a remembrance," said Angus firmly. "He may remember you, and you him. The two of you are good friends, I trow."

His words, plain and simple enough, made her feel uneasy, and she watched with some suspicion as Angus gathered the charms and stuffed the full pouch into the bag on Luran's shoulder. Did the man realize the depth of feeling between herself and Calum? Or had he mistaken that feeling for friendship alone? "Thank you again, Angus," she said slowly, looking straight into his eyes. She let him lift her onto Luran's back, then glanced about, searching for Calum. The man had once more disappeared. Why, it was he, not Angus, who should have given her the memento. "Where's your brother gotten to?" she asked, her hands trembling on the makeshift reins.

"Yonder, mistress." Angus pointed toward the ridge that hid the remains of Bailebeag. "At Catriona's cairn. 'Tis his practice each morning. Weren't you after knowing that? He has visited her cairn every day since . . . since he saw what had become of Bailebeag."

Abby bit her lower lip, trying to hold back the fear and disappointment gathered in her throat. It was only to be expected that a loving husband like Calum pay his respects to his dead wife, and yet Abby wished he had forsaken the cairn, for that morning only. He had not even given her a proper farewell. Could a man who abandoned her when she needed him most truly love her?

Well, she didn't need him, after all. She could manage quite well on her own, thank you. Waving to Angus and the children, Abby turned Luran's head away from the croft and started down the gentle slope, following Niall's broad back. The three oldest children and the deerhound ran beside Luran to the foot of the hill, then wearied of their game and dropped behind. Abby looked behind her only once. A dark figure stood on the crest of the hill behind the house, its hand raised in a solemn salute. She turned back and stared straight ahead into the veil of mist surging over the mountains.

# *Eleven*

### *The Dark Island*

The journey to the kyle took two full days of weary riding. Abby slipped from Luran's back more than once as the stallion scrambled up rocky hillsides and slid down frost-covered slopes. Thanks to Niall, though, who managed to break her fall each time, she was bruised and breathless but unhurt. Riding along a high ridge, Abby gasped at the beauty of a long line of snow-encrusted peaks and at the savagery of the north wind as it tore her breath from her mouth.

As she rode, Niall plodded before her, whistling or singing, always easy to hear, even above the howl of the wind. She found that, when he spoke slowly, she could understand him tolerably well.

"You must be a great lady, Avvy," he told her once, breaking a long stretch of silence between them as they descended the ridge into a broad, windswept glen. Like many Gaels, including Angus' children, he had some difficulty wrapping his tongue around her name.

Abby chuckled in surprise. "Must I? Why is that now? As you can see, I have nothing save the clothes I wear."

"Why, because you are a friend of Calum Og's," he replied, "and Calum is a gentleman."

Abby clutched Luran's mane and pulled herself forward over his withers. "A gentleman? Calum Og? What do you mean?" She had never guessed Calum was anything but a simple country person, a farmer with a charming smattering of scholarly knowledge and awkward dignity.

"Aye," puffed Niall. "A landed gentleman. Before the burning of Bailebeag, he owned more head of cattle than anyone in the district, save one chieftain and the Mac-Donald himself, of course."

"Now he has nothing."

"Not so, m'lady. Come spring, he will have just as many cattle as he had before. Every family in Glenfinnan will find a calf or a stirk or a steer or a heifer or two to give Calum. When you have as little as my people have, you cannot let a gentleman do with less."

The simple strength and honesty of Niall's words made Abby draw back in awe. As much as she loved Calum, she could scarcely believe even he could inspire such generosity among a destitute people. She thought of her last night at the Rose Cottage, forsaken by everyone who had ever claimed to be her friend. The "better sort," as Roger had called them, who had fawned over her in happy times, had even refused her the silver to give her husband a decent burial. The gravedigger, a rude but kind-hearted fellow, had finally undertaken the horrible task without payment.

Abby shook her head to rid herself of such dark memories. "And Bailebeag? Was it very beautiful?"

"Beauty is for Lowland houses, mistress," snorted the drover. "Bailebeag was large and sturdy and well-built. Good shelter from the cold. The wind would flow over its round corners like water before the prow of a boat. And it will again. You'll see. That is, if you return. It will rise again, and Calum will take another wife and sire another brood. There is no stopping life. It goes on like the seasons."

Perhaps she should ask Niall for his best guess at the identity of Calum's future wife, she thought. But no, she was tired of speaking in Gaelic, and she was not certain she wished to know his opinions on the subject. Her silence seemed to suit Niall, who walked on ahead, singing merrily to himself.

Abby pulled her shawl from her face and let the icy wind blast against her skin. The pain helped her think. So Calum was nobility, as least by Highland standards, an idea at once comforting and distressing. On the one hand, Calum was most certainly well-respected and hence no doubt honorable, with more means than she had at first conjectured. On the other hand, he was also of high enough estate that he could woo and wed any woman he wished. Despite what he had told her that last night, then, did she have any right to expect that his first choice would be a penniless vagabond from the land of his most hated enemies?

Once again she tried to put the thought from her and concentrate on seeing Lydia again, but now her mind was full of doubt and indecision. Would Lydia recognize her, especially if the girl had been used badly? And what sort of lies might Lydia have heard? Would she want to return to the mother who, she might believe, had abandoned her?

Just then the wind shifted, and Abby smelled the sharp tang of salt in the air. "The kyle!" shouted Niall, pointing to the west. "We are almost at the coast. One good night's sleep at the inn at Abairuan, and noon will see us at the ferry."

*"Gle mhath!"* Abby called back. "Very good." Soon, one way or the other, with joy or great sorrow, her travels

would come to an end. Or was it not an end at all, but the beginning of a new eternity? One more night and day, and she would discover if she had any claim to the past. Anything beyond that point was too immense and frightening to contemplate.

"Twenty-four." Major Racker's voice cracked. He took a sip of Marsala from his flask as the sergeant raised the flog yet again and brought it down with a smack on the Jacobite's bare back. The youth cried out, a strange, strangled sound. The major felt himself grow tense and hard in the breeches. "Twenty-five."

"That's enough for the lad, don't you think, major?" said Campbell. The red gashes in the boy's skin bloomed like roses. The smell reminded Racker of the hunt, of the hounds snapping at the flanks of the frantic stag. "He will scarcely take thirty."

"Twenty-six," counted the major. Blood dripped from the creature's wounds and puddled beneath him, dyeing his naked feet rhododendron red. His eyes rolled white and wild, his tongue lolled from his mouth. The few Gaels who had gathered outside the major's billet to watch the punishment turned their heads aside and began to howl like a pack of wolves as the sergeant again plied the flog. The major's hands twitched at the smack of leather against flesh. "Twenty-seven. Stuff and nonsense! You asked that he be disciplined, did you not? We shall try for fifty. Tell me, Captain, why are your countrymen so confoundedly loud?"

Campbell's face was drawn and white. For all his savage swagger, thought Racker, the captain had at heart no more spine than a cowpat. "They wail for the suffering and the dying," he whispered.

"Twenty-eight. Dying, bah! Fifty lashes will not kill. Oh, see! The whoreson! You Gaels have no more sense of privacy than brutes!" The major nodded at the youth as water streamed from him and splattered into the pool of blood. Steam rose from the frozen ground. "Twenty-nine."

At the forty-seventh blow, the felon slumped against the wooden frame that held him captive. One slender hand actually tore free from a hand-iron. His body fell toward the ground, only to jerk to a stop, inches from the crimson earth, suspended by the remaining manacle. The villagers set up a fresh chorus of howling and shrieking.

"Damn your eyes, captain!" cried Racker. "You were right! He could not bear fifty!" He passed the Marsala to the Scot, who drank slowly and steadily without pause, his scowl fastened on the major. Racker returned the Gael's cold, blue gaze. "There's one MacDonald who shan't be throwing dung at you again."

Sunrise leaked pink through the mist, the beginning of another wretched day in a wretched country. Briefly the major thought of marching southward, but the time was not right. Although they had conducted far too few reprisals for his liking, they would have to weather the winter before they could continue. He had certainly made a mark on the land. But he had not subdued it.

The major retired to his billet to write, but his head began throbbing halfway through a letter to Diana, and only a few lines later the pain was so great he could not keep his hand steady enough to guide the quill over the page. He leafed through his journal, but even thoughts of Edwin could not soothe the warfare raging within his skull. A lean breakfast of oat porridge and milk did not please him, and at last he thrust himself out again into the cold.

The head pains subsided somewhat, as if taken by surprise. He noticed a patch of crimson ice where the flogging-frame had stood, and an idea leaped into his aching head.

"Saddle me a Highland horse," he commanded the first grenadier he saw.

"A Highland horse, sir?" muttered the soldier. "Begging your pardon, sir, but it couldn't carry you far. Shall I saddle the gray instead?"

"A Highland horse!" roared the major. He felt the tension that invariably preceded pain ripple across his forehead, and he felt a powerful urge to twist his words into rhymes. "Must I use force? The largest and strongest of its kind you can find. Saddle it, addlebrain. Bridle it, idler. And make haste, lest you taste my displeasure."

Racker stalked about the village in the cold until the grenadier returned, leading a short-legged black mare, the cavalry saddle and trappings absurdly large upon its scrawny frame.

"The largest nag I could find, sir," apologized the soldier, cinching the girth a little tighter around the animal's belly. "Of the Scotch sort, that is."

"It will do for my purposes," said the major. He flung himself onto the horse's back, nodding to himself as it grunted under the shock of his weight.

"It won't carry you far, sir," said the grenadier, repeating his earlier warning. "It's nothing but a pony, really, not even a proper lady's horse. Mind yourself, sir, lest it fall under you."

"Or I under it," replied the major, ripping the reins from the soldier's hands. He set his spurs into the mare's flanks, gouging it into a gallop, and in moments he was careening down the slope toward the open moor, toward the sea.

His head pains returned, jolted into existence by the wild motion of the horse and the burning chill of the wind against his face. He struck one hand against his temple. The pain faltered a moment, then flared back stronger than before. Under him he felt the mare straining, her sides heaving. Foam flew from her mouth. Agony united man and beast.

Disasters blurred past him, narrowly missing him. Large stones rose from nowhere. A cleft in the earth opened up before him, barely cleared by the weary horse. A stretch of boggy ground sent the mare slipping right and left. A fallen tree lay in wait for him, clawing at him and the horse with brittle branches. The nag leaped the trunk, stumbling as her hooves hit the frozen earth. The major pitched forward, his head pains suddenly gone. For a moment he saw Edwin very clearly before him, arms outstretched, beloved phantom. Instinctively the major threw his weight backward over the horse's flanks and righted himself in the saddle. A bolt of pain flashed through his forehead, shattering the image of Edwin. Racker spurred his laboring mount until blood dripped from his bootheels, but the animal would go no faster. Insolent brute! It was hardier than he had expected. How far would it run before its heart burst, its lungs exploded? How far before it killed itself? Or him?

On he rode across a dark valley, up a slope to the crest of a ridge, the mare's breath coming in great, harsh gasps, her hooves slipping in the scree and ice. When he reined in the staggering beast at the summit, she fell into a fit of trembling so violent that he was forced to dismount. The major felt his own lungs laboring under his ribs, in sympathy with the mare.

The major's eyes raked the landscape before him. In the near distance lay a vast gray-green meadow of foaming water. The Atlantic. What Atlantis waited for him, under that foul-smelling expanse of wet nothing? And how far might a rider go in that roiling wasteland until the waves pounded his head apart and pulled him under, sucking the air from him, filling him with brine?

No, absurd thought! Edwin would wish him to live, not snuff himself out in the sea or scatter his brains about the moorlands of a godless country. It was his head pains which sent him on these devil's errands. He must take care to beware of them, to force his poor, agonized mind to resist the demons of dementia.

The major turned to mount the mare, but as soon as he placed one boot in the stirrup, the animal commenced to shudder, its legs folded under it, and it slumped onto its side at his feet. Racker stared at the horse for some time, but it did not move. He kicked it, twice in the head, twice in the belly, four times under the tail. A red stream opened from within its body and trickled over its haunches, but the beast was far past feeling. Racker wiped his boot on its shaggy hide. He pulled a violet-scented kerchief from his sleeve and held it under his nose to dispel the sudden, evil odor that filled the air. So it was not quite as hardy as he had thought.

Carefully he stripped the carcass of the saddle and blanket, then slipped the headstall over the wide, white eyes. The mare's teeth were clenched hard in death upon the bit, and it took the major some doing to pull the heavy steel from the frothing mouth. As he lifted the saddle to his shoulders, he thought he saw the briefest shadow of a movement, the whisk of a horse's tail, the flick of a plaid. He sensed eyes upon him, heard the hushed breathing of a frightened person.

The major spun around so quickly the saddle slid onto his neck and struck him against the back of his head.

Some fifty paces from him, on the slope of the ridge leading to the sea, stood a Gael and a woman on a gray horse. All three eyed him with grave intensity, as if he were a dangerous creature which might spring on them at any moment. He touched the hilt of his saber. It would be a very simple matter to overpower the man and commandeer the horse.

Yet something made him hesitate. It was the woman. The wind had blown back the shawl from her face, and he could see in a glance that she was no pinch-cheeked, hard-skinned Gael. Her face was rounded and tender, her nose a pearl set between the luminous gemstones of her eyes. She gazed back at him, curious, impertinent, and perhaps a little fearful. He had seen hundreds of such faces before, but none quite so arresting. If he had cared at all for the beauty of women, he admitted to himself, he might find this one worthy of him. After all, he was certain, she was an Englishwoman.

England! How he yearned for England! The bronze leaves of the beech trees, the larks in the morning, porcelain teacups, linen sheets like soft hands on one's body. And here before him was a living echo of England, a lovely vision whose fingers might lift a silver teaspoon, whose voice might politely request a biscuit, a comfit, a slice of lemon. What such a creature might be doing among the dead heather, in the company of a skirted savage, scarcely seemed important just then. In a fit of longing, the major swept his tricorn from his head and bowed as low as the saddle would permit him. "Mistress."

The moment she saw the officer lower his head, Abby knew she had nothing to fear. He was a gentleman. A lone gentleman with a dead horse in the midst of no-where—scarcely too threatening a figure. "How do you do, major? It is major, isn't it?" Roger, who had loved the military life as long as he could view it from afar, had taught her, as a social grace, to recognize the various insignia of all His Majesty's officers. The gold braid on the major's tricorn was unmistakable.

"Yes, indeed, mistress. Most perceptive of you. Major Thomas Racker of His Majesty's Fifth Regiment of Foot, your humble servant. May I be of assistance? It's surely not safe for a person of your sensitive constitution to be abroad in this barbaric country."

Abby paused, hiding her confusion with a cough. She knew she must reveal as little as possible about herself to strangers. Yet she must say something to the major. She glanced at Niall. The poor man held himself as rigid as an arrow, ready to fly. He could not possibly have a clue as to what they were talking about. "Why, sir, my constitution is hardier than it appears, I suspect. I have kinsfolk here, and this honest fellow is leading me to them."

The major's smile lit up his handsome face. His features reminded Abby of a hawk or eagle, leaner and more angular than Roger's, yet finer than Calum's, as if sculpted by a clever artist. "And might I inquire what part of this accursed country is so fortunate to be the destination of one so fair?"

Abby frowned. Her face felt as stiff as a mask. She knew so few destinations in this unknown land. She could not mention Bailebeag, lest she endanger Calum and Angus. The truth would have to do. "Duninnis, on the Isle of Skye," she murmured.

"Staunch Loyalists," said the major. Abby thought she heard a sigh of disappointment in his voice. He was doubtless in search of Jacobite supporters. What if she had answered him with the name of some rebel stronghold? How might he have reacted then? "Strong opponents of the rebellion and the Stuarts as well. You'll be perfectly safe with them."

Abby felt the muscles of her face relax. She had given a safe answer. She smiled at Niall, to reassure him, but the Gael simply shifted his weight and tightened his hold on Luran's halter rope. If flight were necessary, Niall was ready for it. "Thank you for your concern, major, but it seems to me you are in more need of assistance just now than we are." She pointed toward the flock of hoodie crows which had descended on the ridge behind the major. Some of the bolder ones had even lit on the head of the unfortunate horse and were pecking at its eyes. "You've lost your mount, it seems."

The major snorted and cast a look of disgust behind him at the hapless animal. "Useless beast," he muttered. "It simply collapsed under me, without warning or cause. But have no fear for me, mistress. My encampment is quite close." He gazed hungrily at Luran, and Abby nervously turned the stallion's head away, ready to set off at a gallop if the major took a step toward her. " 'Tis you I fear for, so far from civilization, surrounded by thieves, rogues and barbarians."

"Thank you, I can manage quite well." Something about the man made Abby feel uncomfortable, despite his genteel way of talking, despite his Englishness. Though he spoke with all the grace and ease of a dandy at a ball, wooing the ladies, his true intentions were far more serious. He would kill Calum if he ever found him. No doubt he had already killed many people and burned many houses. He was not unlike a certain hound that Roger had once owned, a handsome animal that enjoyed being petted and coddled. But every so often the dog would snap at Roger for no reason, and had once bitten Lydia's hand. After that, Roger had had it destroyed. Abby shuddered at the memory. She pulled her shawl tightly over her head to ward off the chill of the rising wind. "Good day to you then, major."

"And to you, dear lady."

Abby nodded at Niall, and he led Luran away at a brisk trot. Once she shot a brief glance over her shoulder at the major and saw him disappearing over the ridge, bowed under the weight of the heavy tack. As much as she loved the sound of his voice—so mannered and so out of place on the wild moorland—she was relieved to be rid of him. He smelled of blood.

She was close enough now to Lydia she could almost see the child before her, could almost catch the scent of the irises of Brenthurst, could almost hear her daughter's laughter as Roger chased her through the garden. Abby shook her head. It was all gone, all of it, withered and uprooted. Save Lydia. Lydia was real. And alive.

At the kyle, Niall found an innkeep who promised to stable Luran for no coin, in return for the privilege of trying to breed his own mare with the spirited horse. Finding a boatman to cross the kyle was far more difficult. The wind had whipped the waters of the sound into a mass of wild waves, and the villagers were certain it was only a matter of days before the kyle would begin to freeze.

At last, with the help of many cups of whisky and most of her remaining silver, Abby convinced one ferryman to risk the short crossing to the island and back. The journey took less than an hour, a most frightening hour. Waves crashed into the little boat, threatening to rend it apart, while the boatman swore and shouted and stabbed his oars into the water like broadswords.

"Do you wish to return?" Niall asked her once, but Abby shook her head, her wet hair dripping into her eyes.

"Lydia," she gasped, as salt spray dashed into her face. "All I wish is to find my daughter."

After what seemed a lifetime, Abby saw a huge black cliff materialize before her, breaking through the mist. "The island!" shouted the boatman, and he thrust one oar into the water, heeling the boat about sideways. They reached the shore of the island, dripping like seals, in the darkness of the early evening. Niall went about his business, collecting debts, as he told Abby, while she followed the boatman into the warmth of his tiny house. The family shared their supper with her, oatmeal fried in suet, and big bowls of milk yellow with cream. Afterwards Abby crawled among the boatman's twelve children and fell into an exhausted sleep by the fire.

And then someone was shaking Abby awake. She saw the delicate hand on her arm and heard the anxious whisperings of a child. She sat up, rubbing sleep from her eyes, but all the children were gone, the boatman and his wife were gone, even the stone walls of the cottage had disappeared. In front of her stood Lydia in a cornflower blue frock, rimmed with lace, a gift from her father. Abby stretched out her hand toward the vision, but Lydia seemed to be drifting away from her, further and further back into a gray void.

"Mama, please hurry!" cried the phantom. "The dark island! The dark island! Mama, Mama!" Abby rose and tried to follow the vision, but gray nothingness, like smoke, billowed around her and blinded her eyes. She fell and kept falling, falling, until suddenly a strong hand caught her and the air beneath her feet somehow solidified. She turned toward her rescuer but could see nothing of his face save two beautiful, lapis-colored eyes . . .

*Calum!*

Abby woke with a gasp. "Calum? Lydia?" she whispered, but she was back again in the boatman's croft, surrounded by squirming children and the smells of sea salt and cooking fat. Abby lay back down on her plaid, panting. "I'm coming, Lydia, my darling," she whispered to herself. "I promise you, I'm on my way. Whatever happens, I shall find you. I promise you."

Abby could not fall back asleep, but lay motionless, her eyes unable to shut, waiting for the morning. When dawn came, she was the first one afoot. A short time later, dressed in dry clothing borrowed from the boatman's wife, Abby set out for Duninnis, alone.

There was no need to search for it. The fortress, something like a small castle or a squat, ugly manor house, was perched upon a hill very near the shore, surrounded by naked rowans, birches and aspens, all about half the size of mainland trees. Despite the urgency of the phantom the night before, Abby walked slowly past the dwarfed trees, feeling strangely diminished, as if they would not allow her to move any faster. Overhead seamews and gulls wheeled and dived, their shrieks ripping apart the silence of the morning.

Abby stopped to rub her feet, freezing in her sea-damp shoes. "Don't go barefoot before Duninnis," Angus had warned her. "A chieftain of his stature will be sure to ignore a woman without shoes."

At the gates of the fortress, a man with a musket tried to drive her off before she could explain herself, but she howled and cried and shouted so much that she drew a small crowd, who listened to her with some sympathy.

She had learned one thing about the Gaels: whoever among them made the most noise got the most consideration.

At last a man with grizzled hair and a fierce expression appeared and scattered the crowd with threats and curses. *"Am Broc! Am Broc!"* cried the people, as they tramped away. "The Badger! The Badger!" *Badger? They mean this fellow,* thought Abby, as the stocky islander gripped her by the hand and led her through the gate and into the courtyard. She knew at once he must be a gentleman of some note, a *duine uasal,* as Niall had called Calum. A single eagle's feather pointed straight upward from his bonnet, like a horn, exactly the same insignia that Calum wore in his cap. She wished her red-haired protector were with her now; the stone walls, the pain of Badger's grasp and the anger in his face were draining her courage.

"You don't speak like a Gael," said Badger.

"I am not a Gael," said Abby, in as stout a voice as she could muster. "I am an Englishwoman."

"A Saxon, eh? What business can you have here, woman? Spreading disease, are you?"

Abby wrenched her hand free and glowered at the man. "I am here to speak with your master, Duninnis of Duninnis. Tell him Abigail Fields is here to see him." By now a small group of armed men had gathered around her and Badger, and Abby glowered at them as well. "Abigail Fields," she repeated.

"Why should the master of Duninnis wish to see a Saxon wench such as yourself?" growled Badger. The other men began whispering among each other, and Abby guessed they had their own answers to Badger's question.

"It's a personal matter, really," Abby replied. The men fell silent a moment, then began to roar with laughter.

"Not what small minds might be thinking," she added. "Duninnis will be most unhappy, I believe, if you prevent me from seeing him."

Badger snorted, tossed his head and rolled his eyes. "Keep her here," he barked to the others. "I'll shoot the man who lays a hand on her, at least until I return." With surprising grace, Badger turned and trotted up the stair-case leading to the fortress, his plaid whipping in the wind, and was soon swallowed up in shadows. Abby tried to speak with her guards, but they were close-mouthed and sullen. At least, she thought, they did not try to touch her. Perhaps they where afraid of Badger, or perhaps they simply did not find her attractive.

Some time passed before the burly Gael returned, his face oddly blank, almost kind. Again he took her by the hand, this time with some semblance of courtesy, and led her toward the stone staircase. "Abigail Fields, you are welcome here. Duninnis will see you," was all he said.

Abby followed Badger into a huge dark hall, past a gaggle of servants who stared at her with mouths agape. Badger hurried her on down several gloomy corridors, his feet echoing against the stone flags. He paused once to address a serving girl. They spoke so quickly that Abby missed much of what they said, but she gathered that Badger was trying to locate his lord. Finally he led her to a large hallway, its walls covered with parts of animals: heads of wildcats and lynxes, eagle wings, stags' antlers, and whole pelts of wolves, martens and four-legged badgers.

"Wait for me here, Saxon." The big man vanished through a brass-bound door.

Abby flattened herself against a wall and breathed deeply, trying to quiet the wild hammering of her heart. She could not bear to look at the animals. It was too easy to imagine Lydia up on the wall with them, a hunting trophy, a lifeless skin. Could it be true that her daughter was actually in this dark, dead place, like a garden flower blooming in a bog, a ditch, a cemetery? Abby sniffed the air for the scent of irises, roses and dianthus, but smelled only dust, peatsmoke and the ever-present sharpness of whisky. Perhaps she was making a terrible error. Perhaps Janet was mistaken, or her informers misinformed. Lydia could not possibly exist in such a tomb.

Yet what of the vision in her dream? That Lydia had urged her to hurry. What if Lydia were in danger? What if she had been on the island and suffered some tragedy?

"Abigail Fields!"

Abby started upright. Badger stood before her, beckoning her toward the open door. "Go on with you, woman. Duninnis is being so good as to let you see him. Don't keep him waiting, now."

She slipped past Badger into the chamber and heard the door close behind her with a creak and a thump. In contrast to the rest of the fortress, the room was bathed in pale light which streamed through two tall, narrow windows set with decorative sections of ice-blue glass. Her eyes were still becoming accustomed to the light when a soft, low voice addressed her in English. "Mistress Fields, I presume? Charmed to meet you. I am Alasdair Mor of Duninnis, Alexander MacLeod, you would say."

Abby turned toward the voice and beheld an older man standing before a stone fireplace. He was tall and lean, dressed very simply in white English breeches, a tartan waistkit and flowing linen shirt. The graying remains of a long, thick head of red hair fell in wisps over his shoulders. He had been handsome once, she thought, though now he seemed frail and bloodless, less like a man than the withered remains of a man, preserved and animated. Was he ill, or was it the light which made his skin look so pale? What would such a man want with her daughter? If he had harmed Lydia, Abby would strike him until he collapsed into a pile of dust. "How shall I address you, sir?" she asked, dropping him a curtsey.

"Duninnis will do," said the man with a smile. "Come, have a seat." He motioned toward a plain, stiff chair with a thin, embroidered cushion covering the seat. "Then you can tell me what brings you here, mistress. We are not frequently graced with visitors from your country, but I am very glad to have you. It gives me an opportunity to practice your tongue, always a challenge for me."

After Abby had seated herself, Duninnis pulled a larger, thickly padded chair up close to her and eased himself into it, as one eases a sore foot into a hard leather shoe. He poured a measure of whisky from a flask on a nearby table into two glasses and handed one to her. "I daresay you need a dram on a cold day like this," said the old man. "I do, for my heart is old and tired and can't abide the cold."

Abby sipped at the whisky. It burned her throat, but she forced herself to swallow it. The pain helped her think. "As you have deduced, sir, I am here for an explicit reason, and have indeed risked life and limb, and the life of a friend, to beseech your assistance."

Duninnis raised one white eyebrow. "How now? How may I be of service to you? Speak freely, mistress."

Abby took a deep breath. "I am searching for my daughter, Lydia, Lydia Fields." As she mentioned her daughter's name, Abby thought she saw a shadow pass over Duninnis' ashen face. "I have been told on good authority that my husband Roger—God rest his soul!— entrusted Lydia to your keeping, for whatever reason I do not know. Therefore I have reason to believe she is here now and, therefore, I am asking for her return."

The old Gael tossed back his whisky in one swallow. "I am afraid you have come all this way for naught, mistress. Your daughter isn't here, nor do I know where she might be. Faith, I know nothing of her, nor of you nor your husband."

Abby froze in horror, her fingers taut on the glass. She wasn't hearing him aright. "I pray you be candid with me, sir. If some ill has befallen my daughter, I must be told."

"And I am telling you I know nothing of her, ill nor good." Duninnis poured himself another dram and drained it. "Whoever told you she was here on Skye was either mistaken or purposely leading you astray. If there were a young Englishwoman on this island, you can be sure I would know of it. Not a cow has a calf but my gillies tell me every detail of the birth. I will remember you, though, and her. Perhaps she is elsewhere in the north. There are many men such as myself, you know, landed chieftains with a little money and a great many poor clansfolk. Your daughter could be among any of these gentlemen."

"Lydia herself told me she was here. She came to me in a dream."

"A dream, you say?" laughed Duninnis. "Why, mistress, if dreams were real, then we would all of us be dead, or pursued by demons and dragons and suchlike monsters. If you saw your daughter in a dream, it's no more a sign that she's here than if you had dreamt of dancing seals and raspberry tarts."

Abby took another sip of whisky. "I don't know, sir, I am much confused. Perhaps you would be so good as to let me walk about the grounds and chambers. In case she is being hidden from your eyes," she added hastily.

Duninnis shook his head, his long hair rippling on his shoulders. "You're a bold one, aren't you? Do you know to whom you speak so saucily? No? You know nothing of me. I am the twenty-fifth of my line, and the last, perhaps, as I have no heir of yet." The old man drew himself up straight. "My forefathers used to make the chiefs of the north tremble like aspens. They were great warriors, great leaders, and great scholars to boot. A raid by Duninnis, it was said, was like a visit from the devil: nothing would be left that wasn't burned or broken.

"I'm no great man, but I am of a race of great men. And if I tell you your daughter is not on Skye, you may be certain she is not on Skye. And if you won't take the word of Duninnis of Duninnis, then you're not welcome on this island."

"I'm not . . . I don't . . . I'm quite sure you mean . . ." sputtered Abby, rising from her chair as Duninnis stalked to the door. But before he could reach it, Badger burst in, and Abby realized he had been standing just outside the chamber during the entire conversation, listening to every word.

"The lady is leaving now," Duninnis told Badger. "Escort her to wherever you first found her, and be certain she does not return here. Our business is at an end."

"I beg you, sir, reconsider," pleaded Abby. "Let Badger accompany me around the grounds for a short time." A ribbon, a scrap of lace, the scent of irises, any such small thing would be enough to confirm Lydia's presence. " 'Tis all I ask." Had she really offended the chieftain, or was he concealing the truth? She remembered a line from the Bard of Avon, and thought that Duninnis was indeed protesting much too much.

*"Adieu,* mistress," said Duninnis. "Your loss has made you quite desperate, and it's sorry I am that I can't be of more help to you. Badger will see you out."

Badger all but dragged Abby from the room, her arm locked under his armpit. She knew it was stupid to struggle, but she did so anyway, kicking at the Gael's bare legs and trying to wrench her arm from his. All she succeeded in doing, however, was making Badger so determined to be rid of her that he tightened his hold on her arm and pushed her through the corridors as fast as she could walk. Faces and paintings of faces blurred past her and, at one point, the sad eyes and pink tongue of a small, black and white spaniel.

"Tip!" Abby dug her feet into the floor. She stopped so quickly that Badger stumbled and fell to his knees, his hands flying in front of himself to break his fall. Pulling free, Abby raced back to the dog and found him in Lydia's arms, only ten paces away. The high forehead, the sculpted cheekbones, her father's eyes—unmistakably Lydia, though her face was turned in profile as she held her pet, pressing kisses on his shaggy forehead. She was older, taller than Abby remembered, her delicate beauty heightened by a look of utter melancholy.

Abby struggled for a word, a sound, anything to catch the girl's attention. Lydia's name was on her lips when she felt the crush of Badger's arms encircling her ribs and felt the word fall noiseless from her mouth in a rush of breath. Badger lifted Abby into his arms and ran with her down the corridor, his hand clasped so tightly around her throat that she could scarcely whisper, could scarcely even breathe. From the corner of her eye she saw Lydia turn her head toward the corridor. Then Lydia was gone. Had she seen her mother, or only a faceless blur, a flash of tartan that could be easily explained away?

Outside in the courtyard, Badger pushed Abby down hard on the ground. "Be off with you!" he shouted.

Abby scrambled to her feet, choking as the air rushed into her swollen throat. "You have her!" she gasped. "Give her to me!" She ran forward straight into Badger and ducked under his elbow, but he was too quick for her. She screamed as he caught her by the hair and threw her back down on the flagstones. Again she heaved herself to her feet. She felt something tickling her skin; a sticky liquid was dripping down the back of her neck. "Lydia!" she called, but her voice came out hoarse and hushed. She saw Badger approaching, but hadn't the strength to flee from him. There was a breeze in her face, an impact, and blackness.

---

The faces of half a dozen children were before her when Abby awoke in the boatman's hut. Her jaw ached, and she resisted the temptation to touch it. *"Lath mhath,"* she whispered. "Good day."

*"Tha i beath!"* shouted the youngsters. "She's alive!"

The boatman's wife came running in with a cup of warm milk. She patted Abby's trembling hands, then stood aside as a big shadow entered the room. "Faith, Mistress Avvy, it's good to see you back in the land of the living. Have you been in a brawl, then?" asked a familiar voice.

It was Niall. Abby wept to see the drover, her one and only link to Glenalagan and Calum Og. "Niall! Oh, I'm so happy to see you! How did I get here? And how did you know I was here?"

Niall knelt beside the heather bed and wiped away her tears with the hem of his plaid, neatly avoiding her swollen jaw. "Well, mistress, it was a bit of a surprise to me,

I don't mind saying. One of Duninnis' gillies found me at the alehouse and asked whether I was the man who had come across the kyle with an Englishwoman. I was, I said, and the creature led me here and I found you, half dead, so I thought. She has taken a bad fall, the gillie said, which I knew was a handful of dung, for the mark of the fist that struck you is still very plainly written on your chin. But I said nothing, and I have been waiting most of the day for you to awaken. Now pray tell me, mistress, what truly befell you?"

"Oh, Niall! They have Lydia! Lydia is in the fortress, with Duninnis. I saw her!" Between sobs of rage and pain, Abby told Niall how she had asked for the chieftain's help, only to be told he had never seen Lydia and knew nothing of her. It was a lie, Abby said, since she saw Tip, and then Lydia herself, only for a moment, but alive and well and unmistakable. Then Badger had forced her out of the house, and it was very likely he who had struck her.

"A man striking a woman!" cried Niall. "Now I have heard everything! The brute! A true Gael would never strike a woman."

"I am afraid he is far more a dupe of his master than he is a true Gael," sighed Abby. "But Badger is not important. Niall, we must rescue Lydia. Spirit her away somehow."

"Nay, mistress," said Niall, shaking his head. "A poor drover and a woman against Duninnis and his men? Very bad odds, indeed. We'll get ourselves killed, and what's the use of that? There's only one creature, possibly, who might be able to talk some reason into Duninnis' old head."

"Who is that?" snapped Abby. The back of her head hurt as if it were being pierced with needles, and Niall's face swam in front of her, now clear, now a blur. She clenched her teeth, and the pain faded. "Who?"

"Why, Calum Og, of course," said Niall. "Duninnis owes Calum a little silver from the sale of some cattle several years past. Calum hasn't pressed him for it, since they are distant kin, you know. But it would not surprise Duninnis to see Calum on Skye, asking for his due. Perhaps they can strike some bargain. Perhaps Calum can wheedle Lydia from the old man. I don't know. But Calum can charm the very devil himself, if he has a mind to. And the sooner he speaks with Duninnis the better, I'm thinking."

"Why? Is Lydia in danger?"

Niall laid his hand on hers. "The news isn't good, mistress, and I feel sorry to be the one to tell you. Are you well enough to hear me out?"

Abby shut her eyes, blacking out Niall, the cottage, the island, everything real around her, only the dark, secret center of herself, the strength that had taken her so far into the unknown. "Yes, I am prepared," she said, opening her eyes. She could withstand anything if it brought her even a hand's breadth closer to her daughter. "Go on."

"Well, before I left Glenalagan, Angus and Calum bade me keep my eyes and ears open and learn anything I could about the girl, Lydia. So I did, mistress. I have many friends here, and they are all very willing to tell their news to a mainlander, especially after they have had a dram or two. And this is what I learned from them.

"It seems Duninnis is diseased. He has the bad disorder, and it has left him unable to sire a child. There is a belief among my people—a stupid one, mind you—that the touch of a Saxon maiden applied to the privates can undo the disease. Shall I continue? Well, Duninnis hasn't much faith in poor people's remedies, mind you, but when he was in Glasgow last autumn, he heard of your husband's misfortunes galore at the gaming tables. When he saw Lydia for himself, he decided he would win her and see what might happen."

Niall paused, as if recovering from the horror of what he had just said. Abby stared at him. She was blank, she was without feelings. She could bear whatever he had to say, if only he would hurry. "Pray continue."

"Well, then. Your husband had a run of bad luck playing whist with the chieftain. But he was a feverish man, driven by devils when it came to gaming, so I'm told."

"Yes, I know. Do go on." She was stone, impervious to feeling. She was marble, incapable of tears. Better still, she was a rose, an iris, a foxglove, able to absorb all and feel nothing. Nothing could harm her, as long as she knew the truth.

"Aye. Well, at last your man had nothing left to stake save Lydia, which of course was Duninnis' wish. And they played long and hard for her, and Duninnis at length got the best of your husband and won the child. It sore aggrieved the father, but there was naught he could do. He took her to Duninnis' coach the next morning, and Duninnis drove away with her. They say he rode after the carriage, and that was when he was waylaid and murdered." Niall looked up at her and stopped. "Shall I go on or not?"

Abby felt the tears brimming in her eyes and spilling onto her cheeks, weeping as no stone ever had. She could see Lydia's face before her, uncertain and wary. Had he told her she was going to visit relatives in the North, that he would fetch her back presently? What else could he have said? "Continue," she whispered.

"As you wish, mistress. That's nearly all of it. My

friends had no way of knowing exactly what use Duninnis has for your daughter, but they think she's not . . . she's not suffered the worst. Indeed, they think he cannot do the worst to her."

"But even if she were ravished, that is surely not the worst."

Niall nodded. "Aye, true enough. Duninnis could grow weary of her and find a way to be done with her. Or she could find it herself, if she were aye unhappy with her lot."

Abby sat up and swung her legs over the bed, but her head reeled like a drunkard and sent her sprawling back upon the plaids, half senseless. "As soon as I can walk, I shall return to Duninnis and find her."

Niall pressed a cool, wet rag to her forehead. "Nay, mistress. As soon as you can walk, you and I will cross the kyle and fetch Calum. Unless you wish to have three deaths on your head."

Niall began singing. It was a tuneless children's song that Angus frequently crooned to little Sorcha. For some time Abby lay silent, lulled by the coolness of the water on her skin and Niall's soothing voice. Some of the boatman's children came to the bedside and sat on the floor at Niall's feet, staring shyly at their strange guest. "Niall, where is my stringpurse?" she said at length.

Niall reached inside his plaid and pulled out the bag. "I meant only to keep it safe," he explained.

"I understand." Abby fumbled with the contents of the purse. At last her hands touched something cold and hard. She drew forth the little double frame that had traveled so far, through so much, and opened it. The two faces, her own and Roger's, stared back at her, as if in astonishment, oddly distant and unfamiliar in the blue smoke of the peat fire. With great effort she worked

Roger's portrait out of its brass prison and handed it to Niall. "This was Roger, my husband."

"A handsome man." The drover turned the watercolor round and round, as fragile and lovely as a butterfly captured in his big hands. When he tried to return it, Abby pushed the painting back toward him.

"Into the fire with it, Niall."

"Mistress Avvy?"

"Put it in the fire." Roger was gone. She didn't want to see him again, didn't wish to carry him about with her anymore, a constant reminder of Lydia's suffering and his own treachery. "Into the fire."

When Abby slept that night, she dreamed of herself and Lydia at Brenthurst. They were picking raspberries and gooseberries in the sunlit garden, and every sort of flower—pansies and peonies and chrysanthemums alike, regardless of their place in the seasons—was in full bloom.

# *Twelve*

### Winter and a Thaw

Calum was on his knees on the frozen earth at the foot of Catriona's cairn when he felt the sting of ice on the back of his neck. He looked upward into a swirling mass of snow crystals. Some landed in his eyes and mouth, and he leaped to his feet, brushing his face with the tail of his plaid. The black and red tartan glittered with white specks, like a trout in sunlight. The first snow, and Abby nowhere to be found.

He hurried into the house and the warmth of the fire, the smell of oatcakes on the griddle and the noise of the children. There was never any sound at Catriona's cairn, not even the cries of birds. All living things seemed to avoid the place. "Calum, you were gone so long I was worried you had frozen yourself stiff," Angus berated him. "Did you bag anything?"

"Nothing worth speaking of."

Calum unbelted his heavy plaid and let it drop to the floor. "Here now, let me help you gather it up," offered Angus. "You're as much bother as the weans."

"It's not me you should be worried about, man." Calum sat down by the fire, picked up Sorcha and set her on his lap. The little girl nestled against his chest and promptly fell asleep. "Abby and Niall should have returned days since, or if not Abby, at least Niall. Perhaps they've run into a mischief, and I wouldn't put it beyond Duninnis to have had a hand in it, if they did."

"Have a dram, brother." Angus crouched beside Calum and handed him a cup full of whisky. "Your Abby is well enough, I warrant, what with Niall beside her and Luran underneath her. You'd like to see her again, I think."

"Aye, if she'd have it so."

"Because she's your friend and you wish her well?"

"Aye, indeed."

"And also because you love her?"

Calum looked into Angus' blue eyes, as deep as twin oceans, and knew he could keep nothing secret from his foster brother. Angus grasped the answer to every riddle, even riddles of the heart. "Why do you say that?"

"Why, man, it is written all over your face whenever you're with her. You cough and blush and preen like a bridegroom. And what's more, I saw her go to your bed the night before she left Glenalagan."

"You can be sure I did nothing to shame her."

"Of course you didn't. But do you love her? Did you love her, even before you found Bailebeag burned to the ground and the cairns on the hillside?"

"Perhaps. Sometimes I believe I love her. Jesus and Mairi! It's not an easy thing to know just what I feel sometimes. Perhaps it's nothing more than desire. A hard *slat* is a demanding master."

"Well, a man never died of that ailment." Angus rose and drew aside a corner of the plaids which covered the doorway. A swirl of white flakes flew onto his whiskers, and he let the plaids fall back into place. "A heavy snow-fall. I hope neither man nor beast is out tonight in this."

"Nor woman," added Calum, wishing at once he had not said a word.

"Nor woman neither," murmured Angus. "Calum, be truthful with yourself, *mo luran*. It's not your stick that's ailing you but your heart. Isn't it so?"

"As I've said, I don't know." If it were true and he did love her, he wasn't much of a husband. A good husband wouldn't be sighing and fretting over another woman, with his own wife barely cold in the ground, would he? Calum stroked Sorcha's damp forehead. She wasn't much younger than his own poor little gosling. Shot through the heart, Angus had told him. Tears welled up in his throat and he choked them back. "I loved Catriona, that I know."

"Well, what do you think Catriona herself would say about Abby?" asked Angus, hunkering down beside Calum.

"What do you mean?" said Calum, though he had asked himself the same question many times and never found an answer he believed.

"Do you think Catriona would disapprove of her? Of you both, together? Nay, I think she'd be uncommon glad that you'd found another love, someone decent and pretty, someone to help you start a new family. She was aye a giving, generous woman, your Catriona, and she always wished for nothing but your happiness."

"I'm not happy now, now that she's gone, even though I may be free to wed Abby, if she'd have me." Calum laid Sorcha beside the fire and held his face in his hands. "I don't know what I'm thinking, brother." He had never felt more aimless in the head than he felt just then.

"You weren't hunting, were you, Calum? Leastways, not hunting beasts nor birds."

Calum shook his head. He hadn't told Angus or the children about his plan to kill his family's murderer, lest it worry them, but somehow Angus had guessed the truth.

There was no hiding anything from Angus. "I was hunting the man who killed Catriona. The man who put a bullet through my baby's heart. Recker is his name."

"An odd thing to call a person, but the Saxon have aye odd names. How do you know he's the man you seek?"

Calum raised his head and poured himself another cup of whisky. "I didn't find him, but I found two of his kind—deserters, grenadiers both of them. They tried to shoot me on sight, that's how much they think of our people. I blew the head off one with the Girl from Madrid," he said, patting his Spanish musket. "The other ran and I brought him down with my broadsword. They're a useless lot, without a weapon to hide behind."

Calum sipped his whisky. It was a good malt, well-aged and not bitter, like some. "Before the creature gave up the spirit, he told me what had happened to Bailebeag, how this man Recker had ordered it destroyed because it was the house of a Jacobite. I would have helped the grenadier, tried to save him." Calum emptied the cup. "But it was too late for him. He had given over."

"And this Recker creature . . . do you know where he is?"

"Nay, the grenadier was gone before I could ask him."

Angus draped his arm around Calum's shoulder and pulled him close. "My poor brother! It must lie heavy on your heart, knowing the man who slew Catriona and the weans is still as free as a lark and likely killing other men's families."

"He spared you and the weans, thanks be to God."

"To God, aye," sighed Angus, "and to my brave clansfolk, who made the Saxons believe I was a very sick man. They are ever fearful of illness."

"They will be deathly ill when I'm done with them," said Calum grimly.

"But there's naught you can do, brother, not now, not until the snows melt and you're free to roam the hills and root the devil out. The snow has him imprisoned, mind you, wherever he is, for he cannot march through it without losing most of his men. And wherever he stays, he will have little food for his troops. Many will desert, and he will be easy game for you come spring."

"Spring is far off yet." A mighty gust of wind shook the little house until the rafters creaked and moaned in complaint. Abby was out in the storm, wandering through the snow with Niall and Luran, lost, perhaps, cold and frightened. It terrified Calum to think that he had no more idea where she was than where the Saxon murderer was. He could do nothing to help Abby and nothing to hurt the Englishman. "Should I look for her, do you think?" he asked, barely aware that he spoke aloud.

"Nay, nay, don't fear for Abby, Calum. I saw her in my dreams, well and happy, playing with her daughter. You'll find your Englishwoman safe and sound in a day or two, I'm certain of it. If you must search for her, at least wait until the storm is over."

"I will find Abby, I promise you," murmured Calum, "and I'll find this Recker, too, before he has a chance to hurt her." Again a tide of grief and guilt rose up inside him, and this time he trapped it in his brain and forged it into red-hot anger. He shook his cup over the blazing peats and watched as several drops of whisky struck the flames and flared into wide, red eyes of fire. "He'll sore regret ever having heard of Bailebeag or Calum Og Mac-Donald."

* * *

"Do you think we should go back, Niall?" Abby clung to Luran's ice-encrusted mane. The wind whipped snowflakes into her eyes and mouth, and she wasn't certain she could maintain her balance on the stallion's back much longer.

"Indeed, mistress," Niall shouted above the screaming of the wind. "To go back is as bad as to go forward." If she had not felt so fearful of freezing, or worse yet watching Niall freeze to death, Abby might have laughed at the poor drover. Only his eyes were visible through a mask of ice that dripped from his beard and eyebrows. "But neither will do just now, I think."

"Have we an alternative?" Abby thought she could see her words rise from her mouth and take shape in swirls of mist.

"A cave," answered Niall. "Close by, if I can but find it. Herders use it in bad weather, which is most days in Glenfinnan."

"I cannot go on," moaned Abby, but Niall ignored her. She sank into a sort of half-wakefulness in which everything was warm and cozy. It was a summer's day, she held a cup of tea in her hands, and she was bathing in a tub of lovely warm water, perfumed with lavender. As she sank deeper into the half-dream, she thought she felt someone in the tub with her, a hard, masculine presence with a salty, masculine smell. She was oddly unafraid. Was it Calum?

When she turned to catch sight of him, a sudden jolt destroyed her dreams of summer. Luran had come to a stop, and Abby was rolling off his back, into the snow. The touch of ice on her bare hands and face made her gasp in pain. "The cave," said Niall, helping her to her feet. He brushed handfuls of snow from her *arasaid*. "I'll go ahead, holding your hand. You follow with the horse."

The mouth of the cave was barely wide enough to admit Luran. The stallion snorted and shivered as Abby tugged on his halter and dragged him into the darkness. She patted his velvet muzzle and felt his warm breath against her fingers. "It's all right, Luran, you've nothing to fear," she reassured him, sounding far braver than she felt. In the depths of the granite blackness, she could see nothing, could hear nothing save Niall's uncertain footsteps shuffling about in the void.

Suddenly a light tore open the darkness. Niall must have struck a flint. Abby could just make out the lines of the man's body as he crouched over a tiny fire. As the flames grew larger and stronger, she could see the walls of the cave itself, like the inside of a black kettle. Abby held herself stiff and straight, trying to take up as little space as possible. Soon she began to feel almost warm again. "Are we to stay here until the storm is over?"

"Nay, mistress, not unless you're weary of living. These few sticks and straws will make just enough of a fire to keep your blood from freezing for a short while, long enough, I trow, so that I'll be able to find proper shelter."

"Proper shelter? You can't intend to go back into the snow?"

"Indeed I do, mistress," said Niall, holding his bonnet under Luran's jaws. The cap was full of melted snow, and the horse drank it dry in a moment. "We're no but a mile or two from Glenalagan, if I have reckoned aright. I'll find Calum and Angus and lead them to you. And if I've reckoned badly, then at least I'm sure to find a house where I can get dry clothing and a fresh horse and food galore for you."

"You'll be lost in the storm!"

"Not with Luran beside me," said Niall. "He knows just where he's going. Haven't you noticed how he stops now and then, sucks the wind, and changes his direction? He's searching the air for the smell of horses and cattle. He'll make straight for the nearest byre, and I'll be with him."

"Let me go with you, then." Why was it that those she trusted were always leaving her, or she them? She remembered the horror of waking up in Rose Cottage and finding Lydia gone. "I'd rather walk through the snow than wait by myself in this miserable mousehole."

Niall laughed and shook his head. "If you're weary enough to fall off Luran's back, then you're too weary to continue. Rest and content yourself as best you can, mistress. Feed the fire slowly, lest you burn all your fuel too quickly or smoke yourself out into the cold. The sooner I leave, the sooner I'll be back. Don't fret, now."

"I beg you, don't leave me alone!" cried Abby, grabbing hold of Niall's plaid, but the drover only smiled and removed her hand. With great care he maneuvered Luran around the fire and led him toward the mouth of the cave.

"Wait for my return!" he called back to her, his voice as light as the falling snow.

Abby crouched by the fire and tried to think. The snow on her clothing had melted and formed a pool of icewater under her feet. She pulled off her shoes and edged her toes as close to the flames as she could bear.

What recourse did she have but to wait for Niall? She had to assume he would return for her. And of course he would, provided he did not lose Luran, injure himself, or freeze to death.

But would he return in time? She thought she had quite a bit of kindling, but she could not tell how long it might last. Nor did she have anything to eat or drink.

She had survived hard times before, to be sure, but at least then she had the comfort of other people, if not the most friendly people. And she had had Calum. He and she together, she was sure, could endure anything. But how long might she survive alone?

Abby chewed on a rowan twig to stave off the empty feeling in her stomach. Instead of feeding herself she would feed the flames, just a little morsel at a time, a few straws, a stick of fir, a chunk of pine. The little fire responded with a crack and a pretty burst of blue sparks.

Abby experimented. Different woods produced different effects: sometimes a spurt of tiny fireworks, red, blue or white, sometimes brightly colored flames, and sometimes only smoke. She tried to avoid the smoke, but that meant burning no peat at all, nor any green needles. The fire amused her so much she was barely aware of the passage of time or the great icy belly of the cave that lay just beyond the puny glow of the flames. She fancied the fire was a living thing, a pleasant little animal whose only desire was to make her feel comfortable. In return, she would feed it bonbons and watch it snatch the treats from her fingers with its red-orange tongues.

*Abby.*

She looked behind her but saw only blackness. No one had spoken. Abby was sure of it. Nevertheless, she had heard her name. Perhaps she was talking to herself. She shivered, suddenly aware of the damp chill that filled the cave. The fire was no longer a cheerful beast, but a lifeless spot of warmth, woefully small and inadequate.

To her horror, Abby noticed that the pile of kindling was more than half gone.

She must be more careful, she thought. She didn't need such a large fire, actually, when a bed of hot embers would do just as well. If she wrapped herself in her *arasaid* as the men wrapped themselves in their plaids, she could curl up by the warm remnants of the fire and fall asleep. When she awoke, Niall might be there to cheer her, or, if not, she could stoke the fire and wait longer.

Abby unbelted her *arasaid* and lapped it round about her until she could scarcely see. This must be how a butterfly feels inside a chrysalis, she thought, and began to doze. When she woke, her first thought was for the fire. She felt sorry for it. After all, she had petted it, cozened it like a lapdog, and then so rudely denied it all her affections that it had sunk low to the ground, black and disheartened, casting only the feeblest shimmer of light.

Abby sat bolt upright and reached for a twig. As she laid it on the embers, it burst into flames with a loud *pop!* She was just settling herself back into sleep when she heard another sound.

*"Mama?"*

Shaking herself free of the heavy *arasaid,* Abby leaped to her feet. Outside the embrace of the fire, the air was as cold and sharp as steel. "Lydia?" Abby peered into the nothingness of the cave. She was sure she had not been talking to herself. But how could Lydia be in the cave with her? It wasn't possible. Was it?

*"Mama?"*

Again the voice! Her daughter's musical, sweet voice. Abby drew the *arasaid* up around her shoulders and turned about in the darkness. "Lydia! Where are you, pet? Lydia, come to me, my darling!"

Outside, the wind purred inside the entrance to the cave. Inside, the fire gave a halfhearted snap. Ashes fell with a soft, shirring sound. Was Lydia gone? "I cannot see you, my love. If you're here, pray speak to me."

*"Come with me, Mama."*

This time the voice clearly came from the mouth of the cave. Abby belted her *arasaid* around her waist and draped it about her as best she could. Everything seemed to have fallen asleep. The fire was again black and quiet, the wind had died down, even her heart seemed to have stopped beating. She inched toward the entrance.

*Stop, Abby, stop!* a voice cried out inside her head. Abby heard the warning, considered it, and ignored it. Why was she talking to herself when Lydia was obviously just within hand's reach?

Abby forced herself out to the mouth of the cave, then past it into the cold beyond. The snow had stopped falling. Every hill and rock and tree was swaddled in white. And in the very center of this blinding whiteness, amid a heap of snow-buried rocks, stood Lydia, as fragile as a Meissen figurine.

But she was not really standing. She was floating. Her feet, encased in blue satin slippers, were well off the ground, her thin pink frock billowing about her in the wind. "Lydia!" cried Abby, and rushed toward her. But the girl was gone by the time Abby reached the rocks. Lydia appeared again, more distant this time, and again Abby raced to meet her, kicking up clouds of snowdust as she ran. Again she was too late. Lydia was far down in the glen, hovering between two silvered pines, her arms outstretched, beseeching.

Abby stared at the image which looked so much like—and yet unlike—her daughter. The cold began to take hold of Abby, starting with her toes and fingers, devouring her inward, turning her legs and arms into numb branches. She stumbled forward in a stiff-legged trot, but when she reached the silver pine trees, she knew she had made a terrible error. She had entrusted herself to a shadow, a memory, a fancy of a distracted mind that saw life where there was none. Sensible Calum would never have let her make such a mistake.

Abby sat down in the snow, too weary and stiff to play touch-and-begone with apparitions any longer. To her surprise and delight, the snow was pleasantly warm and inviting, like her big featherbed at Brenthurst, only softer and somehow alive. *I'll take care of you,* whispered the wind over the snow.

*"Mama, pray do not lie down."*

Abby looked up. The phantom Lydia floated only an arm's length away from Abby's face. "Oh, my darling! To think that I have come so far . . . gone through so much . . . and have lost you, all the same!"

*"Will you take my hand? I shall help you up."*

Abby struggled against the snow's comforting embrace. With considerable effort she stretched one hand forward and placed it in the nonexistent grasp of the unreal Lydia. Lunging forward, Abby pushed herself up from the ground and tottered ahead a few paces. She could not see Lydia now, but she continued to clench her fist, as if holding hands with the beautiful vision.

A fir tree stood before her in the near distance, its branches spread out in welcome. Abby staggered toward it and after an eternity found herself leaning against the tree's thick trunk. The ground under the fir tree was wet but almost free of snow. It smelled of spices and the inside of friends' houses. Abby curled up at the foot of the tree and felt herself grow warm again.

*"Mama!"*

The voice came from the ground, as if the phantom were crouching in the snow. Abby roused herself and sat up. Large, strange markings marched in two straight lines across the white hillside, only a few paces from where she lay. These meant something, she knew, and the more she stared at them, the more familiar they became.

They were the hoofprints of a horse and the footprints of a man, half-buried in snow.

Abby smiled to herself and fell back against the protective treetrunk. "Thank you, Lydia, my love," she whispered. "Now I shall just sleep for a little while, until *Papa* comes home."

Her dreams were deep and disturbing. She found herself in the garden at Brenthurst, standing at the lily pond where the path branched in opposite directions. To the left stood Lydia, holding out her hands and smiling, and to the right stood Roger, his face distorted with fear, shouting to Abby, begging her to join him.

Abby wanted nothing to do with Roger, but she could not make herself walk toward Lydia. Some great force was at work, drawing her down the righthand path, into Roger's grasp. The grass looked softer where he stood, the blossoms brighter, the sun warmer. She could rest forever under the flowering cherry and let it bury her under its petals. She felt herself sinking into Roger's arms, right through the flesh, onto the bone. The sun grew dark. The flowers faded and crumpled into pieces.

"Abby! Abby! Rouse yourself, love!"

Was someone calling her? Not Lydia. But who, then?

Suddenly someone caught hold of her shoulder and began pulling her back. She felt herself sailing upward through layers of sleep, like a trout on a line, being dragged skyward out of the dark, deep water. When she broke through to the surface at last, she gasped for air, her lungs filling with cold. Her eyes snapped open for a moment and met two other eyes, as bright as blue flames. She smelled the familiar, heathery smell that never quite seemed to leave her memory. "Calum?" she croaked, her voice shuddering with cold. "Why are you at Brenthurst?"

"Oh, Abby, *a'ghraidh,* I'd thought I'd lost you!" The Gael buried his face against Abby's neck, and she felt the heat of his tears on her skin. Then his strong arms were underneath her, lifting her against his chest. Something warm was wrapped around her, and a hot, sweet liquid filled her mouth. She thought she heard Angus' voice, but Lydia and Roger had vanished completely.

Abby could not feel her feet, and her fingers were only so many icicles adhering to her hands, but none of this troubled her. She had Calum back. Lydia had led her to him. She nestled against him though she could not see him. The cold air had frozen the tears in her eyes, making it impossible to open them.

*"Mo ghraidh, mo chreidh, mo lurag, mo lemhan,"* she heard him say, and thought to herself, *my love, my heart, my jewel, my darling.* "Now you are home."

For days Abby lay silent in the second room, used only by visitors and invalids. She drifted between waking and sleeping, shivering even under the warmth of five plaids. Calum and Angus took turns chafing her limbs, wrapping her feet in nettle poultices, and spooning noxious liquors down her throat. All their activity seemed distant to her, as if she herself were far removed from the poor, feeble woman on the bed. That was not Abby. Abby was a theater-goer watching a rather dull performance she did not especially care to see.

One morning she awoke to see little Sorcha standing by the bed, peering down into her face. *"Matainn mhath,* Avvy," murmured the child. "You're not dead, are you?"

"Good morning. No, I don't believe I am," whispered Abby. Suddenly she became aware of her hands. Her fingers felt as if they were part of her again. They were clutching the coarse wool of the bedclothes, and Sorcha was stroking them, her touch as light as eiderdown.

At the sound of her voice, Calum was at her side. "You spoke, Abby! You're awake!"

"I was coming back to Glenalagan," she tried to explain.

"So Niall said. He told us what happened with Duninnis, that you saw her dog and the child herself holding him, but the old devil refuses to admit he has her. I'll get him to give her up, I promise you, if I do nothing else in my life."

"Thank you. Yes, we must go back for her. But what I meant was . . . that is to say . . ."

"You needn't talk, my love."

Abby struggled to make sense out of the rush of words that tumbled about in her brain. "I must say this. I love you, Calum Og MacDonald. I need you, yes, but I also love you. If you send me away, I shall simply keep returning, like swallows in the spring, until you keep me. Or destroy me." Her mind wavered and went blank for a moment. "There. Now you know all I have to say. I came back, not only for Lydia, but for you. It's you I want, however you'll have me. If you won't have me as a wife, so be it. I am prepared for that. If being with you means a life of sin, then I will choose sin, rather than be without you."

The Gael stared at her, his face ebbing and flowing before her eyes. "Abby, I'd wager you have never said so many words at one time before in your life."

"No, perhaps not." Her brain was floating inside her skull, as light as seafoam on the crest of a wave. "Did they make any sense?"

"Aye, but you needn't have said anything at all, for you mean more to me than food or drink or life itself.

And if anyone thinks it is wicked or unseemly to say so, let the devil take him." He bent over her and kissed her mouth, a breath of a kiss. But when he saw she could bear it, he kissed her deeply, a proper kiss, with his tongue between her lips. She felt as if she had melted and were seeping into the heather bed. "I love you, Abby. I think I have loved you from the very first, at the Heart's-ease, with me in Saxon rags and you with fear in your heart."

Abby heard a faint sound, like the breathing of a very small animal. "Sorcha!"

The little girl sat beside the bed, playing with two skeins of yarn, blue and red. When she heard her name, she looked up at Abby and Calum, a shy smile flickering across her face. "Here are the babies," she said, holding up the yarn. "I am the sister. That pebble is the dog. And you are Ma and Da."

Abby lay back in the bed. She was falling into sleep and could do nothing to save herself. "I'd like that very much."

Days passed, weeks passed, fortnights passed. Feeling returned to Abby's feet, though she could not walk more than a few steps without stumbling. Angus urged her to be patient.

Calum was almost always at her bedside, telling her about the weather or the children or some silly story about his family and clansfolk. He had six books, including the Bible, *Pilgrim's Progress* and *Le Morte d'Arthur,* which he read to her over and over, until she could have recited them aloud as he read. He read to her from *MacBeth* and made her think how little the Bard knew about real Gaels. She could not imagine Calum betraying either his king or his friend, and she was certain the kind

Highland women she had met could never be one half so fiendish as MacBeth's maniacal lady.

Calum played chess and backgammon with Abby, though he was a poor player. More than once she stopped the game, pleading weariness, rather than let him suffer another loss. Sometimes he was away for long periods of time; he would never tell her where he had been, but he smelled of snow and granite and always spoke softly afterward.

Most nights, when Angus and the children were sleeping, he came to her little room in the hushed glow of a candle, only his shirt covering his freckled hide. Those nights they lay on the bed together, Abby under the plaids and Calum on top of them. They kissed, he touched her and she touched him. She ran her hands over his back, marveling at the hardness of his muscles and the breadth of his shoulders. She stroked the satin parts of him between his legs and let him stroke her, up and around and inside, until she could no longer breathe. Sometimes she would feel him tense, as if he had been struck a great blow, and then his head would jerk back and his hips would thrust forward, and a white stream of infinitesimal Calums would burst forth from him, into her empty hands.

"I want a child," she told him one night, after he had exhausted himself beside her. "I want you to give me a child."

"A child? My child?" he replied. He had taken to speaking in English with her in the nighttime, because, as he explained, the Saxon tongue seemed better suited for darkness. "And us not wed?"

It was the first time he had ever linked the two of them with the possibility of marriage. Abby shuddered. She knew that, in some way he could not explain to her, he still thought of himself as Catriona's husband. "Is there no hope that we can be man and wife?"

"I love you, Abby, but I cannot wed you, not now. Not until I've paid Catriona what I owe her—the head of her murderer. It's a fearsome condition, I trow, but the best I can manage." He sighed and stroked her face. "And, if you have a child, I'll provide for both of you."

"God bless you, my love!" She pulled his head down toward hers and kissed him tenderly. She felt as giddy as a little girl, as wild as a filly turned out into spring pasture. She had never been allowed to feel so free before, and it worried her a little, as if she had stepped into the midst of some great danger and did not know she should be afraid.

Calum's face was undecipherable. Had she said something stupid? "I am a Jacobite, Abby, remember that. I always will be, and if you consort with me, you're as good as a Jacobite yourself, for you can't be loyal to Georgie and Jamie at the same time. If you stay with me and have my babe, you'll very likely never return to England, nor see your beautiful Burnthouse again."

"Brenthurst." Abby thought for a moment. She was an Englishwoman, that could not be changed. But there was nothing in England for her now, nothing save the ashes of her youth and the dim memories of a distant happiness. Brenthurst was gone forever, sold to some London swell as his country estate. "Very well, so be it. I can live without England, my love, but not without you."

"Abigail, *mo chreidh*."

They drank deeply of each other. Calum ran his hands over her breasts, lapping at her, nuzzling her, all but swallowing her. Roger had never loved her so fiercely. She quivered under Calum's touch like a taut harpstring only a moment away from snapping.

Something had changed. Abby sensed the difference but could not name it immediately. It was the bare caress of his skin that finally made her understand: he was lying naked under the plaids with her. "Shall I?" he whispered. "May I?"

"Yes. Yes."

The Gael surged over her like a wave of the ocean, drowning her, smothering her in heat and motion. Her body arced to meet his, and wondrously became his, thrusting, pulsing and writhing, caught in inescapable currents of being and becoming. He was a great fish, a leviathan, that had caught her in his jaws and was devouring her, ripping the limbs from her body and scattering her flesh all over the waters of oblivion. She pressed her face into his wet neck and breathed in the ocean smell of his glistening skin. From deep within her something sparked and caught fire, and in one desperate, gasping second she burst into flames, no longer a woman, no longer a woman and a man, but a torch blazing inexplicably at the bottom of an ocean, shot through with rippling, white-hot elixirs.

The flames died down, the depths receded, and Abby felt herself wash up on the shore of consciousness. So that was what Roger had experienced, what he had kept to himself, this exquisite sea garden of the senses. The generous Gael had shared it with her.

Calum still lay atop her, his head to one side. "Abby, I love you," he panted, stroking her throat with one finger. "You are so warm and beguiling, so full of love and spirit. *Dia!* I've never seen a woman like you at all."

*Nor have I,* thought Abby. Never in all her life had she been so attuned to her own body, and she knew she had Calum to thank for it. "What did she look like?"

"She?"

"Catriona."

Abby felt his arms tremble in the darkness. "Why, she was beautiful, mistress. Surely I've told you that before."

"Her hair?"

"Black, raven black. And her eyes the color of amber. Very beautiful she was. So beautiful I hate to think of it, knowing I'll never see her again."

"More lovely than I, I suppose," murmured Abby.

Calum laughed sadly. "No, not more lovely than you, dearest calf, but different. The trout and the salmon are each a beautiful fish, but the salmon is shimmering silver and the trout is all the colors of the weaver's dyes. Magnificent, each one. But not the same sort of magnificent."

Abby fell silent. She had never heard anyone compare beautiful women to fish before. Roger had called her a swan, had said her cheeks were like roses and her eyes like violets. But Roger could never make her feel as beloved as Calum made her feel. Perhaps all things considered, it was better being a fish. She wound her arms around him and held him tight against her, afraid that at any moment he might vanish like the phantom Lydia. "Pray don't leave me, Calum."

"Nay, you've bagged me now, mistress," he murmured. "I can't leave you, nor would I ever wish to."

They fell asleep, side by side, and when Abby woke with the gray light of dawn she found Calum curled up behind her on his side, encircling her breasts with his powerful arms. Something nudged her on the bottom, though the man was fast asleep. She rolled over and peered at what had prodded her so earnestly. She touched its velvet tip, and it nodded. Calum nodded in his sleep and smiled. When he woke, he would love her again, become one with her again. She could enfold him, encircle him, engulf him, take him into the deepmost center of her heart and breathe in unison with him, at least for a short time. She did not dare think any further ahead than that.

Days passed, and so did nights of loving. But sometimes Abby lay still in Calum's arms, speaking to him about the happy years of her childhood and Lydia's, listening to him talk about Catriona and the children. She loved the rough feel of his skin against hers, the heat, the hairiness. Sometimes she stroked the smoothest places of his body, his eyelids, his ears, his horse-like haunches and the silken underside of his stones. Her fingers had almost forgotten what it was like to touch someone with love.

Late one evening, as she sat talking before the fire with Calum, Angus brought them each a cup of wine. *"Slainte mhath,"* he said. "To the good health of the bride and the groom."

Abby felt her cheeks begin to burn with shame. "What mean you, 'bride and groom'?" asked Calum warily. "Who told you anything of the sort?"

"No one told me anything," answered Angus. "I can see it well enough for myself." He cocked one eyebrow. "You're not to be wed, then?"

"I don't know," snapped Calum. "When the time is right, perhaps."

Angus looked from Calum to Abby in horror, then back to Calum. "Not wed? Is it because of Catriona, Calum? I'm certain there's no harm in wedding Abby, then seeking vengeance."

Abby gulped down the wine, and Angus poured her another cupful. "I am perfectly content to wait."

"Aye," said Angus sharply. "But you're not waiting,

are you now? It's not decent, bedding each other without being pledged."

"It can't be helped," grumbled Calum. "Abby and I are as much in love as if we were man and wife, but I made a vow, and I must keep it."

"A vow?" Abby touched his arm, but he shook off her hand.

"Indeed. A vow to Catriona. At her cairn, in the midst of the snow and ice and cold. I gave her my word I'd destroy the man who slew her and the children before I wed again."

"Foolish creature!" stormed Angus. "How long might that be? You might never find the fiend!"

Calum smiled. "If I remember correctly, 'twas you who told me I'd track him down once the snows melted. Leastways, you are complaining far more than Abby. She understands."

Angus turned his eyes upon her, and Abby turned away. She could not look into his honest eyes, eyes that tore the truth out of one's heart. "Is this true, Abby? You're willing to live as Calum's bedfellow, without his troth, until he avenges Catriona?"

Abby nodded. She forced herself to look at Angus, and was not sorry she did so. His face was full of compassion and affection, and not a little disappointment. "I am, Angus. What else can I do? Calum and I love each other, and he must do what he has sworn to do. The only alternative is to leave him, and that I'll never do."

Angus shook his head sadly. "If it must be so, then it must. You'll find the people of the district more accepting of your choice than your countrymen would be. And at least Calum will see that you don't live in want."

Calum laughed bitterly. "Come, Angus! I have nothing to give Abby. You are her provider, not I."

Angus took Abby's hand between his own. His eyes shone like lanterns in midnight darkness. "For the moment only. Come spring, mistress, Calum will rebuild Bailebeag. We were speaking about it while you lay ill. Half the people in the district will come to help us, and by harvest time we'll have a fine house, fit for a chieftain's wife."

Abby recalled what Niall had told her. It was true, then; Calum was Highland gentry, though possessions and position meant almost nothing to her now. Roger had inherited great wealth, but what good had it brought to him or his family? It all went into the bullpen, the cockpit, the card hall, the gaming den, into the pockets of cheats, rakes and scoundrels. In the end it had killed him and thrust Lydia into the hands of a madman.

Abby had seen the poverty of the Gaels. It was brutal, but not shameful. It ground families down but did not destroy them, as Roger's riches had destroyed him.

Abby stroked Calum's cheek and patted the great blue scar that had frightened her so badly at the Heart's-ease. "I should like a house, Angus. But if having Calum meant living outdoors under a plaid in the wind and snow, it would be enough for me."

"A pretty fancy, mistress, but not true," snorted Calum. "You did not fare very well in the snow, if you remember."

"A little house then," she conceded, "just the essentials of living. A few utensils, some pottery, warm clothing and sufficient victuals . . ."

". . . A formal garden, a clavier, a dozen servants, a coach and six . . ."

"Nay, sir! You mock me!" She knew Calum was teasing; still, she could not resist giving the Gael a good thump on the shoulder, which only made him laugh. "I need nothing save you. And Lydia, of course."

"Well, you have me, mistress," he admitted. "Not the way you'd prefer me, perhaps, but I will do what I can to remedy that." He wrapped his iron arms around her and kissed her forehead. "While I have breath, you will always have your Calum Og."

That night, in Calum's arms, Abby dreamt of her wedding. But it was she and Roger being married, not she and Calum. The ceremony was long and tedious, the worthy old minister properly stiff and sour. Abby did not know any of the people present, and kept looking under furniture and in dark corners for Lydia and Angus' children. During the ceremony afterward, she wove between people who had no faces, calling Calum's name, while all around her swirled an endless noise sprinkled with snippets of gossip and the sounds of glasses breaking. Hundreds of sweetmeats lay heaped on tables all around her—chocolate raspberry tarts, cocoa-dusted cremecakes and meringues with chocolate syrup centers—but disappeared when she tried to bite into them. She caught a glimpse of Calum gliding past her, but she could not run fast enough to catch him. When she gave up the chase and sought the wedding feast, it too had vanished, and she found herself standing alone in a small field of snow, surrounded by five small cairns.

She woke weeping.

"What is it, mistress?" said Calum, his voice hoarse with sleep. He fumbled for her with one arm and pulled her against his bare chest.

"Nothing, my love," she said, almost choking as she spoke. Perhaps she was quite wrong. Perhaps Angus was right: what they were doing was indecent. Not the same sort of indecency practiced at the Heart's-ease, perhaps, but something more passionate, more personal. She had not the slightest doubt about her devotion to the man; she cherished him. She had given up everything for him: king, country, and all the small joys that she had grown accustomed to. In return she had Calum's love and a strange new life in a strange country. But did the man indeed love her as she loved him? Would his heart ever belong to her alone? "Oh, Calum, do you think . . . do you think we shall ever wed?"

For several moments she lay in silence, listening to his heartbeat. At last he kissed her and patted her hands. "Go back to sleep, my darling," he said. "I'm sorry I can't do better by you. You have my love and pledge of faithfulness, and for now those are the best I can offer you."

His answer brought her no peace. She had the feeling she had slipped into some long ago time or deserted land she could never comprehend or fully accept. She remembered one of Roger's riddles: four legs like a horse, the tail of a horse, the head of a horse, but not a horse. She was the answer to that maggot: the shadow of a horse, the insubstantial semblance of something with substance.

Calum put his arm around her in his sleep, and she knew she had been mistaken. Her life did have substance, was in fact rich in meaning. She did belong there, right by Calum's side. She was whole, and what they were doing, while not exactly right, could not be wrong.

Time glided by like wild geese, first fortnights, then months. Abby was so happy with Calum that she had to remind herself that all was not entirely well, that Lydia was still imprisoned on a cold, dark island, her future uncertain and perilous. And Lydia was not her only worry.

Calum regularly left the house, sometimes for hours. When she asked where he'd been, he would hesitate and shrug his shoulders. He had been by himself, thinking, he'd say. A man needed time to be alone with himself.

"Calum still visits Catriona's cairn every day, doesn't he?" Abby asked Angus one morning when Calum was away.

"And the cairns of the children, too, mistress," he added. "You can hardly expect anything less of him, can you now? He loved them, loved them deeply, and they are still part of him, no matter how distant. You will have to accept this about the man, I think. He will always grieve for them. He'll never forget them."

"I shan't ask him to forget them," retorted Abby. Was she being too stubborn? Was it hoping too much to expect Calum's complete devotion? "I shall ask him to release them, however. Angus, my monthlies are a week late. Calum doesn't know. It could mean nothing, or it could mean I'm with child already. How can I share him with phantoms and memories? Once a year, twice a year, yea, four times a year . . . such memorials are appropriate. But not daily vigils."

"Well," sighed Angus, "you Saxons are different than we Gaels, as you well know. You put death away from you, bury it up and remember it only when you choose. But death walks with the Gael every day. 'Tis a part of our life, just as winter is part of the year. When a Gael visits the cairns of the dead, he puts a stone on each one, a sign that he is thinking of those who will never awaken. If a clansman goes to war he takes a stone with him, to be added to his cairn if he's slain. Often you'll find two Calums or two Morags or whatever in one family, so the name will go on, even if one child dies. Faith, Abby, you've heard our stories and our verses. The more deaths in a tale, we say, the better the tale. There's a certain happiness to be gained in recalling the dead and being grateful that you're not among them."

"Yes, yes, like the ancient Greeks," said Abby. "Angus, you must admit I have given up a great deal since I met Calum. I've given up my country, my language, my modesty . . . heavens! I even dress like a Gael! But I cannot let Calum pummel himself with guilt over something he could neither foresee nor prevent."

Angus stroked his chin. "You've given up some things, Abby, and received others in return, not least of which is Calum Og. Tell the man how you feel, Abby. Tell him about the child, too, once you're certain."

Abby waited. The ice began to melt in the streams and the shores of Loch Shiel. Icicles dripped from the thatch. The heather thrust green fingers through the snow and violets bloomed in the bogs. Once Abby saw an osprey in a dead pine. Still her monthlies didn't come.

She rose early one morning and walked to Bailebeag. Patches of snow still clung to the hillsides. The gray sky was streaked with yellow sunrise banners and the mountains were capped with mist. She found Calum at Catriona's cairn, on his knees, his head in his hands. "It was not your fault they died, you know," said Abby, coming up behind him.

Calum leaped to his feet, his sword half-drawn. "Forgive me, love. You shouldn't come here. It's no place for you."

"But it is for you, isn't it?"

Calum pulled her into his arms. "Abby, you are my only love. But I have some debts to repay before I sleep well at night."

"And I too, I assure you. I pray you please give up this ill-starred venture. If we never wed, so be it. You will be killed, and I will once again be destitute and alone."

"List, Abby. The man who killed Catriona and the weans was an Englishman named Recker. Now that the winter's dying, I can track the devil down and be done with him."

Recker, Recker. Why did the name sound so familiar? Abby remembered a flash of scarlet, a tricorn hat, a handsome, angular face, a dead horse—the major on the moor. "I met an English major on the road to the isles, just before I reached the kyle," she whispered into his chest.

"What? You met what?" Calum pushed her away and held her from him at arm's length.

"An English major. Ricket, Rackham, Redland . . . oh, I can't remember! But he was a proper gentleman."

"Proper gentleman, my arse!" spat Calum. "That was the man, I'm sure of it!" He would have bolted from her, but she gripped his belt and held it fast.

"Where are you going?"

"Why, to the kyle, of course, woman, to find this Recker-ricker-racket and relieve him of the task of carrying his head about with him."

"Nay, Calum! You must help me rescue Lydia first. You swore you would. Have you forgotten? No, of course you haven't. Calum, your vengeance can wait, but Lydia cannot. Every day she is more brutalized, more abused, more degraded."

"Abused? In what way?"

"Intimately, I believe, in some fashion. I don't know. But Niall said you were the only man who had any hope of wresting her from Duninnis."

"The dog!" Calum slammed his fist against his scabbard. "Harming a lass! He'll have nothing to hurt her with when I'm finished with him, the wicked *bodag!* Very well. That decides it. Duninnis first and the good major second." Again he began to pull away from her, and again she kept him close.

"A moment more, pray. My love, you should know this. 'What journey do all living make, yet none a single step must take?' "

"A riddle? Now? You Saxons! Well, life, I suppose. Nay, nay, the journey through the womb. Birth." Suddenly Calum stared at her as if she had instantly materialized before him. "Abby, is it so? Have you taken already? Me, a da again?"

Abby placed his hand on her still-slender belly. "It is. I am. You are."

Calum's face seemed to break into a thousand pieces as he smiled, grinned, then threw back his head and bugled exactly like a red stag. Abby shied away, then laughed and threw her arms around him. Someday, she told herself, she would become used to the wild ways of the Gaels. "Now you see?" crowed Calum. "I must hurry and make good on my vow, so we can be wed before we become ma and da."

They were halfway home, his plaid around her shoulders, when he broke away from her and loped back toward Bailebeag without a word of explanation. In a very short time he was back by her side, sweating and panting. "Where were you, love?" she asked. "Is something amiss?"

"Not now," he puffed. "A stone. I had to put a stone on each cairn."

Abby walked home beside him in silence.

# Thirteen

## Chess Games

March 25, 1716
My Dearest Diana,

Oh, for an English spring! Cherries blossoming along the lanes, the smell of hyacinths, lambs gamboling in green meadows . . . all these I deeply miss, as well as your dear company, beloved Diana!

The weather here is foul. Prolonged rains, mitigated only by an occasional hour or so of palest sunshine. At least the snow and ice are greatly diminished. The inhabitants of the village where we are encamped have undertaken some hunting excursions, which is well, as my men are heartily sick of oat flour and well nigh famished. This is very poor for morale, as you may well imagine. The spirits of the Scotch troops are somewhat less dampened, since they are accustomed to mean fare and miserable weather.

Good news for us, my dear. I shall soon be returning home, as I have had explicit orders to march south and await reappointment. It is highly likely that a permanent garrison of His Majesty's troops will be established in this area to prevent further uprisings and revolts among these warlike people. You will be pleased to hear, I'm sure, that your own dutiful husband is being seriously *considered to lead this enterprise. Although, of course, this would mean some absence from you for some time, it would be a great honor as well as an excellent opportunity for me to be of service to His Majesty.*

*With good luck, I should return to you within the next two months. Until then, I beg you keep your spirits high and pray for my safe and rapid return. The messenger who brings you this letter may be entrusted with your own to me.*

*Ever your humble servant and devoted husband,*
*Thomas*

The major sealed the letter and delivered it himself into the hands of the courier. It was only right and proper that Diana be the first to be advised of his approaching good fortune, since she would be the one most hard-pressed because of it.

Two grenadiers sidled out of his way, saluting, as he stalked past. There had been seven more desertions during the past fortnight, despite the serious punishments meted out to those who were caught and returned. One erring private had even perished under the lash. Some of Captain Campbell's men had also stolen off, but the Gael never seemed able to retrieve them.

"Bring me my gray," the major commanded one of the grenadiers.

"Riding to the hounds are you again, major?" Racker turned and saw Campbell not five paces from him, his rheumy Scotch eyes rolling wildly in his head. "Take care you don't break your neck. What would your lads in breeks do without you to hold them in line?"

"They could most surely not depend on you," answered the major. "The only thing you Scotch can line is a female."

"Perhaps," growled the captain, "but there is a thin

line between doing one's duty and abusing one's men. Perhaps you've crossed that line, major. 'Tis my opinion that, should you drive any more men away, you'll not have enough left to hold this position. From Jacobites, of course. Sir."

The grenadier arrived with the major's mount, and Racker vaulted into the saddle. "If I were you, captain, I would not be giving suggestions to my superiors on how to comport oneself. You have come dangerously close to defying my orders on occasion. And if I ever have proof of your insubordination, I promise you, there shall be lines on your back and perhaps one round your neck."

The major cantered off toward the broad white beach, the captain's laughter drifting away behind him. Perhaps, perhaps there was some way to hasten the inevitable destruction of Captain Campbell.

The next morning the major rode along the shore again, drawn by impulse. A woman walked along the strand, gathering seaweed and shellfish in a wicker basket she carried on her head. Racker gazed at her for a long time before riding away. The next day he returned with a Campbell soldier, and together they watched the same woman plucking kelp and pulling mussels from rocks.

"Is it she?" asked the major. "Is she his?"

"Indeed she is, sir," replied the Scot. "Sorcha Bheag, she's called, the joy of the captain's heart."

"I thought as much. Are you certain?"

"Aye, certain. You wouldn't be wanting her for yourself, would you now, major, sir?"

"Insolent dog! A dirty creature such as this, crawling with vermin and hardened by labor? Let the captain have her. You are dismissed. Speak to no one of this."

The man stared up at him, frightened but intrigued. "As you wish, major. I am silent."

A storm set in for four days, and when it cleared the major returned to the beach, alone. The woman was far up the shore among the rocks, where the wind had driven the kelp. He rode up behind her, calling out to attract her attention, wishing that he knew just a few words of her language. The woman turned toward him. The smile on her face faded when she saw his red uniform, his wig, his stern expression. Still, he was sure she suspected nothing.

She murmured something in her strange tongue, and whatever she said seemed deferential enough. She was actually rather attractive, with long yellow hair and bright eyes that matched the green of the ocean. Had he cared at all for women, thought the major, he might have considered sparing her. Ridiculous! That would have ruined his plan.

With a headache building inside his skull, the major drew his pistol and trained it on the woman's forehead. Her eyes grew as round as coins. He could smell her fear. Any moment she would fling her basket from her head and try to flee.

Racker fired.

The woman collapsed. A red hole gaped where her right eye had been. The smell of blood mingled with the smell of seaweed, decaying fish and saltwater. The major felt his stomach lurch inside him. Wheeling his horse about, he galloped back to Ardnamurchan with triumph in his heart.

"Calum, this place frightens me so!" Abby shivered as she stepped from the boat and looked up at the fortress of Duninnis, black against the slate-gray sky. "Do you really think we have any hope of saving Lydia?"

"Certainly so, woman, or I wouldn't have brought you here," answered Calum. "I will proceed, you and Angus will be right behind me. You have nothing to fear."

"Only keep your shawl about your head so they don't perceive who you are straight away," advised Angus.

"And keep your neb shut, too," added Calum. "You talk like a Saxon, even when you speak the Gaelic."

Abby let them rush her along, up the path from the beach to the fortress, through the forest of diminutive trees, now hesitantly green. She wished Niall were with them, or even Angus' children. The drover was always so practical and reassuring, and his wisdom had once saved her life. As for the children, she had come to miss them almost as much as she missed Lydia. But, no. As Calum had told her, he and Angus were enough for the task; the children were happy staying with their auntie, and there was no need to bother Niall, who had a family of his own to care for.

Their arrival at the gate caused a small commotion among the guards and the clansfolk there, but after Calum had had a few words with the sentries, all three of them were shown inside. Abby recognized Badger among their armed escort, and drew her shawl so low over her face she could scarcely see. She could hear her heart pounding. Her breath came short and fast. Lydia was only rooms, perhaps only footsteps away from her! She could smell roses and hear the sound of her daughter's voice, pleading with her to hurry.

Duninnis' men ushered them into a small, cozy chamber aglow with firelight. Turkish carpeting covered the floor and shelves full of books lined the walls. Abby searched the room, peering into each shadow, but Duninnis was not there. She inched herself onto a straight-backed chair and waited, clenching and unclenching her hands in her lap.

Calum took a book from a shelf, paged through it and replaced it. "This is some sort of gaming room, I ween," he said, pointing to a small wooden table with a marble top contrived in black and white squares. "Here's a chessboard."

Abby looked about and saw that many of the book-shelves contained boxes of gaming pieces: chessmen, cards, dice and dicecups. The room reminded her of the many forays she had made into gaming houses in London and later Glasgow, trying to persuade Roger to return home. She had never been successful. She had even gone to a bull pit to fetch him back, but only once. The cries of the dogs and the terrified roaring of the bull had frightened her away before she could find her husband.

"I detest this room, Calum," she whispered.

"Aye, but it suits our purposes, if worse comes to worst."

He was about to say more when the latch rattled and the door swung open. Two deerhound bitches bounded into the room, followed by their master. Duninnis was dressed in skin-tight tartan trews that made him appear even leaner than when Abby had first seen him. He strode into the room slowly, gracefully, his head high and a little to one side, as if one ear were heavier than the other. Badger entered behind him and closed the door.

"My dear cousin!" cried Duninnis.

"My lord," replied Calum. The two men embraced each other with stiff arms. The deerhounds came up to Calum and thrust their muzzles under his sporran. "Hallo, Brida! Good girl, Luath! You recognize me, I see," he crooned, stroking their bristled faces.

"Back, back, ill-mannered brutes!" snapped the chieftain. "It's fortunate people have better eyesight than dogs, isn't it, Calum? Now, let me see . . . I know your foster brother, Angus," said the chief. "And the lady?"

"A dear friend who wished to accompany me."

Duninnis bowed. Abby gave a little nod, though every inch of her flesh prodded her to return the bow with a curtsey. If he recognized her through her shawl, he gave no sign of it. "I was sore grieved to hear of your loss, cousin," said the chieftain, "though for certain you brought it on your own head. There are no red soldiers here, you see. Now, if you were to place your allegiance where it should be, with the House of Hanover and Scotland's true and only king, then you'd never have to live like a coney, in constant fear and worry."

"I did not come to Skye to speak of politics," grumbled Calum, seating himself in a heavily embroidered chair. "Have you no whisky for your weary kinsfolk, cousin?"

Duninnis immediately pointed to a black lacquer cabinet, and Badger opened it. Inside were at least a dozen flasks and decanters full of ruby wines and tawny liquors that sparkled in the firelight. "I am indeed a poor host," murmured Duninnis, "but what I lack in grace I can make up in quantity. You see, I am never very far from the water of life. It sustains my heart and fortifies my poor, sick body." He sank into a chair, and the dogs curled up at his feet, sighing.

Badger poured whisky into four glasses and distributed them around the room. "Now," said the chieftain, "just what brings you to Skye, cousin?"

"To be frank, my lord, you are obliged to me for a sum of silver," said Calum.

"Aye, it's true. Badger, fetch my sporran."

"Wait a bit, if you please. I'd just as soon have the debt repaid in other coin."

"What?" Duninnis sipped from his glass, and it seemed to Abby that the man was smiling. Perhaps he thought Calum had arranged some jest or game or amusement, which, in truth, was not too far from the mark. Abby closed her eyes. Dear God, she prayed to herself, let me not lose a sweetheart as well as a daughter. "What sort of coin is this?"

"Well, not a coin at all, cousin," said Calum. Abby noticed that Calum's fingers were white from gripping the arms of his chair. He may not have been afraid, but he was most definitely alert. "You have here a young girl named Lydia Fields. It's her I want."

Duninnis sprang to his feet at once and fell back in his chair just as quickly. The dogs whimpered and started. Abby saw a flash of steel. "Calum! Badger's sword is drawn!" she cried in English. She jumped up so suddenly her shawl fell to her shoulders.

"You! The Saxon woman!" gasped Duninnis. "What is this, Calum? Would you slay your own kinsman for the sake of a child you've never seen?"

"My love's child," Calum corrected him, rising. "And therefore as close to my heart as any child from my groin. But I have no intention of slaying anyone. Unlike your man, there."

The chieftain glanced at Badger and waved his hand. "Put away your blade. There's no need for bloodshed, not among cousins." Badger sheathed his sword. Duninnis' face was as gray as ash, and Abby feared he might fall into a faint at any moment. "Now tell me, Calum, why have you come here, my buck?"

"Why, for not other reason than to return Lydia to her mother," Calum explained. "You have the child here, there's no point denying it. And it's widely known you're treating her without decency."

"I treat her very well indeed," snorted Duninnis, "but it would make no difference whether I did or no. Lydia is mine. You understand I can do her no real harm, no more than the caresses which are so common among lads and lasses. Less than you and this woman partake of, I ween. And while Lydia has done nothing to cure me, she has made my wretched life a little sweeter. No, I cannot part with her. I won her fairly, and there's many who'll bear witness to it."

"No!" shouted Abby. She could restrain herself no further. "You didn't win her fairly. She was never yours to win. Children are not coins or horses. You cannot rip them from their parents' bosoms. My husband had no right to wager Lydia's freedom to turn her over to you as a plaything for your amusement. He most assuredly did not have my permission to do so."

The chieftain shrugged. "Nevertheless, mistress, I have her. You do not. Calum shall have the silver I owe him, and then I must ask all of you to take your leave."

Abby looked at Calum. He shot her a quick glance and clapped his hand on his sporran. They were not done gambling just yet. "Do you care to make a wager, cousin?"

"Wager?" The chieftain's eyes gleamed with anticipation.

"Aye, a wager for Lydia." Calum fished six dice from his sporran. They were weighted, Abby knew. Playing with those dice, Calum would never lose unless he wished to. "If I win, she comes with us. If you win, we swear to forego all claims to her."

"And?" Duninnis brought his hands together, then

spread them out wide. "Come, come, cousin! Make your wager worth my while."

Calum sighed and gave a nervous laugh. "I have nothing to ante."

"Not at the moment," said the chieftain, smiling. "But you will, probably within the year, if I am good judge of men and women. A little son or daughter that I can bring up as my own."

*"Nooo!"* Abby tried to scream, but her voice was the whine of a frightened child. The two bitches turned their bearded faces toward her in astonishment. "Absolutely not!" How could she risk losing one child for the sake of saving another? Only a demon would make such a request.

"Abby, we have no choice."

"Aye, you do," said Angus quietly. "You can wager my house. I own it and the lands it sits on."

"In that case, we have no game," said Duninnis with a scowl. "What use do I have for a house in MacDonald country? Get yourselves gone."

His words echoed in silence. After a moment Abby spoke up. "Very well," she whispered. "But the game must be dice. Calum is very lucky with dice."

"Nay, nay, no games of chance," said the chieftain, fanning the air with his hand, as if to brush away her suggestion. "A game of skill, a game of cunning and strategy, where fate plays no role in the victory." His hand fell outspread upon the checkered top of the little gaming table. "Such as chess."

"Done," said Calum.

Abby stared at him in terror. Her clever, practical lover had gone completely mad. "No! That is . . . Calum, you cannot play the game."

Calum gave her a wink. "True enough, mistress. But you can."

"You? A woman? A chess player?" jeered the chieftain.

"Yes, if it please you," returned Abby. Roger had loved the game and had taught her well. She had often played for pin money and usually won it. But besides Roger, she had never played anyone but several of his pot companions, who were often too deep in their cups to play very skillfully, and Calum. If Duninnis chose chess as the game, it was undoubtedly because he was an expert player. But if she did not play, Lydia was lost.

"I don't play against women," snorted Duninnis.

"Fancy that!" cried Calum. "A man afeared of losing to a woman!"

"I am afraid of no one," said Duninnis gravely. "But I don't wish to take advantage of the poor *quean*."

Abby swallowed hard. "I pray you, if we must contest over the freedom of my unfortunate child, let me be her champion. If I lose the game, I promise I shall cause you no further embarrassment, and you shall have the child within me this very moment." Duninnis cocked one eyebrow. "Only I beg of you, send your man away. His presence unnerves me."

"Done!" barked Duninnis. "Begone, Badger. Wait outside the door. Angus, you join him and await the outcome. Calum, you I trust. You may stay and witness my victory. It will be a brief match, I assure you."

The old man poured himself another cup of whisky from a crystal decanter, and Abby could not help but see that his hands trembled as he held the glass. Was he as ill as he claimed to be, or did he simply drink too freely? Whatever the answer, she could not afford to play a timid game; on the contrary, she would not allow the chieftain a moment's rest.

Abby settled herself opposite Duninnis. When he thrust out both hands before her, she chose his left. In it lay a white pawn, giving her the advantage of the first move. She sent out her king's knight. On her next move she dispatched the queen's horse, then briskly opened up her front line of defense, sacrificing a third of her pawns and one knight in the first few minutes of play.

"Mistress, we needn't prolong your ordeal. You may concede whenever you wish," murmured the old chieftain, as he stooped to caress one of the hounds. Two crimson spots now glowed on his death-pale face and his jabot rose and fell with the labor of his breath. He took another sip of whisky.

Abby felt Calum's strong hand on her shoulder. "Why, my lord, she has scarcely begun." She began a vicious attack with the queen, working the piece close to black bishops, knights and pawns, always just a hair's breadth from capture, always forcing the chieftain to defend himself.

Time slipped past without meaning. Abby forgot why she was playing, forgot that Lydia existed, forgot the firm hand that never left her shoulder. The only things that mattered were her relentless attack, the growing sheen of sweat on Duninnis' forehead, and the decreasing whisky in the decanter. The board was a jumble of black and white, yet she saw a beautiful order begin to take place upon it. She had thirteen pieces remaining; the old man had lost but three pawns.

"There is no point in playing any further," whined Duninnis. He ran his kerchief over his dripping face. "The game is mine, as any fool can see."

"Well, this fool cannot see it," growled Calum. "The

woman is playing for her child, man. Let her play as she wishes, to the bitter end." His grip on her shoulder tightened, and Abby wondered whether even he might have begun to doubt her gamesmanship. A drop of water fell from her brow onto the board but she did not disturb it.

When she had but six pieces left, Abby moved her queen into certain capture. It was a calculated move, intended to set Duninnis' mind at ease and tap him toward the abyss of over-confidence. Roger had used the same tactic against her to successfully distract her from some larger, more lethal business. The chieftain's hand swooped down toward the queen, then paused and hung in mid-air. Duninnis looked about the board with great concern before finally nabbing the piece and tossing it into a small box, nearly filled with white chessmen.

"I suggest you concede now, mistress. What use is there in continuing?" Pearls of sweat ran down the chieftain's long nose, and he dashed them away with the cuff of his sleeve. "This game is not meant for the delicate sensibilities of your sex."

"I'm sure her sex has nothing at all to do with her skill at chess," said Calum.

Abby heard the men as if they were standing at one end of a bridge and she at the other. Their words were distant, insignificant and meaningless. From somewhere a clock struck the hour, but she could not count the strokes. She heard the dogs panting and smelled their musty, outdoor odor. She had never felt so sure of herself before, so tense with power and control. Not a breath was taken but she commanded it, not an atom moved but she was aware of it. Her flesh had turned to steel, her nerves were the cogs within the fine German timepiece Roger had once borne so proudly in his pocket. From the shadow of a black square she urged her last horse forward into the arms of Duninnis' bishop. The chieftain studied the board for some time, then, with shaking fingers, removed the knight from the board.

Abby watched her hand sail across the board and land on one of her two remaining pawns. The polished wood felt as cool and smooth as Calum's silver swordhilt. She wished she could remain forever at the chessboard, locked in that moment, the elegant chesspiece eternally poised for conquest. Apparently under its own volition, the pawn glided forward two squares until it stood diagonally opposite the imposing black king. The royal victim, surrounded by its own men, had no route of escape. The white assassin, guarded by Abby's own king, was unassailable. Her hand, its duties over, retreated into her lap. She closed her eyes and clenched both fists. Thank God for Roger! The game hadn't absolved him, but it made him cease to be evil. She saw him clearly now, a pathetic creature driven, not by reason, but by sickness. He would have been proud of her. "Checkmate, m'lord."

Duninnis stared at the board, his face as still and white as carved marble. "Impossible," he whispered at last. "I have not lost a game in three years."

"Why, if you haven't lost, then take your turn," urged Calum. Abby opened her eyes as his free hand leaped onto her shoulder with a mighty clap. His voice rang with pride and relief. "Go on, then, take your turn. What, would you let a mere woman defeat you in a manly game of skill? Go on with you, cousin!" The Gael brought his lips next to her ear. *"Gle mhath, mo ghraidh!* Brilliant! Ingenuous!"

Abby allowed herself a small smile. Every muscle in her body seemed to sigh and give way, and as they did so, a hundred tiny pains ran up and down her arms, legs and back. She felt her skin begin to burn with anticipation. "I would like to see Lydia now, Duninnis."

But the chieftain did not seem to hear her. He continued to gaze at the board as if it had bitten him. His cheeks glowed blood-red. His eyes swelled until they seemed to occupy his entire face. And then, like a bubble burst with a pin, he folded into himself and collapsed deep in his chair. The two bitches sat up, sniffed his legs and began to whine.

"Calum! He's in a swoon!" cried Abby.

"Can't abide losing, can he?" mumbled Calum. He hurried to the chieftain's side and tried to rouse him. He rubbed the old man's cheeks and pinched his wasted arms to no avail. The dogs growled and whimpered, staring at Calum with solemn, amber-colored eyes. *"Nighean mhath, nighean mhath,"* he comforted them, scratching their ears.

Duninnis did not awaken.

With a growing sense of dread, Abby noticed a dark stain spreading across the front of the chieftain's trews. "My love, he's lost his water," she whispered.

The Gael looked at the stain and cursed. He grabbed the old man's wrist, then laid his head on his kinman's narrow chest. Calum's face grew as white as the chieftain's. "Abby, do not raise your voice lest Badger come running. List to me, now. The old devil has won, after all. He's as dead as a drowned rat."

"Dead!" Abby mouthed the word. "Are you certain?"

"Aye, I am," sighed Calum, rising. "Though he could hardly have chosen a more awkward time."

"Why, then we must tell Badger!" Abby started from her chair.

"Nay!" cried Calum, under his breath but with such force that Abby sank back into her seat. "We'll tell no one, save perhaps Angus. If Duninnis' people know he's dead, they'll not be likely to listen to reason, and we'll have some unpleasant explaining to be doing. So . . . Duninnis is sleeping. Do you hear, mistress? Don't look so aghost at me, woman!"

Calum moved the black king to a place of safety on the board. "There, now. This game was never finished, Abby. Do you see? Never finished."

"I don't understand," said Abby. An icy fear had completely replaced her brief glow of triumph. "I've won Lydia. The board proved I won her. Now all is as it was before, and we are powerless to free her."

"Abby, list to me!" Calum caught her by the elbows, and for half an instant she thought he might strike her. "Duninnis is asleep. He fell asleep during the game, before it could be completed. Badger won't dare try to rouse him. If he thought the old man had lost the wager, he'd be suspicious, wouldn't he? He'd wonder how Duninnis could have fallen asleep after such a loss. It wouldn't do to pretend he won, either, for the same reason. We'll tell Badger you have conceded the game and that we'll be leaving and not coming back. By the time Duninnis' people discover the truth, we'll be back safe in Glenfinnan, halfway to Glenalagan. It will look as though the old creature passed away in his sleep. Indeed, there's not a mark on him."

"But . . . but what about Lydia?"

"I don't know."

"With Duninnis dead, these people won't have any use for her, Calum. They'll kill her!" She began to weep.

"No, they won't," he assured her. "I'll find her." To her complete surprise, Calum knelt by one of the grieving dogs and dabbed his kerchief under her tail until the cloth was soaked with the animal's essence.

"What in God's name are you doing?" she hissed through her tears.

"Lydia has a lapdog, hasn't she?"

"Yes, Tip by name. She is never without him."

"Well, I have a crazy-mad idea, but pay me no mind. If anything can be done for our Lydia, I'll do it. I swear it on my heart. Go on weeping, if you will. Tears will make you look defeated."

"The dogs?" she sobbed.

" 'Tis better to leave them than try to remove them, I think."

Calum returned to the dead chieftain and rearranged the corpse so that, to the unsuspicious, it would appear as if Duninnis had fallen asleep. Calum drew the man's eyelids shut and hid the telltale stain with a mohair blanket Abby had discovered on a chair. When the work was finished, Abby could almost believe the old man was still alive, nestled in the blanket, his sunken face half hidden in the soft folds of the cloth.

Angus and Badger were sitting just outside the chamber, perched on the edge of two hard chairs. Had they moved at all during the game? wondered Abby. The face of the standing clock in the anteroom made her gasp: the deadly wager had lasted three full hours.

"You've been playing with the dogs," muttered Badger, wrinkling his nose.

Abby barely listened to Calum as he spun his story to Badger, and could scarcely nod her head when Calum asked her if she had conceded the game. Somehow she found herself moving through dark corridors, almost floating in Calum's and Angus' hands. Somewhere in this darkness Lydia was waiting for her, searching for her, calling to her.

"Something is wrong, brother," she heard Angus whisper to Calum. "Your mouth and your eyes are saying two different things."

"Duninnis is supping with the devil tonight," answered the Gael.

*"Dia!* He's dead? Did you strike him?"

"Not a bit," snorted Calum. "Abby played like an angel. She whipped the fellow like a dog, and he rolled over and died. The old man aye hated to lose a bet."

By the time they reached the courtyard, Abby could not feel her feet upon the flagstones. Her mind could not tear itself away from the awful thought that she had both won and lost. She had done as she was supposed to, played well, even courageously. But what use was any of that? Fate had wanted to keep her from Lydia. She could fight forever, but she could not defeat fate.

Abby felt Calum's hand on her cheek, but as she turned to look into his face her eyes saw only smudges of color, a flash of blue, a blur of red. Her exhausted body began dragging her down toward the earth and a comforting, velvet-black nothingness seeped into her mind.

All she longed for was sleep.

# *Fourteen*

*Calum Tries His Hand at It*

"Abby!" Calum crouched beside her and cradled her head in his hands. "She's fallen into a faint, brother."

"What shall we do, Calum?"

"Why, take her to the boat. Tell the boatman you must cross tonight. If he won't take you, find a boat yourself and row across."

"Me?" murmured Angus. "I'm not an oarsman."

"Any man worth his porridge can row a boat across the kyle," grumbled Calum.

"And you? You won't be with us?"

"Nay, I will just have a hand at trying to find Lydia. Don't be fretting over me, now. With luck, I'll have until morning to find her and get her over the kyle. I can row with the best of them, if need be, ye ken."

"That's with luck. And there's ice in the water still," warned Angus.

"Not so much, and anyway, it can't be helped. A little ice won't trouble a stout boat."

Calum lifted Abby into Angus' arms and gave her a swift kiss on the forehead. Then he slipped her ever-present stringpurse from her wrist.

"You'll be needing that?" asked Angus.

"Aye, I hope I will. Farewell, brother. Take good care

of my dear one and the little lamb. God be with you and them, and if He sees fit, with me and my new daughter."

Calum turned and trotted back inside the fortress. Not a soul came up to stop him from entering, but he hadn't taken three steps on the wooden floor before Badger was beside him. "You were just leaving," said the big man.

"Aye, but your master generously allowed me to look about a bit before I go," stalled Calum. "I have never seen such a fine house. Not even my chief's can match it."

"Out with you now," said Badger, with half a smile. He was not being vicious, Calum knew. Only efficient.

"You wouldn't turn me out without my silver, would you now? I've traveled aye far for it."

Badger shook his wild, rat-colored hair away from his eyes. "I can fetch the sporran, but I cannot give you the silver, man. Only Duninnis can do that. Shall I wake him for you?"

Calum drew a deep breath. *It's a pity you cannot,* he thought. "Nay, don't bother the old gentleman. He needs his rest. Be so good as to find me a place to stay the night, and I'll ask him for my silver come morning."

"Can you not stay with your brother and the woman?" growled Badger.

Calum grinned and shrugged his shoulders. "I might, if I knew where they were. Abby was not well, and Angus hurried her off before I could speak with him. 'Tis too cold and dark to go looking for them now, don't you think?"

Badger grunted, stroking his charcoal-black chin. "I suppose. Come with me, son of Donald." The man led Calum through a narrow corridor and down an even narrower staircase. The sounds of laughter and excited voices were distinct at the top of the stairs and grew stronger and louder as Calum descended. At the bottom, the stairway opened into a wide, bright kitchen, filled with all manner of men and women in various degrees of inebriation. At once Calum understood: the servants of the house were taking full advantage of their master's long chess game and longer nap to indulge in a little sport of their own. They roared in welcome when they saw Calum's unfamiliar face and dragged him and Badger into their midst. Someone pushed a full cup of whisky into Calum's hands and he drained it dry. It seemed that sleep was not on anyone's mind that night.

Calum waited for an opportunity to leave. When he saw Badger down his fifth cup of whisky, Calum pulled his plaid well over his head and made his way up the staircase, trailed by a cloud of song and laughter. Not a soul had missed him, he was certain. Before him, the house divided itself into a Chinese puzzlebox of hallways, rooms and staircases. How long would it take him to find Lydia in such a place? How long did he have to find her? He pulled the kerchief from his jacket and held the offensive cloth as far out in front of him as he could reach. The corridor filled up with the stench of a bitch in heat. A good dog might bark if he smelled a stranger walk by his mistress' room, reasoned Calum. Or he might not, if he were accustomed to strangers. But if the stink of the kerchief didn't seize the attention of Lydia's spaniel, then nothing would.

With soft, slow steps he made his way up a darkened staircase, past the trophy-heads of many a stag and wildcat and the painted heads of many long dead chieftains of Duninnis. He stalked every hall and narrow passageway, every niche and alcove, guided only by the feeble light of tallow candles in bronze sconces on the walls. Once two serving girls rushed past him, far too intent on some gossip they were sharing to pay him much mind. A boy saw him, and later an old man, but both only nodded to him before scuttling past.

Just as he was about to curse himself for a complete fool, Calum heard a bark. He waited, and again the barking of a dog, a small dog, came echoing to him from overhead. In no time at all he found a stairway and ascended it, his feet flying up the steps, the kerchief thrust before him.

A bark, a yip, and the faint music of a female voice, hushing the dog: the sounds were clear and sweet.

Calum rushed through a passage, following the sounds, and nearly ran into a door that rose out of nowhere, straight against his nose. A dog whimpered, and a scrabbling of claws rattled the door. The scent of lavender was almost cloying. "Badger, is it you? Please, tell the master I cannot see him."

Calum halted, one hand frozen on the latch. If he had not known Abby was far away, safe with Angus, he would have sworn she was behind the heavy door, badly frightened, her voice ashake and aquiver. That voice had to belong to Abby's daughter. Would the terrified girl open her door to a stranger? he wondered. "Aye, Lydia, 'tis Badger," he answered, imitating the big man's well-deep tones. "I must see you. The master has naught to do with this."

Silence followed. Finally Lydia spoke again, her voice a little steadier. "Open up, then, Badger. You have the key, haven't you?"

*Dia!* The sons of hell kept the poor creature under lock and key, denying her even the poor freedom to roam the cold, dismal halls. Without hesitating a heartbeat, Calum spread his plaid over the latch and pulled his steel pistol from his jacket. With one clean stroke, he smashed the weapon's hammer-like butt against the latch. The door swung open.

Before him stood a younger, very much smaller Abby, wearing a white silk nightdress and cradling a small dog in her arms. Her nut-brown hair fell to her shoulders in smooth, glossy waves. Her mouth was wide open in a soundless scream. Calum had never seen such a beautiful creature before; he could not keep himself from staring at her, imagining Abby in her childhood. "Lydia? You are Lydia, are you not?"

The girl snapped her mouth shut and nodded. The dog growled, and she hushed him into silence. "Who are you? Is Badger here? Please, I beg you, don't touch me. Don't let Badger see me."

Calum shook his head. "No one is going to harm you, lass, least of all myself, and Badger is occupied with other pursuits. My name is Calum Og MacDonald, and I've come to fetch you from this hell on earth, if you wish to leave, which I'm sure you must."

"Fetch me?" breathed the girl.

"Aye, bring you to your mother. She would be here herself, but she was a bit faint and had to leave the island. I'll have both of you together before cockcrow." If God grants me a miracle, he added to himself.

"My mother is dead."

Calum could not help but laugh. "Nonsense, lass! I spoke with her less than an hour ago."

The girl stood transfixed, her eyes like silver coins glowing in the candlelight. "Duninnis said she was dead. 'Your mother and father are both dead,' he told me."

"Damn the brute!" Calum cursed under his breath. "Duninnis was lying, child. Your da is dead, 'tis true. He suffered a . . . mishap. But your mama is as alive as I, or more so." Suddenly he remembered Abby's bag and wrenched it out of his sporran. Ripping open the string-purse, he held up a small square of white cloth rainbowed with embroidery.

Lydia touched the kerchief with a trembling hand, then sniffed her fingers. "That's my needlework," she whispered. "I gave it to my mother, years ago when I was little. I can smell her rosewater on the linen." A single tear glistened on her cheek. "Where did you get it?"

Calum touched the girl's arm, as much to assure himself that she was real as to comfort her. Lydia shuddered. *What have they been doing to the poor thing?* wondered the Gael. "From your mother, of course, *mo nighean.* Now come. We've no time to tarry. Dress in your warmest clothing and your strongest shoes."

For a moment the girl remained motionless, then suddenly flung open the immense wardrobe that dominated the chamber, pulled out a few garments, and scurried behind a lacquered screen. In a short time she emerged, red-faced and breathless, wearing a frock of heavy green velvet and sturdy leather boots. Calum nodded in satisfaction. "Aye, that's grand. I hope there's nothing you wish to take with you."

"My Bible." Lydia searched a nearby shelf, seized a slim volume and slipped it into her camisole. "And Tip, of course."

Calum glanced down at the spaniel, lying on his mistress' feet. "I'm afeared you must leave him here, lass. One yelp from him and we'll be discovered."

Lydia looked up at him, desperation and defiance flickering over her face. How often he had seen the same conviction in her mother's eyes! "Then I shan't go."

"Devil take it!" snorted Calum. "Would you endure Duninnis and slight your mother for the sake of a worth-less tyke?"

The girl trembled but said nothing.

He could force the hoyden to obey him, but she might cry out and alert the house. Then again, the dog might do the same. He searched his mind for a solution. Lydia loved Tip, that much was clear. She probably thought she had no friend on earth save the brainless tailwagger. "Very well, child. I'll bind the creature's muzzle and take him with us. But keep him quiet, or your mother will be sore disappointed come the morrow."

Calum tore a strip of linen from Lydia's bedsheets and, with her help, bound the little dog's jaws tightly shut. Tip growled as Lydia picked him up and held him to her chest. "He is very discomfited."

"I'm none too comfortable myself, lass, what with twenty strong gillies within earshot of us and Badger not far behind them. Now enough of this! In you get!" Calum spread open his plaid, forming a roomy pouch.

The child's face grew as pink as a rose. "Into that? I am to go into that?"

"Aye," he answered. "Shepherds carry lambs this way, and you are my lamb now. We can't risk letting you be seen, can we, my heart? Don't fret yourself. 'Tis clean and dry and smells like heather on a summer's day. In with you, now! Hurry, and mind the tyke."

Lydia hesitated, then climbed into Calum's plaid with Tip in her arms: Calum lurched sideways. Who would have thought such a dainty creature could have weighed so much? He shifted his broadsword to his other hip to balance his burden.

Step by step he retraced his way through the twisting puzzle of passages, now and then passing a serving maid or gillie. They all nodded their respects to him, his due as a very, very distant cousin to their master. He stopped only once to catch his breath and reassure the quivering lamb within his plaid. His heart filled with tenderness for the brave lass, and he imagined how joyful Abby would be to see her beloved daughter again.

Finally they reached a side door opening onto a narrow staircase. On each side of the doorway lay two strapping fellows, each with a Spanish musket sprawled across his lap. Both men were dead to the world with drink and snoring like dogs in a kennel. Calum could scarcely believe his good fortune. Had he known it would have been such an easy matter to spirit Lydia from Duninnis' fortress, he thought, he would have left the spaniel unmuzzled to make the task a little more of a challenge. He would certainly have to invent some dangers and disasters when he retold the story to Abby and Angus.

Calum stepped over the slumbering sentries as if he were traversing a narrow mountain path, but he was still so off balance he brushed one fellow's outstretched arm. *"De tha seo?"* cried the man. "What is this?" Calum stopped dead, his heart frozen within him, and began breathing again only when he realized the guard was speaking in his sleep.

Halfway down the stairway, Calum thought he heard a shout from within. He paused to listen, then went on his way. The servants would pay for their revelry with headaches in the morning, he thought.

Once down the stairs, Calum helped Lydia disentangle herself from his plaid and took her by the hand. Together they hurried toward the beach, Calum forcing himself to take short strides that allowed Lydia to keep pace with him. The poor lass was hobbled by her frock and panted as she ran.

At the boatman's house all was dark. Calum decided not to wake the fellow, since Angus had clearly not had any luck convincing the boatman to take his vessel out that night. The ferryboat lay beached close by, gleaming in the moonlight like a great white horse. The breakers crashed on the shore, just out of reach of the sleek wooden craft.

"To the boat, lass!" cried Calum, giving her a gentle nudge. He fished a few coins out of his sporran and laid them on the boatman's threshold, reminding himself to leave the boat on the other side of the kyle where the fellow could easily find it on the morrow. What a pity it was, thought Calum, looking wistfully at his silver, that Duninnis had not had time to repay his debt.

Calum scrambled up onto a cliff overlooking the ocean. His heart had not beat so fast since he had nearly laid down his life for his king at Sherrifmuir. Below him lay the silent, moonlit beach and beyond that the bluff where the fortress stood watch in the cold spring night. There was naught else to be seen. He was back on the strand when a deep voice assaulted him. "Stay where you are, son of hell!"

Calum whirled. Before him stood a broad, black shadow of a man, his plaid rippling in the wind. Calum's good humor sank like a stone when he saw the man's clouded face. "Badger!"

"Himself. Give me the lass, Calum Og. You've no need for her."

His words puzzled the Gael. Had the man found Duninnis' body? If so, why was Lydia of more importance to him? An answer came to him, and his stomach sickened at the thought. Perhaps Badger was no more decent than his master. "I'm taking Lydia to her mother, Badger," he rumbled. "Duninnis has no claim to her, leastwise no honest claim."

Badger lurched forward a few steps. It was clear he'd had a dram too many. "Duninnis has no claim to anything, even life. He's as cold as clay. I was about to rouse the house when I saw you creeping over the moor with a bundle in your arms."

Calum sighed in relief. Only Badger knew. "He was seized with a sickness and died before my eyes."

The big man nodded, and his entire body, unbalanced by whisky, appeared to nod with him. "I believe you, son of Donald. You're well known as a man of honor, and a man of honor would never slay his kinsman."

"Duninnis' death grieves me sore, Badger." Calum spoke slowly, choosing his words with care lest Badger misinterpret him. "I only wish I could have prevented his passing, but I'm grateful that you understand I had no hand in it. Now, if you'll be so kind as to let me past, I'll be on my way and you can mourn your chieftain. My lady is ill and pining for her daughter."

"Well, Calum Og, I am also heartsick and pining for the lass."

As Calum stared at the Badger, the sick feeling grew even stronger within him. He shot a glance toward Lydia; the girl stood by the boat, aglow with moonlight, as still as death itself. Now he knew the meaning of her plea, "Don't let Badger see me." Calum faced the *duine-uasal*. "What do you mean, man?" Badger was not speaking of marriage; the creature had a wife already, Calum knew, and four young children besides.

"Calum, she doesn't belong to Duninnis now. She's mine. He himself told me I should have her, once the sickness had taken him, and I intend to wrap her properly, rip into her where she's narrow and suck the sweetness out of her. Duninnis could not, but I can, and I will."

Calum winced. He had not wanted bloodshed, but he could see no way to avoid it. Any man as depraved as

Badger could not be suffered to live. "You can have her, Badger." The big man smiled. As he ambled forward, Calum drew his broadsword, sprang from the rock and landed precisely in front of the grizzled devil. "But you will have to slay me first."

"A hundred thousand murders!" gasped Badger. "I'll not fight you! Nor do I need to. A few hundred men of Clan MacLeod should settle your mischief, Calum Og, as long as they believe you've killed their chieftain." He turned and gathered himself for a run.

"Wait, Badger!"

The man stopped in midstep, poised like a startled roebuck. Drunk though he might be, he had a great lead on Calum and would likely outrun him. What might stay the man?

"Your wife is a whore!" shouted Calum. "Her loins sag on the ground and stink of other men's seed!"

Badger staggered forward a few steps.

"Your children are the spawn of seals! They are fairy children! Their father was an English grenadier!"

Badger lumbered to a halt, then trotted forward again. Calum jogged after him, showering him with the vilest insults he could imagine. "Your mother lay with dogs! Your father was the devil himself! Your *slat* is a hazel twig, a blade of grass, a dead fish!"

Badger slowed, then loped away faster than ever. Calum broke into a run but could not catch him. The whisky which kept Badger from walking normally had not affected his speed in the slightest. "Your cattle are sickly and scrawny!" cried Calum, in desperation.

Badger slowed to a trot, then a walk. At last he stopped, turned about and reeled back toward Calum. "My cattle are round and beautiful," he murmured. "Every man on Skye knows my cattle are fairer and fatter and more graceful than most women. What cheek you have to mock them."

Calum's heart rejoiced. He forced his face into sullen lines. "Your cattle," he drawled, swaggering toward the *duine-uasal,* "are no better than dogs with horns. Your cattle have the scours and they bleed beneath the tail. Your cows give birth to two-headed calves and your bulls have pintels no bigger than a baby's finger." Badger drew nearer, his mouth an angry red slash in the middle of his face.

How stupid he was to have wasted so many epithets on Badger's manhood! thought Calum. It was the bulls he should have been twigging and grass-blading and dead-fishing all along. "You cover your own cows, because your bulls are not manly enough to do so."

The man drew his sword. Calum drew his, and suddenly realized he had made a serious error. In any other circumstances, Badger would be no match for him. But he could not slay the creature, not with a blade. Every man of Clan MacLeod would be looking for the man's murderer. Badger struck and Calum parried. Badger struck again and missed, falling on his knees in the sand.

*I must lead him back,* thought Calum, *back toward the sea.* He taunted Badger without mercy, feinting and parrying, leading the man on an aimless, drunken chase over the open beach and finally up the rocks and through the brambles to the top of the cliff where Calum had been standing only minutes before. "Why, the meat from your cattle is rotten the moment the beast is butchered. No one has yet had the courage to touch it, much less . . ."

Suddenly Calum was on his back amid the rocks and Badger was standing over him, aiming a blow at him. Calum rolled onto his belly. The man's blade drew sparks as it clattered harmlessly from stone to stone. Calum lurched to his feet. His sword lay some distance from him, and between him and his weapon stood a swaying, heaving, snuffling Badger, his face dripping blood from a hundred briar scratches. "Retract your words about my cattle," he mumbled.

Behind him Calum could hear the waves striking the rocks below. He was no more than an arm's length from the edge of the precipice. *Oh Abby, if I fail you, forgive me,* he pleaded in silence. *No matter what, I shall always love you.*

"Your cattle are lumps of peat, pig turds, drunkards' vomit, stinking seaweed, lifeless carcasses . . ."

Badger lunged, his sword outstretched. Calum flung himself aside an instant before he would have been run through, and Badger soared past him, landing on one edge of the cliff. He thrashed his arms furiously, treading the air, looked at Calum and snarled in defeat.

"Your cattle are bonny!" cried Calum, and gave Badger's shoulder a mighty shove. " 'Tis you who stink!"

"Son of hell!" gasped Badger, even as he lost his footing. His back arched, his arms spread out beside him like wings, and he sank down head foremost toward the breakers. Calum watched. Badger took his time falling and made no sound when he hit the waves. The silence seemed fitting; Badger deserved no dirge.

When Calum reached Lydia, she was still standing beside the boat where he had left her. "Badger won't be bothering you ever again," he told her.

Her face relaxed and broke into a shimmering smile as lovely as her mother's. "Thank you, Mr. MacDonald," she whispered. "I am so glad to hear it."

"Hurry, my heart!" Calum nodded toward the boat. "In you get! I'll push you into the water."

The voyage across the kyle was short in distance and

long in terror. As Calum maneuvered the boat into the surf, the waves grabbed the little vessel like a gift, and Calum had to swim to reach it. He pulled himself aboard, seized the oars and began rowing, shivering with sea-cold from his wet clothes. Lydia cowered in the gunwale, clinging to Tip. Five times Calum felt the boat bump into chunks of ice; the sixth time, the wooden slats creaked, splintered, and finally gave way in the stern. Death-cold water rushed into the gunwale. "Mr. MacDonald!" shrieked Lydia. Tip, his jaws still bound, whined in her arms.

"Be still! Keep your seat!" shouted Calum, but it was too late. Lydia leaped up. The boat rocked, pitching the girl to one side. Calum felt the deck rise under his feet. An instant later he was in the water. He heard Lydia screaming and saw her plunge into the waves.

*I'll not lose her, not now that I've found her,* Calum vowed. He shucked off his plaid, then paddled about until he found the lass. Taking care to keep her face above water, he tore at the lacing of her frock until he managed to strip the heavy garment from her. She struck him in the face with one fist. "A short life to you!" he barked. "Just like your mama! I won't harm you! You must shed this heavy thing."

Calum began swimming into the darkness, towing behind him a very frightened, weeping little girl. He swam toward the far shore, pulled more by a feeling of rightness than by a sense of direction. Water surged into his mouth and nostrils but still he struggled on. Twice he lost consciousness and woke with terror in his heart, still swimming, still holding his precious lamb. Numb with cold, he paddled on until he could remember doing nothing else.

Calum opened his eyes and immediately shut them. He lay on his back on a cold beach. Weak morning sunlight washed over his face and seabirds screeched over-head.

"Mr. MacDonald?"

Calum squinted up at a drenched angel in petticoats and camisole. Her hair hung over her shoulders in brown strings. "Lydia? Ah, Lydia! *Mo aingeal!* You're not drowned, are you? Nor am I, I trust?"

The angel laughed. She shivered, and Calum realized he was so cold he could scarcely move.

"Mr. MacDonald? Thank you for saving my life."

"Child, fetch someone."

"Yes, sir, I've done that."

With the last of his strength, Calum forced himself to sit upright. Not a stone's throw away from him stood five Highland soldiers, their chests blazing with the scarlet jackets of King George's army. Their faces were turned toward him, and all were leering.

*Sherrifmuir,* thought Calum, sinking down onto the sand. *Sherrifmuir again.*

# *Fifteen*

## *Close Kin, Distant Kin*

"Abby! Mistress Abby! Awaken!"

Abby felt herself ebb into consciousness. Why was her bed rocking and bobbing about so? Why did everything smell of salt and fish? "Calum!" she called. "Where are you?" Her bladder was hard and heavy and ached inside her. She had no idea how long she had been sleeping, but her head throbbed and her stomach grumbled like thunder.

"Abby, 'tis Angus! Calum's not here!"

The fog before her eyes began to clear, and soon she could discern the shape of her dear friend, rising and falling, rising and falling. They were on a boat, a round leather coracle of the kind she had once seen fishermen sailing on Loch Shiel. She saw the shifting, gray mountain peaks of the ocean waves and heard their shirring voices. "Angus? Where is my Calum Og?"

"Mistress, there's no time to lose!" Abby had never seen Angus look so frightened; his voice quaked, his eyes bulged, and his hands, clamped to the oars, were stark white. "Take the oars from me and guide the boat, Abby! I'm going into it. I can feel it coming over me."

*Going into it?* Abby stared at him, trying to understand his meaning. Suddenly he groaned and slumped onto the bottom of the boat, his body writhing and convulsing. The oars swung freely in the water, held captive only by thin straps of leather. The little boat began spinning in the waves like a leaf trapped in an eddy.

The same feelings of terror and control that had gripped her during the chess game with Duninnis flooded over Abby. The falling sickness, of course. Angus could not help her now. With a calmness which she knew was far too calm, she groped her way past her wriggling kinsman and caught hold of one oar, then the other. She had never rowed a boat before.

With the first pull of the oars her shoulders began to burn with pain. The coracle stopped its whirling dance. With the second pull, the pain grew worse, and she knew she could not give a third effort. After the third pull, she was certain she could not give a fourth. And so she continued, in constant pain and unshakable determination. Between the cresting waves she saw the fortress of Duninnis, and rowed with all her strength away from it. Like a well-trained hound, the coracle obeyed her and began heading toward the mainland. She glanced over her shoulder. The boat was somewhere in the middle of the kyle, she reckoned; she could see cattle grazing on the hills.

The boat gave a sudden leap straight into the air, and Abby felt her bottom rise off the wooden seat. She looked into the waves and saw a shard of ice the size of a young child sliding past within her reach. It must have struck the boat, she thought, and gripped the oars tighter as she settled back on her seat. As she rowed, she saw and felt many more ice children bump against the coracle, nosing into its leather hide, straining the wicker ribs. If the boat had been stiff wood, more easily shattered by a hard blow, what would have become of them then? she wondered. "Thank God for your resilience!" she praised the little craft.

Abby counted the passage of time by each stroke of the oars. The wooden shafts had torn the skin on both her hands, and to take her mind from the pain she concentrated on the progress of the boat, the swells of the ocean, and Angus moaning in the depths of the coracle. She had been rowing for a lifetime when she felt one oar strike a hard surface below the hull. Before she could decide what to do, a breaker dashed into the boat and swept her and Angus out. Abby sat down hard in the chilling, thrashing surf and screamed. "Angus! Calum! Angus! Calum!" She caught a glimpse of the little coracle, riding the tide nearby with effortless grace, as though patiently awaiting her instructions.

Strong arms gripped her shoulders and dragged her to her feet. Suddenly she was standing on the beach with Angus beside her, gasping and shivering. Seawater ran from their hair and clothes, and the smell of fish was stronger than before. "My God, Abby! Calum did well to find you! Without you, we'd be food for the herrings!"

Abby brushed aside his adulation and began wringing the water from her soaking *arasaid*. Something squirmed within her belly, and she realized the child inside her was still alive and well. What a wild ride for one so young! "Angus, what has happened? I can't remember leaving Calum. Where is he? Where is Lydia?"

But Angus only shook his head and refused to answer so many difficult questions until they had found shelter and warmth. The man seemed to have fully recovered from his fit, for Abby found it no easy task to follow him as he trotted along the beach and over a field of rocks. Finally they reached a croft, where a very kind, very stout woman hurried them in to sit by the fire and dry their clothing. Abby was shocked to hear that they were only a few miles north of the village at the Kyle of Lochalsh. She had rowed much straighter than she had thought.

"See? You are a born sailor!" Angus congratulated her. "I could not have done better myself."

After they had warmed themselves by the fire and devoured the mound of oatcakes offered by their sturdy hostess, Abby again plied Angus with questions. His answers did not calm her fears. "Abby, you fell into a faint the moment you left the fortress and got a lungful of cold night air. You slept one entire day and most of another, and woke for the first time on the coracle. It was the only boat I could find, by the by, and 'twas a lucky thing. A wooden boat would not have braved the ice so well.

"Now, when Calum saw you had fainted, he bade me take you back across the kyle, and when I asked him where he'd be when you and I were crossing the water, he says, 'I'll try my hand at finding Lydia.' And that was the last I saw of him, mistress. Where is he? Where is your daughter? *Arrah!* I wish I could be knowing that! It's Calum I cherish above all other men, and not knowing where he is, or if he is, wears heavy on the heart."

Abby's own heart grew heavy as she began to fear she might never see her beloved again. She had very nearly already abandoned Lydia to the fates, but did she have to sacrifice Calum as well? The thought was more than she could bear, and she fell to weeping in Angus' arms.

That evening, when the crofter returned from his work in the fields, Abby asked him many questions. Had he heard of a drowning? Had he seen a tall, ginger-haired man with a badly scarred cheek? Had he seen a little English girl? Had he any news whatsoever from the Isle of Skye? But the man knew nothing, though he was uncommonly embarrassed for being so unhelpful.

Abby and Angus stayed the night with the kind clansfolk, and set off in the crisp chill of morning for the village where Angus had stabled Luran. The heath glowed with flowers and the air was rich with their scent—asters, yellow flags, butcher's broom and harebells—all covered the hillsides in shades of blue and gold. But Abby barely noticed the beauty of the mountains. Her thoughts were with Calum. She knew he was alive; she could feel the air pumping in his lungs and the blood coursing through his heart as though she were inside his body or a part of it. But where was he? Locked away in a prison inside Duninnis' tower? Struggling for life in the waters of the kyle? How could she ever hope to find him?

If he returned, she would never again complain about his visits to the five cairns. She would never beg him for marriage. She would go with him and help him mourn his missing family. He could do as he wished, he could spend all morning in mourning, if only he would return.

The child moved again, striking her belly with a miniature hand or foot. Yes, she still had the child. And if she had lost Calum, if he were gone completely from her life forever, at least she still had his child, his creation, a small but living gift from the man who had teased her, led her, infuriated her, listened to her and loved her as no one had ever done before. She would never truly believe he was gone from her life, she thought, and, as long as she had the child, she would not be deceiving herself.

\* \* \*

Fires, plaids, summer and whisky. They were the warmest things Calum could think of. The Campbell soldiers had taken his shoes and hose, leaving him nothing but his damp shirt and warm thoughts to bring him comfort. Tremors of cold ran through him from his feet to his neck. He shivered in such misery that a soldier offered him a dram of strange, clear liquor. Some English drink, he thought. The fiery water stung Calum's mouth as he swallowed it, but it burned a warm streak through him, too.

Only three Campbells remained. One had taken Lydia away, and Calum had suffered a blow on the head when he had tried to intervene. He hoped she was being treated with decency. Another soldier had been sent into the hills by the others, for what purpose Calum could not guess. "Give me a plaid, for the love of God, lest I freeze!" he begged the three.

The soldiers laughed, and one slammed the butt of his Brown Bess against Calum's thigh. "Jacobite pig! Let your treachery keep you warm!" he growled.

"I am devil the bit a Jacobite," answered Calum, rubbing his leg. At least they had not seen fit to bind him. "I am loyal to no one but Dunvegan of Dunvegan, chief of all of Clan MacLeod, and he takes no stand between Stuarts and Hanovers." There, let them chew on that, though it was not quite true of Dunvegan. A small party of MacLeod clansmen had fought and died at Sherrifmuir. As for himself, his loyalty to James was at the bottom of the kyle, along with his snuffbox. To admit allegiance to the Stuarts in front of Clan Campbell was to ask for the hangman.

"Where is your home?" asked the man who had the liquor.

"On Skye, in Auchnagarridh."

The man scratched his whiskers and exchanged frowns with his fellows. "MacLeod, eh? Then what brings you so far from home in hard seas, especially in the company of a Saxon lass?"

"She came to me and begged me to row her across the kyle," lied Calum, hoping Lydia had said nothing to refute his answer. "She was so bonny and frightened I could not refuse her."

"Faith, I could not refuse her neither, if she would only lie down beside me," chuckled one of the soldiers. Calum was deciding whether or not to strike the insolent creature when someone cried out, "Look yonder! The captain! Old Donni Campbell will take care of you, MacLeod."

"One way or the other," laughed the lecher.

Calum heard hoofbeats and looked up to see a stocky man on a Highland horse, approaching at a gallop. The rider reined in just a few feet from Calum and leaped to the ground. "Well, Archie, what have we here, man? A rebel, I'll warrant."

"Nay, captain. He says he is a Skye man, and neither fish nor flesh," offered Archie, the gin-man.

Calum studied the captain, every muscle, every mark, every thread on the man. He was a fine looking fellow, perhaps not overly clever, judging from the blank, bland look on his face. But the Campbell was strong, broad-built and handsome, and his eyes lacked the fierce blue glow of hatred so common among his clansmen. As Calum stared, he realized the captain was examining him with the same dark scrutiny. That could only mean one thing: the Campbell was not sure whether Calum was lying or not.

"What do they call you, chappie?"

A wild but beautiful idea blossomed in Calum's mind.

It was a great risk, but, compared to leading an English-woman across the country and rescuing her daughter, it seemed almost trifling. The English were fond of saying all Gaels were related; here was a chance to put that notion to the test. "Why, Alasdair, of course, Cousin Donald. Don't you recognize me?"

Calum's words slapped the captain in the face. "What? Cousin?" he sputtered. His men sniggered amongst themselves to see their master so perplexed.

"Aye, after a fashion," said Calum. "Don't you re-member me? We met only once, at your sister's wedding. She married my second cousin, in Argyle, it was. I have never been so far south before or since."

"My sister?" snuffed the captain.

Calum felt a sweat break on all over his body. High-land families were large; even ten weans were considered a middling brood. But now and then they ran to boys. Surely the good captain had a sister or two. "Why, Mairi," he replied in a chastened voice, choosing the most common female name in all Gaeldom. Every family had its Mairi, and some even had a whole string of them: Little Mairi, Fair Mairi, Young Mairi, and so on. Still, it was a great chance to be taking. Calum clenched his fingers.

The captain eyed him sideways. "You must mean Morag," he said at last. "We call her Mairi sometimes, for she is as modest as the Virgin. At least, she used to be. You're Peadair's kinsman, you say?"

"Aye," said Calum with a grateful sigh. He would never have been able to guess two names correctly. "Dear, dear Peadair. I haven't seen him these twelve years or more. It feels like a lifetime."

Again the captain glared at Calum, then walked around him in a complete circle. "It has been many years since the wedding, Alasdair, but I have a good memory. Pray tell, why can't I remember you?"

"Perhaps because he was not there," mumbled one of the soldiers.

The captain chose to ignore the remark, and again Calum sighed. "Well, Donald, with all due respect, you weren't in much of a way to be remembering anything, what with two quarts of excellent whisky in your belly and a little claret besides. Don't you recall spilling a cup of wine over Mairi's skirts, and Peadair giving you the back of his hand across the face?"

At that the soldiers broke out laughing, and the captain shook his head, as if trying to scatter an unpleasant thought. " 'Tis true, I had a dram too many at the wedding," he conceded. Again he fixed a long, hard stare on Calum's face. "You've been in a row, my friend," he said, tapping his cheek.

Calum stroked the dark scar on his own face. "Aye, cousin. A misunderstanding between myself and a cattle buyer. He fared far worse, I assure you."

Campbell's smile held no mirth. "Well, cousin or no, we can't leave you here on the shore, arse-naked and wet as a sprat. Your boat's a heap of kindling, but perhaps we can find you another. Fergus, give the man your plaid. Not another word out of you, son of the devil. Give him the plaid. Aye, that's grand. Well now, we'll be off and return to camp. There are some folks there who would like to see you very much, Alasdair, though I fear you'll be wishing they didn't."

Every hair on Calum's arms leaped to attention, in spite of the warm plaid draped around him. A fear he didn't understand prickled his skin and made his sword arm creep toward his missing sword. But he said nothing and allowed the soldiers to push him forward, toward the hills where the captain had come from.

The camp was a ragtag affair of patched tents and straw pallets. Calum marveled at the grenadiers, whose tattered uniforms were not much better than the rags of the poorest clansfolk. He scanned the camp for a sign of Lydia but saw nothing of her. "Where are we, Cousin Donald?"

"I charge you not to call me that," grunted Campbell. "We are about a day's march from Ardnamurchan on the coast. I myself have just spent a week scouting in the south and was surprised to find the major here instead of in the village. He said there was some trouble with Clan Donald and he was forced to flee Ardnamurchan. We are heading back to Argyle—thank the Lord!—and the major on to England."

"Major?"

The captain nodded toward a man on a gray horse near the largest of the tents. Calum felt his heart drop into his belly. He could not see the face of the rider; it was the horse that gripped his eyes. Dappled all over with silver splotches, lean and long-legged, the beast had no tail to speak of and no ears at all. It was the horse of the devil who killed Catriona.

"Major Thomas Racker," said the captain, speaking each word as if he were spitting out poison. "Stretched-on-the-Racker, we call him."

Racker! That was what the dying grenadier had been trying to tell him, thought Calum. Here was the very devil who had destroyed Bailebeag and slaughtered his wife and weans. But how could he avenge Catriona now? He hadn't so much as a dirk or pistol. And even if he could break free and snap the whoreson's neck, he would certainly be shot dead on the spot. And what then would happen to Abby and the child? "You don't much care for the man, I take it, captain."

"I do, my friend," said the Campbell. "I care for him to have his throat torn out by dogs, and I'm sure he cares for me just as deeply."

Calum watched in helpless anger as the major turned his horse and cantered toward him. The Englishman's uniform may have been faded, but his black boots shone and his scarlet jacket was clean and neatly mended. Racker halted beside Campbell and pointed his riding stick at Calum. "And what, dear captain, is that?"

"Craving your indulgence, major, but we found this fellow on the shore not far from here. He says he crossed the kyle, so the waters must have carried him far south. 'Twas he with the lass."

For a moment the major's dagger-sharp face relaxed, and Calum thought he looked very handsome indeed for a black-hearted demon. Then he realized he had seen that very face long ago or very recently or in another life, much distorted with fury and darkened with hate. His cheek twitched, and he remembered: Sherrifmuir! The saber cut across his face! The wrenching pain, the blood in his eyes! This man was the cause of it all. "The lass? You mean the English girl I'm harboring in my tent?"

At once Calum looked toward the large tent on the edge of the camp. *Dia!* His dear lamb, Abby's sweet child, was a prisoner once again. God Himself only knew what the major might do to her, and another rescue didn't seem possible. Calum began to fear he had torn the poor girl off the griddle and into the coals.

"Aye, major, the very one. The fellow says she asked

him to row her across the kyle, and he did so. Does the lass agree with that account?"

From the great height of his horse, the major gazed at Calum and frowned. "The poor child is stupefied with fear and cannot speak a word. If you've harmed her, Scotchman, you'll fare ill for it. Does he speak the King's English, captain?"

"Aye, sir, that he does."

"What is your name, Scotchman?" demanded the major. "Your allegiance?"

Calum held his head up as high as his aching body would allow. "Let me see the lass."

The major reared back his whip and slashed it across Calum's chest. Calum staggered backward at the sudden pain. "Now, whoreson, your name."

*Faith, you'd not talk so bold without a weapon in your hand, Englishman,* thought Calum. "I am Alasdair Mor of Clan MacLeod, and my allegiance is to my chief, Dunvegan of Dunvegan. He is his own king, and not beholden to your southern governments."

The major snorted and flicked his whip. "Damn redshanks! They all believe they are the descendants of royalty!" Racker closed one eye, leaned far over the saddle and stared into Calum's face. "There's something familiar about you, redtail. You claim to be neutral, but I'm loath to believe you. No man is without loyalties regarding king and country. Captain, perhaps you'd best put the man down."

Calum gasped. He turned to run, but the two strong soldiers on either side of him gripped his arms and held him fast. The captain coughed nervously. "Your pardon, major, but the creature is distant kin to me, and my master, Argyle, would not be pleased with either you or me if our hands were red with the blood of Campbell kin.

Do you not think you could assign him to my care and let me deal with him? If one word he says isn't true, I'll bring him low myself."

"Yes, I'm sure you will," murmured Racker. He pulled a white leather glove from one hand and waved it carelessly to and fro, as if brushing away midges. "Very well, captain. But I promise you, I shall hold you responsible for the fellow. And, as rations are low, he shall eat only what the others leave behind."

"Good enough, sir," grumbled Campbell. He winked at Calum, and Calum nodded his thanks.

The major wheeled his horse about and was riding back to his campaign tent when he reined in and swiveled about in the saddle. He sniffed at Calum, then turned his attention to the captain. A cold, blue light shone in the Englishman's eyes. "I say, captain, do you know a woman named Sorcha Bheag of Ardnamurchan?"

"Know her? In every sense, sir!" cried Campbell. "As you yourself ken, and none to your credit, sir. I was just thinking of asking your permission to visit the dear woman."

Calum saw the captain's face glow with tenderness. Cousin Donald has a sweetheart, he laughed to himself. Even a Campbell couldn't live without love. Immediately he thought of Abby and wondered where she might be, but his musings brought him nothing but sadness. Unless he were lucky indeed, he might never see his own dear woman again.

"You cannot visit her, I'm afraid," said the major. "She's dead."

The captain looked as if he had walked into a stone wall. Calum's guards began muttering to each other, and again Calum tried to pull free. The men held him firm.

"Dead! How can it be?" sobbed Campbell. "She was hale and happy when I left her."

"A tragic mishap," drawled the major. "She was shot, apparently mistaken for someone else. Or perhaps she caught a stray bullet. Or perhaps she came between a hunter and his quarry. She's just as dead in any case." The major glanced at one of Calum's guards. Calum felt the man's hands tremble. "No one knows exactly what took place."

Calum clearly heard a lie hiding behind the major's words, and wondered if the officer had a hand in the death of the captain's woman. His heart ached for the Campbell. The fellow's loss was no worry of his own, to be sure, but he did owe his life to his new "kinsman."

Racker urged his horse away from the captain and began to ride away at a shuffling trot, but the grieving Campbell ran after the major, weeping and howling in despair. "Find the murderer!" he cried, clawing at the Englishman's white breeches. "Find the whoreson!"

The major reined in and spoke, but Calum could not make out a word. The two soldiers dragged him to a rowan tree nearby, just beginning to take leaf, and bound him securely to the rough trunk. Calum chafed against his bonds, but they were made of good English twine and refused to give. From the center of the camp he could hear the wild, broken-hearted keening of the captain, howling a *coronach* for his love.

There was grief of another sort in the major's tent.

"Where's my dog? I want my dog. Where's Tip? Will you please find him for me?"

Major Racker looked up from his writing desk and gazed at the angelic-featured girl, sitting stone-still on a stool in one corner. Her petticoats and camisole were gone, and in their place she wore a grenadier's long, white blouse as a makeshift dress. A small but pleasant thought drifted into the major's mind. A pretty frock, clean tresses, a few weeks' of good food, and the little creature would be absolutely exquisite, the sort of child Diana would appreciate.

He lay aside his pen and ink. "My dear, for the hundredth time, I don't know where your wayward beast is, but if I find him, I shall present him to you posthaste. Why will you speak of nothing but the dog? Be a good lass now and tell me your name. Sarah? Cynthia? Chloe? Where are you from? London, I'd guess from your speech, at least you were born there."

"I want my dog," whimpered the girl. "Where is Tip?"

"Who is the man we found on the shore, child?" Those merciless blue eyes, that rusty hair, that proud tilt of the head and defiant line of a mouth—Racker had seen the man before. But where? He was not who he claimed to be, surely. But who was he? "What is his name, my pet?"

"Tip, sir. He's black and white and small, and he cannot eat nor drink, for his mouth is tied shut with linen. Would you look for him, please? I'm so afraid for him."

"My poor bewildered princess! Your ordeal still disorients you. In time, I wager, you will be able to speak of something other than your precious Tip." *You'll tell me the name of this interloper,* thought the major, *this piece of Scotch driftwood that has burrowed its roots into my brain.* He picked up his pen and resumed his letter.

*My love, I have some remarkable news for you. Fate has thrown into my arms a truly enchanting and beautiful child, a little girl no older than ten years. She is English, an orphan. She has suffered through great danger and has not yet fully recovered from her experience. The poor child is sorely in need of kind attention, and I am certain that no one could shower her with more mother's love than yourself. I am bringing her with me to Ivy House.*

*You may expect us both within the month. By that time, I am sure, she will have completely forgotten the hardships of her past and be happy to escort you down Elm Hill lane, with every swain in town agape at her grace and beauty.*

*With love and respect as ever, your unworthy servant and dutiful husband,*

*Thomas*

The major smiled at the child. "Once I find your little dog, my dear, you and I are going to have a long, delightful conversation. And then I am taking you home to your mother."

The girl stared at him, and for a moment he expected her to speak. Suddenly, a great blast tore apart the silence of the tent. The child dived onto the floor as if the explosion had blown her there.

"Damnation!" roared the major. The girl crept behind his campaign trunk.

Racker ran from the tent and beheld four ragged grenadiers laughing and congratulating themselves. A cloud of black smoke rose in a column from a distant spot on the open heath. A group of Campbell sluggards stood about, shaking their heads and rolling their eyes as they pretended to clean their flintlock rifles. "Who is responsible for this disruption?"

Three of the grenadiers pointed to the fourth. It was Marly, the sergeant. "Begging your par . . . pardon, sir," stammered the man. "We was just having some practice at pitching the grenades, sir. You . . . you ordered us to practice, if I recall c'rectly."

"Not next to my tent, imbecile!" The major pointed to the plume of smoke. "What possessed you to throw a grenade so close to the camp?"

"The . . . the dog, sir."

The major stiffened. "Dog?"

"Aye, sir. A little spotted dog. Just standin' starin' at us. Hawkins here bet me a day's wages I couldn't hit it. Blew it to bits, I did."

The major's lips curled upward in a tight smile. "Congratulations, sergeant. You have won the wager. You have also won twenty lashes, which I shall administer myself. Now begone!"

Racker stalked down to the hole the grenade had created in the heather. Wading through the smoke, he found something white and red on the ground. Gently he retrieved it. It was a bloody strip of linen. *Bastard!* he thought. *I'll make him bleed!* The strange Scot's identity had been within his grasp; now it was still locked within the brain of the silent seraphim in his tent.

# *Sixteen*

## In Rout

As Angus and Niall had both predicted, the people of the district had not forgotten Calum. Abby saw the first sign of their respect while she was trimming the children's hair in the yard, with a pair of shears she had bought from a tinker. "You'll make us English!" the youngsters complained.

"That is not as hideous as you might imagine," Abby scolded them. "However, all I intend to do is make you look respectable and perhaps keep the vermin away. No, of course it doesn't hurt! Diarmid, stop squirming about so! I can't . . ." She stopped and looked over the top of the boy's shaggy hair. Someone was driving a small herd of cattle directly toward the house.

She leaped up, shears still in hand, and ran to greet the drover. "Do you wish to stay the night?" she asked.

"Nay, mistress," he said. "Are you Calum Og's Englishwoman? These cattle are for him, from Keppoch, Clanranand and Culanish. And there are others coming, have no fear. 'Tis not in every peat bank that you'll find a man like Calum, you know. He has friends galore!"

After that, Calum's friends came by the droves, bringing so many beasts that Abby could not keep count of them all—shaggy red and gold Highland cows and calves, a short-haired black bull of a type even Angus had never seen before, two mares for Luran, dozens of sheep and goats, even hens and cockerels. All of Clan Donald, from the highest to the lowest, sent whatever they could spare to replenish Calum's herds and flocks.

The river of gifts flowed on for many days. Gangs of men arrived at the house, and Angus put them to work hauling stones and felling timber for a new Bailebeag. Soon a framework was erected, and stone walls began to rise around it. When Abby brought the men their meals, she often closed her eyes halfway and gazed at their work. She could almost see the finished house with its round corners and low doorway, nearly hear the laughter of children and the whistle of the wind through the thatch.

"Oh, Angus!" sighed Abby one evening, holding a lamb sent by an especially poor family. "Your people are unspeakably kind! If only Calum were here to see it."

"Nay, Mistress Abby," he said, smiling. *"Your* people are kind. You're as good as a Gael yourself now. Your clansfolk would aye like to see you and Calum wed, but indeed I've not heard a single person speak ill of you, not even so much as a grumble by some jealous alewife. No gossip, they say, is the highest praise. And do you know why no tongues are wagging, mistress? Because Calum is a decent man. He has come to the aid of the clan many times, not just at Sherrifmuir, but in countless small ways. Why, should a byre blow down in a storm or a man lose his milk cow, Calum will be there as quick as a crow can steal your supper. I've known him to give meat off his own table to feed another man's family."

Calum! Goodness ran so deep inside his heart that she might never plumb its depths. "Angus, we must find him! The baby will have arrived by harvest time, and I

shall go perfectly mad if Calum is not with me then. You
do believe he's alive, don't you?"

"I do, mistress," said Angus gently. "I feel he's living,
just as I feel myself living. Sometimes I go to Catriona's
cairn myself and run my hands over the stones, and it is
as if she is speaking with me, telling me that Calum is
alive and well. They say the dead know everything.
Whether it's true or not, I beg you be patient. Calum will
return, or else he'll send word to us. He would never
desert you, as you well know yourself."

At sunrise Abby went to Bailebeag alone. The framework of the half-completed building stood like a skeleton
in the morning mist. She sat down at the foot of Catriona's cairn and spread her hands over the cold stones,
but they carried no messages from the dead. She tried
to imagine the woman who lay beneath the cairn, but the
only face she could see was that of Calum Og.

"Oh, where is he, Catriona?" pleaded Abby, her voice
catching on a sob. "Speak, I pray you! I promise you
I'll never wed if you wish it, only let me see dear, dear
Calum once again. You know as well as I there is no
equal to him, in Scotland or England or perhaps the entire world. I beg you, as one woman in love to another
in love, give me some sign! Tell me whether he lives or
has perished."

Abby waited. The stones remained cold and silent. A
cloud swallowed the sun and the sky turned gray. What
a fool she was for thinking the dead had any news for
her!

When she returned to Angus' croft, she found a red-
haired boy standing in the yard. "Is this the house of
Calum Og?" he asked.

Abby stared at him but could not remember his face.
"It is," she replied. "He's not been here for many a day."

"Aye, I'm knowing that," puffed the boy. "Are you English?"

"Indeed I am." Abby frowned. What could the child want? "Have I seen you before? And why do you wish to know my heritage?"

The boy bounced about so that his freckles seemed to dance across his face. "Mistress, my family is from Ceilarag, some miles inland from the west coast, by Albhinnen. We've heard an Englishwoman was living in Glenalagan at the house of Calum Og, and so I was sent to tell you."

"Tell me what?" Abby toyed with the fringe at the corners of her *arasaid*. Getting answers from a Gael, she had found, was like plucking scales from a fish, one at a time.

"That an English girl is being held in the company of red soldiers near Ceilarag, not far from Turachbeann, not far from Ardnamurchan, headed toward the spot where the Children's River crosses Altcannaich, the Stream of the Mountain-down. Do you know that place?"

Abby shook her head. All Highland place-names still ran together in her mind. "It's not important. I shall find it if I need to. But why did you come to me?"

"Why, we heard you were missing your daughter, and here she is, or if not her, one just like her. Brown hair, aye? Hands that never saw work, aye? And eyes just like your own, gray and beautiful."

"That must be Lydia!" Abby gasped. "But how do you know so much about her?"

The lad smiled as he hopped from one foot to the other. "Faith, mistress, news travels throughout Clan Donald like a hound after a deer. In Glenfinnan, a man may get word that his plaid is on fire before he sees it for himself."

"Astounding." Abby sat back and tried to collect both her breath and her thoughts. Lydia, alive and well! It was too much to have expected. "But what of Calum Og?" she asked the child. "Have you heard aught of him?"

"Oh, aye," said the boy. "He's with the lass. But she's treated like a chieftain's daughter, while Calum is trussed up like a calf at the slaughterer."

"Calum a captive of the King's army?" cried Abby. She clapped her hands over her head, trying to suppress the great fear that leaped up inside her. It was exactly as if Catriona had heard her plea and sent a messenger. Abby pushed the thought from her mind. "Why didn't you tell me immediately?"

"My conscience, thrice over, mistress! You didn't ask about him until now. I was sent to tell you about the lass, not Calum Og."

Abby blinked. Sometimes the Gaelic ways still made no sense to her at all. At least she knew that Calum was alive, although no doubt in grave danger. "Thank you," she murmured to the lad, but as she returned to the house and sat down by the fire to mull over her next move, she heard the messenger boy singing to himself outside.

Little Sorcha waddled over to her. "Give the boy?"

" 'Give the boy?' " Abby echoed. "Oh, yes! Give the boy something!" The wonderful, disturbing news about Lydia and Calum had overwhelmed her. She sent Sorcha and Mairi out to the lad with a basket of blueberries, half a dozen eggs, a goodly portion of smoked venison and a spoon carved from a cow's horn. The boy accepted his gifts without a word or smile of thanks.

That evening Abby told Angus about the boy's message and her own plans to effect a rescue. "You and I will journey to this . . . this Altcannaich and find Lydia and Calum," she explained.

Angus gasped in horror. "And the two of us take on King George's soldiers? A pregnant woman and a man with the falling sickness? What a mad idea! It was risky enough trying to win Lydia from Duninnis, and we are still suffering from that adventure."

"Quite true," Abby conceded, remembering the heartache and bad dreams that had kept her awake the past few nights. She thought of all the clansfolk who had sent gifts and helped Angus rebuild Bailebeag. "But surely there are many strong men in the district who would be happy to help rescue Calum after all he's done for them."

"No doubt," said Angus. "But you cannot ask our clansmen to lay down their lives for a *duine-uasal,* no matter how fine a fellow he is. A chief, perhaps, possibly a chieftain, but not Calum. No, mistress, if there's any rescuing to be done, 'tis myself should be doing it. You stay here with the weans. You're in no condition to travel, and even if you were, 'tis no journey for a woman."

"No journey for a woman! Angus, fie on you! *Troch e!* May the devil give you a good slapping next time he sees you!" Abby squared her shoulders and looked the man full in the face. "I traveled most of the road to the isles to find Bailebeag burned and Calum's family murdered. And I traveled the last stretch of the same road twice to Skye to find my poor daughter and failed each time. I should think that any road I travel now will hardly pose an obstacle, not when the lives of my man and child are in the balance."

Angus stared at her with a look that was half respect and half pure glee. "Mistress, your Gaelic has much improved. It's true, you're quite the firebrand, but a firebrand with child, nevertheless. A long journey might tire you and endanger the wean."

"Nonsense! I'm not so very far along, you know. But

if it will put your mind at ease, I shall ride Luran. I'm quite safe on him. You mustn't argue with an English-woman, Angus. We have all the answers. There is noth-ing, *nothing* you can say which will move me from my resolve to find Calum and Lydia." She drew herself up as tall as she could and found to her dismay that Angus was still a good head taller than she. She had not thought of him as a tall man until then. "And I do so hope you'll agree with me."

Angus smiled and lit his pipe, blowing twisted smoke-rings into the air. " 'Give a woman her way and live in peace,' as they say, mistress. Only I hope you know what you're about. From what I've heard of the red soldiers, they're not to be taken lightly."

"I don't take them lightly, but neither do I fear them," said Abby. She was an Englishwoman herself, after all. In the main, her countrypeople were a reasonable, prac-tical folk who would not resort to violence without great provocation. Roger's murder and the destruction of Baile-beag were rarities, oddities, perhaps even mishaps; she reminded herself that she had not witnessed either tragic event. All she wanted was her daughter, a most logical request. Calum's rescue would be a trickier matter, but she had no choice but to attempt it. "I believe this ven-ture will not be one half so challenging as you suggest."

"I was afeared you'd say something of the sort," an-swered Angus, sucking mightily on his pipe, but Abby pretended not to hear him. She was already making lists of provisions in her head and trying to think of just the right words of love she would use to greet her restored family.

"Tomorrow I shall get all in readiness, dear Angus, and the day after we can set forth. Do you know where Altcannaich is, and the Children's River?" Angus nodded,

and began explaining the route they should take to pro-
ceed as swiftly as possible without breaking their necks.
Abby listened but only half heard most of what he said.
Her mind was on rescuing Lydia, and her heart was with
Calum Og.

Abby could think of nothing else that night. When Angus and the weans fell asleep, she smoored the fire and
crept into a bed that was far, far too spacious for her
alone. She slept poorly. Several times she thought she
felt Calum beside her, thought she could hear his deep,
slow breathing and smell the warmth of his body. But
when she stretched out her hand toward his side of the
bed, she found nothing but his empty plaid.

Oh, God in heaven, how she needed Calum! Needed
his impertinence, his peculiar logic, his lopsided wit, his
kisses, his arms around her waist. She longed for a single
night with him. Her belly ached to contain him, and for
a moment she thought she could feel him inside her,
filling her up so full she would never feel complete without him.

Most of all, she needed to tell him how much she
loved him.

Near dawn Abby fell asleep, wrapped in Calum's plaid.
She awoke alone in Rose Cottage. Instead of rushing to
Lydia's room, she ran to the garden door with its frosted,
frozen irises and pushed it open. Behind the door was a
plate of sheer glass, and behind the glass were Lydia and
Calum, carrying on some quiet conversation. "Calum
Og! My love! Lydia! Oh, Lydia!" screamed Abby, but
the beloved girl and man continued to speak with each
other, not even casting a glance in her direction. Abby
pounded on the glass with her fists, but she could neither
shatter it nor attract the attention of either beloved. Suddenly a bright flash of light struck the glass, splintering

it into shards. Abby felt slivers of glass fly harmlessly through her, and suddenly Calum was standing beside her. But when she stretched her hands forward through the huge hole in the glass, trying to touch Lydia, her fingers struck something hard and cold.

Another pane of glass.

Days passed like years for Calum. A soldier was beaten, for what reason Calum could not guess. The poor creature's cries tore the air like a dirk, and made Calum wince as if his own flesh were being stripped from him.

A day after the flogging, the soldiers broke camp and marched southward, dragging Calum with them. A heavy rain took them unaware, drenching him to the marrow and forcing the soldiers to pitch a second camp only a few miles from the first. During the march, Calum caught a glimpse of Lydia twice, once riding on a cushion behind Racker, and again, gliding like a small white spirit through the mist, accompanied by burly blurs of red-coated grenadiers.

After the rain had passed, Campbell brought Calum warm, dry clothes and a long string of curses aimed at the major. Calum listened, filling up every pause with words of sympathy and understanding. " 'Tis sorry I am, cousin," Calum said, as he finished dressing. "You've suffered a great loss these few days past."

His erstwhile kinsman bound him once again to yet another tree. "Thank you, cousin, but the time for weeping is over." The captain struck his palm against the tree like a hammer on an anvil. The blow made the supple fir tremble and forced Calum's teeth down on his lip, drawing blood. Campbell, deep in his own troubles, did not notice. "Do you know, they say Stretched-on-the-

Racker himself shot my Sorcha. Perhaps it's lies, but it would be just like the creature to slay the woman closest to my heart, then pretend he knows nothing. Jesus and Mairi!" he whispered, with such intensity that his spittle flew into Calum's face. "What a thought just came to my mind! I should have done something such as this much sooner."

Calum struggled to understand the flood of angry words that gushed from Campbell's lips. Racker, it seemed, did not stop with killing Jacobite warriors. And, if the major recalled that Calum's face was familiar because he had nearly cleaved it in twain at Sherrifmuir, then yet another murder might be added to the Englishman's credit. Calum wriggled his wrists together to free himself, but the twine held. "What thought, cousin? Something such as what? Faith, your speech confounds me!"

The captain smiled and patted Calum on the cheek. "That's grand, cousin. And well you should be confounded." The Campbell's face was that of a skull, all grin and staring emptiness. "That way you'll not be accused of conspiring with me. Don't fret; I'll see you unbound and safely on your way once it has begun. And if you are truly not my kinsman . . . well, good luck to you in any case."

"Once what has begun?" asked Calum. "What of the girl? Will you free her as well?"

The captain didn't answer; he was already striding back toward the center of camp, whistling *Baile Ionaraora,* Clan Campbell's fierce pipe music. A few of his soldiers snapped their heads up as he walked past, but the captain paid them no mind.

"What do you make of that?" Calum muttered to a pair of crows that had descended on the remains of his scant breakfast. "Deaths and gossip and conspiring and mysterious 'its' that threaten a man's weal. Unless I'm much mistaken, my dear cousin has insurrection on his mind."

The next morning, Calum saw Lydia yet again. She sat behind Racker on his dappled gray, her face almost the same color as the horse's skin. The major rode quite close to the tree where Calum stood prisoner, and for a moment Calum caught the girl's attention. She gave him the smallest of smiles, but even that was enough to assure him that she had likely not been mistreated. *May the angels go with you, lass,* he thought, then realized what a stupid notion that was. Not even the bravest angel would come near the major.

"Now, my dear, this should convince you beyond a doubt." The major swept his hand before him, indicating the great dark moorland before them. "Your little dog is quite, quite irretrievable." He tried to make his voice as soft and soothing as Diana's, but the wind blew cold into his face and turned his words into grunts and snorts. The girl looked away from him, tears trickling down her Devon peach cheeks.

The major jostled her shoulder, wishing he could also jostle some sense into the child's scattered mind. "Come, come! Try to be reasonable! We have ridden all over this beastly countryside, in the rain and the mire. There's not a hair to be seen of the brute. Now, now. Won't you talk to me? There's a lass. You can trust me, you know. I'm English born and bred, just like you. Please speak to me. Only a few words. Won't you tell me your name?"

The girl looked up at him, her eyes glassy and full of sorrow. In some strange way he could not quite fathom, she seemed different. "Lydia," she said. "Lydia Fields is my name. I want my dog. I want my mother."

Racker reached his arm around her in a sudden burst of parental joy. "My dear child! My dear Lydia! You have been through so much. Come, let's return to my tent. You may have some hot chocolate and tell me more about yourself and what has brought you to these barbarous mountains."

"I want to go home," sobbed the girl. "Take me back to my mother. Mr. MacDonald promised me he would take me to *Mama*."

"Mr. MacDonald?" roared the major. "The man who was with you on the shore? Hell and damnation! So he was lying, the bastard!" He glanced at the girl and saw her eyebrows leap so high they nearly met her hairline. "My apologies, miss," he murmured. "But you've just given me some very important news. Your mother? But of course I shall take you to your mother!" The child's face relaxed, but her eyes were still wide and wary. "We're bound for her directly. But first, I must attend to a small matter."

The major wheeled his horse and spurred it into a gallop. Soon, soon, soon! He would have the stranger beaten, hanged, drawn and quartered, fed to wolves. Damned, deceitful, degenerate Jacobite!

In his haste the major forgot the girl, his mount, his grenadiers shivering in the camp, even the very ground beneath him. The gray ran into a bramble thicket, shied and reared. Racker very nearly fell from the horse's back and turned in the saddle just in time to see Lydia slip sideways from her cushion and tumble into the thorns.

The major vaulted from his horse and knelt by the girl. The wretched child was entangled in the briars, yet she did not weep; instead, she panted like a cat tormented by beggar boys.

"Poor child! Do forgive me! Here, let me help you." Racker eased the brambles from the girl's arms and legs, then helped her sit up. Her hands and face had been torn by thorns, and one especially nasty cut ran full across her cheek, under one ear. "Take my kerchief, child and . . ."

The major stopped, his hand unable to pull the kerchief from his pocket. He stared at the girl's face. *Blood on the cheek. A terrified scream. Falling, falling, falling.* His forehead began to ache. A voice called to him within his skull: *Thomas! He's the one! He's the one who slew me! He slew your dear Edwin!*

Edwin!

A wall in Racker's mind collapsed, and memory poured forth: Edwin at Sherrifmuir, lunging at a Highland warrior. The Jacobite parrying with his heavy broadsword, the blade slithering along the length of Edwin's saber and into the young lieutenant's neck. Racker thundering up a moment later, but such a long moment! Edwin lying dead, his neck half severed. His baffled murderer, bloodied sword still in hand, glaring upward as the major's horse bore down on him.

All was lightning-clear now. Blue, red, proud, strong and hard: the face that carried the major's saber cut was the face of the man in camp. Racker smiled. At the camp, he had dismissed the scar on the prisoner's face as an insignificant scratch. He hadn't disfigured the whoreson as badly as he'd hoped, but that could be rectified.


Snow-cold water struck Calum in the face and jolted him from dreams of Abby. "Son of hell!" he snarled. In front of him stood Donald Campbell, an empty drinking cup in one hand.

"Be silent, whey brain!" muttered the captain. "Or have you grown so fond of this tree you'd like to stay here and sprout needles?" With a flick of his dirk, he slashed Calum's bonds. "Now, be off with you, Alasdair!"

"The girl, Donald. Where is she? Has she returned?" As much as he wanted to set off running toward Glenalagan, Calum would not let himself return to Abby without Lydia.

"How am I to be knowing that?" growled Campbell. "And why should you be caring at all about the wench? Flee while you can, cousin. And good luck to you." Campbell trotted off.

Calum leaned against the tree, rubbing his sore wrists. *What in the devil was happening? Was the "it" that Campbell had talked about before about to break loose?* He looked about the camp. The sun had just set, leaving red and purple banners still drifting in its wake. All seemed quiet. A fire glowed in the center of the camp. He could see grenadiers gathered about the flames, eating and drinking. Their tall, ridiculous hats shone in the twilight like silver fish standing on end.

The tent. The major's tent. It glowed ember-red, clinging to the last rays of the sunset. If he could just creep up on it unseen, as he had crept up on so many stags and roebucks in his lifetime, perhaps he could subdue the major and free Lydia.

Calum slid into the shadows of the surrounding forest, using its cover to get as close as he could to Racker's tent. When he broke free of the trees' protection and entered the camp, two Campbell soldiers spotted him immediately. He poised to run, but to his amazement they beckoned him forward. He ran past them and made his way to the tent, where a third Campbell kept watch. Calum was wondering how to overcome the fellow without blade or pistol or dirk when the sentry saw him and nodded.

Calum nodded back. If a mutiny were taking place, it was indeed an orderly and civilized business. Without a word the Campbell held the flap of the tent open, and Calum slipped inside.

Calum blinked in the half-darkness of the tent. In place of the major or Lydia were two Campbell soldiers, industriously stuffing Racker's pens, papers, weapons and other possessions into their sporrans. Anything too large to carry they smashed to bits. The two snorted at Calum when he entered the tent, and one gestured for him to join them. "The major won't be pleased to see how you've rearranged his furnishings," mused Calum.

One man laughed. "The major will be past caring about anything if Donald Campbell has his way," growled the other.

As the two continued their work, Calum examined item after item, then handed each one over to the Campbells. Sifting through the remains of the major's writing desk, he came upon a small leather notebook, full of entries and stuffed with wrinkled letters. Calum leafed through a few pages, then tucked the journal into his plaid. How he loved to read! Even the scribblings of a devil like Racker would do to fill the emptiness of words within him.

No sooner had he turned back to the desk when a great commotion arose outside the tent. All manners of men seemed to be bellowing, shouting and cursing at each other. Finally a voice piped up above the confusion.

"Major, are you within? The lads and me heard some noise and wondered if you needed us."

Calum recognized the razor voice of Sergeant Marly. Many's the time the sergeant had kicked Calum while he stood tied to the tree, or struck him on the legs with a willow switch. At the sound of the sergeant's words, the two Campbells grasped the hilt of their swords. Calum shook his head, and the two men waited, scowling.

Calum cleared his throat. He remembered a very frightened Calum, years and years ago, who had knocked over a tea table at a Glasgow stew. "Damnation, sergeant! Of course I am within! I am not well. In fact, I stumbled into my desk and overturned it, but I've righted it myself. Begone, now. I'm quite ill. I need privacy, not assistance."

There was a long silence on the other side of the tent flap. Sweat broke out on Calum's forehead and poured down his neck. The two Campbells, their eyes wide with admiration for Calum's imitation major, stood as still as two lit grenades.

"Aye, sir," came Marly's voice at last. "As you say, sir. Sorry to trouble you, sir, but I thought you were still . . ."

"When I wish your thoughts, I will give them to you," barked Calum. Blood rushed into his face. Didn't his voice sound a little steadier, a little bolder? "Now be off, or I'll have you flogged!"

"Sir!" The sergeant's voice quavered and cracked. Calum heard the sounds of boots turning in the mud and stamping away.

The Campbell sentry poked his head into the tent. "Son of a roasted pig! Is the major here?"

" 'Twas only me," murmured Calum. He could not keep from smiling.

"Well, so you're useful for something," said the sentry. "Hurry and flee, all of you! I trow it will begin any moment. The Saxons will discover your clever prank in a heartbeat or two, and then neither you nor I will be able to keep them at bay."

"The girl! Where is the girl?"

"Damn the Saxon hussy!" hissed the sentry. "She's still with the major, I ween. Don't fret over her. Begone, lest a grenadier blast you into a handful of powder."

Calum ran from the tent, at the heels of all three Campbells. A thunderous explosion rocked the ground beneath him, and he dived into the heather. Grenades! All about him came the shouts and screams of men and the roar of flintlocks. The unnamed "it" had assuredly begun; the Campbells were deserting with a vengeance.

Calum lunged to his feet and sprinted toward the dark shapes of trees just beyond the camp. A burning pain flared through his arm. He smelled the stink of singed flesh. He turned his head and saw where a musketball had driven a furrow into him, just below his shoulder. With one hand on his wound, Calum dashed through the lingering twilight and into the cool, fir-scented depths of the forest and kept running. Branches lashed out at him as he pushed his way into the startled trees. Where the devil were Lydia and the major? He would never find them now in the dark and confusion. One white-hot thought possessed him: Abby. He had to get back to her.

# *Seventeen*

## In Spate

Abby led Luran forward a step at a time. The ground was slippery from a recent rain. Angus had warned her not to ride, but had let her pick her way through the morning mist, ahead of him, while he sought a privy, comfortable place in the heather.

Luran lifted his head. His ears sprang erect and his velvet nostrils bloomed open like red roses as he inhaled a breeze. "Easy, lad. What is it?" whispered Abby.

Horses had keen senses, Roger had told her, once. They could smell another horse's urine a mile away, or hear a man's footstep at half that distance. Abby felt the halter rope grow damp in her hands. What sound or smell had attracted Luran's senses now? A mare in season? A wolf? A troop of grenadiers? "Luran?"

Suddenly the stallion surged forward. The halter rope slid from Abby's hands, tearing the skin from her fingers. She yelped in pain and dropped the rope. The horse flew from her, his great hooves splashing her with mud. "Luran! Luran! Come back!"

Abby waddled after the horse. Her sense of balance, never too strong in the best of conditions, was sorely hampered by her swollen middle. Twice she fell in the mud, and once she became so bewildered by the swirling

mist that she despaired of ever finding the wayward stallion. Worst of all, she had no idea where she was or how
she might even begin to return to Angus.

A ringing whinny brought back her sense of direction.
She followed the sound through the scattering mist until
she came upon what she thought at first was a patch of
solid gray vapor. It was Luran, and at his feet lay a sorry
lump of tartan, arms and legs, besmirched with filth and
dripping with water.

Abby laughed, then wept, then flung herself down by
the groaning bundle. "Calum! My love, I've found you!
Are you all right?"

Calum sat up and stared at her, his eyes bright points
of blue light in a mud-black face. "Father, Son and Holy
Spirit! Abby, is it you? Your Gaelic is nigh perfect."

Abby sank against him, running her hands over his
face and chest and arms, remembering the feel of him
through her fingertips. "Oh, Calum! I thought I'd lost
you! My God! You're hurt!" She wiped a trail of blood
from his shoulder with the edge of her shawl.

" 'Tis naught, Abby. A scratch, no more. Tell me, my
swan, how did you know where to look for me?"

"Well, I didn't know exactly. Catriona sent me news
of you and . . ."

"Catriona?"

Abby nodded, burrowing her face into the dear warmth
of his chest. "I know it sounds mad, but I went to her
cairn and begged her assistance. Then a messenger appeared . . . well, perhaps it meant nothing after all. Perhaps it was sheer happenstance. It was Luran who found
you, not I."

"Speaking Gaelic like a bard, talking to the dead,
tracking horses over the moor . . . mistress, we'll make
a Gael of you yet!" He pressed his mouth against hers

and thrust his tongue between her lips. Suddenly she could not get enough of him. She wanted to swallow him, to surround him, to take him inside her and fuse with him into one enormous being, neither Gael nor English, neither man nor woman, but as large and giving as love itself. "Beautiful Abigail!"

"I am not so beautiful now, I fear," said Abby. "The child has distorted me."

"Nay, nay! The child has made you more lovely than you were before, if such a thing is possible."

Abby smiled at his kind words. Gently they toppled backward into the muddy heather, and she felt her *arasaid* drift away from her, as if the very air were carrying it off. She clawed at Calum's belt, and he obliged by ripping it from his waist. His plaid poured off his body, and Abby felt herself being swept into a pool of warm, male fragrance.

*Yes,* she thought, *Yes, let this tiny scrap of time linger forever!* She would be content to spend the beginning and end of eternity in the arms of this man she had once deemed "savage." His hands were at her breasts, sending streams of pleasure through her body. She would die of delight, she was sure of it. But such a death!

Calum entered Abby and she welcomed him, arching her back and thrusting her hips against his. They became a river, flowing together in spate. Her body ceased to belong to her; it rippled of its own accord. Fire raced through her and turned her to vapor. She felt Calum shudder atop her, then subside.

"I love you, mistress," he whispered into her neck.

Abby kissed his long, straight nose. She looked at her loins, still joined to his, and realized that both she and the Gael were coated with mud from sodden head to dark brown foot. "Never leave me, Calum, I beg you. I could not withstand even the thought of losing you."

Calum wrapped his filthy plaid around both of them and held her close. "My beloved Abby! What an addle-pated goat I've been! I fear I've wronged you, though I didn't wish to. I brought Lydia over the kyle, but I fear she's gone."

Abby cried out in pain. "Dead!"

"Nay, love, but at the mercy of Major Thomas Racker, Stretched-on-the-Racker, the Campbells call him. I believe she is well but I can't be certain. I myself have also been the guest of King Georgie these past few days and have had a great deal of time for thinking. I could have slain Racker, could have leaped on him and cracked his demon neck in twain, but could not, for fear of being slain myself and leaving you alone."

Abby hugged him closer to her. She heard his great heart thudding deep within him and smiled to herself, despite her fear for Lydia. The Gael loved her every inch as much as she adored him, inside and out.

"I am taking back my promise to Catriona, Abby. It was foolish to begin with, and, as they say, a good retreat is better than a bad stand. *Mo Dhia!* What I mean to say is, will you have me, dearest Abigail? Will you have me for your wedded husband?"

God in heaven! She had waited long for those words from his lips! "If you can stomach a Saxon for a wife, then yes," she laughed. "Calum, you know there is nothing you could say that would make me happier. If Catriona were here, I'm sure she would be just as pleased as I."

He helped her to her feet and both began setting their jumbled clothes to rights. "We'll start searching for Lydia at once, if you wish," muttered Calum, pulling his belt tight about his middle. "As soon as we give ourselves a wash and find Angus."

Abby envied him his waist, slender by comparison to hers. "Angus? Good heavens, Calum! I know not where he is. I left him far behind when Luran dashed off into the mist after you." She peered about the heath with anxious eyes. "Where has that horse gone now?"

Calum laughed the laugh he always gave whenever something she said amused him. "Why, my dearest! Both Luran and Angus have been here and gone. They're close by, I ween."

"Here and gone!" gasped Abby. "You mean to say Angus saw us . . . saw us in . . . that is . . ."

"In congress, as you Saxons say?" chuckled Calum. "Perhaps. He was most discreet, with his back turned toward us all the time."

"And how did you see him?"

Calum opened his eyes as wide and white as they could go. "A Gael sees everything, mistress. Behind and before. No one can take us off guard. And, as for being bashful with Angus, remember this, mistress—he has been in the house every night that we have been together."

"Oh, dear! You're right, of course." Abby felt her face begin to glow. After all she had been through, she thought, she could still not say even one frank word. It was the English in her, she thought. She reached out to Calum, and together they walked off, hand in mud-caked hand, to find Angus.


Racker reined in at the crest of a hill overlooking the camp. He may as well have been gazing into the mouth of hell. Fires raged all about the clearing, lighting up the deepening dusk. His tent was a pile of smoldering coals.

"Damnable redshanks!" he screamed. His head throbbed in pain. "Not one of them can be trusted!" The only cure for the Scotch, he thought, was the cure for wolves and vermin: purge the land of them.

The child behind him shuddered. His horse snorted and stamped its feet. Damn them both! They were safe enough. He tightened his reins. "Be still!" he scolded the child.

"Sir, someone is coming."

Now Racker heard it, too, the sound of legs brushing through heather. He turned and saw a handful of sooty grenadiers, not more than ten or twelve, tramping up the slope toward him. The major galloped up to them. "What has happened?" he shouted. "Come! Speak up!"

"Oh, major, sir, it was horrible!" cried Marly. "Thems as wasn't killed outright or fled with us was roasted alive. We fought back, didn't we, lads? But 'twas no use. We was surprised. The redshanks run off and we . . ."

He had waited so long to chase Campbell over the heath; now the captain's folly was of no more importance to him than a gnat. It was MacDonald he wanted. "Where is the stranger, the man who calls himself MacLeod?"

"Poor Vickers had his head sliced off neat as a pin," lamented Marly. "Little Tommy Barnes was skewered through the middle like a sausage, and . . ."

The major held himself perfectly straight. Once more he was a rock. He was in command. "You will suffer a fate far worse, sergeant, if you don't answer my question. Where is the man called MacLeod, the supposed kinsman of Donald Campbell?"

"Bless me, major, I don't know. 'Twas all fire and smoke and swords and muskets. Boys, did you see MacLeod?" The men mumbled amongst themselves, shaking their heads. "I suppose he's gone, sir, like the captain and the others."

"Gone!" shouted the major. The wind tore into his face. He felt the girl-child squirm on her seat behind him. "Come, fall in, you men. We must find the bastard."

Again a rumbling rose from the grenadiers, like the buzz of humblebees. "Fall in!" cried Racker. The men remained where they stood. "This is insubordination! You shall all be flogged, nay, hanged! Fall in!"

A flash of silver caught the major's eye. Lydia shrieked and dug her nails into his ribs. Marly held a flintlock pistol trained on Racker's heart. "Beggin' your pardon, sir, but the men is all done in. It wouldn't be neither safe nor wise, would it, sir, to go running off into the night after shadows? Better to move on toward the river and find some shelter for the night."

"Mutiny! My own grenadiers!" bawled the major. "Impossible! Marly, you shall be the first on the gallows. Which of you wish to join him?"

A grenadier next to Marly raised his voice. "Unless I'm mistaken, sir, you're not in the best position to be asking such questions. Now, the way I reckon it, you may order us to fall in and move on . . ."

"Or we'll bring you down like a dog," Marly added. A decidedly cruel sneer played over the man's face. "Sir. With your permission, of course." The grenadiers broke into peals of laughter. " 'Tis as you wish it, major. Either we all march over the border together, with some pride in our bellies . . . or we march without you. And the stripes on me back is tellin' me *that* that would be the far better choice."

The major hesitated. Beneath him, the gray pranced and jerked its head. Behind him, the girl panted wetness into his coat. Pain hammered at his forehead. The men had been driven mad by the savage Scotch. That would explain their traitorous actions. It could just be possible that he would have to humor them and wait for an opportune time to explain the whole unfortunate affair to a superior. "Fall in," he said in as calm a voice as he could muster. "And seek shelter in the rocks ahead."

Marly stuffed his pistol into his coat and the grenadiers, whooping and cheering, fell into ragged ranks. Drooping at their lead, the major rode forward, his back still straight but every other part of him crushed in defeat. The girl's grip on his sides slackened; she kept herself stone-still on the pillion behind him. "Thank you, sir," she whispered into his back.

The major clenched his teeth and nodded. "Don't mention it, my dear. Soon you'll be home with your mother. Soon we shall all be home."

From atop a high ridge, Abby glared down into the darkening glen. A glittering ribbon of a stream flowed into a churning, peat-brown river, both swollen with rain and melting snows and roaring in fury. "Hardly a children's river, I'd say," said Abby. "More like an entire battalion of His-Majesty's-Buffs-at-a-charge river, I should think."

"Come, we'd best start down and await the major," said Calum, glancing overhead. "My love, ride slow and easy. There's rain in it for certain."

Abby saw his concern; the entire sky had grown black with shifting, threatening storm clouds. Thunder drummed in the distance and the air smelled of lightning. She squinted at the slender plank structure that maintained a tentative hold on both banks of the unruly *Abhainn nan Cloinne*. "I hope the bridge holds, Calum."

Before he could answer, a white flash lit the sky, followed by a shattering crack and clatter of thunder. Luran squealed in fear and wheeled about, but Calum and Angus held him fast. Abby had just enough time to throw her shawl over her head before the rain came down in sheets.

Slowly they crept down the hillside, sliding and slipping over wet rocks and mud-covered moss. They had not gone more than one quarter of the way down the slope when Angus gripped Abby's arm and pointed to the right. "Look, mistress!"

Abby squinted through the veil of rain. A small blotch of red was working its way over the floor of the glen toward the bridge. "Royal troops?" she wondered aloud. "But there are so few."

"That will be Racker," said Calum grimly. "And Lydia with him, most likely."

Abby strained her eyes for a glimpse of her daughter, but even the red stain on the hillside was as misty as a dream.

"We will never reach them, I fear," said Angus. "Unless we risk breaking neck and tail on this rockface. If you like, I'll run after them."

"Nay, Angus." Abby gulped back her fears and tightened her grip on Luran's halter rope. "What good could you do? They might even open fire on you. Let us stay together and make all haste. The major may fire a few rounds at a man, but I doubt even he would shoot a woman."

"I would not wager on it," grumbled Calum. His words made her flesh crawl.

Every step down the ridge Abby fought back the desire to pull the rope from Angus and kick Luran into a gallop. It would be certain death, of course, but to plod on at a nag's pace while Lydia was so agonizingly close was just as unthinkable. When Luran's hooves at last reached level ground, Abby urged him into a canter. To her surprise, Calum and Angus loped along at the horse's side, without so much as a puff or pant between them. The rain slashed at her eyes, but she raced on.

Abby watched the troops gain the bridge and scuttle across. With fortune she might be able to reach them, but even so, what then? Simply ask for her daughter? Amid the roar of the storm it seemed like an absolutely preposterous idea. But what else could she do? She could not send Calum back into Racker's hands.

A loud crack shattered the night. There was a rumble, a terrified shout, and a splintering crash. The wild waters grabbed the bridge and broke it like a dog crushing a bone in its jaws. Abby pulled Luran to a halt. She saw the last man on the bridge rise into the air screaming, then soar headforemost into the river. A flotilla of planks, poles and bits of boards swept over him, driven by the raging waters.

And on the other side, drenched but safe, was Lydia. A bolt of lightning lit the sky and there was no mistake: it was Lydia, her mother's dearest lamb, sweetest rose, loveliest angel. The child shared a horse with a miserable looking man who rode with his chin tucked into his chest, not casting one glance behind him.

"Lydia! Lydia!" screamed Abby. How could the poor thing hear her above the storm? She couldn't, of course. Still Abby howled her daughter's name. "Lyd-i-a!"

The troops collected themselves and marched on. Abby and Calum hurried on to the river, but the bridge was all but gone. A single plank fixed to a beam jutted out over the water like a waving arm. "Gone! Oh, Lydia, my love!" wailed Abby. Tears mixed with raindrops on her cheeks as she slid from the stallion's back and ran to the very edge of the roiling waters. "Will I never see you again?"

Calum rushed up to her and caught her in his arms. "Abby, my calf. Say but the word and I'll cross the river for you. I'll try to wrest Lydia away from that hobgoblin, I promise you. Say but the word!"

Abby looked at the river, then at Calum. Then at the river again, and at Calum again. It was madness. She would lose both of them. "Stay, my love. Please don't go!"

Calum stripped his soaking plaid from his shoulders. "Say but the word, Abby!" he shouted. "Say but the word! You are my chief!" His eyes burned like torches. She could see every muscle on his face, neck, and forearms.

His fierceness frightened her. What army could stand up to a legion of Calums, as fierce as wildcats, as dangerous as drawn swords? She touched his glistening chin. "No, my dearest. Stay with me."

He turned away from her, glaring at the river, and she guessed how powerless he must feel. She knew this was important to men; it had been for power, not for money, that Roger had gamed away all his inheritance. Again she stroked Calum's face. Power meant nothing to her, but losing Lydia meant losing half a lifetime.

At the touch of her hand, Calum crumpled into a ball at her feet and began sobbing. He wept as mightily as he had at Bailebeag, for his lost wife and children. And then Abby understood: Calum had given up. He never expected to see Lydia again.

She collapsed beside him, holding him close to her in the rain, and tried to sing.

# *Eighteen*

*Harvest*

"Calum?" Abby felt his weight shift on the bed. His hand glided warm and hard over her ribs and slid under one of her heavy breasts. Her skin tingled, not from passion but from dread. "Calum, I cannot."

"Cannot, my love?"

"No, Calum Og," said Abby. "Not tonight. Yes, I know it is our wedding night, wedding morning, actually." The faint glow of sunrise washed through the skin windows of Angus' house. "But I cannot." She sighed, remembering the brief pledging ceremony that had finally united them as man and wife before a dozen respectable witnesses. Oh, how she had longed for that wedding! Sought it, pined for it, lived for it. But without Lydia, even being the wife of Calum Og did not seem so important anymore.

"No matter. Another time, then. I am a very patient sort." He clasped her hand in the semi-darkness. She loved no one, not even Lydia, more than this highly forthright yet secret man who accepted her without complaint, without question. Why then could she not overcome her sorrow and go on loving him, properly, as a wife should love her husband, as she desperately wanted to love him? She almost wished he would shout at her, curse her, and regret his hasty marriage. Nothing could hurt more than his forgiveness.

"It's Lydia, isn't it, love?" murmured Calum. "Since that night on the river, you have been another woman. You have lost all the joy of living, mistress. It isn't good, not with the babe so close to its birthing."

"Calum! My beloved!" Her voice tore on a sob. It was a poor time indeed to be marrying the man she loved and having his child; her happiness could not overcome her grief. Calum gathered her into his arms, and she clung to him like a tree in a storm. "I can still see Lydia's face, so white, so stricken." Poor thing! She had looked so helpless upon that tall horse, behind that tall rider, like a mouse in a corner. Only Abby's love for the child inside her had prevented her from riding into the foaming river after her daughter. "I cannot believe I have lost her yet again, and this time forever."

"Love, let me go after her," said Calum. Abby felt his body thrumming beside her like a gigantic clockspring wound too tightly. "The river will be shallow enough for me to ford now. Perhaps the bridge has been rebuilt."

"Yes," she sighed, "and what if you should cross? Where would you go, love? You cannot search the length and breadth of the country for one small girl. In any event, I would never let you go unless I was at your side, and I can scarcely walk a mile." She laid his hand on the great soft mound of her belly. The babe wriggled, and Abby felt Calum's hand press down on her flesh, trying to touch his unseen child.

"Mistress, there's this you should know," said Calum, his voice as soft as the sunlight trickling into the room. "The major is a wicked man who delights in making people suffer. It grieves me sore to think of Lydia in that creature's clutches. Duninnis was a brute, but the major is a fiend."

Abby shuddered. She could not, would not believe an English gentleman, no matter how severe a solider he might be, would harm an English girl thrust into his care. Calum had no doubt suffered under the major's mercies, but Lydia's fate would be different. "I am certain the major thinks he is saving Lydia from a life of hideous cruelty and barbarous treatment. Whatever he does with her, I know in my heart she will be safe."

She felt her husband let out a long, deep breath. "I wish I felt as confident on that account as you do, love. It is nearly time to rise, you know, and today—but wait! I have a present for you."

Abby watched him rise and feel his way about in the gray gloom. He returned very quickly, bearing a lit candle in one hand and a small muslin package in the other. Inside the cloth was a tin box, and in the tin, by the light of the candle, lay a sizeable clump of fine brown powder from which issued a tantalizing fragrance. "Taste it," Calum urged her.

Abby poked her finger into the substance and licked it. "Chocolate!" She remembered the chocolate house in Glasgow, the scholarly gentlemen, the rich smells rising from thick, white mugs. She blinked to force away her tears. "Calum! Chocolate! But it is sweet, not bitter. Where did you get it?"

"A drover friend of mine. He was in Aberdeen of late. He says they sell it to travelers that way, with the syrup dried to a powder and the sugar already mixed in. Well, do you like it, *a'ghraidh?*"

"But indeed! Chocolate north of the Highland Line! You are an amazing man, my love. And to think, you are *my* amazing man now." Calum bent low and tried to kiss her, but at the last moment she turned her head aside. "I cannot, my darling! Oh, forgive me, but I cannot. Thank you, thank you for your love. And the gift."

Abby placed the tin of chocolate on the floor beside her. It had not been so very long ago that she had considered flinging hot chocolate into this dear man's face.

Spring gave way to summer. The broom died on the hillsides and the heather flourished, covering all of Glenalagan, Glenfinnan and the surrounding countryside with dusky purple robes that reminded Abby of the phlox-covered terraces at Brenthurst.

As summer began to brown into autumn, Calum and Angus turned their attentions to the harvest. Reaping and tying and lifting corn were all too much to ask of Abby, but she helped wherever she could. She cared for the children, mended clothes, herded cattle and cooked every meal, though she was getting bigger and rounder with each passing week and often needed help from Mairi and the older weans. As the harvest wore on, Calum hired two serving girls to make Abby's tasks that much lighter.

The new house at Bailebeag was rising quickly from the ashes of the old one. Every day, when the weather was dry enough for the men to work and her swollen legs permitted her to walk some distance, Abby paid a short visit to Baile-Ur, as it was called: The New Home. All four stone walls stood tall, connected at the top by an intricate structure of heavy wooden rafters.

One day she came to Baile-Ur and found it nearly complete, lacking only the thatching of the roof and frames for the windowskins. Calum and two other men were busily at work, but she did not call out to them. Instead she wandered around the cairns of Catriona and her children, adding a stone to each. They were a part of her now, no longer a threat but a sad reminder of things past.

She stopped at Catriona's cairn and placed her hands on the stones, waiting. Her palms grew clammy, her wrists ached, her hands felt as if they would sink right through the rocks. And she knew what she had to do.

With great deliberation she chose one stone, then another and another. She formed a little circle of stones next to one of the children's cairns, then added more and more until a small heap began to take place. It was hard work, this monument to her lost child, and sweat mixed with tears on her face as she labored.

A clear voice rang out behind her. "Wait, Abby, wait. You have no need for building cairns. Cairns are for the dead, not the living."

She turned and saw her husband, straws from the thatching still clinging to his hair. His dripping arms circled round her. She loved the smell of his sweat. It made her think of lying in bed beside him while a cold wind blew outside. "Build her cairn in your heart if you must, my dearest, but not here."

"Calum, I must bury her. I cannot live, cannot be a wife and mother, with her memory still alive."

Calum stroked her cheek. His ocean eyes gleamed bright with tears. "Abby, I know what it's like to lose a child. But mine are truly lost, while yours is still doubtless alive and hale. Time passes, and you will not always need to think of her. But sometimes, in a storm, perhaps, or whenever the wind rises from the west you will think of her and mourn for her. You will never forget her."

Abby turned and scattered the small pile of stones. She didn't need it, after all. "Calum, the house looks grand."

Abby let him lead her up to the walls of Baile-Ur. "Think of the child within you, mistress, not the one that's gone. Oh, Abby! See how straight the walls are, how firm the rafters, how nicely the thatch is coming along. You will have your little house soon, I trow, before the babe comes, if all goes well."

"Then you shall have to hurry," she replied. "My water broke just this morning."

"God save and preserve us, woman!" gasped Calum. "You should have told someone before now."

Abby felt her lips turn up in half a smile. "No one asked me until now, love." Calum looked so distraught that Abby had to laugh. "Besides, the midwife says it's not my time yet."

Calum swept her up into his arms and hurried her back to Angus' house. That night she went into labor, and Diarmid was sent to the village to fetch the midwife.

All through the long night and well into the morning Abby lay panting, trying to rest. When a contraction tried to rip her insides apart, she held tight to the midwife's hands and stared into her eyes. The woman had delivered two hundred live babies, or so she said; her eyes were gray and serene and almost glowed with confidence. "Mistress, you are doing well indeed," the midwife assured her. Abby nodded and groaned through another contraction. She tried to remember Lydia's birth, but all she could recall was a sweet, wrinkled, red infant in her arms.

As the labor grew fiercer, the midwife began to prepare for the birth, and, in her stead, Calum knelt at Abby's side. How like the Gaels, thought Abby, to let a husband lend his strength to his wife. When her children were delivered, Roger had been shut away in the hall, estranged from his wife and the babes he had fathered.

Suddenly, amid the worst of the pain, Abby had a wonderful thought: this was Calum's child she was suffering over, not Roger's. This child was the product of joy and passion, a living testament to her love for the amusing, somewhat peculiar man she had married. For a moment she hated him for causing her such agony. Then she gave a great push.

"A thousand murders!" yelped the midwife. "Mary, Blessed Virgin, be with me now! Mistress, I have the head! Another push such as that, and you'll have the child."

"Oh, my poor lass," murmured Calum, stroking her hair.

Abby pushed. She felt as though her entire body were being turned inside out and twisted into love-knots. Something slid from her, and she heard a gush of water splatter on the floor. She moaned, though the pain was gone.

"Grand, grand, grand!" cried the midwife, snatching up something between Abby's legs and wrapping it in a lambskin. She raised a dirk in her hand, and Abby panicked. *She'll kill the child!* Calum pushed her back onto her bed with one huge, gentle hand. "The cord, Abby. That's all it is."

Abby lay back, exhausted, and let Calum whisper loving words into her ear. She was not even certain what he was saying. After some time the midwife gave her a wailing, squirming bundle of white linen. "A boy," said the woman, "and as fine a one as I've ever seen."

Abby stared into the tiny, crushed-rose face. The baby stopped crying and gazed back at her, his eyes large and luminous. Abby felt tears of weariness, love and loss rising in her throat. She would do anything for this child, she thought, to keep it with her forever. She would never be parted from it, and it would never have cause to ask, "Where is my mother?"

Calum took the baby from her while the midwife delivered the afterbirth. He unwrapped the child's swaddling cloth and examined its body closely. "It is a boy," he said, in wonderment. "And a strong one, too. Oh ho ro, little bog-frog!" Calum caressed the infant's seashell ear with one fingertip. "Shall we call you Calum Beag? Little Calum? Would you like that?"

"If it is all the same with you, love, I'd rather not have another Calum about the house," sighed Abby. "I am so used to one name for one person that any other arrangement will confuse me. But call him what you will, for I am too tired to debate it."

"Then what of the name Donald?" he asked. "A man named Donald saved my life once, and I never had the chance to thank him properly."

Now that she knew the child was alive and well, Abby wanted nothing more than to sleep, for a day, perhaps, preferably a week. Donald seemed like a good name for a Gael. *"Taghadh ghasda,"* she said. "An excellent choice."


After the harvest, the days grew shorter and cooler. When Baile-Ur was finally complete, Abby left Angus and his family and went to live at the new house with her husband and child. Baile-Ur was clean and tight, its walls unblackened by peatsmoke, its plank floor free of mud and mildew. A smell of turpentine wafted down from the rafters.

Abby slowly began to assemble what she needed to begin her new life. Clanswomen brought her baskets and pottery jugs, Angus made a cradle for Donald, and Abby bought copper pots, pans and candle-sconces from a passing tinker. One evening she returned with Donald from a day of shepherding to find that Calum had built a shelf for his small store of books. He stood beside it, lost in his volume of *MacBeth*.

"I say, Calum, you are better read than most London gentlemen," laughed Abby. She laid her sleeping babe in his cradle, then joined Calum. "Oh, look, a Bible!" Abby pulled a book from the shelf. "Why, this is Lydia's!"

"Aye," said Calum. "I found it by the river. She dropped it, I suppose. Forgive me, my heart, for not remembering to tell you about it sooner."

Abby crushed the little book to her chest. She thought she could detect the scent of Lydia's hands among the pages. "It's all right, Calum. At least now I have a keepsake of her. There is another book I don't remember seeing before."

Calum scanned his little library. "Och, aye! The one I pinched from Racker's tent. His day book, I think." He grabbed the wine-colored notebook and a handful of parchment pages sailed to the floor. "Letters," he murmured. "The major has a wife or sweetheart, as strange as that may seem. Who could love him?" He retrieved the papers, then opened the book to the first page. " 'Major Thomas Racker,' " he read. " 'Journal of events from a campaign, in the year of our Lord 1715.' Hmmm, I don't think I shall care to read much of this, after all. Angus must have found it and placed it here with the others."

"May I see it?" As Abby leafed through the major's journal, her hands quivered so badly she could hardly feel the paper between her fingers. Nearly every page was an account of some atrocity: a soldier flogged, a house burned, a Jacobite man or woman shot or run through.

"Is it bad?" asked Calum.

"Very bad, I'm afraid," she whispered. She handed

him the notebook. "Read here," she said, pointing to a brief notation. It was headed *November 30, 1715, Bally-beg.*

As Calum read, his face turned gray and his mouth sagged open in a silent scream. "God in heaven!" he cried. "Is there no such thing as justice? My family slain like dogs, and the brute runs free. *Dia!* I was so close to wringing him off. Some day I'd like to hold his stones in my hand."

"My darling, I'm so very sorry. But I thought you would want to see the worst of it."

Calum glanced through the front of the book, then stopped, his eyes fastened to one page. "My God, Abby! That was not the worst. We must bring Lydia back at once. And this time, we must not let a river stop us. Look, love!"

He thrust the book into her hands and she began to read. *Dearest Edwin . . . time I spent with you . . . nature of our consort . . . meet you in flames . . . unquenchable fire. . . .* Abby clapped the book shut. "Ca . . . Calum," she faltered. "The major is a . . . a molly!"

*"Olach,* we say," growled Calum. "In love with another man. You cannot have such a creature taking care of your child, Lydia. He might not hurt her, but he might unwittingly present her to people who would."

Abby stood like a rock, like one of the five cairns at Baile-Ur. An idea as warm and bright as summer sunshine lit up her troubled mind. "Calum, news of such a thing would ruin the major's military career, would it not?"

"Aye, likely," answered the Gael. "Along with his social standing and any inheritance he might have. Why, dearest?"

Abby tucked the journal into her *arasaid*. "I think, love, that justice will out, after all." She picked up her sleeping child and headed for the doorway. With a speed she did not expect even from him, Calum bolted ahead of her and blocked her way. "Where are you going, mistress?"

"Back to the road, Calum, the road to the isles. But now I shall have to follow it south, back to Lydia, wherever she may be. It must be done. You said so yourself. And you are correct—this time I will let nothing stop me, not rivers nor oceans nor barkeeps nor madmen." She paused and looked into his eyes. Fury was gathering in his face. "Nor even my husband."

"You don't even know where she is," said Calum. "Much less the major."

"I have no doubt but that we will find some reference or place-name in the journal which will point us in the proper direction. If not there, then perhaps in the major's letters. How far can he be? Even if Racker resides in the bowels of hell, we shall find him."

"We? Us?"

Abby paused. It would be a perilous journey for her but doubly dangerous for a man who had fought for King James at Sherrifmuir. "Perhaps you should not go, Calum. You have the look of a Jacobite about you, and I should think the wounds of the rebellion are far from being healed in England."

"Jesus and Mary, woman! Do you think I am afraid of a bunch of Saxons? I gave them the slip before, ye ken. Why not let me go alone? I almost brought Lydia back with me."

"And twice I very nearly did," said Abby. "No, love, I am going, with you or without you. And no power, celestial or demonic, will prevent me, I assure you. Will you come?"

Calum snorted, snuffed, growled and coughed. He twisted this way and that. Abby had never seen him so lost for words. "A hundred thousand devils!" he thundered at last. "Why is it a woman must always have her way? Very well, I'll go. And if I have an opportunity to give the major a little pain, so much the better. But I am in charge of provisions."

Abby solemnly shook his hand. "Agreed. Your oatcakes are far better than mine."

For the next two days, Abby could think of nothing else save preparing for the journey, but when the morning finally came to leave, her old fears attacked her once again. Lydia had not seen her for a year; perhaps the girl would not recognize her, or worse yet, not want to return to the country of her captivity in the company of a mother who had failed to protect her.

She spoke her mind to Calum and Angus, but they were unmoved.

"Devil the bit will you turn about now, mistress," said Calum. "And if you do, then I shall ride alone."

"Lydia will not spurn you, Abby," added Angus. "An old woman in the village who reads bones promised me that Calum would soon have two children, and that could only mean Lydia's return."

Abby was not convinced, but she knew she had but two courses: seek Lydia yet again or leave the girl's future to the fates.

The next morning, Abby woke before dawn and went to the five cairns. She had to leave a stone behind to prove she would not forget Calum's other family.

She found Calum at Catriona's grave already, speaking into the stones. When Abby approached, Calum fell silent and gazed up at her. It was the first time she had seen him praying by the cairnside in over a fortnight. "I was just making my farewells," he said.

"Aye, as well you should," murmured Abby. Both of them laid stones on the cairns, but Abby saw Calum slip a small chunk of granite into his sporran. "What is that for, love?" As she spoke, she realized she knew the answer.

"Why, in case I die, mistress," Calum replied. "If I must be buried in a strange territory, then at least I shall have a little piece of Glenalagan with me."

"Then I shall, too." Abby picked up a piece of glinting white quartz and thrust it into her bodice. "For if you die, love, I certainly don't intend to live."

Abby's mind was aswirl with fears, doubts, hopes and plans as they returned to Baile-Ur and Calum helped her up onto the back of a sure-footed bay mare. He swung himself onto Luran and nudged the stallion into a trot, directly southward. Abby followed him, humming to herself. It was a glorious day, clear and crisp, and the entire glen was full of the drumming of grouse and the barking of roedeer. Donald lay slung in a plaid before her, rooting at her breast. Angus stood waving to them from the doorway of Baile-Ur. His children ran alongside Abby for some distance, just as they had run after her when she had set out for Skye. She still had Angus' charms, no longer stuffed in a saddlebag, but clutched in one hand as she rode along. If such a thing as magical assistance did exist, she thought, she would have grave need of it.

# Nineteen

## The End of Time and Space

"I tell you, Diana, it is a plot to undo me!" Major Racker shook a rolled up piece of vellum in front of his wife's face. He felt his rage thundering inside his brain, awakening his head pains. "Have you read it?"

Diana nodded. She picked up her embroidery and began tying a French knot. "I beg you, Thomas, keep your voice low. You know the child cannot abide loud noises. Poor thing! She is so delicate, so easily disturbed. One might think she had been badly used. I do so hope she will speak of it one day."

"Damnation, Diana! *I* am speaking now. Did you read it?"

His wife looked up from her needlework, her round face slightly atilt, like a full moon beginning to wane. " 'His Majesty's military advisors do hereby happily announce that the fortified garrison to be established at the mouth of Loch Shiel in the area of Glenfinnan in the lands of Clan MacDonald is to be commanded by Major Augustus Selby. The major's past valor and sagacity have proven him more than worthy of this crucial post, and there is every reason to believe he will succeed in the most pressing task of keeping the King's peace in the north.' You see? I have read it many times."

The major glared into her blank eyes. "Are you mocking me, Diana?" He raised his hand, and she dropped her needlework.

"No, Thomas," she pleaded. She shook her head. Her brown ringlets danced up and down. "You know I would never mock you. I only wanted you to know that I have been listening very closely."

"Selby!" The major slammed his fist down on a small table and sent it crashing to the floor. "That ass! That goat! That preposterous, bum-licking, brainless buffoon! Why not I? Why . . . not . . . I?" Had his superiors found him out? But no! He and Edwin had been so discreet. It must have been the disgrace of losing so many grenadiers. But that had been the damn Campbell's fault, not his. "I tell you, Diana, I am being blamed for a situation that was beyond my control."

His wife touched his hand. He pulled it away. "I am sorry that you are so keenly disappointed, Thomas. But now perhaps you will be able to spend more time with Lydia, go riding with her, take her to the theater, like a father should."

"How could I expect you to understand?" fumed Racker. He flung himself out of the sitting room, through several hallways, and into the courtyard. "My horse!" he bellowed. "Harry, saddle my horse."

"See, Abby? There he goes! *Dia!* It looks as if a hundred devils are after him." Calum pointed to a gray horse, rapidly disappearing in a storm of dust.

Donald whimpered, and Abby slipped her nipple into his mouth. "Don't worry, my sweeting," she crooned. "Soon you shall meet your sister and all will be well again." At least, that was to be hoped. "Come, Calum."

This was the moment they had awaited for so long. "I've stood so many hours behind this hedgerow that I'm sure I will soon take root. Look you! My shoes are worn right through in the heel. Oh, I feel so dirty! Tell me, am I truly hideous, or simply miserable?"

Calum looked her up and down. "Faith, mistress, I think you're grand. But Lydia might be frightened to see you in Lowland dress instead of a proper frock. Pull your shawl over your face, lest she see you before you wish to reveal yourself."

Abby did as he told her. He was quite right, of course. Their pathetic clothing, borrowed here and there from acquaintances on the road, made them look like tinkers, or possibly thieves. Nothing fit properly, and Calum's breeches had been mended so often they threatened to come apart and expose him with each move he made. She longed to see him back in his belted plaid and jacket. "I only hope the servants will let us in."

"They will have to," answered Calum.

Ivy House, the major's home, was one of the prettiest houses Abby had seen in her brief journey through Norwich. It lay just outside the town, surrounded by rambling gardens on one side and beech forest on the other. The house was not unlike Rose Cottage, small but elegant. The entire face of the building was made of flint, which shone in the autumn sun like wet stones on a shore.

The maid servant who answered the door was loath to let them enter. "The mistress doesn't 'low no beggary here," she sniffed.

Abby was firm. "Tell her I am here to see Lydia Fields," she said. "Tell your mistress that Lydia's mother is here."

The maid's eyes widened. She hurried them inside, down a hall and into a small room full of shelves, pots, and muslin bags. It smelled of onions. "A pantry!" cried Abby, once the maid had left. "She's led us to a pantry. I suppose we are too horrid to let into an anteroom."

"No matter," drawled Calum, picking up a turnip and biting into it. "As long as she sees us, a pantry is as good a place for a meeting as any."

They did not have long to wait. The maid entered first, followed by a small, somber-faced lady in blue and green brocade. Abby offered up a silent prayer to the heavens; the woman seemed a decent sort.

"Did you wish to see me?" said the lady. Abby nodded. The maid left, though Abby could almost smell the wench, crouching at the door, listening.

"Yes, madam," said Abby, dropping a curtsey. "I will be brief. I am not as destitute as I appear, but for our safety we have thought it wise to dress low. My name is Abigail Fields, and this is my husband, Calum Mac-Donald."

Calum bowed low. "Your servant, mistress."

"We understand you have been more than kind to our daughter Lydia," Abby continued, letting each word drop from her mouth like a gemstone. She must be careful not to frighten the woman. "For that we are very grateful, and we are truly sorry for any inconvenience her stay has afforded you. Now we have come to take her home."

The woman's nose twitched. She had the look of a rabbit taken by surprise. "Am I to understand you are Lydia's parents?" she squeaked at last. "I was given to believe that Lydia was an orphan."

"No, indeed, madam," said Abby. "I am her mother, and I assure you I have traveled far to see her. If you would but fetch her, you will find out presently that I am telling the truth. Mr. MacDonald is her stepfather, though Lydia may not be aware of that fact. Mayn't we please see her?"

"Show me your face, please," said the woman. "It is so dark in here, and your clothing . . ."

Abby drew the shawl from her face for a moment, then replaced it.

The major's lady blushed, stammered something Abby could not understand, and fled the pantry. Abby felt her heart drop low in her chest. "Calum! What shall we do?"

Calum smiled and seized another turnip. "Why, simply wait, my dear. She will return. Here, have a neap." He offered her the white and purple tuber.

"No, thank you."

Abby waited, pacing round and round the pantry, furious with Calum for being so sure of himself. At length the maid returned and bade them follow her. They ascended a great staircase. Abby marveled at the plush feel of carpeting under her feet as she followed the maid down a wide hall, then into a narrower corridor. The last hall carpet she had seen had been at the Heart's-ease.

The lady of the house stood at a door, expectant. Her head was held high, as if the slightest provocation would send her racing down the hall. "Lydia is within," she told Abby. "I have said only that she has visitors. If you don't mind, I shall accompany you."

Abby laid Donald into his father's strong arms. "Here, love, 'tis best you carry him." She held her breath as the woman released the latch and opened the door. The simple movements lasted an eternity.

"Mistress Diana?"

Abby bit her lip to keep from crying aloud. It was Lydia's voice, sweet and clear and sad. And there at a window, her back turned on a landscape ablaze with red copper beeches and yellow poplars, stood Lydia, very small but upright, dressed in a white frock embroidered all over with red strawberries.

"Your visitors, my dear," choked the major's lady. She stood back, and Abby entered the room. She could hear Calum following her, but she could not feel the floor beneath her feet nor see anything save the girl in front of her. The smell of irises was everywhere.

"Mr. MacDonald?" breathed the child.

"It is he, Lydia," said Abby, when she was an arm's length from the child, "But do you know who I am?"

Lydia trembled. Her eyes, gray and empty only a moment before, flickered with an emotion Abby could not name.

Abby lowered her shawl.

The girl blinked, then gave her head a shake, as if to chase away some troubling memory.

" 'I have a garden, a garden so rare . . .' " sang Abby. Her voice was a whisper. It cracked and stopped, and she could sing no more. "Oh, my poor, sweet Lydia! Do you not know me?"

The girl's face seemed to melt. Her features shifted, her eyes sank, her mouth slid open, even her nose was not where it had been a moment earlier. *"Mama!"* she gasped.

Suddenly Abby felt herself crushed in an iron embrace. Lydia's face was sunk in Abby's chest. She could feel the child's breath hot and sweet upon her neck. "Lydia," murmured Abby, stroking her daughter's beautiful hair. It was indeed as brown as chocolate.

"Oh, dear God," whispered the major's wife. "I'm so very, very sorry."

Abby tried to move, but Lydia clung to her like a mussel on a rock. "Please don't leave again, *Mama,*" she begged.

Abby felt her bodice grow damp with the child's tears. "My poor, dear love. My dearest Lydia. I shall never leave you, I swear it. I have been searching for you an entire year, my dearest. I do so hope you believe me. I would never abandon you." She too began to weep, until she thought the two of them, mother and daughter, would turn into one large puddle of saltwater.

A large, warm hand enclosed Abby's. "Ladies, I understand your feelings, but we do not have the luxury of giving them full vent just now." It was Calum, ever practical, ever inventive in his speech. "Might I remind you that a man lives in this house who would just as soon see me hanged and gutted like a coney, and, unless I'm greatly mistaken, he would not be too pleased with any of us."

"Oh, the major!" cried Lydia, burying her face even deeper into Abby's bodice.

"Yes, you are quite correct," said the major's lady. "Thomas has a terrible temper, as Lydia well knows. If he were to return now and find you, he would be most upset. Although 'tis strange—I don't think he cares a fig for poor Lydia or for me. But he is a soldier, and soldiers like to have command."

Together Abby and Calum helped Lydia from her room. Diana scurried about, packing frocks, shoes and woolens into a brocaded bag. "Please hurry. Betty will take you to the garden door. I don't think you will be seen from there if you keep to the wood."

Abby glimpsed a flash of black and white on a cushion by the window. "Lydia, don't you wish to take Tip with you?"

"That's not Tip, Mama," sighed Lydia. "It's Pip. Tip was lost. The major bought this dog for me. He's a good little fellow and he looks like Tip, but he's not the same."

*No,* thought Abby. *Nothing will ever be the same as it was.* But Lydia was right not to accept a substitute for love. "As you wish," said Abby. She looked at Diana, busy cramming a final pair of gloves into Lydia's bag. "My lady, you are more than kind," said Abby. On an impulse she leaned forward and kissed the woman's cheek. "You don't love the major, do you, mistress?"

"I thought I did when I was younger. But he simply will not let me love him."

"What will become of you when he returns?" asked Calum.

The lady shrugged, an unusual gesture for one so genteel. "Pray do not worry about me, my friends. Take care of your daughter and husband. I shall defend myself."

Then Abby remembered. "Indeed you shall." She fished the major's battered notebook out of her cloak. "Here, Calum. Present this to the lady."

"Me? Why not give it to her yourself, mistress?"

Abby smiled. "What, and deprive you of your vengeance?" Calum had wanted to hold the major's privates in his hands. Now, in a way, the Gael could do just that.

The major's wife stared at them in puzzlement. Calum's face took on the joyful radiance of the suns Abby had seen painted on the maps her father had kept framed in his library, "The Sunne in his Glorie." Grinning, Calum took the journal from Abby and handed it to the baffled woman. "Here, mistress. Read it well. Read it carefully. Most of all, read it now, before your husband returns."

Diana gripped the book in both hands. "I shall. Good fortune follow you. Farewell, Lydia. We had a very nice visit, didn't we?"

Abby saw tears form in the woman's eyes. Dear soul! She had done her best. Perhaps, in her own way, she loved Lydia too.

Lydia looked up at Diana and smiled. "Thank you for the lovely time," she said. "Thank you for the clothes."

And then the new family left the room, Lydia holding tightly to her mother's hand.

The major rode home to find his stablemaster most indignant. "Oh, sir! Poor Greylegs!" The man stroked the horse's soaking neck. "He's all done in! Ride him again like this, sir, and you might just as well give him to the gypsies, sir."

"Gypsies, Harry?" The major leaped from the back of his shuddering mount. "There are no gypsies in Norwich."

"Yes, sir, there are. Saw them with my own eyes, I did. A man and a woman. If you look through your bedroom window, sir, you may even see them yet."

The major dashed into the house, grabbed his spyglass from his writing desk and hurried upstairs. *Gypsies on the grounds of Ivy House! What if they had stolen something?* At his bedroom balcony he paused and looked out over the gardens. Was that a movement among the beeches? He held his glass to his eye and saw three figures weaving through the forest shadows. One was swathed in Lydia's blue wool cape.

*How dare a thief take the child's clothing! It had cost a pretty penny, too.* The major ran to the library where he kept his musket and pistol. He and Harry would soon catch them up and find out what else the filthy beggars had taken. He would . . .

The major stopped short at the library door. There, seated at a small writing table, was Diana. And on the table, under her hand, was a notebook bound in burgundy leather.

"Thomas," said his wife. She had a peculiar, masculine look on her face. The major winced as sweat dripped from his forehead into his eyes. Pressure was building up inside his skull. "You've returned."

"The book . . . Where did you get it?"

"That is not important."

"Have you read it?"

"Yes." Her voice was firm, strong, vigorous. All of the timidity he had become so accustomed to had disappeared.

"Have you read all of it?" He thought his own voice sounded feeble, childlike. His head began to pound.

"Enough." Diana smiled, but it was not a pleasant smile at all, a grimace, a smile like a wolf's, all teeth.

She knew!

The major's mind raced like a whipped horse. She would ruin his life . . . tell his officers . . . tell the minister . . . tell some gazetteer, who would tell all of England. He could kill her, claim that the gypsies had done it. No, no, no! Diana's father was a powerful nobleman. If the old man found out that the major was lying . . . "Diana, may we talk this over sensibly?"

"Oh, yes," she said, cradling the journal in one arm, like an infant. "I'm so glad you want to talk, Thomas, for I have something to tell you. Lydia is gone."

"Lydia!" he roared. "Gone, you say!"

Diana frowned. "Mind your temper, Thomas. Some day it may be your undoing. Yes, Lydia has left with her mother and stepfather. But you needn't worry. I intend to replace her."

Pain wracked the major's temples. He could not be sure he had heard his wife aright. "Replace her?"

"Yes." Diana ran her fingertips over the cover of the journal, tracing an embroidery design on the worn leather. "I have been thinking that perhaps it would be best if you resigned your officer's commission. You could spend more time here, working in the garden, perhaps, or helping me. I'll be needing a great deal of help with the children, you know."

"Children?" gagged the major.

"Did I tell you I received a letter from my sister Amelia today? No? She has been visiting friends in Glasgow, and she tells me the streets are full of children orphaned by the rebellion. I should so like to bring some of those poor, unfortunate waifs back to Ivy House. They would have a lovely home here, don't you think?"

Racker fell back against the doorpost. "Damn you," he growled. "What would you do? Turn the house into a beastly orphanage for a litter of penniless Scotch bastards?"

"Oh, how callously you put it, Thomas. A home for orphans. An excellent idea, isn't it?" She laid the journal back down on the table and tapped it with one finger. "You do agree that would be best, don't you, my dear? Don't you?"

The major shivered. His groin felt cold and damp. Looking down at his breeches he saw that he had wet himself. "Diana, in the past, I may not have treated you as well as I should have, but all that will change, I assure you."

"You'd like to have me murdered, wouldn't you?" Her wolf's smile never wavered. "A poisoned cup of tea, a tragic fall—you'd think of something. It's too late for that. *Papa* and his solicitor know about your wretched escapades. I sent letters to them already. In light of that, you do agree with me about the children, don't you, dear?"

His head throbbed. He wished to God and the devil that he were elsewhere, anywhere else, even in the north. "I . . . agree with whatever you say."

And so he should have to, he thought. Forever.

# Epilogue

November had come round again, chill and damp, silvered with frost in the mornings, clear and knifeblade-cold in the evenings. Lakes, rivulets, even certain trees stood out clear in Abby's memory. She trudged along the invisible road with Calum in front of her, just as she had before. Only now she rode, with little Donald at her breast and Lydia—beautiful, petite, sad-eyed Lydia—beside her on a spavined pony.

Lydia spoke very little and smiled only at Donald. Sometimes, for no reason Abby could see, the girl broke into tears, and they would all have to pause and await her recovery before continuing. It would be a long time, Abby knew, before Lydia was well again; the child had returned from a long, hard journey, and she had suffered much.

One afternoon they stopped to eat and rest in a small clearing. "Do you know where you are?" Calum asked Abby as she helped him gather faggots for a fire.

Abby looked around the granite hills and dead heather. The countryside seemed both familiar and unknown, like the landscape of a dream. "The ruins of your kinswoman's house are nearby," she said at last. "This is the place we found the *triegte.*"

Now and then, especially just when waking or falling asleep, the image of the tortured girl's face drifted into

Abby's mind. The ruined eyes, the hollow cheeks, the face clenched like a fist—Abby could never forget them. She heard Donald squeal and cast a glance toward Lydia, who sat on the ground beside the baby, teasing him with a bit of lace ribbon. "The *triegte.*"

Calum understood Abby's meaning at once. "No, Abby. Lydia is not so very troubled as that. She is strong. She will endure. She will push past whatever pain she has suffered, no matter how frightening it was, and shine through. It will take time, of course. Time is always the kindest, surest healer. But she will heal."

"I would be so much happier if she looked happier," Abby worried aloud. "The little girl from Rose Cottage is gone, or perhaps only hiding. Mayhap we should be telling her riddles. She always adored riddles and maggots."

"Then I shall throw her one," promised Calum.

That evening they camped at the remains of a shieling and rose in the morning early, just as the mists were beginning to lift. Sitting by the breakfast fire, Abby sipped a mixture of whisky and water as she cuddled close to Lydia and nursed the baby. Abby had very nearly fallen asleep when she heard Calum clear his throat. "Lydia?"

"Mr. MacDonald?" Abby felt the girl's body shift and turn beside her.

"Call me 'Da,' my dear," said Calum. Abby opened her eyes and smiled at him. He would be a better father to Lydia than Roger had been; he had faith in the child. "Now, lass, do you like riddles?"

"Yes." The girl wriggled on her seat and leaned forward. "Yes, Da."

"*Gle mhath!* Riddle me this, Liddie," said Calum. " 'I am the beginning of eternity, the end of time and space, the beginning of every end, the end of every race. What am I?' "

Abby nearly choked on her whisky. Such a persistent man! The puzzle was still a flea in Calum's ear, nearly a year after he had first agonized over it.

Lydia glanced away, stroked the baby's arm and looked at her mother. Suddenly the girl's eyes began to glow with a knowing light. "The letter 'e,' " she said.

Abby burst out laughing.

"The letter 'e,' mistress," growled Calum. "The letter 'e!' That cannot be the answer!"

Lydia glanced from Abby to Calum. "It is, isn't it, Mama?" A smile began to flicker on the girl's face, growing on one side, then the other, until she was grinning.

"Yes, my pet," gasped Abby. "I am afraid that your stepfather does not see the humor. I told you, Calum Og, that you would throw me in the nearest stream when you heard the solution."

"And so I will!" The big Gael rose and swept Abby into his arms. She whooped, she squeaked, she felt her body twitch and bob about in spasms of hilarity.

Lydia, alarmed but still smiling, reached out and pinched Calum on the knee. He yowled and dropped Abby, gathered his new daughter into his arms and began tickling her ribs. "See how you like this, saucy miss!" he cried.

Then Abby heard a sweet, delicious sound she had not heard in many dark months and had feared she might not hear for many years: the delighted shrieking of her daughter. The noise that burst from Lydia was part laugh, part battle yell, part shout of rage, and, in the midst of the laughter, woven into it, the puny scream of some black nightmare spirit hurtling out of the child and into the ether.

Abby threw herself on her husband, tickling the back of his neck. Poor Donald, abandoned and still hungry, began wailing. Soon all four were huddled together, laughing and weeping.

Lydia threw her arms around her mother and dissolved into a fit of hiccoughs. "Oh, Lydia!" gasped Abby. "It is so good, so very good to have you back, my dearest!"

A dark shadow lifted from Abby's heart. The emptiness that she had carried about for so long inside her vanished in a tide of relief and love. *Lydia has returned,* thought Abby, *and she has brought peace back to my spirit. But were she to be torn away again, I'd do it all over, the searching, the fighting, the rowing, the weeping, the despairing. For her. For me. For Calum. For us.*

The little group rode on through the Trossachs, past the falls at Linn Solas, through Glen Mhor and past a dozen lonely villages. Abby saw no outlaws, no ghostly misfits, no smoking ruins. The reprisals were at an end, Calum told her. Racker and his ilk had disappeared from the land of the Gael.

"Forever?" Abby wondered aloud.

Calum shook his head sadly. "I cannot think forever, mistress. For a while, perhaps, until the land heals and another rising runs its course. My people are not happy with a foreign king, and to them King George is every bit as much of an outlander as a Frenchman or a Spaniard. But there will be peace, I think. For a time."

One lovely moonlit night they arrived at the house of one of Calum's many kinsmen, a landed gentleman who greeted them with all the good cheer he could muster, including a supper of roast beef, well-hung grouse and mashed turnips. Lydia had her first taste of brose and curled up for the night on a soft featherbed, with Donald in her arms.

Abby crept to her daughter's side when the rest of the house was sound asleep. She listened to Lydia's steady breathing and stroked the girl's still hand. Such a simple thing, to touch a sleeping child, and yet so wonderful, so nearly celestial.

Abby's skin tingled. Was someone standing behind her? She craned her neck over her shoulder. It was Calum Og. Perhaps she was finally learning to "see" like a Gael.

"Asleep?"

"Yes, Calum," she whispered. "Both Lydia and Donald. And I do believe you were correct about time and Lydia." Whatever had happened to her daughter, Lydia had been strong enough to endure it. Someday, when the time was right, the child would unburden herself to her parents, tell them about her grief for her father, her ordeal on Skye. But only when she chose to.

"Ach, Lydia will be fine, just. She's a lovely lass. And strong." Calum took Abby's hand and led her to the door. "Now come with me, mistress. I have something to show you."

"Chocolate again?" laughed Abby in a whisper.

"Nay, something far better. Pull your *arasaid* snug about you, for we must walk a bit through the cold."

Calum's "bit" turned out to be at least a mile through the dark and damp. The moon shone over the moor, lighting their way. Finally Calum pointed to a familiar column, silver in the moonlight.

"The tower," said Abby. "It's the tower we stayed in the night . . . the night before we found Luran."

"Aye." Calum threaded his arm through hers, and together they made their way up to the glittering ruin.

Everything was as they had left it a year ago; even

the ashes of the fire Calum had made lay undisturbed. Abby gazed about in awe. It was as if time had been bottled up inside the ancient building and refused to go forward. "I am so weary," she said, leaning her head against Calum's chest.

"Mistress, do you remember that you lay in my arms in this place?" whispered Calum. "Long after the *firchlisneach* had faded in the skies, you and I slept together like a hart and a hind in a thicket, just keeping each other warm."

"I remember," said Abby. The thought stirred something inside her, something that had been slumbering far too long. "Calum?"

"Mistress?" The tall Gael leaned his head close to her. She could feel his breath on her face and smelled the sweet peat-scent of whisky.

"Will you lie down with me now? Wrap me in your plaid to keep me warm. Put your arms about me and stay the night next to me."

"I will." Calum spread his plaid on the stone floor and knelt on it. Gently, he clasped Abby by the hips and eased her down beside him, under him. She moaned as a sweet stab of desire cut through her.

"Good night," said Calum, then rolled away from her, taking most of his plaid with him.

"Calum! I shall freeze!"

The Gael chuckled and turned to face her. "Then come closer, so I may keep you warm."

As Abby pressed herself against him, her thighs felt him rise against her, prodding her skin. He brushed his lips against her ear, and suddenly the fear and sorrow that had held her apart from him melted under the flames of a searing passion, an undeniable yearning to be part of him. She sought out his mouth with her own and shiv-

ered when his tongue pressed against her lips, parted
them, and entered.

Abby's hips thrust against his. She felt the brief journey of the man as he found his way inside her and arrived
at her hearth, the glowing center of her existence. Then
she knew with splendid certainty that she was home once
again. Home again.

Afterward, Abby ran her hands over Calum's face, lingering on his scar, his sculptured ears, his absurdly high
cheekbones. He was still inside her, pulsing but not in-
sistent. How could she have existed so long without this
man's love?

"My calf," he murmured. "My jewel."

"Calum. My beautiful, beautiful man. I love the feel
of your *slat* within me."

"As he delights in your company, mistress. And glad
I am that you can finally speak of him aloud."

She combed his long, red-gold hair with her fingers.
They had come so far together, suffered so much pain,
learned so much about each other. Like the road to the
isles itself, their path had never been clear, yet somehow
they had managed to end up exactly where they wanted to
be, far from Brenthurst and Rose Cottage, in a wild land
she was learning to think of as her own. She had traveled
her own road to her own particular isle—one man, one
place, one unwavering passion. "I love you so."

"And I you, mistress." He paused, his ragged breath
like a question mark in the darkness. "Abby, will you
tell me something?"

"Anything I can, love."

"Mistress, my English," whispered the Gael. " 'Tis not
as good as I care to think, is it? Many of the words I
say . . . there're not right at all, are they now?"

His English: it was such a mark of pride with him.

Abby kissed him on the tip of his too-long nose. "My love, your English is absolutely perfect, to my ears, anyway. I would rather listen to a scolding from you than a worldful of praises from any other man."

"Mistress, I would never, almost never, raise my voice to you."

Calum's teeth gleamed in the moonlight. Once, long ago, she had been frightened of that ferocious smile. Now she knew it was only an expression of a fierce, consuming love.

Dear Reader,

I clearly remember the very moment I knew I was destined to fall in love with the notion of the romantic Gael. I was seven years old, in an airport terminal in London, accompanying my parents on a tour of Europe. Browsing through a display of comics in a kiosk, I came across a "Classics Illustrated" version of Jane Porter's novel, *The Scottish Chiefs*.

It was essentially a comic book, but oh! what a comic book! The glossy cover bore a glittering picture of a handsome kilted Highlander on horseback. This was ostensibly the 13th-century Scottish patriot, Sir William Wallace, although he was dressed in the fashion of 18th century Scotland, a minor technicality that I did not realize for many years.

I was immediately entranced by the illustrated Scot and commanded my parents to buy the comic, which they fortunately did. Looking back, I'm certain I would have burst into tears had they refused, so taken was I with the evocative picture.

The flimsy book at once became my most adored possession, though the pages soon grew tattered and yellowed from constant use. I virtually taught myself to read poring over the printed balloons ("Ah, Scotland! What evil has come to thee?") and eventually went on to read the original, a much more challenging but even more unabashedly romantic novel.

I was a lonely child, and my youthful romantic obsession with all things Highland saved me from a dreary, isolated existence. The key to my freedom was my own imagination, and my *Scottish Chiefs* comic gave it an opportunity to run wild and flourish. Not content to simply read this literary wonder, I also illustrated it, copying the cover picture over and over in pencil on scraps of tablet paper. One hot summer day I even *squirted* countless portraits of the hero on the wall of my house with a water pistol, so obsessed was I with the bravery and dignity of Sir William. I still possess the treasured booklet, covered with bits of Scotch tape (appropriately enough) in various stages of advanced age.

Thus was born my consuming passion for the history, romance, tragedy, adventure and glory of the Gaels and their cousins, the Celts, a passion which has never left me. It is bigger than I am, and I am grateful to it, for it is the single most powerful impetus which drove me to take up fiction writing. The very first story I ever wrote (at age eight) was intended as a novel about William Wallace and Sir Robert the Bruce. I was extremely disappointed when I discovered how difficult it was to transfer one's thoughts and imaginings from the mind, where they arose fresh and colorful, to cold, hard paper, where they lay like dead worms. Not only did my ideas lose a great deal in the translation to the written word, they came to no more than two pages of childish babbling. Still, it was a start.

My romantic image of Scotland allowed me an avenue for creating and expressing ideas, images and stories; even more important, it made me think better of myself. It gave me the courage to believe in love, beauty, creativity, the power of emotions and the nobility of the human heart, which are the essence of romance. Later, when I learned how miserable life really had been for 18th-century Highlanders, I was nevertheless able to reconcile the grim reality with my romantic notions. The Gaels had an unbreakable spirit and boundless sense of joy and celebration that no hardship could destroy. It was this inner strength that I had glimpsed on the cover of my "Classics Illustrated" many years ago and had instinctively bonded with.

It was also this strength that encouraged me to write *Road to the Isles* as a sort of tribute to a culture long gone. In this book I have attempted to show the people, landscapes, and daily life of the 18th century Highlands in a form that combines the romantic intrigue of my beloved comic book with historical accuracy and an entertaining, accessible story. I hope I have succeeded. In many ways I feel as if I have followed my own road to this particular destination to deliver you this book. It is a road which I have traveled with delight and thankfulness, ever since it began in a kiosk in Gatwick Airport over almost four decades ago.

*Megan Davidson*

*If you liked this book, be sure to look for the June releases in the **Denise Little Presents** line:*

**Sweeter than Dreams** by Olga Bicos    (0142–9, $4.99)
". . . Finely crafted . . . will keep you mesmerized from first page to last. . . . An unforgettable, magical read!"
—*Affaire de Coeur* in a five-star review of *More than Magic*
From the moment that Leydianna Carstair, lovely book-keeper and uncontrollable dreamer, comes into the orbit of Quentin Alexander Rutherford, Lord Belfour, nothing is impossible. Lord Ruthless, as she calls him, is handsome, wealthy beyond imagining, unpredictable, and brilliant. He's also about to have his well-ordered life turned upside down by his impish young employee. Sparks fly when the man who swore never to marry meets the woman of his dreams. It's the beginning salvo in a wild adventure where anything can happen—from kidnapping to kisses, from piracy to passion, and love is only the beginning of the dreams that come true.

**Shades of Rose** by Deb Stover    (0143–7, $4.99)
"Deb Stover spins an engaging tale of a love that defies time and destiny, with some of the most delightful characters to grace the pages of a book!"    —Barbara Bretton
*Shades of Rose* has a little bit of everything in its pages—ghosts, time-travel, a quest for hidden treasure, and a love that transcends time. From the moment that Dylan Marshall begins dreaming about a beautiful woman that he's never met (and these are some pretty intense dreams, let me tell you!), his life is changed. Awake and asleep, he's haunted by her. His only hope of retaining his sanity is to find out what's going on. Trapped between the past and the present, the only hope for then and now, Dylan finds the love of two lifetimes and the answer to his dreams!

*Available wherever paperbacks are sold, or order direct from the Publisher. Send cover price plus 50¢ per copy for mailing and handling to Penguin USA, P.O. Box 999, c/o Dept. 17109, Bergenfield, NJ 07621. Residents of New York and Tennessee must include sales tax. DO NOT SEND CASH.*